Buried Truth

D0645959

The Siren Cove Series

Buried Truth

The Born to Be Wilde Series

Wilde One

Wilde Side

Wilde Thing

Wilde Horses

The Who's Watching Now Series

Every Move She Makes

Every Step She Takes

Every Vow She Breaks

Buried Truth

Jannine Gallant

LYRICAL PRESS
Kensington Publishing Corp.
www.kensingtonbooks.com

LYRICAL PRESS BOOKS are published by

Kensington Publishing Corp.
119 West 40th Street
New York, NY 10018

All Kensington titles, imprints, and distributed lines are available at special quantity discounts for bulk purchases for sales promotion, premiums, fund-raising, educational, or institutional use.

Special book excerpts or customized printings can also be created to fit specific needs. For details, write or phone the office of the Kensington Sales Manager: Attn.: Sales Department. Kensington Publishing Corp., 119 West 40th Street, New York, NY 10018. Phone: 1-800-221-2647.

Lyrical and the Lyrical logo Reg. U.S. Pat. & TM Off.

First Printing: February 2018
ISBN-13: 978-1-5161-0374-4
ISBN-10: 1-5161-0374-2

First Electronic Edition: February 2018
eISBN-13: 978-1-5161-0375-1
eISBN-10: 1-5161-0375-0

10 9 8 7 6 5 4 3 2 1

Printed in the United States of America

*To my daughter, Kristen. You are kind and funny
and beautiful, inside and out.
I wish you much happiness and success
in college at SOU.*

Chapter One

The day from hell was finally over.

Leah Grayson locked her classroom door, fist-pumped the air, then moonwalked backward down the hallway. "Fri-day. Fri-day. Fri . . . day." Her chant ended with a thump as she landed on her heels and met the amused gaze of her coworker as he exited the room beside hers.

"Someone's happy it's the weekend." Sloan Manning tucked a bulging file folder under one long arm before he joined her in the hall. "Not a good sign when the school year is only a few weeks old."

A rueful grin tweaked her lips. "Carina Harris's mom brought in cupcakes for her daughter's birthday. The kids were bouncing off the walls all afternoon."

"There's nothing quite like the unharnessed energy of ten-year-olds on a sugar high."

Leah's leather sandals slapped against the tile floor as she lengthened her stride to keep up with him. "The birthday party was just icing on the cake—so to speak. I already had my students all wound up with plans to bury a new time capsule after we dig up our old one. The kids are super excited to find out what we put in that box twenty years ago. I promised to bring it in to show them after the reunion."

Sloan stopped beside the drinking fountain and turned to face her. His gray eyes darkened behind steel-rimmed glasses. "You still intend to open the capsule we buried when you were a student in my class?"

She nodded. "You bet. Nina, Paige, and I conducted an online poll of classmates we're connected to on Crossroads. Everyone who responded thought unearthing it now was a great idea."

He shoved his free hand into his pocket. "I hate to see you reveal the contents this soon. I always pictured someone excavating that box in a hundred years, not twenty."

"We'll all be dead by then." She gave his plaid shirtsleeve a poke. "Besides, I doubt the items a bunch of fifth-graders deemed worthy of saving would have much historic significance."

"You're probably right."

"Mostly, we're using the time capsule as an excuse to have a class reunion. I'm off to meet Nina and Paige for cocktails and a final organizing session. Since we're planning the event as part of the Fall Festival, we hope to have a good turnout."

"I'm sure you will." He set off again, taking the corner leading toward the double front doors at a fast clip.

She hurried to catch up. "We'll send you an invitation, of course. After all, the original idea was your brainchild."

He paused near the wide front counter, deserted at this hour. "I wouldn't mind seeing what your classmates made of themselves, but damned if it won't make me feel ancient."

"Not a chance. You're still the same cool teacher we loved back in the day." She flashed a quick smile then glanced at her watch. *Almost five.* "Oops, I'd better get moving or I'll be late."

Leaning forward, he held the door open for her. "Leah?"

She glanced back as a gust of wind off the ocean blew her long hair around her like a curtain flapping in the breeze. "Yes?"

He hesitated then shrugged. "Enjoy your evening."

"I'm sure we will. Have a nice weekend, Sloan."

With a nod, he headed toward the parking lot while Leah ran down the steps to pull her pink cruiser out of the bike rack attached to the brick wall of the school. She slung the strap of her oversized purse across her chest, tucked the loose hem of her skirt beneath her, then set off, only to coast to a stop beside the pole where the janitor was lowering the flags.

"Hey, Jesse, how's it going?"

Her former classmate turned with the stars and stripes draped over one arm in blatant disregard for proper flag-folding procedure. "No worse than usual."

"How's your dad?"

His perpetual scowl lightened. "He finished his last round of chemo a while back. The doc says he's cancer-free."

"That's wonderful news. Is he returning to work soon? I've missed all his corny jokes. No one tells a knock-knock joke like Edgar Vargas."

Jesse snorted. "Yeah, my old man's a riot. Pop hopes to start working again in a couple of weeks. When he does, I won't have to fill in for him anymore and can find something a whole lot better."

"Well, give him my best." She pushed off then put her foot down again. "I don't know if you heard, but we're planning a fifth-grade class reunion to open the time capsule we buried."

His heavy brows drew together in a frown. "Why would you want to waste your time doing that?"

"Mostly it's an excuse to see friends we haven't hooked up with in years. I hope we can count on you to come."

"I doubt any of my compadres will show up." He made quick work of folding the flag into triangles and tucked it beneath his arm. "We didn't exactly hang out with the same crowd since I'm from the wrong side of the tracks and all."

Leah rolled her eyes. "That 'poor me' crap isn't going to fly, Jesse. We don't have any tracks in Siren Cove."

A slight smile curled his full lips. "You know what I mean."

"I do, but it's a lame excuse." She glided away. "See you Monday."

Peddling into the wind as she headed toward the downtown area of her hometown, Leah cruised past the park and community swimming pool, then turned onto the main drag lined with shops and restaurants catering to the tourist trade that kept their economy afloat. As she approached Old Things, her friend's antique shop, Paige Shephard stepped outside and waved.

Leah braked to a stop and leaned over to give her a hug. "Good, I'm not late."

Paige grinned, her blue eyes sparkling beneath blond hair drawn up into a complicated knot at the top of her head. "That's because Nina told you we were meeting fifteen minutes before the actual time. After all these years, we know you well enough to make allowances for your perpetual tardiness."

"Smarty." Leah hopped off her bike and pushed it up the sidewalk beside her friend.

Paige gave her an assessing look. "I'm surprised you didn't get your skirt caught in your chain. All you need is a wreath of daisies in your hair to look like the original flower child."

Leah smoothed a lacy peasant blouse over her turquoise gauze skirt. "No one was uptight in the sixties, so I would have fit right in. Anyway, I'm only late because I got sidetracked talking to Sloan about the reunion."

"He'll always be Mr. Manning to me."

"It took me forever to think of him by his first name. Hey, there's Nina." She raised a hand as the third member of their intrepid trio since preschool days parked her Mini Cooper in front of Castaways and climbed out.

Nina Hutton's green eyes brightened with a smile as she waited beside her car. The ends of her short, wispy dark hair lifted in the breeze to flutter around her face. Wearing pencil-thin jeans, paint smudged on one knee, and a shirt the same cherry-red as her car beneath a denim jacket, she still managed to look like a model. Leah had gotten over being jealous of her friend's stunning looks years ago. Between Nina's casual elegance and Paige's petite perfection in a short white skirt and chunky knit sweater, she figured she'd better stop by the restroom to at least comb her hair.

"The gang's all here." Nina reached out to give them each a brief hug. "I've been holed up in my studio all day painting and could use some human interaction. Let's go order drinks and catch up."

Leah lifted the front wheel of her bike into the rack at the edge of the sidewalk and followed the other two women toward the entrance.

Paige glanced back. "Don't you ever lock that thing up?"

"Nobody's going to take it since it can't be worth more than fifty bucks, and there's not a person in town who wouldn't recognize it as mine, even if someone did."

"Good point." She pushed open the door. "Ooh, it's nice and warm in here. With the marine layer rolling in, there's a definite chill in the air."

Out over the ocean, a fog horn blew, long and mournful. Leah paused on the stoop to savor the cool dampness typical of early evening on the central Oregon coast. After a moment, she followed her friends inside.

"Why don't you two claim a table while I make myself presentable? With that wind, my hair probably looks like I battled through a typhoon."

Nina smiled. "Using a comb wouldn't hurt."

With a nod, Leah turned right down a short hallway to the ladies' room. Once inside, she sorted through her bag for a brush. A glance in the mirror made her wince. Her stick-straight, mink-brown hair had looked decent pulled back with a ribbon when she left for work that morning. By lunch, she'd lost the tie, and her mane hung in tangles down her back past her waist. Working out the knots took several minutes, but when she finished, her one concession to vanity shimmered beneath the crappy fluorescent lighting above the sink. Another search through the clutter in her purse turned up a tube of pink lipstick. She stroked on a coat and met her wide, chocolate-brown gaze in the mirror. "Passable."

After washing hands that had touched God knew how many germs that afternoon, she left the bathroom to wind through an assortment of tables to the one occupied by her friends on the far side of the bar. She plopped down on the empty chair, dropped her bag at her feet with a thump, and took a moment to enjoy the view of waves crashing on the beach below. Offshore, the three huge rocks that gave Siren Cove its name were silhouetted by the setting sun. A sigh slipped out. She loved Paige and Nina dearly, but once in a while it would be nice to face a man across the table instead of her old pals. Not that Brock would have noticed nature's splendor on the other side of the window since his gaze would have been glued to whatever sporting event was playing on the TV above the bar.

"What's wrong?"

"Huh?" Leah jerked her attention back to Paige.

"You were making a face like you just bit into a lemon."

"I was thinking about Brock."

Nina picked up the appetizer menu. "Why would you want to think about your loser ex-husband?"

"I've no idea. Chalk it up to a momentary brain freeze. I'm just thankful he won't be coming to our little reunion, since his family didn't move to Oregon until we were in high school."

"Praise be. I—" Paige broke off as their waitress approached. "Hey, Janice. Did you get your hair cut? It looks cute."

"Not cut. Colored." The older woman smiled. "Glad you like it. What can I get for you ladies?"

Nina glanced up. "Margaritas?"

Leah nodded. "After the day I had, you'd better bring us a pitcher."

"And some nachos." Nina slid the menu between a vase filled with blue-tinted carnations and the napkin holder. "Please."

"Coming right up." Janice tucked the order pad in her apron pocket and hurried away.

Paige leaned back in her chair and studied Leah. "Why was your day so rough?"

"Just a long week, plus the kids are beyond excited to create their own time capsule." She smiled. "Although they weren't exactly thrilled when I told them they had to write essays about growing up in the new millennium to put in with their treasures."

"Way to take a fun project and turn it into a learning opportunity. Spoilsport."

Leah laughed when Nina made a face at her. "Yeah, I'm a heartless tyrant. But between bouts of sadistic cruelty, I did reserve the upstairs banquet room at the Poseidon Grill for our reunion and set up menu options with the owner, Arnold Dorsey. Since his son was in our class, he cut us a break. The cost will be a flat twenty dollars per person for food. Soft drinks included. Cash bar."

"That was nice of him." Paige frowned. "I heard George got divorced a while back and moved home to Siren Cove to work for his dad."

"Mr. Dorsey mentioned George is living here now, which is why he'll be able to attend the party." She turned to glance at Nina. "How are the invitations coming along?"

"I just got them back from the printer." She paused as Janice returned, carrying a tray of salt-rimmed glasses and a pitcher of icy margaritas.

She poured a round of drinks then set down the pitcher. "Enjoy. I'll bring your nachos out in a few minutes."

"Thanks." Leah took a sip and looked over at Nina. "You were saying . . ."

"The invitations are ready to send just as soon as we have all the addresses."

Paige straightened. "That would be my cue. Drum roll, please."

Nina thrummed her fingers on the table.

"With my superior powers of detection, I've damn near found an address for every member of our fifth-grade class." Paige lifted her glass in a toast. "To the internet—a most wondrous creation."

Leah regarded her friend in awe. "You're amazing."

"I know." Paige set down her drink and pulled a

sheet of printed labels out of her purse to hand across the table to Nina. "Here you go."

"I'll put the invitations in the mail tomorrow. We have less than a month until the Fall Festival. I hope people will show up on such short notice."

"I think we'll get a decent turnout, especially since over a third of us still live in the area." Leah moved her glass as their waitress returned with a towering plate of nachos. "Yum, I'm starving." She smiled as Janice stepped back from the table. "Thank you."

"You're welcome. Yell if you need anything else."

As they dug into the appetizer, Paige paused with a chip dripping melted cheese halfway to her mouth and glanced over at Leah. "Did you talk to someone at the school about pulling up the bricks in the outside eating area off the cafeteria?"

"Huh? Why would I do that?"

Her friend frowned. "That's where we buried the time capsule. They built the patio over it, what, five years later?"

Nina wiped her fingers on a napkin. "I'd completely forgotten you went to see your grandparents that weekend and missed out on all the excitement."

The confusion in Paige's eyes deepened. "What are you talking about?"

"Didn't we tell her about it afterward?" Leah ran her finger over the salt-rimmed glass and glanced at Nina.

"Her grandpa had a stroke. I guess she was a little preoccupied at the time."

Paige dropped her chip and scowled. "Are you going to tell me what the heck I missed?"

"After the school board approved funding for the new patio, Leah, Ryan, and I decided to rescue our box." Nina grinned. "We snuck out in the middle of the night like a band of thieves, dug it up, and then reburied it in a safer location."

"You're kidding?"

"Nope." Leah scooped beans onto a chip. "Smart thinking on our part, right?"

"I guess so. Where's the time capsule now?"

"In the woods off the parking lot at the school." She took another swallow of her margarita. "Oh, wow, the bartender must have added extra tequila. This drink is making my eyes water."

"Then it's a good thing you're riding your bike and not driving." Nina set down her glass. "Speaking of Ryan, I wonder if he'll show up for our reunion now that he's rich and famous."

"It's not like he's a movie star or a celebrity athlete. So what if he created the latest and greatest social media sensation? Even though Crossroads is undoubtedly making him a fortune, Ryan isn't the kind of guy who would forget about his old pals who stuck by him when the other kids called him a geek." Paige glanced over at Leah. "Am I right?"

Leah's stomach sank along with her mellow mood, and suddenly her margarita tasted like bilge water. Or maybe it was just the lingering aftertaste of failure and regret. "Let's hope he has better things to do that weekend."

Nina leaned forward and frowned. "You don't want to see him?"

"So he can say *I told you so*?" Leah clenched her fists in her lap. "All those nasty comments he made about Brock when we announced our engagement the summer after college graduation were spot-on. I ran into him down on the beach a few days after Brock gave me an engagement ring, and Ryan told me I was making a huge mistake. Coming face-to-face with Ryan Alexander again will only confirm I'm the biggest loser on the planet."

"He's too nice a guy to give you a hard time about your divorce." Paige reached over to pat her arm. "He only blew up about Brock because you broke his heart our senior year."

"We were too different to survive as a couple over the long haul." Leah pressed a hand to the sudden ache in her chest. "I still feel horrible for hurting him, but prolonging the inevitable would have been even worse."

"Hey, we're on your side." Nina's green eyes held sympathy. "But surely you've seen him around town when he comes home to visit his mother?"

"Rarely, and not once since Brock and I split up for good."

"You dumped that cretin two years ago. Afterward, you did one heck of a job putting your life back together." Paige gave her arm a shake before releasing her. "Those old insecurities have no place in your world. You can face Ryan and everyone else with your head held high."

Leah took another swig of her drink. "Damn right." She nudged the nacho plate farther away, the sight of oozing beans and cheese having lost their attraction. "Enough about me. What have you two been doing?"

Nina shrugged. "Just work."

Paige nodded. "The same. I'm afraid my social life has been supremely uninteresting lately."

"God, we're pathetic." Leah picked up the pitcher and topped off all three glasses. "Let's drown our sorrows before we go out and adopt thirty cats each and retreat into our homes, never to be heard from again."

Paige laughed. "Come on, we aren't that bad."

"Anyway, we'll never be completely alone because we'll always have each other." Nina raised her glass. "Am I right?"

"True that." Paige lifted her drink in response.

Leah gave a solemn nod. "Cheers to best friends."

Chapter Two

Ryan Alexander pulled his Jeep up to the row of three mailboxes at the end of the paved road and leaned out the open window to flip down the door to the one on the far left. Grabbing his mail, he dropped the stack on the empty passenger seat, then swung his vehicle around to bump down the winding dirt track that served as his driveway. After half a mile of jolting through the thick pine forest, he entered the clearing in front of his cabin, set the brake, and sat for a moment to enjoy the view. The Three Sisters rose in majestic splendor to the southwest, white-capped after a cold snap and accompanying storm that had rolled through a few days before. Since moving to Central Oregon, he never tired of the panoramic vista.

Whistling beneath his breath, he scooped up the envelopes, then stepped out of his Jeep and turned to lift the bag of climbing gear off the back seat before he headed up the stone walkway to the house. Entering through the mudroom, he pulled off his boots and placed them on the shoe rack, then took the time to empty the bag and hang the harness and ropes on their respective pegs. He carried his mail into the kitchen and went straight to the sink to pour a glass of water before dropping onto a stool to check his phone for missed calls. One from his mom and another from Ursula. He listened to the first message.

"Ryan, why aren't you answering? You better not be screening your own mother. Give me a ring when you have a chance."

A glance at his watch told him he had exactly thirty-seven minutes before he needed to leave to meet Ursula for their date. Plenty of time still to shower and change. He pushed the button to return his mother's call.

"Ryan, I'm so glad you got back to me." His mom's ever cheerful voice filled his ear.

He turned on the speaker and laid the cell on the counter as he sorted through bills and junk mail. "How are you, Mom?"

"Terrific. I've been going to that new spin class, which is where I heard about the time-capsule party. Are you coming home for your reunion?"

His brows knit. "What the heck are you talking about?"

"Didn't you get an invitation?"

He set the power bill to the side as his hand stilled over a plain white envelope stamped with a return address from the Siren Cove Elementary Reunion Committee. "Hold on. It's in today's mail." He lifted the flap, pulled out a square white card with gold print, and scanned the contents. "Interesting."

"Won't it be fun to see your old classmates? And there's the added benefit of getting to spend time with your mother."

He smiled. "I don't need an excuse for that, but I was planning to schedule a Crossroads board meeting for the middle of October, which means I'll be in Portland over that weekend."

"Can't you choose a different date?"

"There really isn't anyone in particular I care about seeing, and I'm dead certain nothing in that time capsule is worth remembering."

"Oh, come on. You'll have a blast. When's the last time you talked to Leah? She and Paige and Nina organized the reunion."

An indrawn breath couldn't fill the sudden hollowness in his chest. "It's been a few years since we bumped into each other."

"She's divorced, you know."

He dropped the invitation on the counter. "I'm aware her marriage to Brock imploded. Not that it matters to me, personally."

"Well, I hope you'll at least consider coming to the reunion."

"Fine, but right now I have to go. I'm meeting a friend for dinner, and I don't want to be late."

"A date?" Her tone brightened. "I won't keep you, then. Have fun this evening."

"Thanks, Mom. Bye." He disconnected, then leaned an elbow on the counter as visions of Leah intruded. Her head thrown back and brown eyes soft with humor as she laughed at something silly and totally irrelevant. Holding her hand firmly in his as they strolled down the beach. Her voice choked with tears when she told him they had to break up . . . He let out a sigh. Ancient history.

He lifted the phone and tapped it to listen to Ursula's message.

"Ryan, I'm running late. A work glitch. I'll meet you at seven instead of six thirty. Sorry for the short notice."

At least she'd had the courtesy to call.

He slid off the stool and headed through the main room, then up the stairs to his loft bedroom. Charlie stretched, muscles flexing beneath thick gray fur before he opened golden eyes a slit and let out a ragged purr.

"You know you aren't supposed to be on my bed."

The cat's only response was a sleepy blink.

Ignoring Charlie's bad behavior, Ryan headed into the bathroom for a quick shower, his mind still on the reunion invitation. After washing off the dirt and sweat from a tricky climb at Smith Rock State Park, he stepped out onto the mat and grabbed a towel off the rack to rub across his chest. A glance in the mirror reassured him he wasn't still that too-skinny, too-smart boy the kids had teased. He had years of life experience . . . and the battle wounds to prove it. A jagged incision across his forearm from a nasty climbing fall a couple years before. Scar tissue on his side where he'd taken most of the skin off sliding down a rough rock wall. Not to mention the tiny lines at the corners of his eyes from staring at code on a computer screen for hours on end. He'd finally ditched his glasses for contacts after breaking too many pairs to count.

Giving his head a shake, he hung the towel on the rack, then stepped into his closet to pull out a polo shirt and khaki slacks. Five minutes later, he was dressed, had brushed the fur off his bed, fed the cat, and was ready to leave.

A fifteen-minute drive into Sisters brought him to the restaurant a few minutes early. Ryan locked the Jeep with the remote as he crossed the lot to enter the brightly lit foyer. He smiled at the hostess and asked for a table for two. He'd only been seated long enough to scan the wine list when Ursula entered and glanced in his direction. She spoke to the hostess then headed his way.

Standing, he pulled out her chair. "You look terrific this evening."

Ursula made the most of her assets, wearing sleek, professional clothing that suited her tall, slim build. As usual, she'd confined her unruly red curls in a knot at the back of her head. She commuted daily to her law offices in Bend and only let down her hair—literally and figuratively—on the weekends. Ryan had nothing but respect for her drive and ambition. He'd been the same way not so long ago. Before he got lucky with Crossroads.

"Crazy day at work." She picked up her menu. "Did you order drinks yet?"

"I haven't had a chance. Shall we choose a bottle of wine?"

"Sure."

He let her make the decision, and only gave his menu cursory attention before ordering a steak with a side Caesar salad. She chatted about her current cases, stopping short of revealing confidential information, while they sipped merlot and ate crusty rolls. He nodded and made an occasional comment, but his thoughts bounced between the climb he wanted to tackle over the weekend, the new code for a website app, and the damn time-capsule reunion he had no interest in attending.

After the server delivered their meals, he took a deep sniff and smiled. "Smells good."

Ursula set down the fork she'd picked up and frowned. "Have you listened to one word I've said?"

He jerked his attention back to his dinner partner. "Yes, of course. Something about a witness refusing to cooperate."

"I mentioned that ten minutes ago. What's on your mind?"

Ryan added sour cream to his potato. "Not much."

"Really?"

"Okay, a challenging code issue, an all-day climb I want to make on Saturday, and the possibility of a trip back to Siren Cove for a grade school reunion."

"Doesn't sound like nothing to me." She folded her napkin into precise squares. "But, if I hadn't forced the issue, you wouldn't have mentioned any of those activities, which are obviously important enough to occupy the majority of your attention."

"I didn't think you'd be interested, since you don't climb and have admitted computer technology makes you crazy."

"Still, they matter to you." Her eyes narrowed. "I've about had it, Ryan."

"Huh?" For the first time all evening, she had his full attention. "What's wrong?"

"Our relationship." She took a bite of her chicken and chewed furiously. "We've been dating exclusively for six months, and I barely know any more about you than I did after our first few weeks together. Except for griping about the way your ex-partner screwed you over, you don't share your personal feelings. Emotionally, you're unavailable."

His stomach clenched, and suddenly his steak smelled less than appetizing. "You want me to complain more? Seems like I bitched plenty about Jay's Judas move."

"I want *you* to want to open up. And not just about work. You mentioned going home. Did it cross your mind to ask me to come with you? Six months of dating, and I've never met your mother."

The knot tightened. "I guess you could come along, but—"

She held up a hand. "You didn't think I'd be *in-terested.*" Her tone was edged with irritation. "Of course, you wouldn't want to come with me if our positions were reversed. When I asked you to spend Labor Day weekend with my family, your eyes practically glazed over."

Were my feelings that obvious? He cleared his throat. "I really enjoy hanging out with you, but I'll be the first to admit I'm slow to take down my barriers in any relationship, personal or professional. Once burned and all that. To me, adding family to the mix is a big step."

"After half a year, you don't trust me enough to meet your mother?" She shook her head. "I've been trying to ignore the obvious, but I don't think I can anymore."

He was afraid to ask. Maybe Ursula didn't stir strong emotions, but she was great company. Smart. Attractive. If he stayed on the defensive, she couldn't take advantage of his unsuspecting nature the way Jay had. As far as he was concerned, a casual romance was close to perfect. For the first time, it occurred to him he might be the only one in this relationship who felt that way.

Time to face the inevitable. "What are you saying?"

"I think it would be in both our best interests to part ways. No animosity. No tears." She wadded her napkin and pushed back her chair. "Not many, anyway. Better to end things now before I let myself fall completely in love with you."

"Ursula—"

She rose to her feet and held up a hand. "Don't." Her voice cracked. "Just don't."

He pressed his lips tight as she hurried across the restaurant. The front door closed with a thump. After a moment he pushed his plate away, then rubbed his temples where a tension headache had taken hold.

"Would you like me to box those dinners for you, Mr. Alexander?"

He glanced up as the pretty young server stopped at his side and gave him a sympathetic smile. "I suppose so. Maybe I'll be hungry later."

She took the two plates and left the bill on the table.

Ryan pulled out his wallet and removed several twenties. A few of the other diners cast curious looks his way and whispered. His cheeks heated as he corked the wine bottle and waited for the server to return with his to-go boxes. When she finally approached with a bulging plastic bag, he practically leapt from his chair to take it from her. "Thank you."

She smiled. "I'll get your change."

"No need. Have a good evening."

"You, too."

Not very likely.

The cool breeze rushed over him as he stepped outside, tempering his embarrassment. In the parking lot, he paused beside his Jeep to release some of his pent-up frustration. *Dumped again.* Okay, maybe the breakup wasn't all Ursula's fault. Maybe he wasn't the most emotionally available guy around. Didn't mean her rejection wasn't still a sharp stab to the gut.

Ryan opened the car door, slid onto the seat and set down his to-go bag, then started the Jeep. Rolling down the windows, he let the cold wind blow out the conflicting emotions flitting around in his head. An irrational mix of anger and irritation—with himself and Ursula. Regret that he'd hurt a woman he genuinely liked. Loneliness he was used to, but this time it came with a surprising hint of relief. The scent of pine along with a touch of moisture in the air soothed his taunt nerves as he drove. By the time he reached his house, he was almost able to convince himself the breakup was for the best. Almost. After unlocking the door, he slammed it shut behind him and jumped when Charlie twined around his ankles.

He bent to stroke the cat's sleek back. What

did he need with a woman when he had a cat for companionship? Wandering into the kitchen, he flipped on a light, set the wine bottle and to-go bag on the granite countertop, then braced his hands on the kitchen sink to stare out into the darkness.

His career was currently on the fast track to unimaginable wealth. He could hardly fathom the popularity Crossroads had achieved in just a few short years, but now that he could slow down and enjoy his success, he had no one with whom to share it. He turned abruptly to pull a wineglass down from the cupboard. After uncorking the half-full bottle and pouring a glass, he took a fork and knife from the drawer and yanked his to-go box out of the bag. Good thing he liked cold steak.

As he ate, Ryan's gaze landed on the reunion invitation, and he picked up the card to tap it on the counter. *Should I go to the reunion?*

He shook his head, dropped the invitation, and returned his attention to the steak. Screw that. He had no desire to parade his success in front of his old classmates . . . or stir up complicated feelings he'd long since put to rest. He didn't need that kind of aggravation when—

A gagging sound interrupted his morose thoughts.

Ryan turned on the stool just as Charlie coughed up a huge hairball on the hardwood floor, gagged for a few seconds more, then lifted his head to saunter away.

The perfect ending to a shitty evening. *Story of my life.*

* * *

He counted ten steps out from the cafeteria door, shortening his stride to allow for the smaller stature of a ten-year-old girl, and stopped to pull on a pair of leather work gloves. This was the place. He distinctly remembered the class electing Leah Grayson to do the honor of choosing the exact spot where the time capsule would be buried. Everyone had liked Leah, who was nice to even the nastiest kids. Kneeling in the dark with only faint moonlight to illuminate the brick pavers, he inserted the crowbar between the cracks and wrenched up the first brick. By the time he'd pulled up a half dozen, he was sweating.

Goddamn women and their stupid idea to open the box after a measly twenty years. He'd figured the truth was safely buried until well after he was dead and oblivious to the fallout. With the two out-of-town detectives nosing around back then—not to mention the panicked look he'd intercepted—he'd been pressed to make a quick decision. The time capsule had seemed like the ideal place to hide evidence that would shock this picture-perfect community. Untainted on the surface, Siren Cove was darker at the core than the good citizens could ever imagine.

The crowbar hit the ground with a clatter. He picked up the shovel and stabbed the metal tip into the dirt. Again and again and again. After digging a good two feet, he straightened and frowned. He should have uncovered the box by now. Was his pacing off, or had he walked out at the wrong angle?

Two hours later, he'd dug up half the area beneath the patio and still hadn't found the damn box. To the east, a hint of dawn colored the night sky.

Shit. He couldn't keep digging and risk getting caught. As it was, news that a vandal had damaged school property was sure to be a hot topic of conversation the second his unproductive excavation site was discovered. Maybe they'd blame a giant gopher.

The spark of amusement faded. No way could he conceal his futile night's work the way he'd originally intended. Not that it mattered much, since the box obviously wasn't under the bricks anymore. The stupid women planning the reunion would be disappointed when they failed to find their hidden fifth-grade treasures. Relief filled him, but only for a moment. He bent to pick up his tools, and after a final glance back at the mounds of dirt and stacks of pavers, hurried around the school toward the parking lot.

If the time capsule wasn't where they'd buried it, where the hell was it? More importantly, who had it now? Maybe the work crew who'd laid the patio had found the box and tossed it in a dumpster fifteen years ago. He could only cross his fingers and pray the roll of film he'd slipped inside at the last second was lost forever.

Chapter Three

Leah rounded the end of the grocery store aisle and stopped with a jerk to avoid contact with the oncoming shopper near a tall display of cereal. "Sorry, I wasn't watching where I . . . Mrs. Alexander!" Her gaze locked with familiar blue eyes beneath short silver hair as she smiled at Ryan's mother. "It's nice to see you."

"My goodness, Leah, don't you look pretty. I swear you haven't aged a day since high school."

"That's sweet. A total lie, but sweet."

Marion Alexander grinned. "I always enjoyed your sense of humor." She maneuvered her cart in closer. "Is the rumor someone ripped up the patio behind the elementary school true?"

Leah nodded. "The popular theory is teenagers did it on some sort of dare." She frowned. "I can't imagine why, though. And what's really strange is that's where we originally buried our time capsule. Did you hear about our fifth-grade class reunion?"

"I did. I've been trying to talk Ryan into coming

home for it." She pressed her lips together. "He says he's busy that weekend." Reaching out, Marion pulled a box of cornflakes off the shelf and set it in her cart. "I wish he'd change his mind because I haven't seen him in a few months." She jerked her head up. "Wait a minute. What do you mean by 'originally buried?'"

"When we were in high school, Ryan, Nina, and I relocated the box before they built the patio."

"Huh. That is strange." She moved out of the way as a harried-looking mother herded two toddlers toward the checkout stand. "Well, at least you'll still be able to open your time capsule at the party."

"I'm certainly happy about that. Nice talking to you, Mrs. Alexander."

"You, too, dear."

Relief lightened Leah's steps as she browsed the produce section and picked out a shiny purple eggplant for dinner. Ryan wasn't coming to the reunion. She'd be able to relax and enjoy herself without his presence as a constant reminder of past foolish choices. Still, a hint of regret niggled. They'd been inseparable before they took their relationship to the next level. Closer even than her friendship with Paige and Nina. Too late to return to that once comfortable platonic bond now. Even if she wanted to.

After paying for her groceries, Leah loaded them into her tote bag and headed out to the parking lot to retrieve her bike. A light rain fell, sending up a steamy aroma from the damp pavement. Pulling up the hood on her jacket, she waved to Marion as Ryan's mother crossed toward an older-model Buick. Beside her, a compact car pulled out of a slot and rolled forward. When a muffled screech sounded from the rear seat, the driver glanced over her shoulder and reached back . . .

"Look out!"

Leah's shouted warning came too late as the front bumper clipped the older woman and sent her sprawling on the asphalt. The paper sack filled with groceries hit the ground, and boxes and cans scattered while a carton of eggs smashed beneath the car's tire.

Releasing her bike, Leah sprinted toward Ryan's mother and dropped onto her knees beside her. "Are you okay?"

A scrape marred the side of Marion's face, and her teeth clamped together on a moan. Her right arm twisted beneath her at an odd angle.

"Oh, my God. I'm so sorry." The driver ran around the car to crouch beside them. "The twins were . . ." She broke off on a cry. "Oh, no. You're hurt."

Leah didn't bother to look at her. "Mrs. Alexander, I'm calling for an ambulance. I think your arm is broken, so try not to move."

"Good Lord, it hurts worse than childbirth." She grimaced then glanced up at the sobbing woman. "Stop that. Accidents happen."

"I feel horrible. What can I do?"

Leah pulled out her cell, not nearly as forgiving as Marion. "Move your car out of the way so the paramedics will have room to work when the ambulance gets here."

Brushing away tears, the woman stood as a handful of people ran toward them. With a surge of relief, Leah recognized one bearded face with steady brown eyes.

"Dr. Carlton, thank heavens. I was just going to call nine-one-one."

"I already did. Move aside, everyone." The doctor knelt on the wet pavement with little regard for his slacks. "How're you feeling, Marion? Let me take a look at that arm."

"I've been better, Arlen." Her gaze was slightly unfocused as she looked beyond the doctor. "Leah, will you call Ryan and tell him what happened?"

"Of course." When a siren sounded in the distance, she stepped back. "I'll stop by the hospital later to check on you. Hang in there, Mrs. A."

Marion smiled at the old nickname, but her voice was shaky when she spoke. "Takes more than a ton of metal to keep me down."

Leah walked back toward the store to get out of the rain as an ambulance and a police cruiser pulled into the lot. With an unsteady hand, she gripped her phone and pulled up the contact list for the reunion Paige had shared with her, found Ryan's cell number and dialed, then hoped he'd pick up.

A voice she remembered all too well answered in a cautious tone.

"Hello."

"Hi, Ryan. It's Leah." When he didn't respond, she cleared the hitch out of her throat. "Leah Grayson."

"This is . . . unexpected. How are you?"

"I'm fine." She drew in a breath. "I'm calling because your mom was hit by a car."

"What?" His voice was sharp. Urgent.

"She's okay, well mostly. An ambulance is taking her to the hospital, and Doctor Carlton was on hand when the accident happened. She has some scrapes and a broken arm. At least it looked like it was broken to me. She asked me to call you."

He was quiet for several long seconds. "Why you?"

"I was in the parking lot at the store where she was hit. I promised to stop by and check on her later, once they admit her. I'm afraid I don't have any more information."

"I'll leave here as soon as I pack a bag. Will you tell my mom I'll see her just as soon as I can get there?"

"Of course."

"Thank you, Leah."

Tears pressed against her eyelids. He sounded hesitant, a little lost. In her mind, Ryan was the boy he'd been all those years ago, unwilling to admit the name-calling from the class bully cut deep. "You're welcome. Drive carefully."

"I will." The connection went dead.

Leah pocketed her phone, then ran over as the EMT loaded Marion into the back of the ambulance on a stretcher. "Mrs. A?"

She lifted her head. "Leah?"

"Ryan will be at the hospital just as soon as he can. I'll stop by to visit you once they have you settled into a room."

"Thank you, dear."

A female medic stepped into the vehicle beside her patient, while her male partner slammed the doors shut and hurried around to the front. A moment later the ambulance pulled away.

Leah stared after it.

"Ms. Grayson, I'm Officer Long. I'll need to get a witness statement from you."

Turning, she faced the cop who'd been talking to the driver and smiled. "I remember you from high school. Your younger sister and I were in the same grade."

She glanced toward the car where both kids were still crying in the back. Their mother sat on the edge of the driver's seat with the door open and looked about ready to collapse onto the pavement. Sympathy stirred as she met the woman's fearful gaze.

Leah turned back to the officer. "It was an accident, a single moment of distraction that ended badly."

"Maybe I could get a few more details, but we can have this conversation over near the store entrance out of the drizzle."

She nodded and followed him across the lot.

Once they reached shelter, he pulled out a notepad. "First, your contact information and relationship to the victim."

Leah reeled off her name, address, and phone number then hesitated. "Uh, Mrs. Alexander is an old friend. I used to date her son back in high school. Since then, we've run into each other now and then." She winced. "Poor choice of words, under the circumstances."

His lips quivered beneath a neatly trimmed

moustache. "All right, let's hear the sequence of events from your perspective."

"Mrs. Alexander was crossing the lot to her car when the woman over there"—she pointed toward the compact car—"pulled out of her parking spot. One of the kids in the back seat let out a yell I could hear through the closed window, and the driver glanced back as she rolled forward. I shouted, but Mrs. A didn't have time to move out of the way before the car hit her."

Officer Long closed his notebook. "Thanks for your help."

Leah picked up the tote bag full of groceries she'd dropped beside her bike, then glanced back at the young mother slumped in the seat of her car. "I feel bad for her but worse for Mrs. Alexander. What's going to happen to the woman?"

"That will depend on whether Mrs. Alexander wants to press charges for negligent driving. Right now, I'll let her get those kids home."

"Oh." She straddled the crossbar on her bike. "Can I leave now?"

"Sure. Have a nice evening."

"You, too."

Leah pedaled hard through the light rain, heading north out of town along the highway. Before long, she turned down the lengthy, rutted drive leading to her family home set on a bluff overlooking the ocean. Before she could get off her bike, Barney bounded over and almost knocked her down.

"Easy, boy. I'm glad to see you, too." She rubbed the soft ears of her big mongrel and tried to avoid sloppy doggie kisses as she wheeled her bike into the carport beside her old Audi wagon. After a detour into the garden behind the house to pick the last of the ripe tomatoes and pinch off a few sprigs of oregano and basil, she headed straight into the kitchen through the back door and set her bag on the counter.

Shedding her wet coat, she toed off her boots and left them where they fell, then dug her phone out of her bag to call the hospital. After identifying herself to the receptionist on duty and requesting an update on Mrs. Alexander, she pried out a few sketchy details from the tight-lipped woman. Apparently, there were complications, whatever that meant. Marion was currently waiting to have her arm set and wasn't expected to be available for visitors other than family until the following day.

Leah scowled as she set the phone on the blue-tiled countertop then glanced over at Barney, waiting by his food bowl. "I guess I'll tell them I'm her niece. But first, dinner for you and me, both."

An hour later, Barney dozed under the table while she ate eggplant with fresh tomatoes. When the phone rang, she reached for her cell, only to realize it was the house phone's old-fashioned clamor, not her cell's muted chime.

"What the heck?" No one called the landline except solicitors and, occasionally, her grandma. On the off chance it wasn't someone trying to sell life insurance or new cable service, she pushed back her chair and hurried into the living room to grab the handset off the end table. "Hello."

"Do you know where the box is?" The voice crackled and broke.

"Excuse me. You must have the wrong—"

"The time capsule." The male voice faded in and out. "What's the point in holding the reunion without the box?"

Word of the patio demolition must have spread. "Don't worry, we still have it. Or, rather, we know where it's currently buried. Who's this?"

The dial tone droned in her ear.

"Huh? That was strange."

When her dog strolled to the door and whined, she hung up and walked over to let him out. Stepping onto the long front porch, she braced her hands on the railing to gaze out across the ocean. The rain had stopped, and the sun was sinking through a thin layer of clouds, giving the sky a rosy glow above the three huge rocks in the cove.

The conversation had been weird. She wondered which of her old classmates had cared enough about the time capsule to call. *Definitely a little odd.* She shivered and rubbed her hands up and down her arms, then went back inside to finish her dinner.

By the time she'd washed the dishes then showered and changed, she felt fairly certain Marion must be settled into a room for the night. She'd promised to visit Ryan's mother, and she intended to keep her word. Grabbing a long sweater off the hook by the door, she headed to the carport.

On the drive to the hospital, memories stirred. Building forts in the woods near the Alexanders' home. Riding bikes through the neighborhood at dusk. Creating science experiments that, on one occasion, had nearly burned down the house. In her teen years, she'd hung out less frequently, mostly because she and Ryan had wanted more privacy by then. Ryan hadn't been the only one who'd expected their relationship to end happily ever after . . . until their differences led to frequent arguments that left her aching and miserable.

Leah pulled into the visitor's lot near the front entrance and parked, then leaned against the steering wheel. The least she owed Mrs. A was a visit to check on her welfare. Ryan's mother would certainly do the same for her. She locked the car and hurried toward the glass doors that slid open at her approach. The young woman who manned the front desk glanced up and smiled.

"Hi, I'm here to see my aunt, Marion Alexander. She was admitted earlier with a broken arm."

The receptionist checked her computer. "I'm not sure if Mrs. Alexander is out of surgery yet. You can wait up in the lounge on the second floor until the doctor has a chance to speak to her family."

"Thank you." Leah's steps echoed on the stone floor as she crossed to the elevator and pushed the button. Worry niggled as the metal doors slid open. Wouldn't a simple break have been attended to by now?

When the elevator rose to her floor and stopped, she stepped out into the hallway and turned left toward the waiting room. Only one other person occupied the area. A man stood facing the window overlooking the parking lot, hands planted on slim hips. A navy T-shirt stretched across a muscled back, and impressive biceps flexed each time he clenched and unclenched his fists. Her stomach fluttered. The hottie must be nervous, but then most people hanging out in a hospital probably were.

When Leah's shoes squeaked on the linoleum, the man spun around. His gaze met hers, and blue eyes widened.

"Ryan?" Why had she made his name sound like a question? The steady blue eyes above a strong nose and wide lips definitely belonged to her old . . . pal. Boyfriend. One-time lover. The man facing her couldn't be pigeonholed into a neat category. Nothing about their relationship had been simple after that first kiss, and he didn't look much like the man she remembered. The ever-present glasses and shaggy, dark hair were gone. Not to mention he'd put on at least twenty pounds since she'd last seen him. All of it muscle. She struggled for composure, hoping she didn't look like the proverbial deer in the headlights.

"Leah." His gaze swept over her, from her hair pulled back in a French braid to hang past her waist, across the sweater belted over a pair of patterned leggings, to her feet encased in ballet flats. "You haven't change at all."

"You have." The words were wrenched from her throat, and her cheeks heated.

"Lately, I spend less time staring at a computer screen and more time outside." He stuffed his hands into the pockets of his cargo shorts. "It was nice of you to come out to check on my mom."

"I was concerned. How is she?"

His eyes darkened. "I haven't spoken to the doctor yet. I only arrived a few minutes ago."

"You made good time from Portland." The small

talk felt awkward. Wrong. Still, she didn't know what else to say.

"I don't live in Portland anymore. I moved to Sisters after Crossroads no longer needed my attention twenty-four seven. I wanted to be close to the best rock climbing around." He shrugged. "What's the point in creating a successful company if you're too busy to enjoy yourself?"

That explained all those muscles.

She pried her gaze away. "I didn't know."

"No reason why you should." He glanced behind her, and suddenly the insecure boy she'd known so well broke through the new, ultra-confident veneer. The hands he pulled from his pockets weren't quite steady. "Doctor, how's my mom?"

Leah turned as a woman in blue scrubs approached. She stepped closer to Ryan and reached for his hand as they waited for the doctor to speak.

"I'm afraid the news is mixed."

He stiffened beside her. "Let's hear the bad first."

Leah squeezed his fingers tight. Typical Ryan, saving the good for last. Facing the worst head-on.

"The break in her arm was a compound fracture. Healing will take longer and require quite a bit of therapy." The doctor smiled. "But I expect she'll make a full recovery in time. Your mother is a real trooper. You should be able to see her shortly."

The tension drained out of him, and he swayed on his feet. "Thank you. I was worried."

The emotion in his voice brought a lump to Leah's throat. Without thinking, she slid an arm around him and hugged tight. His warmth encompassed her as he gathered her against his chest. Being in his arms felt familiar and odd at the same time. She welcomed the comfort, but a zing of electricity startled her. She jerked away.

Their gazes locked, his mirroring the same surprise currently twisting her insides into a knot. He stepped back.

"Thanks for coming, Leah. I'll be sure to tell Mom you stopped by."

She struggled to put more space between them. "Since you're here to keep her company, I should probably go."

He nodded. "It's late. I imagine you have other things to do."

Leah couldn't think of anything, but she didn't argue. He was right. It was late. A dozen years too late to change her mind about Ryan now.

Chapter Four

Ryan paused in the living room doorway and glanced back at his mother. "Are you sure you don't need anything else before I go?"

"If I do, I can get it myself. I may not be able to drive or do cartwheels, but I can fill the kettle with water if I want a cup of tea." She moved her book and rested her good hand on Charlie's back when the cat rolled over on her lap. "For heaven's sake, go for a run or a ride or whatever. I don't need you to hover over me."

He grinned. "If you say so. I'll be back in time to cook dinner."

"You do that. I consider meal preparation payback for all the years I fed you."

"Seems only fair. By the way, you're spoiling my cat."

Her eyes narrowed as she studied Ryan. "I'd rather spoil a grandchild, but I'll take what I can get."

He snorted, then crossed the entry and let the

front door swing shut behind him with a bang. She'd better enjoy Charlie since babies weren't anywhere near his radar. His steps slowed on the brick walk as a handful of shouting and laughing kids rode their bikes past the driveway. Memories of Leah matching his pace as they pumped hard to reach the top of the hill at the end of the street, then crouched low to race back down again played through his mind. He stuffed his hands in the pockets of his windbreaker and headed down the path through the empty lot next door, in the direction of the beach. The two of them had made a good team before she decided they were simply too different to last over the long haul. He kicked a pinecone to send it ricocheting off a rock. Turned out she was right.

He trotted across the road and followed the steep trail down the cliff to the beach. When he reached the sand, he stopped to stretch. He wasn't a runner, but he needed exercise, and he hadn't had the foresight to bring his mountain bike in his mad dash to leave home after Leah's call. Charlie was lucky he'd remembered him. Setting out at an easy pace, he headed north along an endless stretch of sand. Every now and then he passed a couple strolling near the water's edge or another jogger and nodded a greeting, but the cold wind blowing off the ocean discouraged casual beach-goers.

Ryan had run a couple of miles and left the center of town far behind when a big dog loped toward him from the direction of the bluff that edged the beach. The brown and black mongrel looked like some sort of shepherd mix. He slowed as the dog approached, then sped up again when the animal showed no signs of aggression. His new pal fell in at his side.

"Where did you come from?" He squinted against the sun and made out a zigzagging path down the cliff face. "Huh, I didn't know anyone lived this far out except . . . Leah." He stopped and reached a cautious hand toward the dog's collar where tags dangled. One in the shape of a bone identified him as Barney. Pulling out his cell, he scrolled through recent calls to match the phone number on the tag. As he suspected, the mutt belonged to Leah.

With a sigh, he tapped the number to dial.

"Hello." She sounded breathless when she answered.

"Leah, I have your dog."

Silence greeted him before she spoke again. "Ryan?"

"Sorry, I assumed . . . never mind. Yeah, this is Ryan. I found Barney—at least that's what his tag says—on the beach. I thought you might be worried about him."

"Honestly, I didn't realize he was gone. He likes to hang out down by the water, and he never strays too far."

His brows shot up. "You don't keep him tied up or fenced in?"

"No. He never wanders out to the highway, and he's perfectly friendly. Why shouldn't he enjoy his freedom while I'm at work most days?"

Since he didn't figure she wanted to hear a lecture on responsible dog ownership, he kept his thoughts to himself. "Is he smart enough to stop following me when I turn to run back to town?"

"I'm pretty sure he is." She didn't sound the least bit convinced. "Uh, maybe I'll come down to get him. Do you mind waiting five minutes while I get dressed?"

He swayed a little as an image of Leah straight from the shower weakened his knees. He'd only seen her that way once, years before, but the picture had been etched forever on his mind. "I'll run a little farther and be back in five."

"Thank you, Ryan."

"No problem." He stuck his phone in his pocket. Hopefully pounding the sand would knock the mental image of Leah, wet and naked, out of his head. He took off running, with Barney at his heels. Two and a half minutes later, he turned to jog back. As he approached the bottom of the stairs cut into the bluff, one glance told him Leah wasn't on her way down yet.

What a shock. When had she ever been on time? Turning into a stiff breeze, he gazed out at the three monolithic rocks far offshore. Stooping, he picked up a handful of pebbles and tossed them one at a time into the waves while the dog jumped and splashed, then ran back to shake all over him. *Perfect.*

"Sorry, it took me longer than I thought."

He turned slowly to face Leah. She wore a purple hoodie and a pair of faded cutoffs. Long, shapely legs stretched forever. She'd pulled her damp hair back in a ponytail and hadn't bothered with makeup. Her resemblance to the girl he'd loved in high school was strong enough to take his breath away. Everyone else aged, but apparently not Leah.

Barney bounded up to her and planted his front paws on her chest. Though she staggered backward, Leah patted her dog before pushing him down.

She brushed dirty wet prints off her hoodie then glanced up. "How's your mom?"

"Hanging in there, despite her frustration. The doctor says she'll get her cast off in six to eight weeks. Until then, she can't drive to appointments or the grocery store, and cooking is a challenge, so I'm staying in Siren Cove."

Leah dug her bare toes into the sand. "That's awfully nice of you."

"I could hire a caretaker, but Mom would hate having a stranger constantly around the house. I may have to travel to Portland a couple of times for meetings and home again to collect more of my stuff, but my work schedule is flexible." He met her soft brown gaze. "Have laptop will travel."

"If you'll be in town for a while, we're likely to run into each other now and then."

From her tone, he wasn't sure if she was neutral or apprehensive about future meetings. "I was sorry to hear about your divorce."

She stiffened. "Were you?"

He plunged his hands into his pockets. "Yeah. Maybe I thought Brock was an ass, but I never wanted you to be unhappy, despite . . ."

"Well, you were right. I thought his lighthearted outlook on life would be a good match for my own. Turned out he didn't take anything seriously, including our marriage vows. I guess I should have listened to you when you said he'd hurt me."

He clenched his fists. "He cheated on you?"

"More than once. I was too stupid to believe the rumors the first time. Maybe I just didn't want to acknowledge I was such a bad judge of character."

He stepped toward her to touch her arm before pulling back. "Any man who would abuse your trust has shit for brains."

She smiled, and the shadows in her eyes disappeared. "I won't argue with that. Anyway, it's finished. Now, I thank God he wanted to wait to have kids, so I don't have that tie to bind us forever. He relocated up north after we split up, and I moved back into my old childhood home when my parents left town."

"Mom mentioned they moved to California a while back."

She nodded. "My sister lives in the Bay Area now. When Brenda had her second baby, they wanted to be closer to their grandkids since it seemed obvious I wouldn't be producing offspring anytime soon."

"We have that in common."

Leah studied him for a moment. "My grandma is still here, though. She lives in the senior apartments over on the other side of town."

"I always loved your grandma. What a character."

"Gram hasn't changed much. She keeps me on my toes."

Ryan took a step back. "Well, it was nice to catch up, but I'd better get going." Still, he hesitated, reluctant to walk away. "Is it too late to change the response I sent in for the reunion party from a no to a yes? Since I'll be here anyway—"

"Of course not. It looks like we'll have a decent turnout. I was surprised at how many people plan to come."

"That's great." He retreated further, even though part of him wanted to reach out and touch the curve of her cheek then bend in to kiss those full lips. Not the part he used for thinking, however, and he wasn't stupid enough to let attraction overtake common sense. "See you, Leah."

"Ryan?"

He stopped. "Yes?"

"If you feel like company on a run or a hike or a bike ride, give me a call. I try to get out and exercise most days, at least when it isn't pouring rain. Sometimes even when it is."

"Aren't you still teaching?"

"Sure, but I go after class lets out. Or, I get up early." Her quick smile held a touch of uncertainty. "If you'd rather not, I understand. But, we were friends first, before . . ." She glanced away.

"Before we fell in love."

Her gaze swung up to meet his. "Yeah, before that. Maybe we can be friends again instead of passing awkwardly by each other on the street with no more than a nod. Or you can simply tell me to go to hell."

A snort of laughter escaped. "Way to call it like it is, Leah. Your honesty is nothing if not refreshing."

"I don't see much point in pretending we don't have a history together."

"No, none at all." His chest tightened. "Why

not? I'll give you a call. Maybe tomorrow. I still need to go home to get my mountain bike, but we could hike."

"I'd like that." She turned away. "Have a nice evening, Ryan."

"You, too." He took off at a sprint. *Not to escape conflicting emotions I don't want to acknowledge let alone dissect. That isn't it at all.* He ran harder, facing into the wind. *Am I an idiot for letting Leah back into my life, even for an afternoon hike?* Maybe. But she'd stirred up more of a reaction in him in the last ten minutes than Ursula had in six months of dating. An inner voice scoffed. *Trepidation and lust. Not the best combo.*

By the time he reached town, he was sweating bullets. He stopped below the path up into his neighborhood to walk in circles to cool off. A lone figure heading his way made him pause. He recognized the confident stride even before she got close enough to identify.

"Nina." A grin stretched his lips. "It's good to see you."

She ran the last few yards and reached out to hug him.

"Don't. I'm dripping sweat and probably smell like a dirty sock."

"I don't care." She hugged him anyway. "Sorry to hear about your mom's accident."

"Yeah, she doesn't much like having her independence curtailed. She's the strongest woman I know."

"I'll say. She raised you single-handedly after your dad died all those years ago."

"Lucky for Mom, I was a perfect child."

Nina laughed. "I seem to remember a few less than perfect moments." She hesitated then squinted into the setting sun. "Have you talked to Leah yet?"

"I ran into her, or rather her dog, on the beach a half hour ago. We chatted for a few minutes after she came down to get Barney."

"And?"

"What do you mean, *and*? We had a civil conversation."

"That's good, I guess."

"Leah played the friend card. She wants to go hiking and not act awkward when we see each other."

Her green eyes glimmered with humor. "Sounds like Leah. Always the peacemaker. I know she was a little apprehensive about seeing you after she finally kicked Brock's cheating, lying ass out of her life."

He reared back. "Why? I'm not a total jerk, am I?"

"No, and Paige and I both told her you wouldn't make her feel worse about not recognizing the man for what he was sooner, especially since she constantly beats herself up about it." She paused. "Despite how your relationship with her ended."

"You mean with Leah telling me my OCD would drive her insane?"

"She didn't say anything of the sort! Leah's far too gracious to be cruel."

"Okay, maybe she couched her rejection in softer terms, but that was the gist." He glanced out over the rolling waves before meeting her gaze again.

"Leah is right about one thing. We were friends first. Salvaging that part of our relationship would be . . . nice."

"Damn right." Nina patted his shoulder. "If I don't see you again before the reunion, we'll hang out then and catch up on what it's like to rub elbows with the rich and famous. You are planning to come, aren't you?"

"I told Leah I would. For the record, my life is pretty normal. Quiet, maybe even a little lonely, despite the success of Crossroads."

"Huh, sounds like you should do something about that." She retreated a few steps. "And I should get back to work. I only came down here to clear the paint fumes out of my head."

"Sure. Good talking to you, Nina." With a wave, he headed toward the path up the cliff, then paused for a moment to glance back as she walked away.

Nina's long stride quickly increased the distance between them but didn't detract from her lithe beauty. She was stunning. A solitary creature with only a few close friends, they'd always had far more in common than he had with the gregarious Leah. But not the chemistry.

He climbed the steep slope as he contemplated the oddity of coming home again. Time seemed to have dissolved since he'd returned to Siren Cove. Maybe what he needed was a solid dose of Leah in the present to clear away memories of the past, so he could move on.

Once and for all.

* * *

"I tell you, there's no way of finding the stupid box before the reunion committee digs it up again." He ran a hand across the back of his neck as the irritating voice on the other end of the line droned on and on in his ear.

"Look, the only other option would be to somehow convince Leah Grayson to tell me where they buried it, and she's not going to do that without asking questions." He gritted his teeth. "I've no intention of putting a target on my back if something goes wrong."

"Then eliminate the problem. Bring the nosy bitch to the holding room after you get the information from her. We'll need a sacrifice for our Samhain celebration. Why not her?"

"We've avoided detection for well over a century because we have one rule. *Never in our own backyard.* We find our sacrifices elsewhere." His hand shook as he shifted the phone to his other ear. "Twenty years ago, we took one a little too close, and questions were asked, as you very well know. It's the reason I had to hide the film in the first place." His voice rose. "I won't make the same mistake twice."

"The situation was under control, so your panic then wasn't necessary." Heavy breathing followed. "How do you intend to fix the problem?"

"I'll either be there when they open the box or have someone I trust in position. One of us will lift the roll of film before those women notice it, and make certain the damn thing disappears for good." His tone was sharp. "I'll handle the situation."

"You'd better."

Sweat broke across his brow just thinking about the consequences if he didn't. Not that he'd admit he was worried. When he spoke, his voice oozed confidence. "You can tell the others the complication is under control. I'll do whatever's necessary to get the film back so our ceremony can go on as scheduled."

"See that you do. You created this mess, and you'd damn well better fix it . . . or there'll be hell to pay."

Chapter Five

Why in the world had she thought spending casual time with Ryan would be a good idea? Leah yanked weeds out of the ground from around the pumpkins and squash in her garden, then brushed dirty hands down her faded jeans. *I must have been out of my mind.*

She'd spent a mostly sleepless night thinking about what they could possibly talk about that wouldn't lead to touchy subjects like their breakup or the one summer night after junior year they'd caved in and slept together. A first for them both, the experience had been imprinted on her heart in all its sweet but awkward glory.

She pulled hard on a particularly stubborn thistle, then swore when it pricked her palm through her gloves. Maybe if they focused solely on their respective careers, the hike wouldn't be a complete disaster. Down on the beach, staring into Ryan's serious blue eyes and seeing the boy she'd cared so much about inside the man, she hadn't wanted to walk away from him. Not completely. So here she was, stomach tied in knots, pulling weeds and waiting for him to show up.

The crunch of tires on the driveway prompted her to glance over her shoulder then leap to her feet. "Crap!" One look at her watch assured her Ryan was right on time. Where the hell had the morning disappeared to? After dropping the pile of weeds into a basket, she hustled around the side of the house and waved.

He stepped out of his Jeep and smiled then raised a brow. "You're hiking in that?"

Leah glanced down at one of the baggy, long-sleeved dress shirts she'd salvaged when her grandma had packed up her grandpa's clothes after he passed, ancient jeans, and plastic sandals. "I need to change. I was gardening and lost track of time." She pulled off her gloves then pushed a strand of hair behind her ear. "Give me five minutes."

"No problem." He bent to pet Barney when her dog loped over to lean against his leg. "I won't time you."

"Come on in and make yourself at home." She dropped the bucket of weeds in the carport, then led the way to the back door and held open the screen. "You know where everything is, since nothing's changed much in the last few decades."

"Except us." He stepped into the huge kitchen that had seen three generations of Grayson women turn out meals served at the long wooden table. Nothing was modern about the room except the microwave on the counter. "The place looks the same."

"As Grandma always says, 'If it ain't broke, don't

fix it.' " She waved a hand toward the white enamel refrigerator and matching stove. "Back in the day, they made appliances to last a lifetime, not ten years."

"Isn't that the truth?" He pulled out a chair at the table and sat. "Go change so we can get moving. The route I want to hike will take us at least a couple of hours round trip."

With a nod, she bolted from the room. *Two hours?* He must not be nervous about making conversation. She pulled off her shirt and tossed it toward the laundry basket in the corner of her bedroom. It missed, but she didn't stop to pick it up as she hurried to the dresser to pull out shorts and a T-shirt.

Fine. I won't worry about it, either.

She scrubbed the dirt out from beneath her fingernails, washed her face, then slapped on sunscreen, dressed, and braided her hair. She was ready in just under twelve minutes. *Not bad.*

Ryan glanced up from his phone when she entered the kitchen. "I hope you don't mind I connected to your Wi-Fi to check my mail. The service here isn't great."

Leah picked a water bottle up off the counter and filled it then turned with a frown. "How'd you know the password? Did you take Hacking 101 in college?"

"I tried your birthday then your dog's name. Only two attempts to get it right. No hacking skills required."

She rolled her eyes before sorting through the pile of odds and ends on a bench beside the door to lift out a day pack she filled with snacks and the water bottle, then swung it over her shoulder. "Okay, I'm all set."

"Great." He stood to join her. "I thought we'd head up to Cloven Ridge since we can hike straight from here."

"And the views are spectacular. Good choice." She shut the door behind them and whistled for Barney. "Let's go, boy."

Her dog raced around the back of the house and headed down the driveway.

Ryan paused to pull a sturdy canvas rucksack out of his Jeep. "Ready?"

"Yep." Leah snapped her fingers. "Heel, Barney. I don't want you running out in front of a car when we get to the highway."

They crossed the main road to the hiking path leading straight into the woods, with Barney bounding ahead. The trail climbed steadily through a dense forest of fir, madrone, and huckleberry bushes.

Leah breathed deeply of the moist, earth scent and sighed in pleasure. "I always associate this smell with home. Do you ever miss living here?"

"Sometimes. More so during the years I spent in Portland after college. I love Central Oregon, though. The woods around my house aren't as thick as these, nor as humid, but the rock climbing in the area is unbeatable."

"Interesting." She was slightly breathless as the pitch of their ascent increased. "You moved to Sisters in order to climb?"

He nodded. "Climbing's my thing, but I also enjoy bouldering, hiking, and mountain biking." He shrugged. "Whatever gets me outdoors."

"All solitary activities, for the most part. You never cared much for team sports when we were kids, either." She took a couple of running steps to walk next to him as the trail widened and flattened out. "You hated baseball the one summer you played Little League."

"Obviously there's nothing wrong with your memory."

"Nope. You tried to bribe me to join the team, just to keep you company."

"But instead, you took a gymnastics class with Nina and Paige. Wait, how'd that work out for you?"

She returned his broad grin. "Broken leg after falling off the balance beam. Apparently, coordination isn't my thing." The nervous tension drained out of her. "Wow, maybe hanging out together wasn't such a bad idea, after all."

"Huh?" He motioned for her to go ahead as the trail narrowed to cross a stream. "What do you mean?"

She hopped from one rock to the next to keep her feet dry. "Honestly, I was a little worried our conversation would be stilted, but this is . . . nice. More than anything else, I missed our easy friendship after—"

"You dumped me?" He kicked a fir cone out of the path. "It's been twelve years. I hope I'm man enough not to carry a grudge that long." His gaze cooled as he gave her an up-and-down glance. "You may have been my first love, but you weren't my last."

The neat jab hit its mark, and Leah pressed a hand to the sudden sharp pain in her chest. Of course he'd loved other women. Time hadn't frozen when they'd gone their separate ways. The only real surprise was the fact he wasn't at least engaged—

When she stopped abruptly, Ryan smacked into her back. He wrapped one arm around her waist to keep from knocking her over, and his breath brushed her ear.

"Geez, warn a guy before you dig in your heels."

"Sorry." Her cheeks heated, and she stepped away when he released her. But not before the contact sent an odd little quiver through her. He smelled the way she remembered, earthy with a hint of spice.

"Did you see a snake or something?" He held back a branch. "This section of the trail is pretty overgrown."

"I don't think many people come up here. No, I was just wondering . . ." Words she couldn't seem to control blurted out. "Why aren't you married? Last time I got my teeth cleaned, I was flipping through a regional magazine and saw your name on a top ten list of eligible Oregon bachelors. Or maybe there's someone waiting at home for you I didn't hear about." She stuttered to a halt, feeling like an idiot for even asking. "Not my business. Forget I opened my big mouth."

"No, it's a fair question. For years my sole focus was work. Women tend to get irritated when you stand them up over code issues." His lips twisted. "I was a classic workaholic."

Forcing her feet to move, she continued up the trail ahead of him. "You have more time now."

"Yeah, I do."

Apparently he didn't intend to elaborate, but she couldn't let the subject drop. "I hope suggesting we hike together didn't put you in an awkward position . . ."

"My last relationship ended not long ago, if that's the information you're fishing for."

Her neck prickled with embarrassment, and she picked up her pace. "This isn't a date or anything, but still . . . After what I went through with Brock, I wouldn't want some other woman to even *think* I was trying to poach her man."

"You didn't take his name."

He spoke so low, she wasn't sure she'd heard him right. "Excuse me?"

"You're still Leah Grayson."

"Yeah. I was going to change it, but . . . When I was standing in line at the social security office, it just felt wrong not to be Leah Grayson."

"The line was that long, huh?"

She laughed out loud as the harmony between them was restored. "It didn't help that I would have been Leah Hooker."

He gave her a sideways glance, and they both snorted and choked with laughter.

"You definitely dodged a bullet there."

"I guess so. At least I didn't have to go through the paperwork to change it back after we divorced." She clenched her fists at her sides. "The last thing I wanted was any reminder of the colossal mistake I'd made. Live and learn, right?"

"I guess so." He was quiet for a few moments as they trudged steadily uphill. "Maybe the more important lesson is that people don't change. Brock was an ass when we were in high school. A few years didn't morph him into a good guy."

"I didn't have a car in college, so I got rides home with him from Ashland when we ended up living in the same apartment complex our junior year. Brock can be very entertaining, and I was flattered he was interested in me since he was Mr. Popular around campus." She stopped to pull her water out of her backpack and took a drink. "What's done is done. Let's just say I'm not as quick to give people the benefit of the doubt anymore." She held out the bottle. "Want some?"

He nodded and took it. His throat moved as he drank. "Thanks." Capping the top, he handed it back. "You aren't the only one who made a bad judgment call that ended in disaster. I signed partnership papers with my old college roommate, Jay, when we were developing Intersect."

Leah returned the bottle to her pack, then picked up the stick Barney dropped at her feet and tossed it before moving onward. "I tried using your old platform for a while, but the mechanics were clunky."

"Yeah, Jay pushed to launch Intersect before I had all the bugs worked out. After the site took off, I discovered a couple of questionable clauses in the contract that progressively gave him a higher share of the profits."

"You're kidding? Didn't your lawyer—"

"I trusted Jay. He was in charge of the business end, while I was the tech side. When I figured out what he'd done, I walked away from our partnership and gave him everything instead of battling it out in court." Sarcasm laced his words. "Too bad the guy he hired to replace me could never get the program to work right."

She grinned. "He wasn't as good as you, huh?"

"Not by a long shot. Intersect went down in flames."

"And Crossroads emerged from the ashes."

"I came out on top, but you can damn well bet I'll never sign anything again without reading the fine print." His tone was hard.

"I guess we're both a little jaded."

"I prefer to think of it as cautious."

Leah didn't respond. *Jaded* definitely seemed like a better fit for Ryan's current attitude. The drive that defined his personality was still there, but the optimism she'd found so attractive when they were younger was missing. She wondered what changes in her temperament he'd observed, and made a mental note to quit bitching about Brock and focus on the present.

"You still teach fifth grade?"

She was relieved to change the subject. "I do. The kids are great at that age, curious and eager to learn. At least they are when I can present the material in a way that sparks their interest."

"I bet you're the cool teacher now, the way Mr. Manning was back in the day."

"He still teaches, you know. We're coworkers."

"Really?" He held up a hand. "Wait, I can do the math. I guess he isn't all that old since he was probably only in his twenties when he taught us."

"Exactly. Anyone over sixteen just seems ancient to a ten-year-old. Half my students probably think I'm a grandma." She gave him a wry smile. "Anyway, I talked Sloan into coming to the reunion. I figured everyone would get a kick out of seeing him again."

"Without a doubt."

They hiked in silence for several minutes, but the lack of conversation wasn't uncomfortable. When Barney ran back to drop a pinecone at his feet, tongue hanging as he wriggled in excitement, Ryan picked it up and threw it. The dog galloped away.

"What happened to the stick you tossed for him earlier?"

"He probably buried it somewhere. The pinecone will disappear shortly. Barney is weird that way."

"Unconventional, kind of like his owner. You always had your own unique flare."

"Yes, but my individuality doesn't involve burying strange objects. Well, I guess the time capsule was pretty weird, but Barney is the worst. Once, when I was working in the garden, I discovered a hairbrush of mine that had mysteriously disappeared."

"I noticed you have a good-sized garden plot." He grasped her hand to help her over a downed tree that had fallen across the path.

When his palm closed over hers, warm and calloused, she drew in a breath before she answered. "I grow most of my own herbs and vegetables. I dry, can, or freeze what I don't eat fresh to save for the winter."

"So, you live off your own land. Why doesn't that surprise me?"

"Because I was already a budding naturalist way back in high school. Do you remember when I told my parents I didn't want to eat meat any-more? My dad thought I'd lost my mind."

"Nothing wrong with my memory. I had to give up pepperoni on my pizza that summer." His arm brushed hers as he walked at her side. "You must have rubbed off on me, though, because even after we broke up, I kept ordering odd veggie combos."

"Not a surprise since you're a smart man, and they taste great."

"Yeah, they do." Raising a hand, he pointed. "The trees are thinning. I think we're almost to the ridge."

"I haven't been up here in a few years, but I'm pretty sure you're right."

A couple of minutes later they reached the summit of the climb and veered off the trail to a narrow overlook. The hillside plunged downward into a thick bowl of evergreens broken up by splashes of fall color. On the horizon, the ocean shimmered beneath an azure blue sky.

"Wow, spectacular. The view is worth every step of the climb."

Ryan grasped her elbow. "Careful. The ground looks a little crumbly at the edge there. I'm surprised the Forest Service hasn't put up a railing."

"I don't think there's a budget for those types of projects on trails that get little use, and this one isn't marked on most maps."

"You're probably right." He released her to fist his hands on his hips and take a long look around. "Where'd your dog disappear to?"

Leah dragged her gaze away from the endless

stretch of sea and frowned. "I'm not sure." Raising her voice, she called, "Barney, here boy."

A muffled woof came from their left, but her dog didn't appear from between the manzanita bushes.

"I guess I should go see what he's doing. My crazy mutt probably treed a squirrel or stuck his head down a gopher hole."

"Looks like there's a break in the bushes over here." Ryan pulled back a couple of branches. "Can you get through?"

She nodded and pushed past a prickly thicket to emerge in a small clearing with trees on three sides and a sheer drop to the west. Barney sniffed around the base of a large, flat stone.

"Hey, boy, are the chipmunks teasing you again?"

He snuffled and dug furiously, giving an occasional woof.

Ryan stepped past her. "What's that discoloration on the top? Something stained the granite. Kids with paint?"

Grabbing Barney by the collar, Leah hauled him away from the rock, then wrinkled her nose as she took a closer look at the rusty stain on the pale gray surface. "Eww, definitely not paint. Maybe blood? Gross! Do you think a coyote dragged a rabbit carcass up there to eat?"

"Or a mountain lion dined on deer. A while back, Mom mentioned a big cat had been spotted in the vicinity."

Leah glanced over her shoulder into the thick forest. "Uh, let's not have our snack here. I wouldn't want to wind up on the lunch menu of a mountain lion."

"They tend to hunt at dawn or dusk, and that stain looks old and weathered, but I don't mind finding someplace else to eat. This place has an eerie feel to it."

Leah shivered and backed toward the bushes. "Better safe than sorry."

Chapter Six

Ryan pushed the grocery cart down the aisle of the refrigerator section and paused to grab a container of sour cream before moving on. He glanced at the list in his mother's neat handwriting to see what he was still missing. Yogurts and juice. "They should be somewhere around here," he muttered.

When his cart sideswiped the open cooler door, the impact jolted him to attention. "Oops, sorry, I wasn't looking where I was going."

An older man in a gray suit turned, holding a six-pack of beer. "Ryan, how are you? I heard you were back in town."

"I'm fine. It's good to see you, Mr. Brewster."

Mr. Brewster shut the cooler door and reached across the cart to shake hands. "Call me Waylon. You aren't a kid anymore, for heaven's sake. I hope your mother's recovering from her accident. Damn inconvenient having a broken arm, I'm sure."

"She's healing, although not as quickly as she'd like. How's Pete? I haven't seen him since I returned to town."

"Busy making sure our clients get what they deserve. My boy always was a dynamo. He'll be taking over the reins at the law office when I retire in a couple of years." His smile reminded Ryan of a shark. "If you ever need solid legal advice, you know where to come, right?" The attorney gave him a slap on the shoulder.

Ryan controlled the urge to roll his eyes. His memories of Waylon Brewster were of a parent determined to bail his son out of every mishap from playground fights to speeding tickets to bribing teachers into changing Cs to As. Apparently nothing much had change over the years.

"I'll keep that in mind."

"Good. Good." He tucked the six-pack under his arm. "I'll be sure to tell Pete you asked about him. Are you planning to go to that silly time-capsule opening tomorrow night?"

Ryan nodded then edged around the man to pull a bottle of orange juice off the cooler shelf. "Yeah, it should be fun to see old friends."

"Leah Grayson organized the reunion. I remember you two dated back in high school." Waylon scowled. "You'd better watch out for that one. Ever since she burned poor Brock in their divorce settlement, I hear she's on the prowl for husband number two."

Ryan leaned against his cart. "Oh?"

"A woman like that can't go long without a man. I don't know where she got her shyster lawyer, but—"

"I take it you represented Brock in the divorce?"

"Pete handled it. They were good buddies before Brock left town, thanks to that little . . . uh, never mind." Waylon produced another blinding grin.

The man must spend a fortune on whitening products.

"Just figured I'd give you fair warning. Maybe you'll throw a little business our way in exchange."

Ryan responded with a noncommittal smile. "Nice talking to you, Waylon, but I should finish my shopping."

"Tell your mom I said hello."

"Will do." Ryan tossed a few yogurts in the cart without checking the flavors and bolted toward the produce section. Much more of Waylon Brewster's good-old-boy routine and he'd puke. He'd never liked the man, and his son was even worse. Sounded like Leah had been smart enough to look further afield for legal representation.

As for her being in the market for a new man . . . *Is that why she wanted to go hiking with me?*

Ryan shook his head. He couldn't wrap his mind around the implication that the independent woman he'd spent the previous Sunday with needed a male to . . . do what? Open jars for her? She had a steady income, a home she loved, good friends, and a dog for companionship. That left only one thing a man might provide. Sex. He ran a hand beneath the collar of his T-shirt as he set a bag of apples in the cart. As free-spirited and sexy as Leah was, he was pretty certain she wasn't hard up in *that* department. At least she hadn't given him any indication she was interested when she'd left him at his Jeep with no more than a thank-you and a smile. Certainly not an invitation to extend their day to include dinner or anything else.

Maybe Leah simply wasn't interested in him in *that* way. He'd never forget the warm summer night they'd loved each other in the dark, down on the beach, young and oh so eager . . . But he'd be the first to admit he hadn't had a clue what he was doing. With a sigh, he picked up a bunch of bananas to set beside the apples. He sure hoped to God his technique had improved since then.

He finished his shopping, paid, and then carried the bags of groceries out to his Jeep. Driving home, he spotted a pink cruiser bike up ahead. Only one person he knew in Siren Cove had hair that long, streaming out behind her like a flag fluttering in the breeze. A jumbo-sized bag hung over one shoulder to tilt her sideways, but the curve of her ass was still as sexy as ever. He slowed and rolled down the passenger-side window as he drew even. "Heading home from work?"

Leah glanced over and smiled. "Hi, Ryan. Actually, I'm meeting Nina and Paige for drinks. Hey, pull over so you don't block traffic. I have a question for you."

He did as she requested, parking along the curb in the first empty spot.

She coasted up beside him a moment later and stopped. "How's your mom doing?"

"Better. I was just grocery shopping for her." He rested an elbow on the steering wheel. "What's up?"

"I was thinking."

"Always dangerous."

"Witty as usual." Leaning in through the window opening, she met his gaze. "I was wondering if we should dig up the time capsule tonight instead of at the reunion tomorrow."

"Why would you want to do that?"

"Because we'll be dressed in party clothes not conducive to tromping through the woods. We won't open the box until we're at the reunion, but there's no reason the whole class has to be present for the actual excavation."

"Makes sense."

"I intend to ask Paige and Nina their opinions then go get a shovel if they're on board. What do you think?"

He nodded. "Seems like a smart idea. Since we moved the capsule when they built the patio at the school, it isn't in the original location, anyway."

"True." She backed up a foot. "Well, great. I'm glad you approve." She hesitated for a moment. "Would you like to join us for drinks? Paige mentioned Quentin Radcliff arrived in town a few hours ago and will be hanging out with us tonight. Do you remember him? He moved away the summer after fifth grade, but he and Paige stayed in touch."

"Didn't he live next door to her? The two of them were always attached at the hip."

Leah nodded. "That's right."

"Sure. Sounds like fun. I have to take the groceries home first, but I could bring a shovel back with me."

Leah's responding smile made his chest ache a little.

"Terrific. That'll save me a trip out to my house." She hopped up onto her bike seat. "We'll be down at Castaways."

He shifted the car into gear. "I'll see you there." Pulling away from her, he turned onto the street leading into his neighborhood a moment later but kept his gaze on the rearview mirror as Leah pedaled straight toward the main drag, hair flying. He smiled then refocused on the road.

He'd put away the groceries then go meet his old pals. *And pretend a decade plus hasn't changed us all forever.* Maybe the years that had passed wouldn't matter much, but the most important differences were glaring. At the end of the evening there'd be no make-out session with Leah in her driveway before she went inside. No softly spoken words of love. Just memories of broken promises and shattered dreams.

There could be no going back to what might have been. He was too smart to make the same mistake twice.

The door to Castaways opened for the fifth time since Leah sat down, and for the fifth time, she glanced toward the entrance. Not Ryan.

Nina touched her arm. "You're jumpy as a cat. What's up? Paige texted me they were on their way."

"It's not . . . uh, I asked Ryan to join us."

Nina's perfectly arched brows shot up. "Oh?"

"I ran into him on the way here."

"Interesting."

Leah could feel her cheeks heating. "He'll be in town until his mom's arm heals, and it's not like he has anyone else to hang out with . . ."

"So you asked him out of kindness and charity, not because you had a good time on your hike?"

"How did you know—"

"I bumped into him on the beach last weekend, and he mentioned you'd made plans."

"Oh. We did have fun. The camaraderie was still there once we got past a few awkward moments, but at the same time, being together seemed odd."

"No kissing and groping like in the good old days?"

The heat in her cheeks deepened, but she answered honestly. "I'll admit I was tempted. Ryan never used to have all those muscles, that's for sure. But, I'm not interested in starting something I might not be able to finish. Neither one of us has changed much. If anything, our differences have only intensified over the years."

Nina sipped her drink. "I thought opposites were supposed to attract."

"Maybe, but I've had enough conflict in my life. At this point, I'd rather have a smooth path to romance without any bumps."

"Sounds boring." She glanced up. "Here come Paige and Quentin."

"And Ryan's with them." Leah sat up straighter and pushed her hair over one shoulder.

"Great. We can get this party started, although I feel a bit like a fifth wheel."

"Why? Ryan and I certainly aren't a couple anymore, and Paige and Quentin were never romantically involved. They're just best buds, despite the fact he lives in Seattle."

"True, although I've often wondered why there's no chemistry between them. Quentin is smokin' hot if you like the *GQ* casually elegant look. He pulls off jeans and a suit jacket with panache." Nina's lips curved. "Then there's Ryan, straight out of an L.L. Bean catalogue in flannel."

Leah pressed a hand to her mouth to cover a snort of laughter. "Shh, or he'll hear you."

Greetings with hugs all around followed before everyone sat, and the new arrivals ordered drinks when their server appeared. Leah couldn't help comparing the two men, who were so very different in looks and attitude, as they caught up on their respective careers. Quentin's joie de vivre bubbled forth like a fast-flowing brook when he described his expanding chain of high-end restaurants. His blond hair was combed back in the latest style, and those odd, aqua-blue eyes of his flashed with animation. By contrast, Ryan's dark brown hair was cut short and neat, and his deep blue eyes radiated a calm intensity. Both men looked like they hit the gym regularly, but Leah was willing to bet all Ryan's strength had been acquired rock climbing, not lifting free weights.

"Earth to Leah." Paige jogged her elbow. "You mentioned something about the time capsule when you texted us to meet you here."

"Oh, yeah, I . . ." Leah dragged her gaze away from Ryan, who was laughing at something Nina had said, and focused. "I was wondering if we should dig up the box tonight instead of at the reunion. Seems kind of silly for the whole class to drive to the school to watch us shovel dirt then back to the restaurant, when we can simply bring the time capsule with us and open it there." She glanced around the table. "What do you all think?"

"Excellent idea." Nina leaned back in her chair and swirled the ice cubes in her vodka cranberry. "I don't know why we didn't think of it sooner."

"Because we're idiots, apparently," Paige said. "I was considering wearing my low heels tomorrow simply because I knew we'd be tromping through the woods."

"What—the three-inch ones instead of the five?" Quentin looked over at her and winked.

Paige punched him on the arm. "Don't make fun of me. If you were barely over five feet, you'd wear heels, too."

He grinned. "Why do you think I like hanging out with you? I'm not tall, but next to you, I feel like an NBA center."

"Funny. You aren't short, either." Paige planted an elbow on the table. "So, should we go get a shovel?"

"I have one in my Jeep." Ryan thanked their waitress when she delivered their drinks. "Leah mentioned her idea when she invited me to join you this evening."

"Way to plan ahead." Quentin took a swallow of his beer. "Can I dig, too?"

Paige eyed him up and down. "You're too pretty to get dirty. Better let Ryan do the honors."

Quentin choked. "Pretty? Really?"

"You two crack me up." Leah sipped her wine, then set down her glass and flexed her arm. "Maybe I'll dig. Drink up, people, and we'll go get started."

Paige raised her cocktail. "Cheers!"

They finished their drinks amid a lot of chatter and reminiscing. Every now and then Leah caught Ryan watching her, and she couldn't help wondering what he was thinking. His expression gave nothing away, but after they paid their tab and left the table, he walked toward the door with a casual hand on her back. *Habit?* Maybe, but the contact sent a dart of heat straight through her, and every effort she made to ignore the fluttering feeling failed.

Nina stopped beside her Mini Cooper. "I'll see you up at the school."

Paige tucked her hands in her jacket pockets. "What're you all doing this evening? The Fall Festival starts tonight, and the carnival was setting up rides at the fairgrounds this morning. We could re-live our youth by riding the Tilt-A-Whirl."

Quentin gave his keys a toss. "Count me in."

Nina scrunched up her nose. "Those rides make me nauseous. Anyway, I need to wrap the paintings I'm selling at the art auction on Sunday for transport, so I'll pass."

"I'm game if . . ." Leah glanced up at Ryan.

"Sure." His voice held a hint of self-deprecation. "My only plan was to hang out with my mom and watch endless repeats of *Murder, She Wrote*."

"Wow, you really know how to live." Leah pulled her pink cruiser out of the rack near the bar door. "I rode here—"

"You can hook your bike on the back of my Jeep."

"Great." She gave the others a wave as she followed Ryan down the sidewalk. "See you guys in a few minutes."

When they reached his vehicle, he strapped her bike to the rack then opened the passenger door for her. "Hop in."

"Thanks." Leah slid onto the seat and shut the

door. After he climbed in, started the engine, and pulled out onto the street, she glanced over. "Shouldn't you be driving a Ferrari or a Lamborghini or something else equally indicative of your success?"

"I can just see a low-slung sports car trying to make it up some of the off-road tracks to my favorite climbing spots."

"I guess the Jeep is more practical."

"By far. Anyway, I've no interest in acting pretentious."

"No, you're still the same down-to-earth Ryan you always were." She settled back as they turned onto the road leading to the school. "Do you really want to go to the carnival later? I don't want you to feel coerced—"

"I don't, and I wouldn't have agreed if I wasn't interested." He pulled into the lot in front of the school and parked next to Quentin's black Jaguar. "Hey, Quentin has a cool car, even if I don't. I haven't seen him since he moved out of town back when we were kids, but he seems like a good dude. Are he and Paige—"

"Nope. They're just friends, have been forever."

Ryan studied her for a long moment in the glow from the overhead lights. "Apparently there's a lot of that going around." He opened his door. "I'll get the shovel."

Leah stepped out of the car and shut the door. Paige and Quentin had strolled over to join Nina, who waited at the edge of the woods. She smiled at the group. "Let's go dig up that time capsule."

Chapter Seven

As hard as Leah was squeezing his hand, Ryan wasn't sure he'd ever be able to grip an outcropping of rock again. Not that crushed fingers was his top priority at the moment. When the Tilt-A-Whirl picked up speed, Leah screamed loud enough to rupture his eardrum as centrifugal force smashed them together. A teeth-jarring spin moments later slammed him back against the seat before the ride finally came to an end. He was damn happy to have survived with the corn dog he'd eaten earlier still in his stomach. The car lurched and jerked to a final stop, and Leah peeled herself off his lap.

"Oh, my God. Why did I ever think that was fun?"

As the attendant released the bar holding them in place, he grimaced. "I have no idea. Let's get out of here."

Still clutching his hand, she wobbled down the ramp to the trampled grass and let out a long breath. "I'm not going on that upside-down torture chamber over there." She pointed toward the long, snaking line where Paige and Quentin waited their turn to get on the Zipper. "Just saying."

"Oh, thank God. I didn't want to be the one to wuss out."

"I'm glad I'm not the only chicken. Can we ride the Ferris wheel?" Releasing his hand, she gave him a quick smile. "Sorry, I didn't realize I was still clutching onto you for dear life."

"I didn't mind." He flexed his fingers to get the blood flowing. "Not much, anyway."

She linked her arm through his. "I promise to keep my hands to myself. Let's go. There's not even a line."

He wouldn't have minded her holding tight to him again. Memories of endless similar evenings spent with Leah pushed aside old hurt, until he could almost believe they were a couple again. With the colorful lights swirling against the night sky along with the blaring carnival music, slipping into the past was as easy as wrapping an arm around her as they took their seats on the big wheel, then sat back to enjoy the ride.

"Oh, wow, the view from up here is spectacular. The moon is shining over the ocean, and there isn't even any fog." She pointed toward the three huge rocks in the cove. "Check it out. You can even see the Sirens tonight." Leah tilted her head back until it rested on his shoulder.

"Beautiful." Ryan wasn't sure if he was talking about the view of waves crashing on the beach or the curve of her lips and brightness in her eyes. When they reached the apex, he bent and kissed her. He'd meant for it to be a quick caress, but the familiar taste of her and feel of soft woman in his arms turned the kiss into something a whole lot less casual. The wheel had circled until they were back at the bottom before he released her.

Her eyes widened as she stared into his from inches away while the ride whisked them back toward the top. "Why'd you do that?"

"I couldn't seem to help myself. I guess I got a little carried away by the moment. Sorry."

"Don't be. I'll admit I've thought about kissing you more than once since this evening began." She touched his cheek. "Maybe not the smartest move . . ."

"Probably not." He kissed her again, this time twining his fingers in her hair to hold her close, tasting every crevice of her mouth, enjoying each tantalizing second.

When he finally pulled away, a smile stretched the lips he'd so thoroughly kissed. "Wow." She let out a breath. "Just . . . wow."

The rush of air slid over him, cooling his heated skin. The wheel continued to turn while he and Leah stared into each other's eyes. "Now what?"

"I'm not sure. Honestly?"

"Of course."

"Part of me—you can probably guess which part—wants to take this show back to my house and . . ." Her voice caught before she swallowed.

He appreciated her touch of humor. "Do more than make out on a Ferris wheel?"

A quick nod sent silky hair sliding over her shoulder. "A time-out . . . literally. Is it wrong to revisit our past?"

The hesitancy in her voice made him pause before answering. "Not if no one gets hurt in the process."

"Maybe we shouldn't think too hard about that possibility." When the ride slowed to a stop as the first car unloaded, she laid her hand on his thigh. "I'm okay with simply enjoying tonight. How about you?"

Okay didn't begin to describe how he was feeling. Desire, stronger than anything he'd experienced in years, was certainly involved in the equation. But when he covered Leah's hand with his own, and she turned her palm over to twine their fingers, emotions he'd been trying hard to ignore engaged.

His heart thumped in response as he squeezed out a single word. "Yes."

They waited without talking for their car to bump to a stop at the unloading zone. Stepping out, Ryan held tight to her hand as they wound through the other attractions toward the gravel path leading to the parking lot.

"Should we let Paige and Quentin know we're leaving?"

Leah glanced over. "I doubt they'll care." Her steps faltered before she skipped once to keep pace. "But I'll text Quentin in the morning to remind him the time capsule is still in his trunk. Probably best, since I would have been tempted to peek inside."

"Not without pulling out a dozen nails. Whoever hammered that baby shut did an excellent job."

"I think it was Edgar Vargas. I remember worrying about the lid falling off until Mr. Manning sent him to find a hammer."

"That's right—" Ryan stopped and swore. "What the hell!" Releasing her hand, he ran toward his Jeep where glass from the shattered side window littered the ground. His feet crunched through the debris as he wrenched open the door. "Shit!"

"Did they steal anything?"

He glanced back at Leah and frowned. "The CD player is still intact, and the CD case is right where I left it. I don't keep anything else in my Jeep."

"Unlike my car, which is full of crap . . . oh damn."

"What's wrong?"

She reached past him to snag the strap of her tote bag. "I left my purse in here."

"That's a purse? Looks more like a suitcase."

"I have a lot of stuff." She rummaged inside and came up with her wallet. "I stuffed my cash and ID in my pants pocket before we went into the carnival, but . . ." Her eyes were wide when she looked up. "My credit cards are still here, thank God."

"Did they take anything else?"

She dumped an assortment of items that boggled his mind out onto the seat. *Why would anyone keep an ace bandage in her purse? Or a corkscrew?* The toothbrush he could understand, but not the pliers.

"I don't think anything is missing, although I'm not one hundred percent positive." She lifted a pair of earrings that glittered in the glow from the overhead security lights. "These have real rubies, but whoever smashed the window didn't take them."

"Maybe someone hit it with a rock. Could have been an accident."

"Kids screwing around would be my guess. When the window shattered, they probably ran like hell."

"Except the door was unlocked when I opened it." Pressing up against her, he bent to pull a rag out from under the seat. "If you want to put your stuff back into your bag, I'll brush off the glass that fell onto the upholstery."

"Sure." She scooped the collection into her purse then stepped back.

A minute later, he'd cleared the interior of all the small glass pebbles. "I hate to just leave them on the ground."

"No one will puncture a tire. The pieces aren't sharp since the window was safety glass."

He snapped his fingers. "Wait, I still have the shovel." Reaching to lift the cover off the back storage compartment, he frowned. "That's strange. The tarp isn't hooked correctly."

Leah hung over his shoulder. "Don't tell me the idiot who broke the window did it to get your shovel?"

He pulled back the heavy rubber. "No, the shovel is still there." He removed it, then scraped the pieces of glass into a pile and scooped them up.

"There's a trash can over by the fence. Do you think we should call the police to report this?"

"Not much point since whoever vandalized my vehicle is long gone. I'll notify my insurance company in the morning. I have a deductible, but they'll replace the broken window." He dumped the glass in the metal can. "What a pain in the ass, though."

After he'd returned the shovel to the storage compartment, she gave him a brief smile. "Apparently, no one wanted my bike. Riding an old junker means I don't have to worry about someone stealing it."

"Always a positive." He let out a long breath and did his best to shake off his annoyance. "Hop in, and I'll take you home."

She rounded the car and climbed in the passenger side while he started the engine. The breeze blasting through the empty space where the window had been didn't improve his temper as they cruised down the rutted access lane to the highway. Neither of them spoke during the five minutes it took to reach her driveway. After he turned off the engine, silence descended.

She released her seat belt and turned to face him. "I guess the mood is shot."

"Maybe it's for the best."

"If that's what you believe, I guess so."

His stomach knotted. "I'm not against making love to you. The attraction between us obviously never died . . . or maybe I should say has been resurrected. But I'm still that same guy you cut loose our senior year because we were *too different to last.* Your words. Based on the state of your purse, not without merit."

"My purse?" Her voice rose. "Are you kidding?"

"I'm organized and methodical, not to mention fairly traditional. You, on the other hand, are—"

"A haphazard slob?"

"I was going to say free-spirited and a little

chaotic. My point is I expect you'll get bored with my conformity in short order."

She sat back as the fight seemed to drain out of her. "I don't know. Marrying a guy who was a bit of a rebel didn't work out so well for me. Maybe my perspective has changed." A brief smile curved her lips as she lifted her bulging bag off the floor. "If not my habits."

Next to her head, the glass shook as something slammed against the window. Leah let out a scream then pressed a hand to her chest. "Oh, my God. Scare the crap out of me."

Ryan smiled as a wet nose pressed against the glass. "Lucky Barney didn't break it, or I would have had to replace two windows."

"No kidding." She opened the door an inch. "Get down. Off!" When the dog moved, she climbed out.

"I'll get your bike." He stepped out of the Jeep and walked around the back to lift her cruiser off the rack, then wheeled it toward the carport. After leaning it against a post, he stroked Barney's soft cars. "I guess I'll see you tomorrow at the reunion."

Leah nodded in the faint moonlight. "Thanks for going to the carnival with me."

"I enjoyed it." He squeezed past her then stopped. "Well, maybe not the Tilt-A-Whirl, but everything else."

Her soft laugh slid over his senses, and he couldn't stop the hand that cupped her chin. Slowly, he bent to kiss her. "Good night, Leah."

"Good night, Ryan."

As their lips touched, neither moved. His pulse

drummed in his ears. When Barney pushed hard against him on his way toward the house, Ryan nearly fell on his ass. Leah reached out a hand to steady him, and somehow she wound up in his arms. He kissed her again, this time no simple good-bye gesture. Burying his fingers in her hair, his mouth opened over hers. Her bag hit the cement of the carport with a thump as she wrapped her arms around him.

Long minutes later, she asked breathlessly, "Want to come inside?"

He nodded and dropped another kiss on her lips before taking her hand. Leah bent to grab her purse, then led the way toward the back porch. After she opened the door, Barney bolted inside. She flipped on the kitchen light and blinked in the glow from the overhead fixture.

"I need to feed him."

Ryan glanced at the dog, who was prostrate before his food bowl. "He does seem to be nearing starvation."

"You'd think, right?" With a quick smile, she left him to open the pantry and pull out a plastic container.

While she fed Barney, Ryan crossed the creaking wood floor of the living room to stand in front of the window overlooking the ocean. Moonlight glimmered off the incoming waves as the tide receded. He couldn't help wondering if being here now, with Leah, was a mistake he'd live to regret. But when she approached to slide her arms around him and rest her forehead against his shoulder, he decided he didn't much care.

"I think I have a bottle of wine in the cupboard."

He turned to pull her against him. "I don't need anything to drink."

"No?"

"No." He pressed his cheek to her soft, silky hair. "It's been a long time since we hung out together like this. I have to say, I never expected to be here with you again."

"Me, either." She pulled back a little and glanced up at him. "I'll admit there were times in the past when I thought of you and missed what we had. The companionship and respect." Her voice dropped. "The unconditional love."

"You make me sound like Barney."

She smiled in the dim light spilling from the kitchen, her eyes soft and shining. "Hey, I love that dog to pieces, but I don't plan to kick you out of bed the way I do him."

"Good to hear I won't have to share the covers with the mutt." He bent to kiss her. "God, you're pretty. Can we . . ."

"Yes, we can." Taking his hand, she led him toward the stairs.

He followed her up, enjoying the sway of her hips in the formfitting, wide-legged pants. She'd left the jacket she'd had on earlier in the kitchen, and the soft green shirt beneath clung to her curves. He tore his gaze away as she turned into the second bedroom on the left, the one she'd used as a girl.

"You didn't move into the master bedroom?"

She clicked on the bedside lamp. "I haven't gotten around to it yet."

"In how many years?"

"Nearly two. Don't judge."

She bent to scoop up scattered socks, underwear, and shirts, then tossed them toward the basket in the corner. The quilt on her full-size bed was askew, displaying rainbow-colored sheets.

His breath came a little faster when she kicked off her shoes and turned to face him. He swallowed. "Would I do that?"

"I hope not."

"The woman you are now is the same girl I loved growing up. I don't want to change you."

"Then we should get along just fine." She stepped closer. "I don't want to change you, either."

He caressed the smooth line of her throat with his thumb. "Then there's no reason why we can't enjoy ourselves thoroughly for the next few weeks." He hesitated. "Until my mom can function on her own again."

"And you go home." Her gaze held steady on his. "No harm, no foul."

His chest hurt just thinking about leaving her, but he nodded. If he didn't let himself imagine anything more than a temporary affair, he wouldn't be disappointed this time around. Instead of overanalyzing their relationship, he backed her toward the bed.

"Wait."

His eyes widened as she peeled her shirt over her head and dropped it at their feet. The pants followed. When she stood before him in nothing but a bra and panties, he knew without a doubt there wasn't a woman on earth more beautiful than this one.

She eyed him from the top of his head down-ward. "You're overdressed."

"I guess so." When he reached for the buttons on his shirt, she brushed his hands away and deftly parted the soft flannel.

Palms flat against his pecs, she smiled up at him. "This is new."

"Huh?"

"All these muscles. Nice."

His cheeks heated, and the flush spread until he feared he looked like a sunburn victim. "Rock climbing is a demanding sport that requires upper body strength."

"I can see that." Pushing the shirt down his arms, her hands lingered on his biceps. "Very nice."

He seemed to be losing control of the situation. Or maybe he'd never had any to begin with. When she unfastened the metal button on his jeans and released the zipper, he was way past caring.

Her head jerked up. "Commando? I wouldn't have guessed, but I definitely approve."

"I don't like being all bound up." Denim slid down his legs as he stepped out of the pants.

"Not so conventional after all."

"Maybe not." Pulling her close, he released the hooks on her bra, then groaned when her breasts pressed against his chest as the scrap of lace fell to the floor. "I know there's nothing ordinary about what I want to do to you next. You're incredible, Leah."

"See, there's hope we aren't so very different." When he slid his hands down her sides to hook his thumbs in the elastic of her panties, her breath came out in a whoosh. "No fumbling this time around."

"I certainly hope I'm a little smoother at the advanced age of thirty than I was at seventeen." He smiled as she kicked the pink underwear across the room, then he cupped her face in his palms to kiss her.

They fell backward together onto the bed. She raked nails across his back while he explored places on Leah he'd only fantasized about and hadn't had the nerve to touch the one time he'd had the chance. When they were both breathing so hard he was afraid he might have a heart attack, he reached toward the bedside table and froze.

Her room. Not his.

"What?" She stopped kissing him long enough to stare into his eyes.

He probably looked like he'd been skewered. His throat worked. "No protection."

"I'm on the pill. Have been for years, so I didn't quit after . . ." Her eyes darkened. "I trust you don't have something contagious?"

"No."

"Neither do I, so all is good."

"Oh, thank God. If we'd had to quit now . . ."

"I appreciate your concern for me." She grinned down at him. "Even though I feared you might cry."

"I probably would have." He might still. Loving Leah felt that good. So completely right. As he pushed inside her, nothing in the world mattered but the two of them.

They moved in rhythm, perspiration-dampened skin sliding together to create an unbearable friction as the tempo built. When she moaned, long and low in his ear, he came undone, shaking with a release that rocked him to the core.

"Oh, my heavens." She went limp beneath him. "There are no words . . ."

He held her tight, not wanting the moment to end, and couldn't stop smiling against her neck. "Better than last time?"

She laughed out loud. "Just a little. Wow. You should write a manual or something. That one move . . ." Her eyes widened when he pulled back to gaze down at her. "Do you have a name for that? Why aren't women following you wherever you go?"

"I guess you inspired me."

"Ryan?"

He stroked her cheek. "Yes?"

"I'm happy to be your muse."

Chapter Eight

"Wow, this place is packed." Leah scanned the parking lot next to the Poseidon Grill for an empty spot.

Ryan pointed. "Maybe you can squeeze in at the end of the row over there."

"It's either that or go park on the street." Leah edged her Audi in next to a compact car and turned off the engine. The repair shop had promised to fix Ryan's Jeep on Monday. Until then, she was doing the driving.

"Did you see the live music sign out front? My guess is people came for dinner and are staying to hear the band later. That's in addition to our group upstairs."

She opened the door and stepped out. "The merchants are making a killing this weekend on the Fall Festival. Paige said she's had a steady stream of customers through her shop, and they weren't all just browsers."

"These weekend events are great for the economy." Ryan met her at the front bumper. "Speaking of Paige, there she is now."

Leah glanced in the direction of the street where Quentin and Paige approached carrying a large wooden box between them. Thankfully, they'd cleaned the time capsule so it was no longer caked in dirt.

"Hey, I'll get that." Ryan hurried over to take Paige's end.

"Thanks. What did we put in this thing, rocks? It weighs a ton."

"I can't wait to find out. I barely remember what my own contribution was." Leah smiled at her friend. "You look spectacular, by the way."

Paige wore a gold dress that hugged her figure and swirled out around her knees, and a pair of strappy heels that added a good five inches to her height.

"Right back at you. That shade is fabulous with your complexion."

Leah glanced down at her tangerine-colored dress. The scoop neck revealed a hint of cleavage and left her shoulders bare, while the side slit parted high up on her thigh with every step she took. "Is it too much? The saleswoman at All Dressed Up insisted I buy it."

"You look perfect. That clerk knows her business." Paige held the door to the restaurant open for the men.

Quentin grinned as he passed through carrying his end of the time capsule. "You both look extremely hot. Right, Ryan?"

Ryan's blue gaze locked with Leah's in a long

moment of wordless communication. "Even prettier than you were back in high school."

"Then there's Nina." Paige gestured toward their friend, who stood beside a table in the dining room speaking with Dr. Carlton and his wife. "If I didn't love her so much . . ."

Nina wore a dark red, deceptively simple dress that stopped at mid-thigh, displaying legs a supermodel would kill for. She was so beautiful, it almost hurt to look at her.

"Good thing we do, right?" Leah's lips curved. "Jealousy isn't a pretty emotion."

"What do you have there?"

She jumped when a hand landed on her shoulder and glanced up at Irving Stackhouse, their chief of police. "It's the time capsule we buried back in fifth grade. We dug it up last night for our reunion."

"I heard about that." He nodded at Nina as she joined them. "Should be entertaining to revisit the past."

"We plan to have a great time," Paige said. "Are you here to enjoy the music later?"

"Don't I wish." Stackhouse grimaced. "No, my officers and I will be in and out periodically all evening to discourage drunk drivers. My whole force is working overtime on such a busy weekend. Nothing like the local police presence to inspire sobriety."

"We'll keep that in mind." Quentin pressed a hand to Paige's back to nudge her out of the way. "Are we going upstairs? This thing is heavy."

"Yep, straight up." Leah smiled at the veteran

cop, who'd been a fixture in town as long as she could remember. "Good talking to you, Chief."

"You bet."

Quentin and Ryan led the way up the stairs with the time capsule between them. When they reached the open room at the top, decorated with the welcome banner and streamers Leah and Paige had strung up earlier, the handful of people already present cheered.

"Put it on the table by the back wall." Nina directed the men toward the rear of the room.

Ryan let the box down with a thump. "I can't wait to see who included the gold brick."

"No kidding." Quentin dusted his hands on his slacks. "Where's the bar? That was thirsty work."

As more of their old classmates arrived, Leah mingled, catching up with a few friends she hadn't seen in years. Still, her gaze returned again and again to Ryan. The previous night had been perfect, but—

"You look pensive."

She glanced up and smiled at Sloan. "You changed your mind about attending. The reunion wouldn't have seemed right without you."

"I'll admit to feeling my age in this group, so I asked Edgar to come along with me. After all, he helped a couple of the dads with the actual hole-digging during the burial party twenty years ago."

"I'm thrilled Edgar's back to work after kicking cancer's ass. Oh, there he is over by the window, talking with Jesse and Ryan. I'll make sure to tell him I'm glad he came."

"You do that. The man dotes on you."

Leah grinned. "That's because I laugh at his jokes."

"Or you're just a lot prettier than I am. I'll talk to you later, Leah."

"Sure."

After Sloan strolled away, she headed over to the food tables to consult with Arnold Dorsey. Assured by the restaurant owner that dinner was ready to serve, she clapped for attention and announced the buffet was open.

Fifteen minutes later, plate in hand, she slid onto a chair next to Nina and let out a sigh. "I think the party's going well. Everyone seems to be having a good time."

"I'd say so." Her friend paused with a skewered prawn halfway to her mouth. "You're positively glowing. Great sex tends to do that for a woman."

Leah choked on the water she was sipping. "What makes you think—"

"Ryan has been watching your every move all evening and is wearing the same satisfied expression." Nina lowered her voice as a laughing couple passed behind them. "My superior powers of deduction tell me you two heated up the sheets last night."

"God, are we that obvious?"

"Only to someone who knows you well. So, are you and Ryan—"

Leah gulped more water as her face heated. "Doing it? Yes, and it was pretty darn amazing."

"I was going to ask if you're officially a couple."

"Not really."

"Why not?"

She shrugged one shoulder. "We agreed this is temporary . . . just until he goes back home."

"That works for you?" Nina asked.

Leah pressed a hand against her chest and rubbed. "I'm determined to live in the moment."

"Hmm."

"What the heck does that mean?"

"Nothing." Nina glanced up. "Hey, Ryan, have a seat."

He pulled out the chair beside Leah and sat. "Paige and Quentin are on the way over, and I ordered a round of drinks for us."

"You're the best." Nina gave Leah a quick glance. "Some people should keep that in mind."

"Huh?" Ryan frowned. "Did I miss something?"

"Nope." Nina leaned an elbow on the table. "So, tell me what's next for Crossroads. Or is that classified info? Would you have to kill me if you leaked your secrets?"

"Not kill, but I'd expect you to sign an oath of silence in your own blood . . ."

Leah's grin faded as she met Pete Brewster's gaze from several yards away. He leaned against the wall beside Sloan Manning and George Dorsey. She responded with a brief nod. The man had been a bully when they were kids, and nothing much had changed over the years. The fact that he was her ex-husband's best friend and lawyer had always irritated her.

After a moment, he said something to Sloan then approached. Stopping a meager foot away, he triggered an urgent need to put some space between them, impossible with the table hemming her in.

He crossed his arms over his chest. "I haven't spoken to Brock in a while. How is he?"

Her stomach tightened. "I don't have a clue. We aren't in touch."

When Paige and Quentin arrived, carrying full plates, Pete finally stepped back. "I heard he has plans to be in the area soon. If you do talk to him, tell him to look me up." Turning on his heel, he strode toward the bar without waiting for an answer.

Leah shivered. "Jerk."

Beneath the table, Ryan laid a hand on her thigh and squeezed, but he didn't comment as a server approached with a tray of drinks. His silent show of support dissolved some of her tension, and she let out a long breath, determined not to let mention of Brock ruin her evening.

Paige held up her glass. "To old friends. Cheers, everyone!" Around the room, others echoed the sentiment.

Leah met Ryan's gaze and clicked the edge of her glass to his. "Cheers to us."

"Are you okay?"

She nodded in response to the concern in his voice. "Absolutely. Let's eat. These salads look delicious."

He regarded her for a long moment before picking up his fork to dig into the chicken pasta on his plate. "Rabbit food, but to each his . . . or her . . . own."

"Darn right."

An hour later the buffet had been cleared away, and most of the group had assembled around the table where the time capsule rested. The gather-

ing had expanded to include a few curious specta-
tors, mostly family members of classmates, who'd
come upstairs to watch the unveiling along with
the local community events reporter from the
newspaper. She stood with her camera poised as
Ryan and Sloan used crowbars to wrench off the
cover.

With a hard yank, the nails came loose, and Ryan
set the lid off to the side. "Finally." He smiled at
Leah. "Who plans to do the honors?"

Nina joined her up front with Paige, who rubbed
her hands together. "Let's see what we have in
here."

Leah stared down at the contents and laughed
out loud. "Oh, my goodness, we really did put a
rock in the box." Reaching in with both hands, she
lifted out a large, flat rock decorated with artwork
and signatures from every member of the class.
"I'd totally forgotten about this."

Nina pulled out several books. "*The Lion, the
Witch and the Wardrobe, Matilda,* and *On the Banks of
Plumb Creek.* Wow, a few of us had great taste in lit-
erature when we were ten."

"Not so much in music." Paige waved a Hanson
CD. "Remember these guys? Who's the guilty
party?" When no one fessed up, everyone laughed.
Next, she produced a dog collar complete with a
bone-shaped name tag. "I hope the dog wasn't still
attached when we buried the capsule."

"Hey, that was my contribution." Quentin took
the collar from her and grinned. "My mom couldn't
figure out how Rowdy lost this."

Leah fluttered a long, black feather. "Looks like
someone plucked this out of a raven."

"I shot it with my BB gun first." Pete Brewster glanced over at his father, who'd joined the group. "Hey, Dad. Do you remember that? None of the birds were safe in our yard."

Leah's stomach turned, and she dropped the feather on the table. Gritting her teeth, she reached into the box and held up a purple bear. "Who still has their old Beanie Babies? This was my contribution."

"Typical Leah." Paige fished out two VHS tapes. "I contributed *The Parent Trap*. Who put in *Jumanji*?"

"That would be me." Ryan grinned. "I still love that movie."

"We also have a Lego dinosaur and *Jurassic Park* trading cards." Nina set them on the table. "Hey, what ten-year-old boy doesn't love dinosaurs, right?"

"That T. rex was mine." George Dorsey left the buffet table, where his father was clearing away serving dishes, to approach. Blue eyes gleamed as he picked up the Lego dinosaur. "I bet I still have a box full of Legos at my dad's place."

"Some things you just can't let go." Nina cradled a small red book sporting a miniature lock. "Oh, wow, this was my diary. You know, I think I still have the key at home in my jewelry box."

Leah nudged her arm. "Great. I'll be able to unlock your journal and read it to my class on Monday morning when I share our time capsule with them."

"Not on your life." Nina stuffed the diary into the purse slung over her shoulder. "I remember some of the things I wrote in there, and they aren't anything I want to share with the public."

"Spoilsport."

"Call me all the names you want, but I'm still not budging." She reached in to lift out a framed glossy photo. "Here's a picture of our whole class, including Mr. Manning."

Their former teacher stepped forward. "Oh, Lord, look how young I was. Do you think I had enough gel in my hair?"

Leah shot a smiling glance at Sloan. "You were a cool dude back then."

"*Sure* I was. Are we finished here?"

"I think so . . . wait." Leah held up a roll of film. "Who did this belong to?" When no one took credit, she shrugged. "Must have been from someone who couldn't make it to the reunion." She slipped the film into the black silk purse she'd brought instead of her usual jumbo bag. "I'll get the pictures developed to share with my students. The official portion of our evening is over, folks, but please stick around to enjoy yourselves. Sounds like the live music has started downstairs."

"Can I get a group photo for the paper before this breaks up?" The reporter stepped back and lifted her camera. "All the former students with Mr. Manning and the time capsule. Crowd in closer. That's great." She clicked several times before nodding. "Thanks, everyone."

Ryan took Leah's arm and led her away from the table where a few of their classmates gathered to check out the photo and the painted rock. His hand was warm on her bare skin, and the glow in his eyes heated her further.

"Do you want to head downstairs?"

"Sure. The local band playing tonight is really good." She stepped closer when someone brushed against her from behind, and Ryan drew her tight to his side. She was slightly breathless when she spoke again. "Anyway, I have to hang around to take down the decorations and pack up the time capsule once everyone leaves."

"Then we'll listen to the music for a while first."

They joined the throng of people on the stairs, and Leah teetered precariously as they neared the bottom.

"Careful." Ryan grabbed her around the waist.

"Wow, I almost fell on my head. My purse caught on something, maybe the handrail. Good thing I zipped it closed earlier."

"As much crap as you carry, that would have been a disaster for sure." He guided her toward the bar area, where the band was playing a lively bluegrass tune. "Hey, they are good. I don't see any empty tables, though."

"Looks like Sloan and the Vargases just got one. Maybe another will open up soon. This place is packed." When her purse vibrated, she unzipped it to pull out her cell and glanced at the display. "Uh-oh."

Ryan slid an arm around her as Chief Stackhouse brushed past, headed toward a rowdy group in the corner that had been joined by Pete and Waylon Brewster. "What's wrong?"

"My grandma just texted me, and I quote, 'You'd better come over here. Damn bastards.'" Leah's grip on the cell tightened. "Crap."

"Interesting language coming from a senior citizen. Your grandma knows how to text at . . . how old is she now?"

"Eighty-two. Yeah, she's up on all the latest technology, and she's been known to use colorful language when she's upset. Damn, I wonder what she pulled this time."

"How much trouble can an eighty-two-year-old get into?"

"You'd be surprised." Leah stuffed the phone back into her purse. "Do you mind leaving now? I need to get over to the senior apartments."

"Of course not."

She gave him a grateful look, then reached out to snag Nina's arm as she passed them on the way toward the bar. "Ryan and I have to leave. Can you and Paige clean up without me and take the time capsule home with you? I'll pick it up tomorrow."

"Of course, but why the rush to get out of here?"

"Grandma texted."

The concern in Nina's gaze turned to amusement. "What's she done now?"

"God only knows, but I'd better get over there pronto."

"Go. Paige and I will handle everything here."

"Thanks. You're the best." Grabbing Ryan's hand, she tugged him toward the door.

"Call if you need bail money," Nina shouted after them.

His steps faltered. "Is she kidding?"

"Not in the least."

* * *

He sat alone in the dark office and focused on keeping his temper. He'd failed. Not once, not twice, but three times. Four, if he counted the pointless hours spent digging under the paving stones at the school the previous month. On sheer gut instinct, he'd followed Leah and Ryan and the others the previous night when they left Castaways to head up to the grade school. Sure enough, they'd dug up the box. He'd nearly shouted with glee when they'd turned down the access road to the carnival afterward. He'd only had to wait twenty minutes for an opportunity to break into the Jeep. But the damn time capsule wasn't inside. One look at the blinking light on the dash of the Jaguar Paige Shephard had been riding in told him the alarm was set on the expensive vehicle. He couldn't risk getting caught red-handed stealing the box.

He slammed his fist down on his thigh and swore. Earlier in the evening, he'd edged up through the crowd surrounding the time capsule while those idiotic women lifted out "treasures." A bunch of ridiculous crap not worthy of the attention they'd given it. But he hadn't been able to slip the film into his pocket before Leah stuck the roll in her purse. *Stupid bitch.*

"I'll get the pictures developed to share with my students," he mimicked in a high-pitched voice. Wouldn't that be the ultimate show-and-tell? Those kids would have nightmares for the rest of their lives.

When his phone beeped, he pulled it from his pocket and glanced at the text. **Did you get it?**

With a grunt, he typed a response. **Not yet.**

Fuckin' A!

He tapped furiously. **I'll take care of the problem.
One way or the other.**

   You'd better.

He threw his phone down and let out a shaky breath. He'd save their collective asses, even if he had to break their cardinal rule in the process. If he couldn't get the film any other way, he'd kill Leah Grayson on their home turf. And damn the consequences.

Chapter Nine

Ryan glanced over at Leah as she pulled into the lot next to the apartment complex and parked in the first vacant spot. "What, exactly, are you afraid your grandmother did?"

"Based on past behavior, the possibilities are endless." She released her seat belt and opened the door. "Let's see, there was the time Gram serenaded an elderly gentleman from out on the lawn and woke up all the other residents. She also spearheaded what she called a skivvy raid. For the uninformed, *skivvies* is a term my grandpa picked up in the navy for his underwear."

"That's hilarious." Ryan climbed out and pushed the car door shut, then followed her toward the large complex surrounded by a brick wall.

"Not so much since one grouchy old fart called the cops to report the theft. Thankfully, he accepted an apology and didn't press charges, but it took some fast talking on my part to get Gram to say she was sorry."

"Your grandma always was a firecracker. How long ago did your grandpa pass?"

"Five years now. Gram's lonely. She says she doesn't like being single."

He waited while she punched in a code at the entrance gate. "Single, not widowed?"

"Shows where her mindset is."

"Good for your grandma." He laid a hand on her arm and squeezed. "I'm sorry about your grandfather."

"I am, too, but I've gotten used to his absence. I still miss his charm and wit, however." She let out a sigh and knocked on the door to one of the apartments facing a central courtyard. "No police cars out front or uniformed officers prowling the grounds. That's a good sign."

The door swung open before he could respond. *Talk about your blue-haired old ladies . . .* Leah's grandma was short but not hunched. She stood ramrod straight in the doorway. Her eyes snapped with temper beneath curls tinted the blue of a summer sky.

"About time you got here." She transferred her gaze from Leah to Ryan and gave him a slow perusal. "Who's the hunk?"

"Grandma, you remember Ryan Alexander."

"The one you let get away? Of course I do, but you look a lot older now." She snorted with laughter. "Of course, I'm no spring chicken, either."

He responded with a broad grin. "It's good to see you again, Mrs. Grayson."

"You can call me Evie, short for Evangeline, which is a real mouthful. Come on inside." Spinning on a slipper-clad foot, she retreated into a room crammed with knickknacks. Her pink silk caftan with a peacock embroidered on the back floated around her small frame.

"What's the emergency, Gram?" Leah dropped onto a couch upholstered in purple suede while her grandmother paced the area rug in front of it.

Ryan hovered, waiting for the elderly woman to sit.

Instead, she picked an envelope up off an end table and tossed it in Leah's lap. "I didn't get around to opening yesterday's mail until a little bit ago. Read that drivel. I don't know who's to blame, the apartment manager here or some idiot at the bank. Either way, heads are gonna roll come Monday morning."

As Leah read without speaking, her lips tightened. Finally, she glanced up. "I don't suppose you have a recent bank statement handy."

"I think one came a few days ago, but that thing is confusing. Anyway, the machine spits out a little slip that tells me how much money I have when I get cash."

"Can I look at your statement?"

With a flutter of her caftan, Evie headed toward the rolltop desk in the corner. She lifted the lid and returned with an unopened envelope. "Here you go. So it was the bank that screwed up, not the manager who sent the letter telling me I hadn't paid my rent?"

"We'll see." Leah's tone was grim as she ripped open the envelope. Moments later, her eyes widened. "Gram, what's this transfer from your investment account to your checking? It looks like you moved the money back out again a few days later." She pointed at the statement. "You wrote a pretty hefty check a couple of weeks ago, too, which is why the one for rent bounced."

Ryan's gut tightened at the fear darkening Leah's eyes. His gaze swung to her grandmother as the woman's brow creased. "I gave a check to that nice Mr. Woodward to invest in his new housing development. He assured me I'd triple my money before the year ends."

"And the transfers?" Leah's knuckles whitened as she gripped the statement.

"He said I'd want to have capital available for future investments, so I sold my stocks the next day and moved the profits. But that money should still be in my account."

She closed her eyes for a moment. "Did you give this Mr. Woodward your account number?"

"No, but I got out the statement that came before this one for him to look at. He said he didn't want me to write a check for more than I could afford." Her earlier temper seemed to fizzle. "I appreciated him safeguarding my best interests. He was a real nice fellow. Good-looking, too."

"Did he write anything down when he looked at your statement?"

Evie shook her head, blue curls fluttering. "No. He was too busy telling me all about his project and how I was getting in on the ground floor when investing was most lucrative. Then he showed me pictures of the houses in his development he'd taken with his phone. Real luxury homes for a reasonable price."

Leah turned to glance up at Ryan. "He probably snapped a picture of her statement." All the color had leached from her face, and she swayed slightly.

He sat beside her and rested a hand on her shoulder. "How much did he transfer out of Evie's account?"

"A little over a hundred grand plus the check for five thousand."

His grip tightened. "Maybe you can recover most of it. The bank should be able to trace where it went."

Her grandmother glanced between them. "You're scaring me, Leah. What's going on?"

"The letter from the manager is a notice that your rent check bounced. That's because the one you wrote to that man, Woodward, in addition to your other bills, overdrew your account. But the bigger problem is all the money from the stock transfer is now missing."

"I don't understand."

Leah stood and took both her grandmother's hands. "That man was a scam artist. How'd you meet him?"

"Through Bea, who lives two units down. She invested with him, too."

Ryan balled his hands into fists as he rose to his feet. "I doubt they were the only two this crook approached. You'll need to call the police to report him." He met her grandma's tearful gaze. "Don't you worry, Evie. We'll get to the bottom of this."

"But he was such a nice man . . ." Her voice trailed off, and her eyes glittered with temper through her tears. "Shame on him for abusing my trust."

"Not exactly the way I would express my opinion, but close enough." Leah pulled her checkbook out of her purse, scribbled furiously, then ripped off the slip to hand to her grandma. "Give this to the manager so he won't be on your back about rent before we get this problem straightened out."

"Thank you, Leah. I'm so mad I could spit, but Mr. Woodward seemed smart and trustworthy."

"Most con men do." Ryan gave her a reassuring smile. "You aren't the first to be fooled by a predator like him."

"And, unfortunately, I doubt you'll be the last. Don't cry, Grandma."

Evie wiped away a few tears. "I just want to smack myself for being such a sucker."

Leah hugged her tight. "Did you sign a contract when you gave him the check?"

Her eyes brightened. "I sure did. Now where did I put it?" She headed back to her desk to rummage through the drawers, then waved a thin sheaf of papers stapled together. "Here's the copy he gave me."

Leah took the document and dropped back down on the couch. Ryan moved in to read over her shoulder and glanced at the letterhead.

"Woodward Enterprises with a post office box in Portland."

Leah flipped pages. "Looks like a bunch of gibberish to me. Damn." She slapped the papers against her thigh. "I'll take this with me to the police station tomorrow. They'll probably send someone out here to talk to you, but I don't want to deal with the authorities tonight. At this point, I doubt a few hours will make a difference. On Monday, we'll go to the bank during my lunch break."

Evie smiled at her granddaughter. "You take

such good care of me." Her gaze slid to Ryan. "You'd better be nice to my girl."

"No worries. I intend to treat her like a princess." Glancing over at Leah, he hammered it up, hoping to erase a little of the tension carving tight lines around her lips. "Princess Leah has a nice ring to it, don't you think?"

She rolled her eyes and stood. "We have to go now, Gram. Promise you won't lose sleep over this."

"Oh, I won't. I trust you to get me out of this mess the way you have all the others."

"I'll do my best." She dropped a kiss on her grandmother's creased cheek. "Talk to you tomorrow."

"Not too early. I'm taking a walk with Magnus right after breakfast." She turned her attention to Ryan. "Good night, young man. Nice to see you again after all these years."

"You, too, Evie. Sleep well." He hurried to catch up with Leah, who had already reached the door. With a final smile for her grandma, he followed her out.

Leah ran a few yards to lean against a light post. Her shoulders shook as she pounded her fist against the metal. "Goddamn it! I'd like to scream right now."

He wrapped his arms around her from behind. "Hey, don't fall apart on me. You were great at keeping your grandma's spirits up."

"No point in both of us breaking down. I can't believe this!"

"Unfortunately, scumbags prey on seniors all the time. I'll help you through this, Leah."

She straightened, swiped a hand across her damp cheeks, then gave him a grim smile. "I appreciate that, but I'll call my sister in the morning. Her husband is a corporate attorney, so he should have some ideas about recourse in a situation like this. And I'll file a report with the local police so they can be on the lookout for this creep if he's still in the area."

"Your grandma signed those papers two weeks ago, so he's probably moved on by now."

Her lips twisted. "Bilking elderly people in some other senior community."

Slipping an arm around her waist, he led her toward the parking area. "There's nothing you can do right this minute, so let's go home."

She nodded, her hair brushing his neck as she leaned against him. "Thanks, Ryan. I'm glad you were with me."

He hesitated for a moment. "If your grandma needs some temporary financial assistance—"

"I'll figure something out. With the move to California, my parents don't have a lot of extra disposable income, but between them and my sister and me, hopefully we can manage living expenses until Gram's money is recovered."

He kept his mouth shut as he opened the door to the Audi, which she hadn't bothered to lock. In cases like these, often there was little money left to recover. No point in mentioning his fears to Leah and upsetting her, however. Once they were seated and she started the engine, they drove toward town in silence.

Finally, she glanced over. "I'm sorry our evening

ended on such a sour note. The objective was to have fun tonight."

"We had a great time at the reunion. I think everyone got a kick out of the objects we put in the time capsule."

"I'm looking forward to showing our childhood treasures to my students. We plan to bury a new time capsule next week." Streetlights cast shadows across her sober expression as they passed through town. "Maybe in twenty years they'll have a reunion, too."

"Maybe so. And in a couple of decades, your students will look back and be thankful for having had such a creative teacher, the same way we appreciate Mr. Manning."

A real smile lit her face in the glow of the dash. "I certainly hope so."

She turned off the highway and slowed as they bumped down her driveway. After edging around his Jeep, she pulled into the carport and turned off the engine.

He reached over to touch her hand. "I'll walk you inside."

"You don't want to stay?"

"I doubt you're much in the mood to . . . well, do anything."

She grimaced. "Maybe not."

Stepping out of the car, he braced himself with a hand on the hood when Barney sprinted through the doorway and jumped. "Down." His sharp order produced results, and the dog backed away after the initial contact of big paws on his jacket.

"Hey, he minds you." When Barney ran over to her side, Leah scratched his ears. "Good boy."

After brushing off the paw prints, Ryan tucked an arm around her to head toward the kitchen door, where he stopped beneath the glow of the porch light. Bending, he tipped her chin with his free hand and kissed her thoroughly. Both their breathing had quickened when he finally raised his head.

"Maybe I could get in the mood . . ."

"No offense, but you look worn out. I'll let you get some rest."

She pressed her forehead against his chest. "I feel like someone scrubbed the floor with me. Thanks for understanding." She glanced up, her beautiful brown eyes clouded with fatigue and worry. "I may have taken a direct hit, but I have amazing powers of recovery. Do you want to do something tomorrow after I talk to the police?"

"Sure. I'll give you a call." He kissed her again and reluctantly released her. "Good night, Leah."

"Night." Juggling the sheaf of papers and her purse, she opened the door, shooed the dog inside, then gave Ryan a final quick smile before shutting it behind her.

Feeling noble, he turned and walked away as the cool night air swirled around him. She might appreciate his nice-guy qualities, but they sure wouldn't keep him warm tonight.

Leah sat opposite Officer Chris Long on Sunday morning in the nearly empty squad room with the contract open on his desk between them. A steaming cup of coffee and a half-eaten bagel also occupied the space, and Leah felt a little guilty for interrupting his mid-morning snack. Not that he seemed to mind as he flipped to her grandmother's signature at the bottom of the last page and frowned.

"You showed this document to a lawyer?"

She nodded. "I scanned it then emailed the doc to my brother-in-law earlier. He said it's a standard form you can print online after filling in the pertinent information. Basically worthless, and nothing that would hold up in court. He also researched this company, Woodward Enterprises out of Portland, and couldn't find any listing. His conclusion was the same as mine. Thomas Woodward, or whoever this man might be, is a scam artist who swindled my grandma out of all her savings."

"I'll run his name through the database to see what comes up." Officer Long's gaze was sober as he fidgeted with his coffee mug. "We'll certainly do our best to locate him."

"I appreciate that. I can't contact the bank about Grandma's account until tomorrow. Although at this point, that would be sort of like shutting the barn door after the whole herd moseyed out to the pasture. There's nothing but a few dollars left in there to take."

"Maybe we can track where the money was wired. I'll need her account information to look into that angle."

"Gram's statements with the account numbers are at her apartment."

He typed on his keyboard for a moment before glancing up. "Is there anything else you can tell me about this man?"

"I'm afraid not, but Grandma spoke with him face-to-face, and her neighbor also *invested* with this jerk." Leah tucked a strand of hair behind her ear and sat back in the chair. Bea Stenson, I think her name is. Both women should be able to give you a description."

"I'll head over there now to talk to them. Even if he's left town, we can put out an ATL via LEIN across the West to keep watch for him in other senior communities."

Leah blinked. "Huh?"

Chris grinned, reminding her of the boy she'd known back in high school. "Attempt to locate. It goes out through the Law Enforcement Information Network."

"Oh. That would be great." Leah stood when he did, and shook the hand he extended. "Thank you for your help."

"You bet." He released their grip and walked with her out to the lobby. "I'm sorry this ruined your weekend. Kim said she had a lot of fun last night."

"I talked to your sister at the reunion. Catching up with old friends was terrific."

"Sounds like everyone enjoyed themselves." He opened the door for her. "I'll be in touch as soon as I have an update."

"Thanks, Chris." She headed across the pavement toward her Audi but paused when a police cruiser pulled into the lot and stopped beside her.

The window lowered, and Irving Stackhouse rested an elbow on the opening. "What brings you to our neck of the woods on a Sunday morning, Leah? Nothing wrong, I hope."

She squinted against the sunlight as she stepped closer. "Morning, Chief. Unfortunately, some sleazebag scam artist is preying on local seniors, including my grandmother. I just filed a report with Officer Long."

His eyes darkened. "I'm sorry to hear Evie was a victim, but we'll put all our resources into following up on your report." A frown carved lines deep in his forehead. "In fact, I'll personally oversee the case. Can't have our older citizens targeted in their own homes."

"I appreciate that." Leah glanced at her watch. "Darn, I'm late meeting someone. I'll talk to you later, Chief Stackhouse."

"Enjoy your day, young lady, and don't worry about your grandma. We'll make sure she receives justice."

Leah was all for justice and would love to see the cretin who'd taken advantage of her grandma drawn and quartered, at the very least. But her most immediate concern was cold, hard cash. Short of robbing a bank, she wasn't sure how she was going to pay to keep her grandma in her apartment. After opening the car door, she leaned against it and closed her eyes. She'd figure out a way. Somehow.

Chapter Ten

Ryan glanced at the digital clock on the stove. Leah was twenty minutes late and counting. Not exactly unexpected . . . He filled two water bottles at the sink, then turned when his mom entered the kitchen.

"I thought you were going for a bike ride."

When she lifted the teakettle from the stove, he took it from her to fill before returning it to the burner. "I am, but Leah's running late."

Her blue eyes brightened. "I'm so pleased you and Leah are back together again. Of all the women you've dated over the years, she was always my favorite."

"We're not exactly together, Mom. We're just hanging out while I'm in town. What kind of tea do you want?"

"Peach." She used her good arm to reach for a flowered mug on the cupboard shelf, while he headed toward the pantry. "Seems like you're a couple to me. As an adult, your comings and goings are your own business, of course, but I'm not completely clueless."

The back of his neck heated as he returned with the requested box of tea. His mother might not have mentioned the night he hadn't come home, but she'd obviously noticed. "We're seeing each other, but don't start making a big deal out of a rekindled friendship."

"In my day—"

"No offense, but this isn't your day, and since to my knowledge you've rarely dated since Dad died thirty years ago . . ."

"You make a valid point. Fine, I won't meddle in your private life if you don't butt into mine." When the kettle shrieked, long and shrill, she lifted it from the burner. "So, is Leah the reason you brought two bikes back after your quick trip home last week?"

So much for not meddling . . . "She only has that pink cruiser, which isn't designed for trail riding." The hum of an engine caught his attention, and he leaned over the sink to glance out the window toward the driveway. "Here she is now. Only thirty-five minutes late. Not bad."

His mother snorted. "You might not want to lead with that comment if you value this *friendship*."

"Do I look stupid?"

She gave him a quick once-over from his cycling jersey to his bike shorts to his riding cleats. "Currently, you look like those crazy guys on the sports channel who launch their bikes off cliffs. In my opinion, none of them has a whole lot of sense."

"I assure you, Leah and I will stick to the trail today and not do anything irresponsible."

"Good to know." She shooed him toward the door when the bell chimed from the front of the house. "Go let Leah in so I can say hello to her."

"Sure." He left the kitchen and hurried toward the entry. After swinging the door wide open, his smile slowly faded. "You changed your mind about mountain biking with me?"

Leah glanced down past a lavender top to a denim skirt that stopped just above her knees. Not that he was complaining about the view of killer legs, but—

She held up her bulging tote bag. "I need to change. I didn't want to wear bike shorts to the police station."

Relief slid through him. "How'd it go?"

"Okay, I guess." Her soft brown eyes darkened with worry. "They assured me they'll do their best to track down this Woodward person. I just hope they find him before he spends all Gram's savings."

"Maybe he'll slip up now that the authorities are looking for him." Ryan took her arm to tug her inside and shut the door. "Although you'd think other victims would have reported him already. Based on what your grandma said, he sounds too smooth to be new to this game."

"I know, right?" Leah frowned. "Still, Chris called shortly after I left the station to let me know Thomas Woodward isn't in their database."

Ryan stopped. "Chris?"

"Officer Long. You probably remember him from high school. His younger sister Kim was at our reunion. He's the one I talked to this morning."

"Oh. I imagine Woodward is an alias, so maybe they'll turn up a connection to similar crimes in a different town and uncover this creep's real identity."

"I'll cross my fingers, but right now, I don't want to think about it anymore since there's nothing I can do to fix the problem. Can I change someplace?"

"You know where the bathroom is. When you're ready, come find me in the kitchen. Mom wants to say hello before we leave."

"I'd love to see your mom." She glanced down toward his feet. "Who's that?"

When Charlie rubbed against his ankles and eyed Leah warily, Ryan smiled. "Charlie."

"Beautiful animal. I'll be out in a minute."

He waited until she disappeared down the hallway then rejoined his mother. True to her word, Leah returned a few minutes later.

She set down her tote bag then crossed the kitchen dressed in bike shorts and a T-shirt. A helmet dangled from the fingers of one hand, and a single long braid hung down her back.

At the table, his mom rose to her feet. "It's good to see you, dear. Did I thank you properly for your assistance when I broke this darned arm?"

"The snickerdoodles and lovely note you dropped off were more than enough thanks for making a simple phone call to Ryan." Reaching his mom, Leah gave her a quick hug. "When will the doctor take off your cast?"

"If all goes well, early in November."

She stepped back. "I'll keep my fingers crossed for you, although I'm enjoying having Ryan in town again."

"No reason he can't visit often even if he doesn't have to be here to fetch and carry for me, right Ryan?" His mom shot him a pointed look.

"None that I can think of." He stepped away from the counter. "But right now we'd better get moving. There's a strong chance of rain later this afternoon, so we probably want to be back before then."

"My pinochle group is meeting here this evening, so feel free to take Leah out for a nice dinner after your ride." She added a wide smile that would have made a crocodile proud. "You two have fun, now."

"We will." He took Leah's arm and steered her toward the back door into the garage.

She glanced over her shoulder. "See you later, Mrs. A."

"I hope so, dear."

Ryan shut the door behind them. "Could my mom be any more obvious?"

Leah glanced up. "What are you talking about?"

"She's probably in there planning our wedding as we speak. She's always loved you, and the fact that I didn't come home Friday night was the clincher in her mind." He pressed the button to raise the garage door. "I told her we're just friends, but she didn't believe me."

"Is that a fact?"

He gave her a sharp look, not sure how to interpret her comment. "Uh, you can ride my old bike. The frame may be a little big for you, but I lowered the seat." Grabbing the handlebars, he wheeled it out to the driveway.

She took it from him. "This is your old bike? It looks pretty fancy to me."

"Yeah, well, I went off the deep end and splurged on a new one. The shocks are such high quality, I can barely feel the bumps, and it hardly weighs anything."

After he returned with the second bike, she whistled. "Geez, Ryan. Does it pedal for you?"

"Just about."

She straddled the first bike, then stepped off again to lower the seat an inch. "I bet that high-tech machine cost more than my car."

He glanced at her old silver Audi. "Probably. I tend to get a little carried away when it comes to quality sports equipment."

"Don't apologize. You earned the right to have nice stuff." She settled her helmet on her head and fastened the strap in place. "Where are we going?"

He donned his own helmet. "I thought we'd head south. There's a great single track that winds up into the hills about eight miles from here."

"I know the one you're talking about. I used to ride out there with Brock." She pushed off and smiled over at him. "You may have to wait for me on the downhill sections. I'm out of practice."

The mention of her ex sent a quick dart of pain

through his chest. Thinking of Leah with another man, especially her former husband, bothered him far more than it should. He shook off the twinge of resentment and forced a smile. "Not a problem. I'm happy to wait for you."

When they reached the highway, they rode single file at a quick clip Leah had no problem maintaining. Ryan slowed to make the turn onto the dirt single track and waved a hand. "Why don't you lead so you can set the pace?"

"You don't mind?"

"Not in the least." A steady view of the curve of Leah's firm behind as she leaned forward wasn't exactly a hardship.

She was in excellent shape . . . in every sense of the word. They rode uphill at a speed that would have challenged a few of his buddies. When the trail finally leveled off and widened, he pulled even with her and took a drink from his water bottle.

"You ride like a pro. Want to rest for a minute?"

She nodded and braked to a stop, then removed her water bottle from its holder. After drinking steadily for several seconds, she squirted water on her face and wiped it off with her sleeve. "Oh, wow, that was tough."

"You didn't need to go so fast."

She shot him a quick grin. "I didn't want you to think I'm a wimp."

"No danger of that. You're an animal."

Her smile broadened. "A compliment sure to impress any woman."

His neck heated, and it wasn't due to exertion. "I didn't mean—"

"Kidding, Ryan. I know what you meant. Thanks." She tipped the water bottle back again, and her throat moved as she drank. A sheen of perspiration glistened on her chest. Finally, she stuck the bottle back in the holder. "I may not hang out in a gym, but I get a lot of exercise."

He adjusted his shorts. "I can tell. By the way, sweat becomes you. Just saying . . ."

Her gaze dropped before lifting to meet his. "You try to ride like that, and you may hurt yourself."

"I'll risk it." He rolled forward a couple of feet and reached out to place a hand behind her neck. Tugging her forward, he kissed her. "You're extremely hot, Leah Grayson."

Her breath brushed his cheek as she backed up a few inches. "You're damn sexy, too, Ryan Alexander. But, since I'm not down for a round of sex on the trail, maybe we should keep riding."

"Probably a good idea." He released her slowly and moved away. "Lead on, Macduff."

"That's *lay* on. Are we going into battle?"

He stared at her blankly. "What the hell are you talking about?"

"It's a Shakespeare thing. A computer guy wouldn't get it."

"Apparently not. You're an odd one at times. Hot but strange. I appreciate that."

"Sounds about right. I'm glad my eccentricities don't bother you." She pushed off, pedaling hard as the trail narrowed again and climbed steadily.

Ryan got the feeling she'd had someone particular in mind when she'd commented on her unconventionality being a turnoff. Her jerk of an ex-husband would be his guess. If that asshole had made Leah feel bad about herself—

His tire hit a rock at the edge of the trail and jerked left. He went over with a solid thud and landed with his bike on top of him. The breath left his lungs in a whoosh.

He gasped for air. "Shit."

"Are you okay?" Leah dismounted and dropped her bike to run back to him. "What happened?"

"I wasn't paying attention. Really, really stupid." When she lifted his bike, he twisted the shoe still locked onto the pedal to release it, and sat up.

"Did you hurt yourself?" Her wide eyes were filled with concern. "Should you move?"

"Nothing's injured but my pride . . . and possibly a bruise on my hip." He rubbed the tender spot as he scrambled to his feet. "I'm not usually such a klutz."

Apparently convinced nothing was broken, she eyed him up and down and smiled. "You did look pretty funny lying in a heap, and you're covered in dirt."

He brushed ineffectually at the sleeve of his jersey. "Great."

"Turn around and let me."

He did as she asked then glanced at her over one shoulder. "Why do I feel like one of your students who had an accident on the playground?"

Her smile melted his heart as she slapped dirt off his ass.

"Believe me, I don't pat down my kids." Her fingers lingered. "Nothing but solid muscle. This is kind of fun."

"Happy to brighten your day."

She went to work on his back, bending down to brush off his legs. The feel of her fingers on his thighs made any bruises worthwhile.

"There, that's as good as it's going to get."

He turned and pulled her into his arms. "If it got any better, you'd wind up just as dirty as I am." Tipping back her head to avoid bumping helmets, he kissed her . . . and kept kissing her until he was forced to come up for air. "Thanks."

"Glad to oblige." She hesitated for a moment before speaking again. "Is it just me, or does this feel exactly like it used to between us? Friends first and lovers second."

His hold on her tightened. "Is there anything wrong with that?"

"No. The friendship was missing in my marriage, and you know how that ended. What we have is better."

"I hope so." He kissed her again, but the knowledge that their previous relationship had self-destructed niggled at the back of his mind. Best not to worry about the future and simply enjoy the present. He brushed a thumb across her cheek. "Let's finish this. We're almost to the top."

She nodded. "Nothing I like more than to accomplish the goals I set." Her serious gaze met his before she turned away to pick up her bike.

Am I one of her goals?

Did he want to be? He'd originally hoped to keep their relationship simple but feared they'd passed that point some distance back. For them, maybe uncomplicated had never been an option.

A whole lot of heartache might be waiting at the end of the path they were on, but he'd stay the course. Because he couldn't imagine walking away from Leah. Not yet.

Maybe never.

Chapter Eleven

Leah parked beneath the carport awning and glanced in the rearview mirror as Ryan pulled into the driveway behind her. Rain came down in a steady torrent, pinging like shrapnel off the metal roof. At least the sheet of plastic he'd taped across the broken window kept his upholstery from getting soaked. They'd stopped at his mom's house first so he could shower and change, and then had picked up groceries on the way home. After an exhausting bike ride, neither of them had felt like eating out, but she hadn't been ready to end the evening, either.

Even if Ryan had been unusually quiet for most of the afternoon.

She stepped out of the car, grabbed her tote bag from the passenger seat, and slammed the door, wondering what was on his mind. A frown formed when Barney didn't run out to greet her.

"That's weird."

"What's weird?" Dampness and gloom closed in

around them as Ryan locked his Jeep with the remote then hurried to get undercover, carrying the sack of groceries.

"Barney. Usually he would have tried to flatten you against your front bumper by now."

"Maybe he went down to the beach."

"That's a possibility, but he's not a big fan of rain. Thank heavens we made it back to your house before this started." She led the way to the back door, pushed it open, then flipped on the light. Her jaw sagged as she stared in horror at the kitchen. She loosened her grip on her bag, and it fell to the floor with a thump. "Oh, my God!"

Ryan peered over her shoulder. "You're not the tidiest person I know, but even for you . . ." He dropped a hand to her shoulder as she let out a ragged breath. "Someone else did this?"

She nodded. Mail that had been stacked on the end of the counter littered the floor. A basket of odds and ends that usually sat on a bench in the corner had been dumped out on the table. Cupboard doors were open, and the pantry was a jumbled mess with a couple of broken jars of home-canned tomatoes smashed on the floor. Jackets from the pegboard beside the door were in a heap on the tile, a few pockets turned inside out.

"Why?" Her voice broke. Advancing into the room, she stiffened when frantic yelps and scratching echoed from the rear of the house. "Barney!"

She ran through the kitchen, avoiding the tomatoes, and dashed into the living room to flip on a light. Couch cushions were upended, and books had been swept off the shelves. The doors to the cabinet below the TV were open, and CDs and

your fault." He took her arm and hoisted
her feet.

don't forget someone broke the window in
eep." Her voice rose. "Crap like this doesn't
en in Siren Cove. I don't get it."

Honestly, right now all I care about is you. Sit
n, or heat up a can of soup or something. I'll
sh this."

She caved in to his firm tone. "Fine, but you
n't want to eat canned soup. We bought ingre-
ents for stuffed portabella mushrooms."

"Which you're way too tired to cook. Cut yourself some slack, for heaven's sake."

"All right, I'll put together a couple of grilled
cheese and tomato sandwiches and open a bag of
chips."

"Sounds perfect." He dropped the wad of soggy
paper towels in the trash and ripped off a couple
more to finish the mop-up. "I'll go make your
bathroom habitable while you cook. My guess is
you'd like a shower."

She narrowed her gaze. "Are you a mind reader?"

A smile crinkled the corners of his eyes. "Remind me to look for my crystal ball later." He
squeezed her arm. "I'll be back by the time those
sandwiches are ready."

"Okay."

After he left the room, Leah sat for a minute
and simply breathed. She had no idea who'd ran-
acked her house or why, but her skin crawled just
hinking about someone going through her clothes.
What the hell is wrong with people?

First, some loser had taken advantage of her
andma, and now this. A single whimper slipped

old VHS tapes were scattered out onto the rug. Ignoring the mess, she followed the weak barks.
Nails scraped wood again as Barney hit the bathroom door. She jerked it open, and her quivering
dog knocked her back against the wall, whining as
he licked her neck and face. Leah held on tight
and forced herself to breathe.

"He looks okay, just scared."

Tears slid down her cheeks as she glanced over
at Ryan. "Thank God. He sounds like he's been
barking for a long time."

"Whoever did this must have locked him in
there while they ransacked the place. I wonder
what they took. The TV and your laptop were both
still in the living room, so it wasn't electronics they
wanted."

After a final hug, Leah pushed Barney off her
and ran up the stairs. Taking a deep breath, she
flipped on the light in her bedroom, then let out a
moan. Every dresser drawer had been emptied
and the bedding tossed. With her dog pressed
against her legs, she moved through the mess to
the small walk-in closet. Not a single hanger or
item of clothing had escaped and lay in a heap on
the carpet.

"Your jewelry box is open." Ryan's voice, calm
and matter-of-fact, steadied her nerves. "Come see
what's missing before we call the police."

Turning away from the closet, she wiped the
tears off her cheeks and complied. "I don't have
anything really valuable." She tried to focus. "This
is a genuine ruby, my birthstone." She touched the
small gem on the necklace her parents had given
her for her sixteenth birthday. "My pearl earrings

are still in there, and a gold bracelet. I don't think anything's missing."

Ryan slid one arm around her and reached for a heart-shaped silver pendant. "I gave you this." He glanced down at her. "You kept it?"

She nodded. "You fastened it around my neck after we, uh, slept together on the beach. I stopped wearing it when we broke up, but I couldn't bring myself to throw it away."

His hold on her tightened. "We'd better check the other rooms."

"I suppose so."

Her bathroom was a disaster, but not much damage had been done in the spare bedrooms. She finished the inspection tour and headed back downstairs, straight to the landline phone sitting on the end table. "I need to call the police."

"You're sure nothing's missing?"

Leah slumped onto the couch, thankful for Ryan's presence as he moved in behind her and threaded fingers through her hair to knead the tense muscles at the back of her neck. "I honestly can't think of anything. I have no idea what this person was looking for."

"Maybe the cops will find prints." He paused his massage. "Go ahead and make the call. We should report the break-in."

Over an hour later, Leah thanked the officer who'd responded to her nine-one-one call and was about to shut the back door when headlights flashed on the puddles in the driveway.

"I wonder who that is."

"I'll go see." Ryan dropped a hand on her shoulder as he passed. "Go sit down. You look wiped out."

"I am. Thanks." She turned the disaster area that used to be let out a sigh. No way could she made at least some effort to clean She'd lost her appetite, but Ryan wanted dinner, and she hadn't even p groceries they'd bought not two hours seemed like an eternity. Glancing dov sweaty jersey and bike shorts, she grim shower was in order, but that would requir ing away all the supplies dumped out of bath cabinets. The dirt coating her skin from their would have to stay for a while longer.

She was squatting on the floor, picking glass ou of the puddle of tomatoes when Ryan returned. "Hey, I'll do that."

Leah dropped the shards into the trash can and glanced up. "I've got it, but you can hand me a few paper towels to soak up this mess." She gave him a tired smile as he bent to help her. "Who was outside?"

"The police chief, Stackhouse. I guess he heard about the break-in on the scanner in his living room and drove out to get an update from his officer. Technically, this wasn't a break-in because yo hadn't locked your door, just unlawful entry. any rate, he told me he'd follow up with you morrow."

"The man must think I'm a real problem lived in Siren Cove my whole life, except for cc and never once called the cops. Then today, I two incidents inside twelve hours. Un-freak lievable."

out before she squared her shoulders and forced back a bout of self-pity. She'd suck it up and deal since she didn't have any other option. At least she wasn't fighting this battle alone.

Tears surfaced again. Thank God for Ryan.

Leah focused on not losing her temper while her grandma signed forms to transfer the meager amount left in her old bank account to a new one. The manager, Leonard Wilkinson, was throwing in checks for free.

Whoopee!

"This will insure the party who transferred your funds won't have access to any new deposits. Your money is safe with us, Mrs. Grayson."

"Easy to say now that he's wiped out her life savings." Leah eyed the man sitting opposite them with the same degree of mistrust she saw reflected in his dark eyes.

Probably because he's afraid I'll sue his ass.

"We're doing everything we can to trace that transfer, Ms. Grayson. These things take time."

"If your tech guy was as good at hacking bank records as the criminals—"

"There are procedures to follow. Rest assured, we intend to exhaust every avenue to recover your grandmother's funds."

From what she'd learned in the last forty-five minutes, she had little hope they'd ever see that money again. "Terrific." Leah rose to her feet. "I'm afraid I need to get back to work. Are we finished here?"

"Absolutely." The manager gave her grandma a

smile that didn't quite reach his eyes as he held out a hand. "I can't express how sorry we are here at Central Coast Bank that you're experiencing these difficulties."

"Not as sorry as we are," Leah muttered beneath her breath. She pasted on a smile. "I appreciate your help."

Her grandma shook the hand he offered then patted his arm. "I know this isn't your fault, Mr. Wilkinson, and I trust you'll fix the problem shortly. Have a nice day, young man."

The "young" man, who had to be pushing fifty, had the grace to look more than a little contrite. "As I said, we'll do our best."

Once they escaped the manager's inner sanctum, Leah hurried her grandmother through the lobby and out to her car. Rain drizzled down the windshield as she started the engine. "I'll drop you at home, and then I need to get back to my classroom. One of the office staff is filling in for me. I told the kids I wouldn't open the time capsule today unless they behaved for her."

"Bribery is a wonderful tool." Her grandma glanced at her watch and gave her blue curls a shake. "Actually, you can just drop me off at Flo's. I have an appointment in twenty minutes."

Leah pulled out onto the street. "How will you get home?"

"Magnus said he'd pick me up."

"You've mentioned Magnus a couple of times now. Who is he?"

"A very nice gentleman who lives in my complex. Magnus Lindgren." She giggled. "I call him my Viking."

Leah resisted the urge to roll her eyes. "Is he a competent driver?"

"Good heavens, Leah, I'm not a teenager on a first date. I assure you Magnus has all his faculties and drives his Bentley with skill and aplomb."

"His Bentley?" She parked in an empty spot in front of Flo's Beauty Emporium and set the brake. "Are you kidding?"

"Nope. The man has style."

"You'll have to introduce me to him sometime soon."

Her grandma nodded. "I'll make a point of it." She stepped out onto the sidewalk and leaned down to look through the open door. "What do you think about purple?"

"Huh?"

"For my hair instead of blue."

Leah grinned. "Go for it, Gram. You'll rock purple."

An answering smile creased her lined cheeks. "I will, won't I? Thanks for straightening everything out at the bank."

Leah let out a sigh. "We'll see how it goes. Bye, Gram."

With a little wave, she slammed the door and headed into the shop. Leah let off the brake and pulled onto the street. All she wanted to do was go crawl in a hole, but instead she turned up the road toward Siren Cove Elementary and parked her car in the main lot. The rain was still falling as she wrestled the time-capsule box, which she'd picked up early in the morning from Nina, out of the back seat and lugged it and her purse toward the building through the light drizzle.

"Leah, let me help you with that!" Edgar Vargas dropped the lid of the dumpster with a clang and hustled toward her.

She relinquished one end to carry the box between them. "Thanks. I probably would have strained my back. This thing weighs a ton."

His lips curved beneath his thick moustache. "Are you showing your kids all the treasures you buried?"

Leah nodded and huffed a little as they climbed the front steps. When they reached cover, she swiped her free hand across her damp hair and shook. "The whole class is super excited about the time capsule."

"I bet." He hesitated. "I heard you had a little trouble at your place last night."

Her eyes widened as she waited while he opened the door. "That's right. Someone ransacked my house, but how did you hear about it?"

"My wife's cousin is on the force."

She waved to the school secretary behind the front counter as they headed down the hall. "The way gossip spreads around here, I imagine half the town knows about my break-in by now."

"Did they steal much?"

Juggling her purse, she pulled her keys from her jacket pocket. "Actually, they didn't take anything. The police officer who responded thought whoever was responsible must have been looking for something specific, though I can't imagine what. If it was drugs, they were out of luck, and I don't keep cash lying around the house."

"Strange that someone targeted you."

"My house sits alone on the bluff. All I can think

is they took a chance and failed." Leah unlocked the classroom door and pushed it open to a burst of excitement from her students. "Settle down, and stay in your seats," she called out as she and Edgar lowered the box onto her desk. She turned to him with a smile. "Thanks for your help."

"Anytime." With a nod, he left the room.

The office assistant and sometime sub laid a hand on her shoulder. "The kids behaved very well for me. Impressive."

"That's because I bribed them with the time capsule." She pointed at the box. "Thanks for filling in, Sandy."

"Sure. I hope you got your grandma's business all straightened out."

Leah stuffed her purse in her bottom desk drawer then straightened to shrug off her coat. "We did what we could." She raised her voice to be heard over the commotion as the kids literally bounced in their seats. "I'd better open this thing before they completely lose it."

Sandy grinned. "All they could talk about is that time capsule. I hope the contents don't disappoint. I'll see you later."

"Thanks again." Leah waited to address her class until the other woman shut the door. "This isn't going to be a free-for-all, but everyone will have an opportunity to check out the items we buried twenty years ago." She held up a hand as half the kids sprang from their seats. "Hold it. Remember, you'll each pick one object to write a compare and contrast essay describing the similarities and differences to the item you plan to bury in our time capsule."

When a groan went up, she smiled. "Hey, this is a learning opportunity in addition to being fun." She pried off the lid. "Okay, here we go." She held up a purple Beanie Baby. "This was my contribution. Show of hands. How many of you have Beanie Babies? No one? Geez, I feel old." She passed the bear to one of the girls in the first row and dug back into the box.

It was nearly time for the bell to ring before the last item, one of the VHS tapes, was returned to the box. When a hand shot up and waved wildly, she nodded. "Yes, Carina?"

"Is that everything, Ms. Grayson?"

"I'm afraid so." Leah smiled. "Well, there was a diary in here, but the author refused to let me share it."

"Aww, no fair."

"Would you let a bunch of strangers read your journal?"

"No way! Mine's password protected."

"Exactly." Her brows drew together. "Wait, there was also a roll of film, but I need to get the pictures developed before I can show them to you." Her frown deepened as she tried to remember where she'd put the film. It had been in her purse, but she was nearly certain she'd taken it out.

"Why can't you just print the pictures on the computer?" Boyce asked from the back row.

"Because the photos aren't digital. In the old days when I was a kid, pictures had to be processed from film. If anyone wants to write their paper on the differences between film and digital photographs, they can." When the bell rang, she spoke over the clang. "Don't forget to do your math homework. I'll see you all tomorrow."

As the kids bolted out of the room, Leah dropped onto her desk chair and rubbed her temples as the beginning of a headache took hold. Where *had* she put the film? Undoubtedly it would turn up somewhere, and when it did, everyone would get a kick out of seeing the pictures the roll contained.

She'd look for it when she got home. Right after she finished cleaning up the giant mess waiting for her at the house. Tears burned behind her eyelids just thinking about the evening ahead. But feeling sorry for herself wouldn't get the job done.

"Suck it up, Leah." Standing, she dropped the lid on the time capsule box with a thump. As her grandpa had been fond of saying, *hard work never killed anyone*.

Chapter Twelve

Ryan hung the last rumpled shirt in the closet and stepped back to scan the room. Barney lay sprawled on the rug, twitching now and then in his sleep. Everything was neat without a single sign of the break-in left to greet Leah when she returned home. He'd spent the last five hours cleaning up the mess, only taking a break to pick up his repaired vehicle, and every minute was time well spent. She'd been a bundle of nerves the previous night until she'd fallen asleep on the couch out of sheer exhaustion. He'd covered her with an afghan and quietly left, taking her spare key with him.

A glance at his watch told him she'd be home anytime now. He'd hang around until then, maybe offer to take her out to dinner. After the fiasco the previous evening, they hadn't had a chance to talk about where their relationship was headed. He'd made up his mind on the bike ride he needed to know what she was thinking, even if it turned out not to be what he wanted to hear. Like it or not, his emotions were firmly engaged, and he couldn't let Leah blindside him again.

The crunch of tires on gravel in the driveway drew his attention as the dog scrambled to his feet. Ryan glanced out the bedroom window and smiled, then hurried down the stairs to the kitchen. Pushing open the screen door, he followed Barney into the carport and waited for Leah to step out of her Audi.

"Hey, what are you doing here?" She rubbed her dog's ears before standing on her toes to plant a kiss on Ryan's lips. "This is a nice surprise."

"I thought I'd straighten up a little." He took her face in his hands and kissed her back, taking his time.

"You didn't have to do that." She was breathless when he finally released her.

"I know, but I wanted to."

"Well, thank you." She walked beside him toward the back door, then stopped a few feet into the kitchen and turned in a circle. "Oh, my God, Ryan. You didn't just pick up. You *cleaned.* I can practically see my reflection in the floor. The place hasn't been this spotless since my mother moved out."

"What's the point in doing a half-assed job? The tile was still sticky from the tomatoes."

She pressed a hand to her chest as she moved from room to room with him trailing behind her. Finally, she stopped next to her bed. "I don't know what to say. Thank you seems so inadequate."

"You don't have to say anything. You've been under a lot of stress between your grandma's problems and the break-in. I was happy to take on some of the load."

"This . . ." Her voice broke as she leaned against his chest. "I wasn't looking forward to dealing with the huge mess that cretin left. This means a lot. Thank you."

He slid his arms around her. The light floral scent of her shampoo tickled his nose as he rested his cheek on her hair. "You're welcome. How was your day?"

"Not so good at the bank. I sincerely doubt my grandma will recover her money. I spoke to my parents after school let out, and they're as worried as I am. Gram may have to move back in with me since her retirement checks won't cover her rent along with living expenses, and I don't know that our family can make up the difference for more than a few months. It'll be an adjustment for us both."

He opened his mouth, then shut it and cleared his throat. "It's early in the police investigation. Don't give up hope."

"I'm trying to stay positive, but it's hard."

He tightened his arms briefly before letting her go and changed the subject. "Did you share our time capsule with your class?"

"Oh, yeah. They got a huge kick out of all the treasures—and I use the term loosely—we buried. Which reminds me . . ." She glanced up. "Did you find a roll of film while you were cleaning? I remember taking it out of my little evening bag, but I can't recall what I did with it."

"I didn't notice one anywhere."

"Weird. Not that I haven't misplaced things before." She frowned. "I'm sure it'll turn up some-where."

"Unless Barney buried it." He glanced over at the dog, who lay beside the bed gnawing a ragged chew toy. "He was digging in the yard earlier."

"Probably going after a gopher. They make him crazy."

Ryan followed her down to the kitchen and leaned against the counter while she filled the kettle with water.

"Would you like a cup of tea?"

"I'll pass." He stuffed his hands in the pockets of his jeans. "Do you have anything going on this evening, or can I take you out to dinner?"

"Dinner out sounds lovely if we can go a little later. I have science reports to finish grading since I didn't get them done this weekend."

He pushed away from the counter. "Does seven thirty work? That gives you three hours."

"Perfect." She turned on the burner beneath the kettle, then crossed the room to meet him in the middle. "You're unbelievably wonderful. I can't imagine why some woman hasn't snapped you up already."

"A few have tried." He grinned. "But then I'd do something stupid to turn them off."

"Doubtful. They all must have been shy on brain cells. Kind of like I was. Hopefully, I'm smarter now."

"I'd like to believe we're both a little wiser." He dropped a quick kiss on her upturned lips. "I'll see you in a while."

"I'll be ready."

He sincerely doubted the promise but realized he didn't mind—not much, anyway. Tardiness probably wasn't the worst flaw a person could have. As he climbed into his Jeep and backed up to turn around in the driveway, he gave Leah's comments some hard consideration. What had he done to screw up his previous relationships? Expecting 100 percent compatibility and feeling disappointed when he didn't find it probably didn't say much for his intelligence. No one was perfect . . . or even perfect for him. He needed to remember that.

When he reached town, he swerved into a parking spot near Castaways. He'd have a beer and chill before going home to give his mom a hand with dinner, since it seemed like he'd been neglecting her lately, then shower and change for his date with Leah. Maybe if he made a conscious effort to relax more instead of being so uptight all the time, he wouldn't blow it with her.

The rain from earlier in the day had stopped, but low-hanging fog swirled in the air. The thick dampness covered him like a blanket as he hurried down the sidewalk toward the bar. Giving himself a mental shake, he pulled open the door and glanced around. A few familiar faces stood out. Pete Brewster and George Dorsey sat at a table near the windows with a blond man whose back was to him. When he turned to signal the cocktail waitress, Ryan sucked in a breath.

What the hell is Leah's ex doing back in town?

Ryan's gaze locked with Brock Hooker's. Blue eyes widened before he said something to his companions. Both their former classmates turned his way. Pete made a comment, and the other two burst out laughing.

"Ryan."

He jerked his attention away from the trio when a hand touched his arm. Glancing over his shoulder, he smiled at Nina. "Hey, I didn't expect to see you in here."

"I'm meeting someone, but I'm a little early. Want to sit with me while I wait?"

"Better than joining that group." He angled his head toward the three by the window.

"Oh, God. I wonder if Leah knows Brock is in town."

"I'm pretty sure she doesn't. At least she didn't mention it earlier." Taking Nina's arm, he led her through the crowded room toward a table some distance from their old classmates, and nodded at Dr. Carlton and his wife as they passed. "Who're you meeting?"

"A guy named Clayton Smith. You wouldn't know him."

He pulled out her chair. "I was kind of surprised you didn't bring a date to the reunion." He studied Nina's classic beauty combined with modern chic as he took the seat opposite her. "Unless the men around here are all blind or something."

"I don't date much, but seeing you and Leah together . . ." She hunched a shoulder. "You both looked really happy. I figured I'd try again. So, when Clay asked me out, I agreed." She glanced up as the cocktail server approached. "Hey, Janice. How's it going?"

"Just great." Fine lines crinkled around hazel eyes as she smiled. "What can I get you?"

"For now, I'll have tonic water with lime. I need to pace myself."

Ryan laughed. "Keep your wits about you?"

Expressive green eyes darkened. "It pays to be cautious."

"Without a doubt." He turned to their server. "I'll take whatever import you have on draft."

She nodded. "Be right back."

He eyed Nina as she toyed with the strap on her purse. "You look nervous. I hope that isn't my fault."

She glanced up swiftly. "God, no. I'd much rather hang out with you all evening than go on this date."

"Then why'd you tell the guy you would?"

"Because it's been nearly five years, and I need to have a life again."

His chest tightened at the pain in her voice, but he forced himself to ask, "Five years since what?"

"Since my fiancé died. Keith was killed in Afghanistan."

His breath left him in a rush. "I didn't know. I'm sorry."

"Me, too." She seemed to shake off the aura of sadness and squared her shoulders. "Leah told me about the break-in at her house when she picked up the time capsule this morning. I can't believe something like that happened in Siren Cove. We don't have much vandalism here, or any real crime, for that matter."

"I talked to her when she got home from work." He frowned. "The ordeal definitely disturbed her, but I helped her clean up the mess, and she seems to be bouncing back."

"Smart man. The way to Leah's heart is definitely through her vacuum cleaner—as long as she doesn't have to use it."

"Aren't you funny?" He paused when the cocktail waitress returned with their drinks. "Thank you."

"You're welcome." Janice set his beer in front of him. "Let me know if you need anything else." With a quick smile, she hurried off.

Nina sipped her drink. "Yeah, I'm a riot. Seriously, though, how are you and Leah getting along?"

"Pretty well. We seem to have picked up right where we left off, but I'm not exactly sure where we're headed."

She patted his arm. "You know Leah. Sometimes it takes her a while to recognize her feelings. She doesn't make quick judgments the way you and I tend to do." Nina drew back her hand. "At least that's how you used to be."

"I haven't changed much." He took a long pull on his beer. "Apparently Leah hasn't, either."

"Don't push too hard. I honestly think you'd be great for her, but she might need a little time to figure that out. Especially when she has so much on her mind."

"I guess we'll see what happens." He squirmed a little under Nina's steady regard, feeling like his emotions had been laid bare. He ran a finger down the side of his sweating glass and changed the subject. "Leah mentioned her class enjoyed checking out our time capsule."

"I bet. They probably thought the CDs and VHS tapes were antiques. All kids do now is download entertainment to their phones." She leaned back in her chair. "Hey, tell Leah I want to see those pictures once she gets the film we found in the box developed. I assume the photos are shots taken of our class."

"I will, but she misplaced the roll. She'll have to find it again before she can get the film—" He broke off as Pete, George, and Brock stopped at their table. If their slightly glazed eyes were any indication, the threesome had been drinking for quite some time, despite the early hour.

Brock stared at Ryan as he brought his hand down on the back of Nina's chair. His lips tightened when he leaned in close. "If you're into Leah's castoffs, babe, I wouldn't mind getting in line."

Nina shifted to avoid his touch. "Don't be an ass, Brock. Does Leah know you're in town?"

Pete crossed his arms over his chest and swayed a little. "Not yet, she doesn't."

Brock nodded. "I might head out to the house to see what she's up to later."

Blue eyes glittered beneath shaggy blond hair that gave him the same California surfer look Ryan remembered from high school. Based on the biceps pressing against the sleeves of his T-shirt, Leah's ex spent the majority of his time in a gym.

His gut tightened. "Don't waste your time. She's having dinner with me tonight."

Brock snorted. "Figures she'd take up with you again now that you're such a big freaking success with Crossroads. Someone has to pay the bills, right?"

"God, you're a jerk. I don't know how Leah put up with you for as long as she did." Nina didn't raise her voice, but her tone sliced through the sudden stillness.

"Dude, maybe we should take off." George nudged his pal, apparently the most sober of the three.

"Glad to." Brock eyed Nina up and down. "You may be hot, but you're still the same bitch who talked my wife into leaving me. Let's get out of here."

Ryan relaxed his clenched fist as the three men walked away. Letting out a slow breath, he met Nina's troubled gaze. "I should have punched him."

"No, you shouldn't. He'd probably have you arrested."

"Did you really convince Leah to divorce him?"

She shook her head. "No, of course not, but Brock is the kind of guy who has to blame someone for his problems. He doesn't own them." She glanced past him and frowned. "Damn, Clayton just walked in. I was going to call Leah to give her a heads-up, but—"

"Don't worry. I'll do it when I see her."

"Thanks." She pushed back her chair and stood. "Uh, can you tell Janice to transfer my drink tab—"

"I've got it." He rose to his feet. "It was good talking to you, Nina."

"Likewise." She smiled. "You and Leah have a nice evening."

"You, too. Give this guy a chance. You deserve happiness."

Her eyes darkened, but she only nodded before striding away. Ryan finished his beer and signaled

Janice for the bill, paid, and left the bar. He'd gone into Castaways to relax. An epic fail since seeing Brock had strung his nerves tighter than any noose. The man had implied Leah was only interested in him for his money.

Total bullshit.

He should have punched the asshole in his smug face. And damn the consequences.

He cruised along the dark highway, headed back toward town, headlights barely penetrating the thick fog, his cell clutched tight in his fist. "What do you mean she never sent the film off to be developed?"

"Exactly what I said." The voice on the other end of the connection radiated irritation. "A reliable source overheard Ryan Alexander talking to Nina Hutton in Castaways. He mentioned Leah Grayson—who has become a real pain in our ass—misplaced it."

"Well, the film roll sure as hell wasn't anywhere inside her house. I took that place apart looking for it."

"Then maybe she dropped the damn thing in her car."

He forced himself to think. "Or it could be in that giant bag she hauls around everywhere she goes, even though she didn't have it with her at the reunion."

"You'd think the woman would have looked in her own purse."

"Maybe, but I've been close enough to see the thing is full of crap. She could have missed seeing it when she searched through the clutter."

"Then get ahold of her bag. Search her car. Do whatever's necessary to get that damn film roll back. Got it?" The voice lashed out, striking a nerve.

The vein in his temple throbbed. "I'm getting a little tired of your attitude."

"Then do something proactive for a change. Even I won't be able to stop the shit storm if those photos come to light. And while we're on the subject of brainless idiots, I hear your son has been working his magic a little too close to home lately. Aren't you the one who harps about going further afield to choose our sacrifices so no one will come poking around? You'd think your innate caution would have rubbed off on your kid when it comes to his little side business, but *no*."

"His little side business, as you put it, filled our coffers when we were running low on funds, so don't shout at me." He let out a slow breath. "However, I'll speak to him about discretion."

"See that you do. In the meantime, I'll try to cover his ass."

"Your efforts are in all our best interests."

A grunt answered him.

He loosened his grip on the cell as his temper abated. "Has this year's Samhain sacrifice been secured yet?"

"Apparently, the *sure thing* our brother promised fell through. I'm surrounded by imbeciles. I'll try to get a lead on another one."

"I'll keep my eyes open, too. You never know when the perfect victim will present herself."

"You do that, but your top priority is the damn roll of film."

He stared into the dark night as his mind clicked over, sorting and rejecting scenarios. How hard could it be to get ahold of her bag? He gritted his teeth. "Don't worry. I'll take care of it . . . and her."

Chapter Thirteen

Dim lighting, enticing aromas, and low conversation created the seemingly perfect romantic atmosphere for date night at the Poseidon Grill. Leah picked at her tofu stir-fry. Across from her, Ryan savored a steak that oozed blood each time he cut into it. She shuddered.

Finally, he laid down his fork. "What's wrong?"

She tried to smile. "Nothing. I'm just not very hungry."

"I should have waited until after dinner to tell you Brock was in town." He laid a hand over her closed fist resting on the tablecloth. "My mistake, but don't let it ruin your evening."

"I'm doing my best, which isn't very good, I'm afraid."

He tightened his grip. "You have every right to feel anger or irritation or anxiety, whatever emotion is turning your knuckles white. I just hate to see you upset."

She relaxed the hand beneath his, certain she

didn't deserve his consideration. "Sorry. I shouldn't let the man affect me, but he does. He'll stop by the house at some point, ostensibly to visit Barney, and issue some derogatory comment that raises my blood pressure and makes me wonder why I ever married the jackass in the first place. Then I'll spend the next few days trying to remember the good parts of our relationship so I won't feel like such an idiot for falling for him. It's a vicious cycle."

"Sounds like it. A restraining order might solve your problem."

Finally, she smiled. "God, I'd love to see his face if I had him served with one of those. But he hasn't done anything to warrant it, except make a few rude remarks. A judge would laugh me out of court."

"I'm glad he isn't physically threatening."

She grimaced. "Only to my ego."

Ryan turned her hand over to thread his fingers through hers. "Do you still have feelings for him? Is that why he upsets you?"

"No!" The word came out louder than she'd planned, and a few heads turned as nearby diners glanced their way. She lowered her voice. "His cheating killed any love I had left for him, well before our divorce was final."

"Then don't let the jerk get to you. I'll hang around to supervise any dog custody visits, and you don't even have to talk to him."

Some of the tension filling her chest eased. "You'd do that?"

"Sure. He doesn't intimidate me, despite all those bulging muscles."

A second smile slipped out. "He's obsessed with

working out. But, while you're no slouch when it comes to abs, you have a brain to complement them."

His blue eyes glimmered with amusement. "I guess brain before brawn is a good thing."

"Definitely." She pulled her hand away and forced herself to eat. After a few bites, she laid down her fork. "Hey, if bad luck comes in threes, I should be in the clear after this. First Grandma's con man, then the break-in at my house, and now Brock showing up in town. Karma may be sending me a message, but hopefully her point has been made."

He chewed and swallowed. "What point might that be?"

"That you have to take the bad with the good. No one said life is easy."

"And the good would be . . . ?"

"You, back in my life again."

"Is that what you want? I've been wondering where our relationship is headed."

The caution reflected in his steady gaze set off a warning bell. Had she completely misjudged his feelings? The last thing she needed was for—

"Leah?"

"Haven't we been getting along really well? Is there a problem I don't know about?"

He reached for her hand again and held tight when she tried to pull away. "No problem. I'd love to build on what we have and take it to the next level. But I won't pretend I'm not a little worried you'll shut me out at some point."

Her heart ached. "You don't trust me?"

"Let's just say I'm wary." He held her gaze for a

long moment. "I don't want to get hurt. I don't want *either* of us to get hurt. If our expectations are different—"

"I *expect* us to enjoy each other's company. I *expect* to take some time to learn more about Ryan the man, who is a whole lot more complex than the boy I knew so well. I don't want to rush into anything and make another mistake." Her hand tensed beneath his grip. "God knows I've made enough of those in the past. I also don't want to lose you again." Her voice cracked. "I care about you. I value our friendship."

"Hey, I do, too, and I don't want to blow this. We'll . . . date. I've never rushed any other relationship without a long test period first. I don't know why this one should be any different."

"Because we have a history. In some ways, it feels like we've jumped into the deep end right off the bat instead of wading through the shallows to get used to the water first."

"Then I'll back-paddle until I have both my feet beneath me." His smile looked a little forced, but he was obviously trying. "No worries. We both have plenty of reasons to be careful. We'll take this slow and get it right this time around."

"I really hope so."

He released her hand. "Let's finish our meal and get out of here."

"Good idea. Tonight was kind of a bust, which means we have nowhere to go but up. Right?"

"Everyone has an off night, but we still have time to turn the evening around. Let's not talk about anything serious. Just fun stuff. Surely the fifth-graders in your class did something today to make you laugh."

Her morose mood dissolved with a smile. "One of the boys asked if he could put a peanut butter and jelly sandwich in the time capsule we plan to bury, as an experiment to see what it would look like in twenty years. Can you imagine?"

"Now why didn't I think of that? The kid obviously has a brilliant scientific mind."

She snorted then choked on a piece of zucchini. All the awkwardness between them fell away as their conversation became progressively sillier. By the time she'd cleaned her plate, her mood had been restored. "That was the perfect way to destress. How did you know laughter was exactly what I needed?"

"Because after all these years, I may know a thing or two about you." His tone was light, and he gave her a quick smile. "Shall we order dessert?"

"I'm too full, but go ahead."

"Then I'll pass." He raised a hand to signal their server for a check.

A minute later, the restaurant's owner approached to lay the bill on the table. "How was your meal? I hope you both enjoyed it."

"Excellent as always, Mr. Dorsey." Leah smiled at the older man. "You did a superb job with our reunion party. Everyone loved the food."

"Great to hear. George told me he and his buddies had a good time."

Ryan glanced up as he pulled out his wallet and removed a credit card to place on the tray. "I saw your son a few hours ago at Castaways. I'm afraid I didn't have a chance to talk to him at the reunion, but I hope his move back to Siren Cove has been successful."

"So far so good." Arnold Dorsey picked up the tray. "I'll give this to your server. Enjoy the rest of your evening."

"Thanks, Mr. Dorsey." Leah lowered her voice after the man walked away. "Was George with Brock at Castaways?"

Ryan nodded. "Pete, too."

"Perfect. Pete Brewster was always a horrible influence on Brock. Hopefully they'll hole up somewhere drinking and pass out. As long as Brock doesn't come looking for me later, I don't care what he does with his old pals."

Ryan signed the receipt when their server returned with it, slid his credit card into his wallet, and stood when Leah pushed back her chair. "I'll stay with you tonight if you want. Mom isn't going to wonder where I am if I don't show up."

A smile slipped out as she lifted her bag off her chair and slung the strap over her shoulder to head across the restaurant beside him. "You'll make that sacrifice, huh? Strictly for noble reasons?"

He grinned back as he held open the door. "Of course. Do you doubt my motives?"

"Of course not." She waited while he dug out his keys to unlock the Jeep and glanced over as a green sedan turned into the parking lot. "Hey, that's Sloan's car."

Her colleague parked near them, got out, and slammed the door. "Evening, Leah. Ryan, good to see you." Sloan strolled toward them. "How'd your appointment go at the bank? I missed seeing you after school let out."

"Not well. Unless the police catch the creep preying on seniors, I seriously doubt my grandma will get her money back."

"That sucks. I—" Stepping forward, he flailed and grabbed onto her shoulder. "Sorry about that." He regained his balance. "I stepped in a damn hole. Well, I won't keep you. My takeout order's probably ready by now, anyway."

Leah opened the car door. "Enjoy your dinner. I'll talk to you at school tomorrow."

"Sure thing. See you around, Ryan."

She climbed in the Jeep and glanced over as he started the engine. "Once a klutz, always a klutz. The fire department has been out to the school twice after Sloan jumbled up the chemicals during an experiment. Luckily, the only damage was a singed spot on a table and a huge cloud of smoke."

"That must keep everyone on their toes."

"Yeah, right now *I* feel like I need to be on high alert, waiting for the next disaster to strike."

Ryan shot a quick glance her way before returning his attention to the road. "Your luck is sure to change. Karma is on your side, remember?"

"That's right, but I hope she's wearing protective padding, just in case."

He laughed out loud. "I love your sense of humor, Leah. You never fail to amuse me."

"Good to know." She leaned an elbow on the armrest and sighed. "I can handle Brock, but I'm worried about my grandma. That problem isn't going to go away."

He turned down her driveway. "If she needs a loan—"

"She has no way of repaying it. I don't want to think about it anymore tonight."

"Then we won't." After he stopped the Jeep near the carport, the cooling engine pinged in the silence. "Do you want me to come in?"

More than anything. But they'd talked about slowing things down, taking time to make sure they were on the right track. She bit her lip.

"Leah?"

"Yes, I'd like you to come in. If you want to . . ."

"Of course I do. I'm a guy. I may have a brain to go with my brawn, as you pointed out, but I still think with my—"

Paws hit the window by his head, shaking the glass.

Leah grinned. "A timely interruption. Apparently we were taking too long to get out."

He opened the door and gave Barney a shove. "The good news is no one is lurking in the bushes this evening. Your oversized mutt is a good alarm system, even if he is too sweet tempered to bite the bad guys."

"Everyone has to have a skill." She got out and stroked Barney's ears, then strolled beside Ryan toward the house. When he wrapped his arm around her, she leaned her cheek against his shoulder. "Thanks for listening to me whine and cheering me up. I appreciate it."

"Hey, what are friends for, right?"

"True, but I seem to be the one with all the issues." She stopped in the pool of light cast by the outdoor fixture and dug through her bag for her keys. "This is why I never lock my door."

"You could carry a smaller purse. Not locking up isn't an option after what happened yesterday."

"I know, but it pisses me off. I can't remember the last time I felt the need to turn my home into a fortress. Ha, found them." She glanced up and frowned. "Did you roll your eyes at me?"

He grinned. "Only a little. A fortress, really? I could disable that wimpy excuse for security with a credit card."

"I don't do locks." She shook the keys at him. "I'm the trusting sort."

"I'm not."

Her stomach dropped. Once upon a time, he'd been trusting. Was his current cynicism her fault for ending their relationship all those years ago? The thought made her heart ache.

"Are we going inside?"

"Huh? Oh, sure." She unlocked the door, pushed it open, then flipped on the light. "What do you know, clean and tidy just the way we left it." She shrugged off her jacket and hung it on the peg-board near the door.

"That's a relief." He took her hand and followed Barney toward the living room. "Let's sit on the couch, watch some mindless TV, and chill."

"Sounds good. We can even make out like we did in the good old days."

"Except back then I went home frustrated and horny."

"Not tonight." She pulled him down beside her and reached for the remote. When she met his heated gaze, her fingers quivered over the buttons. They weren't the only things quaking in anticipation. "What do you want to watch?"

"I don't care." Pulling her close, his lips trailed down the side of her neck. "I'm not going to be paying much attention."

She let the remote fall to the floor. "In that case, why turn it on?"

"No reason." He turned her to lie full-length against the cushions and came down beside her, then kissed her like he never intended to stop.

"We could just go to bed." She was breathless when they finally came up for air.

"This is kind of fun." He squirmed against her. "Letting the anticipation build." One hand stroked up beneath her shirt to cup her breast beneath the lace of her bra. "Isn't it?"

"Torment of the best kind." She cradled his face in her hands and caressed his lips with one thumb. "I missed this closeness after . . ."

"We had some issues, but chemistry was never a problem." He nipped her thumb with his teeth. "That hasn't changed."

"The attraction has only grown stronger. But what we have going for us is more than simple passion. At least I hope it is."

"Friendship." He rocked with her, holding her tight against him, increasing the tension. "Caring. You matter to me, Leah. Never doubt that."

"The concern and respect and genuine liking I had for you never stopped. I missed you so much, Ryan."

"Me, too." He kissed her again, taking his time. She savored the moment, so caught up in their connection she didn't register the squeak of the kitchen door opening until it smacked against the wall. Barney leaped up from the rug, barking like a one-dog destruction squad to skid out of the room. The barks turned to whines moments later as a deep voice greeted him.

Leah stiffened. "Shit!" She and Ryan were still trying to get untangled and sit up when footsteps stopped in the doorway.

"Real nice, Leah. I just might puke."

"What the hell are you doing here, Brock?" She planted a hand on Ryan's thigh to push herself upright.

"I thought I'd come visit my dog, maybe see if you were lonely." He swayed a little and braced his feet farther apart. "Guess not."

"Using Barney as an excuse is just plain lame." Her grip on Ryan's thigh tightened. "You're drunk. I hope you didn't drive yourself out here."

"George dropped me off."

"Then call him to come pick you up again. What were you thinking?" Her voice rose, and she took a calming breath.

"That my wife—"

"Ex-wife."

"Whatever." He ran a hand through his hair. "I was thinking about crashing here tonight."

"Then think again. I don't want to see you or talk to you. Go away, Brock."

"God, you're a bitch." His gaze settled on Ryan. "Good luck with that. Always nagging and complaining about everything I did wrong. But maybe you're into controlling women. Not to mention sloppy seconds."

Leah gritted her teeth. "Get out. Now!"

"Fine." Brock spun around then gripped the wall to steady himself. "I sure as hell don't need you."

His footsteps sounded against the wood floor as he retreated, and after a moment the back door slammed shut. Barney lifted his nose and howled.

"Exactly how I feel." She turned to face Ryan. "I'm sorry."

"Why? It's not your fault he showed up . . . unless you're in the habit of letting him stay here when he's in town."

She jerked back. "Of course not!"

"Then don't apologize."

Putting a little distance between them, she reached out to stroke Barney's ears when he sidled over to press against her legs. His whole body quivered.

"He gets upset when Brock and I yell at each other. He was still a puppy when I kicked the idiot out for good, but Barney remembers."

"Tension isn't pleasant for anyone." He rose to his feet. "I should probably go."

A lump formed in her throat. Since she couldn't speak, she just nodded.

He took a few steps then turned back and studied her as she blinked away tears. "Are you okay?"

"No." Her voice croaked. "I *hate* when he comes here. Everything about divorce sucks."

"I imagine so. Even a straightforward breakup is bad enough, not that ours was exactly smooth." He stepped closer and drew her up off the couch beside him. "Do you want me to stay? I figured after that little scene you wouldn't exactly be in the mood."

"Maybe not, but I don't want to be alone, either."

"Will he come back?" His tone sharpened. "If you don't feel safe—"

"Not threatened." She sighed. "Just vulnerable and a little lonely."

"Then I'll stay." He wrapped an arm around her and walked her toward the stairs. "Head up to bed. I'll check around outside to make sure Brock isn't hanging around then lock up."

"Thank you." With an effort, she forced back tears. "There's no one I trust more than you. I can't tell you how important that is to me."

His lips tightened. "Steadfast and reliable, that's me, but you already have a dog."

"I didn't mean—"

"I know. I'm a little on edge. Go on up, and I'll be there in a few minutes."

She turned away to plod up the stairs with Barney at her heels. Exhaustion weighed on her. Ryan had every right to be irritated by Brock's comments, but the last thing she needed was attitude. When it came to men, she was sick to death of taking their crap.

Not happening this time around.

Her back stiffened as she stomped up the last few steps.

If Ryan thought otherwise, he was in for a rude awakening.

Chapter Fourteen

Ryan walked slowly around the house and stumbled in the dark, wondering why he hadn't had the foresight to turn on the outdoor lights. Probably because he'd been so damn rattled by Brock's appearance he hadn't used his head. Knowing Leah had been married to the man grated on his last nerve. The reality of the asshole showing up as though he had every right to expect a welcome . . .

A harsh breath hissed out. It had taken every ounce of his control to keep his mouth shut and let Leah handle her ex. She didn't need a savior and hadn't expected Ryan to throw down the gauntlet and defend her honor. She was fully able to fight her own battles.

If part of him wished he could have played hero . . . well, those caveman tendencies would just have to crawl back in the hole where they belonged.

As he stopped near the cliff's edge, faint moonlight shown through the shifting clouds to illuminate the cove and the three monolithic rocks guarding its entrance. Somewhere behind the house, a car door clicked shut, echoing in the stillness.

Brock's ride showing up? Ryan strained to hear the acceleration of an engine, but only silence followed.

"What the hell?"

Frowning, he ran past Leah's garden and stopped near the carport. In the distance, gravel crunched and a flashlight wavered before a car door opened and closed with a *thunk*. When an engine started, Ryan crossed his arms over his chest and stared toward the road. Tail lights gleamed red before the vehicle drove away.

Had Brock been snooping around his Jeep while he waited for a ride? Irritation surged. Surely he'd locked his car. Pushing away from the support post, Ryan strode out to the driveway and tried the passenger side. Locked. Weird. He'd definitely heard a car door.

"Huh. I wonder . . ." He entered the carport and fumbled along the wall until his fingers brushed the light switch. Blinking in the sudden glare, he pulled open the driver's-side door of Leah's Audi. Unlocked, of course.

The interior looked like a tornado had hit it. The glove box hung open, and the owner's manual, registration, and an assortment of paper napkins and ketchup packets littered the passenger-side floor, along with a dozen or more CD cases. Sweatpants, two jackets, a few stray socks, and a pair of running shoes were in a tangle on the back seat. Floor mats had been jerked askew. Striding around to the back, he opened the rear hatch and winced. A blanket lay in a heap beside a small cooler with the lid flipped open, thankfully empty. A cardboard box of file folders had been dumped out. Papers were scattered everywhere.

Leah was going to go ballistic.

"Well, shit."

The back porch light flicked on, and the door squeaked open.

"Ryan, what's going on?"

He glanced up as Leah appeared in the carport doorway. "Slight problem."

"When you didn't come inside, I began to wonder. Did Brock—"

"Someone tossed your car. Maybe your ex-husband, but I can't be positive since I didn't see him."

"What the hell!" Her voice rose as she closed the distance between them and took a quick look inside. "Oh, my God!"

"It's not so bad except for all the papers."

"The science reports I was grading earlier. It's going to take me an hour to sort them all into the right folders." She gritted her teeth. "How many pages do you think won't have names on them? Damn it!"

"I'll help you, but first take a look around. Is anything you keep in the car missing?"

"I don't think so. I actually cleaned out the interior a few days ago, so there wasn't much in here."

He refrained from commenting on the accumulation of clothes in the back seat. "Do you think Brock made a mess just to spite you for telling him to get lost?"

"That's not his style. He's more direct when he

has a problem with me, but I can't imagine who else would have done this."

"Do you suppose the same person who trashed your house came back?"

She rubbed her hands up and down her arms and shivered. "If that's the case, the break-in wasn't some random freak looking for drugs or money. It must have been someone with a specific purpose."

"You have no idea what this guy . . ." He paused. "Although I guess it could be a woman. Anyway, what this person is after?"

"No. What if they return while I'm sleeping? Barney isn't exactly a trained watchdog who will attack on command."

Sliding his arms around her, Ryan pulled her against his chest. "I'm not going anywhere."

"You can't stay indefinitely. You're in town to help out your mom, and once she gets her cast off, you'll go home again."

"That won't be for quite a while yet, so let's focus on right now. Do you want to call the police to report this?"

"Not really. What would be the point since nothing was stolen? I'll mention the—" Her brow creased. "Harassment probably best describes this situation. Anyway, I'll mention it to Chris Long when I speak to him again. He promised to follow up with any new developments on my grandma's con man in the next day or so."

"Fine. Do you want to sort these papers now or in the morning?"

"I'd rather do it tonight and get it over with so I can sleep."

"Smart plan." He released her and stacked the

papers in a pile, then dumped them in the cardboard box. "Lock your car, okay?"

"Yeah. From now on, I'll lock up everything I own. Promise. I may be a slow learner, but I'm not completely stupid."

"You're plenty sharp, just a tad naïve when it comes to trusting people."

"Apparently." She pressed the button to set the locks then slammed all the car doors. "Let's go do this."

Ryan flipped off the outdoor light and locked the back door before setting the box down on the kitchen table. "How can I help?"

Stacking the papers in two messy piles, she laid the folders out in rows. "Match the names on the top of the pages to the labels on each folder. Any without names, put in a separate pile. I can sort those based on handwriting."

He nodded and tackled the task. Ten minutes later, he glanced up as he neared the bottom of his pile. "You couldn't have assigned a shorter report?"

She grinned, the first smile he'd seen from her since Brock walked in.

"Five pages. They've been working on this astronomy assignment for two weeks."

He finished his pile, then went to work ordering the papers in the completed folders while Leah sorted through the pages without names. It was just short of ten o'clock when she returned the last folder to the box.

"Done."

"That wasn't so horrible."

"No, I guess not. Thanks for helping. You've

been great through this, which makes staying annoyed with you harder."

"Huh?" He stared at her. "You're mad at me? What the hell did I do?"

"You got a little pissy after Brock left. Judgmental."

Ryan closed his eyes and counted. He wouldn't lash out at her, no matter how tempted he was to shout that he had every right to be *pissy*. Didn't he? He'd had to listen to Brock's crap and feel like day-old leftovers. The man was a total ass, but Leah had still married the jerk.

Yet she dumped me as unworthy without a solid chance. And I'm the bad guy?

He cared about this woman. Probably still loved her. But he wasn't sure he'd forgiven her yet. Didn't know if he ever could.

He stepped back. "Brock struck a nerve."

"I know that. I've been on the receiving end of his jabs enough times to anticipate the sting. I appreciate how hard it was for you to sit there without taking a swing at him. But that doesn't give you the right to snipe at me."

"I guess it doesn't."

"I'm sorry. The last thing I want is to fight with you, but I have to stand up for myself." She clenched her hands into fists at her sides. "I promised myself I would never let any man make me feel small again."

His heart ached. "That wasn't my intention. My response was triggered by jealousy with a side of pettiness thrown in for good measure."

"Why would you be jealous of Brock when you're ten times the man he is?"

"*I* know that, but . . ."

"You think I don't?" Her voice rose.

"We're both tired and running on adrenaline. Now may not be the best time to hash this out because the last thing I want is to cause you more pain. You have enough to deal with right now without me adding to it."

Her eyes darkened as she held his gaze. "Maybe I overreacted a little. I'm on edge and not thinking straight. I'll go to bed and try to wake up a little less crazy. When I see you next, I promise not to be so emotional."

"What, you plan to ignore me for the rest of the night?"

"I'm sure all you want to do right now is go home."

"Jesus, Leah, some whack job has been creeping around your home. I'm not leaving you on your own."

"The tick in your cheek tells me you're upset."

"Yeah, I am. Frustrated. Confused. Maybe a little angry. I'm still not going anywhere."

"What about your mom?"

"I told you she doesn't expect me back tonight. Anyway, she's doing amazingly well on her own."

"So well you won't have much reason to stick around?" Her voice caught.

"I'm not leaving you here alone." He spoke a little sharper than he probably should have.

Tears filled her eyes, but she blinked them back. "Okay. I appreciate that." Taking his hand, she led him toward the doorway. "Let's go to bed."

In silence, he followed her up the stairs, not too sure what to expect at this point. Maybe that she'd direct him to one of the spare rooms. He paused in the hallway.

She glanced up at him and frowned. "What?"

"Nothing."

He entered her room, which was softly lit by a lamp on the nightstand, and stopped near her bed. A peach nightgown lay in a silky heap beside one of the pillows, but Barney ruined the otherwise romantic image. Sprawled in the middle of the bed, he rolled to his back and stuck all four feet in the air.

"Get off there!"

With a snuffling moan, the dog opened one eye and gave his mistress a skeptical glance.

"Yes, you. Move it."

His lip curled back before he flopped over and stretched slowly.

Leah fisted her hands on her hips. "I'm warning you."

With a grunt, the dog jumped to the floor, shook, then strolled out of the room.

"I'm not very good about disciplining him." She picked up the nightgown and turned away from the bed. "I'll be right back." Her hips swayed as she disappeared into the bathroom.

After a moment, Ryan sat on the edge of the mattress to untie his shoes then stripped off his socks and shirt. Standing, he dropped his pants, glanced down, and grimaced. Since he wasn't 100 percent sure of Leah's mood, he kind of wished he'd worn boxers for a change. Hiding the direction of his thoughts didn't appear to be an option. With a shrug, he flipped back the quilt and crawled into bed.

A minute later, the bathroom door opened, the light went out, and Leah padded into the room on bare feet. The peach gown clung to her curves but somehow still gave her an air of innocence. Or maybe it was simply the vulnerable softness in her wide brown eyes. When he scooted over, she slid beneath the covers and reached over to click off the lamp. Darkness enfolded them.

"Come here." Ryan pulled her close to wrap his arms around her. He rested his cheek against her soft hair as he aligned her snuggly against him. "I know you're tired and stressed. We can just sleep."

"It doesn't feel like sleep is the only thing on your mind." Her voice held a hint of humor.

His lips curved in response. "Natural reaction to holding you. Doesn't mean we have to do anything about it. The problem will go away. Eventually."

When she turned over to face him, he settled his hand on the curve of her waist. "Are we okay? My goal is openness and honesty, which is why I told you how I felt. I want the same from you in return."

He was silent for a long moment. "Truthfully, it bothers me that you married Brock. We're nothing alike. If you were attracted to him . . ."

"I was attracted to you first."

Without conscious thought, his hand slid over her hip. "Yes, but our differences became an insurmountable obstacle in your eyes. Apparently you didn't see those problems with him."

"Obviously I didn't look hard enough. Deep down, I regretted being so black-and-white with you and not trying harder to make our relationship work. I was determined to avoid making the same mistake twice, so I cut Brock more slack." She sighed. "Also, he was better at hiding secrets."

Some of his tension eased as he lowered the hand resting on her hip to her thigh. "You had regrets about me?"

"Of course I did. When my relationship with Brock fell apart, I was able to see that I tossed away something truly special with you. Maybe we weren't perfect . . ."

"Funny, that thought crossed my mind the other day. High expectations are fine as long as you allow room for flexibility."

"I can be flexible." When she slid one leg over his thigh, her nightgown rode high.

Ryan forgot what they were talking about as they lined up in all the areas that mattered most. A throbbing ache overwhelmed him, a need for Leah that obliterated coherent thought.

"I can't argue with that."

"The only friction I want between us is the kind that creates sparks." Twining her arms around his neck, she kissed him with a thoroughness that nearly destroyed him.

Working his hands up under her nightgown, he covered her breasts with his palms, the rasp in her breathing telling him all he needed to know. Leah wanted him as badly as he wanted her. Unable to wait a moment longer, he slid inside her then held still to savor the moment.

"I like being connected to you in the most elemental way." Her breath feathered across his cheek.

"It doesn't get any better than this." He pushed deeper. "Well, maybe a little better, but I'm in no rush."

He kissed her, exploring her mouth with his tongue while he investigated every inch of soft skin within reach of his questing fingers. Only when her whole body quivered with need beneath his did he move slowly to build the tension between them.

"Oh, God, Ryan. I love . . . this. You make me feel so special."

"You're freaking amazing." He gritted his teeth, holding on by a thread. "I want what we have to last forever."

A husky chuckle rumbled through her as she licked his ear. "I don't think I can wait that long."

Not what he'd meant, but he knew when to shut up and go with the moment. He pushed hard again and again until they clung together, shaking in release. Finally he let her go, and she flopped back against the sheet.

Beneath the silky material of her nightgown, her breasts rose and fell in the faint moonlight as her breathing slowed. "Well, that certainly rocked my world."

"We both needed a little stress release." He rubbed her cheek with his thumb. "I'm sorry if I made you feel bad earlier."

"And I'm sorry I got all bent out of shape about it." She leaned over to press a kiss to his chest. "That's why we're good together. Neither of us minds admitting we're wrong once in a while."

He stroked her hair, letting the strands sift through his fingers until he was certain she'd fallen asleep. Slipping out of bed, he pulled on his pants and walked from room to room to stare out into the night. Nothing moved except Barney, who joined him on his vigil.

Ryan nudged the dog with his foot. "You certainly weren't much help tonight."

Barney thumped his tail against the floor.

Nothing but darkness and silence hovered beyond the walls of the house. No hint of light. No scuff of a shoe against the ground or rustle of bushes outside the partially opened window. Convinced whoever had searched Leah's car wasn't hanging around, Ryan shut and locked the window, then made his way back down the hall to stop in the bathroom to remove his contacts. Afterward, he dropped his pants on the floor and slipped into bed. Leah mumbled softly in her sleep but didn't wake as she cuddled against him. With a sigh, he let go of the niggling fear that the woman he cared so much about was in danger. For tonight, at least, she was safe in his arms.

Chapter Fifteen

When a knock sounded on her open classroom door, Leah glanced up from the math homework she was grading. Officer Chris Long stood in the doorway.

He tucked a pair of sunglasses in his pocket and smiled. "Are you busy? The woman at the front counter told me to come on back."

"Nothing that won't keep. Come in." She stood and waved him inside, then hurried over to the corner to drag the only other adult-sized chair up to her desk. "Have a seat. Is there news?"

"Of a sort. We haven't located the man who swindled your grandmother, but I've been looking into similar crimes in the area and found a couple that fit Thomas Woodward's M.O. Unfortunately, the descriptions of the perpetrators don't match, so it may be difficult to get a positive ID on him."

"Does that mean you don't have any leads as to his whereabouts?"

"Not yet, but I'm convinced the same person is

responsible for several crimes." He pulled folded papers from his pocket and flattened them on the desk. "Here are the composite drawings of the men in question." He tapped the first one. "This is the guy who scammed your grandma, going by the name of Thomas Woodward."

Leah frowned. "Looks like he has a modified afro."

"I believe he's Caucasian, but Woodward had one of those curly perms that were popular back in the seventies. Your grandmother said he was wearing a white dress shirt with a big collar and had on a heavy gold cross necklace. The description from the other woman, Bea Stenson, was similar."

"Sounds kind of retro to me." Leah glanced at the other two drawings. "These men don't look much alike."

"No, they don't, but the seniors who provided the descriptions were all focused on the big details—dress, hair, eye color. All those things are easily altered. When the artist asked about facial distinctions, they reported these men were just sort of normal. *Normal* isn't a lot of help to an artist, not to mention the eyesight of the victims describing these perps generally wasn't twenty-twenty."

"Grandma thinks if she squints, she doesn't need to wear her glasses."

"Exactly." Chris pointed to the second drawing of a clean-cut man with light brown hair wearing a traditional suit. "This guy was calling himself Howard Williams from Williams Construction. He was also looking for investors in his housing project. The contract was the same as the one your grandma signed, and his victims lived in a retirement community outside Salem."

Leah frowned. "Seems unlikely more than one person would use the exact same contract to rob seniors in Oregon."

"I agree. Williams was operating about four months ago." The officer touched the third sketch. "Anthony Benedetto was scamming elderly women in Eugene last winter."

"Shaggy dark hair and a bow tie." Leah glanced up. "Looks like all three have light eyes."

"Blue, green, and gray were the colors reported. The perp must use contacts. He only hits a few targets at a time then fades away, which is likely why he hasn't been caught yet."

"Then he creates another new identity." Leah studied the drawings. "There's something familiar about all of them, but I can't put my finger on why."

"You think you may have seen this man, possibly using a different persona?"

"No, it's more a feeling these sketches aren't quite right. Distorted. But that doesn't make sense since, to my knowledge, I've never seen this creep before."

"He's probably in his early thirties. Medium height and build. Your grandma said he was good-looking, tanned, and had a nice smile."

"That could be you."

Chris grinned and touched his moustache. "Except none of his variations had facial hair."

"Maybe his beard is distinctive in some way, so he stays clean-shaven." She planted an elbow on her desk. "What are your plans to catch him?"

"Every law enforcement officer in the state is on alert for suspicious activity in senior communities. Plus, we've put the word out to senior centers to educate their clientele."

"But that won't help my grandma recover her money if he doesn't target new victims for several months, which seems to be his habit."

"I'm afraid not. Of course, we won't stop looking for this man, but the likelihood of him being spotted is slim, since he probably no longer resembles any of these composites."

"That sucks."

"Yes, it does." His tone was serious as he regarded her steadily.

"While you're here, I may as well report my second problem."

He straightened in his seat. "Someone ransacked your house? Yeah, I saw that report. As far as I know, we don't have any leads yet."

"Whoever it was came back last night and broke into my car. At least I assume it was the same person. It was late when it happened, and nothing was stolen, so I didn't call nine-one-one."

"Did you see anyone on your property?" His voice sliced through the quiet disturbed only by the ticking of the clock over the whiteboard on the wall behind her desk.

"No strangers, but Brock Hooker, my ex-husband, had been by not long before. We argued. Still, I don't know why he'd dump a bunch of science reports all over the cargo area of my car or empty out my glove box. Unless he simply wanted to irritate me. If so, he succeeded."

"But you didn't actually witness him near your vehicle?"

"No, and as I said, nothing was taken. If the person responsible was looking for something specific, I don't have a clue what it is."

"I'll file an incident report. What time did this occur?"

"Probably around nine. Ryan Alexander was with me. He went outside to make sure Brock had left and heard a door shut. That's when he discovered the interior of my car was trashed."

"He didn't see anyone, either?"

"No."

"I'll make some inquires, including questioning your ex-husband. Any idea where Brock might be?"

She couldn't hold back a brief smile. "That'll certainly set him off, since he's never felt the need to answer to anyone. Uh, he's probably hanging out with Pete Brewster or George Dorsey. What's weird is that someone broke the window out of Ryan's Jeep when we were at the carnival during the Fall Festival. At the time, we suspected it was just kids, but now I wonder if it was related."

"I'll make a note of it."

"Thanks for your help, Chris."

"You bet." He stood. "I'll let you know if we uncover any new information on either case."

"I appreciate that. Have a good evening."

"You, too."

After he left, Leah tried to focus on the math papers and failed. When someone cleared his throat from behind her, her nerves jumped higher than a spooked cat. She pressed a hand to her chest as she glanced up.

"Sloan, I didn't hear you walk in."

"I didn't want to interrupt while the police officer was here. More problems? Anything I can do to help?"

"Not unless you saw someone skulking around my yard last night. First my home was ransacked, then my car. I don't know what the hell is going on around here."

His gray eyes sobered. "That's more than a little frightening. If you don't feel safe—"

"Ryan has been sticking pretty close. Not that I believe I'm in any personal danger, since robbery or vandalism seems to be the motive here, not assault."

"Better to play it safe and not hang out alone, just in case."

"I expect so." She gathered up the stack of math papers to shove in her bag, then stood and shrugged on her pink denim jacket. "On that note, I think I'll go home to finish grading these."

"I'll walk you out. I was just leaving."

"Thanks." She slung her bag over her shoulder, retrieved her keys from the top drawer, and crossed the room. After locking the door, she walked beside Sloan toward the front of the building. Rounding the corner, she smacked into Edgar Vargas wheeling a mop bucket in the opposite direction. Water sloshed across the linoleum, and her purse fell to the floor with a thump.

"Steady, there." He grabbed her shoulders as she swayed before stepping back. "Maybe I should wear a bell like my old tabby to announce I'm coming."

Leah laughed out loud. "Or I should pay attention to where I'm going. Thank you." She took the bag he handed back to her. "Lucky I didn't dump my students' papers in the collision. They would have been soaked."

"Is that what's in there? I would have guessed rocks. Your bag weighs a ton."

"Oh, it's full of all sorts of crap I probably don't need. Sorry about the mess."

"I'll have the water mopped up in a jiffy. Have a good evening, Leah." He glanced over at Sloan. "I'll see you later."

"Seven sharp." Sloan maneuvered around the puddle.

"Good night, Edgar." Leah followed her coworker past the vacated front counter. "What are you and Edgar doing this evening?"

Sloan pushed the front door wide as a blast of wind whistled through the opening. "Poker night with the boys."

"No women allowed?"

His shoes slapped against the steps. "I don't know if it's actually written into the bylaws, but . . ."

She smiled at his teasing tone. "That's okay. When Nina and Paige and I get together, we don't allow guys to intrude, either." Nearing her car, one of the few left in the lot, she reached into the pocket of her jacket and frowned. "Damn."

"What's wrong?" Sloan turned to face her.

"I must have dropped my keys in that collision with Edgar."

"I can run back—"

"Absolutely not. Go home and enjoy your poker game tonight."

"If you're sure . . ." He hesitated.

"Positive." With a wave, she hiked her bag farther up on her shoulder and headed toward the school.

Behind her, an engine started. The wind whipped through the parking lot, swirling her hair around her face as she picked up her pace. When her cell rang, she stopped to hunt through her purse. Finally, her hand closed over the familiar shape, and she pulled out the phone.

Too late.

She checked the screen. There was a missed call from Ryan. Tapping the notice, she called him back as Sloan's car cruised past behind her, and the engine noise faded.

Ryan answered on the first ring. "Hey, beautiful, are you home yet?"

"I'm currently in the school parking lot, getting blown to pieces on my way back inside because I seem to have dropped my keys."

"Want to come over here for dinner? My mom made enough lasagna to feed half the town. She put spinach and mushrooms in it instead of meat, so you can't say no."

Head down, Leah hurried toward the front steps. "That sounds wonderful. I need to go home first to feed Barney, and then I'll come over."

"Great, I'll—"

Pain exploded behind her eyes, and the phone slipped from her hand. She pitched forward onto the pavement as the world went black . . .

Her head throbbed, a dull ache that made Leah want to curl into a ball to block out the pain. But a voice nagged at her, echoing in her brain. Her name, over and over and over . . .

She forced her eyes open and blinked, trying to clear her hazy vision as strands of hair tangled across her face. Unfamiliar hands brushed them away.

"Leah, can you hear me? Jesus. Hey, Pop, you'd better call for an ambulance."

Awareness dawned as she focused on Jesse Vargas's concerned brown eyes hovering above her. "What happened? God, my head hurts."

"You hit it pretty hard. I don't know if you slipped or what, but I found you lying on your face with a knot on the back of your skull and blood in your hair."

Bits of gravel dug into her cheek. Pressing her palms flat against the pavement, she struggled to push up.

"Here, let me help you." Jesse slid a hand under her arm and lifted her to a sitting position.

Her stomach roiled, and she fought against the tide of nausea climbing up her throat. Taking short breaths through her nose, she conquered the urge to puke. "Oh, geez."

Edgar knelt in front of her beside his son. "I just called nine-one-one. They're sending an ambulance."

She reached up to touch the back of her head. "I don't need . . . ouch!" Her fingers encountered a large knot. "Damn, that hurts."

"Did you trip and fall?" Edgar asked.

Leah glanced from father to son and frowned. "I was talking to Ryan on my cell and . . . I don't remember anything else."

"Here's your phone. Looks like the screen protector saved it when it hit the ground. The case is a little battered, though."

She took her cell from Jesse and stared at the blood smears on the case. "My head must be bleeding."

"Yeah, that's some lump you have. You gave me a scare when I saw you out cold on the pavement when I drove into the lot to pick up Pop."

With her head pounding like a bass drum, thinking was an effort. "How long ago was that?"

"Only about a minute before you came to." When she shivered, Edgar removed his jacket to drape over her shoulders. "I'd just locked the front doors when Jesse stopped his pickup and yelled.

Fragments of memory returned. "I couldn't find my keys. I was coming back to look for them when my phone rang. Ryan asked me to dinner, and then . . ." The recollection faded. "Next thing I remember is Jesse saying my name."

Tires squealed, and an engine roared as a vehicle took the corner off the access road into the lot. A moment later, Ryan stopped his Jeep near them and threw open his door. "Leah!"

"I'm okay." She let out a relieved breath as the other two men stepped back.

"Jesus. You stopped talking, and I heard a thud. Then nothing." He crouched beside her and touched her cheek. "What happened?"

When sirens sounded in the distance, growing louder, Jesse turned toward the road. "Here comes the ambulance."

"What?" Ryan's voice rose. "You're definitely

not okay." Gently, he touched her hair. "There's blood."

Leah leaned against him as a chill shook her. "I hit my head when I fell."

"She was unconscious when I arrived." Jesse crossed his arms over his chest as an ambulance followed by a patrol car rounded the corner and cut their sirens.

Two paramedics got out and hurried over. One carried a red emergency duffel bag.

Chris Long followed. "I heard the nine-one-one call come through. I left here not twenty minutes ago, Leah. What the heck happened?"

"I hit my head. My memory of the specifics is a little hazy."

The female EMT, who was the same one who'd attended to Ryan's mother after her accident, frowned. "If you don't mind, Officer, let us check her out first before you question her."

"Of course." Chris backed up a few steps.

Ryan didn't move. He held Leah's free hand while the paramedic took her vitals then shined a light in her eyes. Her partner pulled on latex gloves before carefully examining the knot on her head.

"Miss, can you tell me what day it is?"

Leah nodded, then winced when the motion aggravated her pounding head. "Tuesday. I'm fine other than a splitting headache. I don't need to go to the hospital."

The paramedic directed the light from her right pupil to her left. "Your name?"

"Leah Grayson. I was a little fuzzy when I first came to, but my memory returned pretty quickly."

Ryan's grip on her hand tightened. "Maybe you should go to the ER to get checked out. You could have a concussion if the fall knocked you out."

The EMT regarded her steadily. "How long were you unconscious?"

"I'm not sure. It's probably been five or six minutes since I woke up." She glanced up. "Jesse, do you know . . ."

"She came to about a minute after I found her, which was when my dad called nine-one-one, but I don't know how long she was lying on the ground before that."

Ryan glanced at his watch. "It's been eight minutes since our conversation was cut off when you dropped your phone. I broke speed records getting over here."

The paramedic behind her stopped probing her wound. "You were unconscious for a couple of minutes, then." He stepped around to face her. Kind blue eyes regarded her from a weathered face. "If you don't want to go to the hospital, I'd recommend you see a doctor for a thorough assessment. I don't suspect a skull fracture, but it's still a possibility. Also, that wound needs to be cleaned and dressed. Do you have any pain in your hands or wrists from breaking your fall? What about your knees?"

"My right arm hurts a little. I must have landed on it. Can Ryan drive me to the doctor's office instead? It should still be open if we hurry. I don't need to go to the emergency room, and I'm not sure what my insurance will cover."

The woman returned her equipment to the

bag. "Of course, but I'd advise you to see a health care provider right away."

Her partner nodded. "You were hit pretty hard, so don't delay treatment."

Leah stilled. "What do you mean, hit?"

"Based on the abrasions on your chin and cheek, I'd say you were hit squarely from behind and fell forward onto your face. You don't remember falling?"

"Just pain exploding in my head, then nothing until I came to with Jesse hovering over me."

"Maybe you crumpled forward rather than going down hard, which probably saved you a nasty wrist sprain."

"You think I was hit?" Her voice rose. "Someone attacked me from behind?"

"That would be my assessment." His gaze held hers. "Are you sure you want to decline immediate medical treatment?"

She couldn't think, couldn't process what he was saying. Tightening her hold on Ryan, she nodded. "Yes. I'll go see my own doctor."

"Make sure you do." He gave her a compassionate smile before he and his partner headed back to the ambulance.

Ryan's lips pressed into a tight line as he slid an arm around her. Slowly, he lifted her to her feet. "Let's get you to the doctor."

Edgar stepped forward to pat her shoulder. "You take care, Leah. I can't imagine anyone would deliberately hurt you. That's just crazy."

She leaned against Ryan. "I have to agree. Maybe the paramedic was mistaken." Her eyes widened.

"Oh, my keys. I dropped them earlier when we bumped into each other in the hall."

"I'll go back inside to find them."

Chris Long crossed his arms over his chest. "You do that, and then I'm going to need to take formal statements from everyone here."

Ryan's grip on her waist tightened. "Can you get one from Leah after she sees a doctor?"

"I suppose—"

"My purse." She glanced around the area and frowned. "Where's my tote bag?"

Jesse raised both hands. "There wasn't a bag anywhere nearby when I found you."

Her knees threatened to buckle as she clung to Ryan. "Are you kidding? Whoever hit me must have taken my purse."

He held her even tighter. "And could have killed you in the process."

Chapter Sixteen

The damn film wasn't in the bitch's purse. He sorted through the pile of crap he'd dumped out on the ground for the third time, shining a light over the accumulation of odds and ends just to be sure. Definitely not there. Math papers scattered in a gust of wind, blowing toward the parking lot. Not that he gave two shits at this point. Everyone had long since departed the school grounds. After he'd ditched the bag in the woods, he'd waited until it was safe to come back to search through it. The last thing he'd wanted was to be caught with the damn thing by some fluke, and he still hadn't replaced that burned-out taillight. Better not to risk having incriminating evidence found in his possession if he was stopped.

Rising to his feet, he shoved the few dollars he'd taken out of Leah's wallet into his pocket to make the cops think it was a simple robbery, then gave the bag a hard kick before heading back toward the parking lot, keeping the flashlight beam low.

What a colossal waste of time watching for a chance to knock the woman out had been. The freaking film was nowhere to be found. Not in her house or her car or her bag. He'd even snuck into the school after hours when he'd found the cafeteria door propped open for a delivery, jimmied the lock on her classroom door, and searched her desk . . . for all the good it had done.

Taking a quick look around, he ran up to the dumpsters where he'd parked out of sight of anyone cruising past the school. No reason to advertise his presence. Breathing hard, he sat in the dark interior of his car and stared out at the night to ponder his next move. When his phone rang, he answered without bothering to check the display, knowing very well who would be calling.

"Yeah."

"Well, what happened?"

"I grabbed her purse and searched it. The film wasn't there."

"Fuckin' A!"

He let out a slow breath and held his temper. "I'm beginning to think she actually lost the roll for good. Maybe tossed it out with the trash or something by accident."

A short silence followed. "That would certainly be a lucky break for us. Still, we can't assume we're safe."

"Then we'll keep our ears open. Surely if the damn thing shows up, Leah will mention it to someone, and word will get back to one of us."

"I guess that's the best we can do at this point."

He slumped against the seat in relief and changed

the subject. "How's the search for a sacrifice going? We don't have much time left."

"Nothing definitive yet. I picked up a prospect hitchhiking, but then she called her boyfriend before I could get the phone away from her. Too risky after that."

Apparently I'm not the only one who screws up. Not that he'd ever say so. Even if he hated the fact he hadn't been voted the Chosen One, he wouldn't show flagrant disrespect to the man who held that honor.

"Too bad, but now that I don't have to focus exclusively on looking for the film, I'll venture further afield. Maybe take a trip over to the university."

"Sounds like a solid plan. Keep me in the loop."

"Right." He disconnected and dropped his cell on the seat, then started the engine. To hell with Leah and the damned roll of film. He'd find a sacrifice instead. Someone worthy. A surge of raw power shot through him in anticipation. Only two weeks until Samhain.

He could hardly wait.

Leah leaned against the counter in his mother's kitchen and sniffed air scented with the aroma of garlic and herbs. "Wow, dinner smells terrific. What can I do to help?"

Ryan pulled the lasagna dish out of the oven to set on the cooling rack. "Sit. Right now, all you need to do is take it easy." Brushing past her, he pulled out a chair at the table and guided her toward it.

"Absolutely." His mom peeled back the foil covering the baking dish. "I can't believe you were attacked here in Siren Cove. At the elementary school, of all places. What is this world coming to?"

"Apparently, no good." Ryan studied Leah's tight lips and wondered if the pain meds she'd taken were strong enough. "At least Dr. Carlton said you only have a mild concussion."

"Isn't that just peachy." Her tone was laced with irony. "No brain damage."

He couldn't help smiling. "Good thing you have a hard head."

She glanced over at his mother. "You raised a funny boy, Mrs. A. I bet you're proud."

"Oh, I am." She paused with her good hand on the refrigerator door. "But I like knowing you can put him in his place."

"Everyone needs a hobby." Leah planted an elbow on the table and leaned her cheek against her open palm. "Thanks for the dinner invitation. I'll admit I'm not up to cooking right now."

"You just sit back and relax." His mother set a salad bowl on the table then returned with plates and flatware, maneuvering competently despite her cast. "Ryan, the bread in the broiler should be done. You can slice the loaf."

He followed orders before loading the waiting basket with the slices. "Are we ready to eat?"

"I'll just pour a round of iced tea. I'd offer wine, but Leah probably shouldn't mix pain meds with alcohol."

She straightened in her chair. "Please, you two go ahead."

"No, we'll all have tea." His mom let out a yell. "Don't even think about it, Charlie!"

Ryan spun, then made a lunging grab as his cat sprang from the tile floor toward the lasagna resting on the counter. He caught him mid-leap and locked gazes with irritated gold eyes. "Bad cat."

"*Bad cat?*" Leah snorted as he set Charlie on the floor and pushed him toward the doorway with his foot. "That's how you discipline your fur ball? And I thought I was lax with Barney."

Using a pair of potholders, he set the steaming casserole dish on the table. "I guess we're both suckers when it comes to our pets."

"Better to be a sucker for an animal than to spoil kids." His mom joined them at the table.

"Oh, I have a firm hand when it comes to my class." Leah took a sip of her tea then squeezed a slice of lemon into it. "I don't let them get away with much."

"I meant if you two have . . ." His mother's voice trailed off as she met his grim stare. "Never mind. Here, have some lasagna." She served Leah a large scoop.

After that, the conversation became general, mainly a discussion of the psychological thriller his mother was reading for her book club. One that Leah had also apparently enjoyed. Ryan was happy to eat in silence. The last thing he wanted was his mom assuming his relationship with Leah was permanent . . . and flapping her mouth about it. At this point, they didn't need that sort of pressure.

"Ryan?"

"Huh?" He dismissed his brooding thoughts when Leah jogged his elbow.

"I asked if you could drive me back to the school to get my car."

"Oh, sure." He pushed away his empty plate.

"Right after I help with the dishes." She rose to her feet, steadying herself with a hand on the chair back.

"I'll take care of those." His mom sprang up from the table. "I'm great at loading the dishwasher one-handed. If Ryan will put the leftover lasagna in the refrigerator first? That dish is heavy."

"Got it." He kept an eye on Leah as he stood. "You look exhausted."

"The pain pills are pretty strong, and they're making me a little sleepy."

"Then go home." His mom shooed her toward the door. "What you need is a good night's sleep."

"I won't argue with that. Thank you for dinner, Mrs. A."

"You're welcome here anytime."

Ryan covered the lasagna with foil and placed the dish in the refrigerator. He squeezed his mother's shoulder as he passed. "Don't wait up. After that knock to the head, I think I'll stick around in case Leah needs anything tonight."

"Excellent idea. Good night, dear."

"Night, Mom." He met Leah at the front door where she'd slipped on her pink jacket and boots. Tucking her hand into his, he stepped out into the chilly evening air. "We don't have to go get your car right now. I can drive you to work in the morning."

"Thanks, but with all the crap that's happened to me lately, I'd rather not leave it at the school overnight."

He nodded. "Okay, but are you sure you can drive?"

"Yeah. It's only for a couple of miles."

"Fine." He opened the passenger door of the Jeep for her, then got in on his side and started the engine. "Uh, sorry my mom was so blatant about her expectations for us."

"Your face was priceless when she mentioned kids." Leah patted his thigh and left her hand resting on the worn denim. "Don't worry about it. I know how moms can be. When I discussed the option of Gram moving in with me, my mother told me I might as well sign a death warrant for any chance of hooking a new husband." She sighed. "In Mom's defense, my grandma's brazenness can be a tad off-putting until you get to know her, and her presence probably will put a crimp in my sex life."

He backed out of the driveway. "Serious? Your mom said that?"

"Yeah, ever since my divorce, she's made it clear she believes I'm doomed to live life as an old maid. More importantly, I won't produce the required grandchildren."

"What, is thirty too old to attract a man?"

"I think it's more about being a bad risk. If I couldn't hold on to Brock . . ."

"Give me a break. You dumped him."

"Yeah, but apparently I should have tried harder to make it work." Her grip on his thigh tightened. "Make the best of a bad situation."

"That's total BS, and you know it."

"I didn't say I agreed with her." She turned to face him when he pulled into the school parking lot and stopped beside her car. "Are you coming back to the house with me?"

"I'd like to. Rest is your top priority, but I need to know you're safe tonight."

"Thank you." Stretching across the center console, she pressed a kiss to his cheek. "I appreciate that."

"I'll follow you home."

With a nod, she climbed out and bent to scoop something off the ground. "You ran over a few papers." She held a white sheet with a tire track across it in the glare from his headlights. "Hey, this is one of the homework assignments I stuffed in my bag earlier. There's another one just out of reach under the Jeep."

He turned off the engine but left the headlights on and opened his door. "Those weren't in the lot earlier."

"Definitely not." She took a few steps then bent to pick up another sheet. "What the heck. There's a whole trail of papers."

"A few more are caught in the bushes over by the woods. I wonder . . ." He headed in that direction, grabbing papers as he went.

Leah hurried behind him. "What are you thinking?"

"If the homework was in your bag, maybe whoever took your purse ditched it nearby."

"Oh, geez, I hope so. I'm not looking forward to going to the DMV for a new license, or canceling all my credit cards. *If* I can remember which ones I have."

He plucked two damp papers out from under a giant fern. "You should keep a list of those numbers in a file."

"There are plenty of things I should do." Her

tone was dark as she used the flashlight app on her phone to illuminate the woods. "A few more pages are caught . . . hey, my bag!" She sprinted through the trees. "Damn. The asshole who hit me scattered stuff everywhere."

Ryan hurried after her. "What the hell? Why spread everything out on the ground like that? Can you tell what's missing?"

Leah opened her wallet. "About twelve bucks in cash. My credit cards are still here, though, and my driver's license. That's a relief."

Ryan retrieved the canvas bag crumpled beneath a tree and stuffed the math homework into it. Dropping to his knees, he gathered together a ruler, a Phillips screwdriver, a box of matches, and a flat container he suspected held birth control pills. *Thank God they'd found those, not that Leah would be in the mood . . .*

She dumped Post-it notes, glue, sunglasses, a bottle of lotion, and a tube of toothpaste into the bag along with her wallet and a checkbook. "I think that's all I had in there."

"So some moron knocked you over the head to steal twelve dollars? Seems unlikely."

"Maybe he or she—whoever—thought I carried around more cash. If that's the case, the person obviously doesn't know me very well."

"We may have lost a few of the math papers." He flashed his light over the needle-coated floor of the forest. "But, I'd say we retrieved everything else. We'd better call the police to report you found your bag."

"I'll do it when I get home." She rose to her feet. "My head is starting to hurt again. Shall we go?"

He stood to slide an arm around her. "Sure. It's been about four hours since the doctor gave you those pills. You're probably due for more."

"Plus, I'm exhausted. I can't wait to go to bed."

He smiled. "Lucky for you, I won't take that the wrong way."

"Good thing, because tonight you'd be doomed to disappointment."

He waited while she unlocked her car with the keys Edgar Vargas had found on the floor in the school, and then followed her home. Thankfully, the house was exactly as they'd left it that morning, with no unpleasant surprises. Barney's greeting, however, made it clear he'd been abandoned for far too long.

"I'm sorry, baby." Leah headed straight toward the dog food container in the pantry. "I'll feed you right now."

"He probably isn't wasting away from malnutrition."

She scooped kibble into his bowl. "He thinks he is. I meant to come home earlier, but after hanging around at the doctor's office, then meeting Chris Long to give him a formal statement . . ."

"Your dog survived."

"I suppose." She clenched her fists at her sides. "I just want life to get back to normal."

"It will." He went to the sink to pour a glass of water. "Take another pain pill and go to bed."

She pulled the bottle out of her jacket pocket. "Excellent idea. Right after I shower. I still have blood in my hair, even though the nurse sponged most of it out."

"Fine. While you're doing that, I'll call to report

we found your bag with the contents intact. Minus twelve dollars."

"My wallet must have been a serious disappointment to the thief." She swallowed the pill, set the glass on the counter, then wound her arms around his neck. "One problem solved, at least. Now if only I could make my grandma's issues go away." Standing on her toes, she kissed him. "Thanks for helping me out. I'll see you upstairs in a few minutes."

He stared after her as she walked away. He knew Leah better than to think she'd been hinting that he could solve her—or rather, her grandmother's—financial problems easily enough. Guilt ate at him, along with the knowledge he had more money than he knew what to do with. Sure, he gave a lot of his wealth to charity and made certain his mother didn't lack for anything she wanted, but if he started handing out cash to everyone he knew . . .

Not just anyone. Leah.

He ignored the voice. Money and friendship didn't mix. Greed had destroyed his relationship with his former roommate and business partner. Uneasiness slithered down his spine. Leah wasn't like Jay. He shook his head. No way. She didn't have a mercenary bone in her body.

Thrusting the disturbing thoughts aside, he pulled out his phone to call the number on Chris Long's business card. After reporting Leah had recovered her purse, he let Barney outside and strolled into the yard behind the dog. A crescent moon rode high in the sky, shedding a glimmering light over the waves rolling into shore. He'd stood in the same spot with Leah countless times in the past. Nothing about the view had changed, but anxiety destroyed his calm. Something . . . or someone . . . with a sinister edge had tainted the tranquility of his hometown.

A chill shook him. Whistling for Barney, he herded the dog around the house to the back door, where a pool of light welcomed them inside. After locking up, Ryan left his shoes in the kitchen before heading upstairs. He brushed his teeth in the bathroom, steamy warm from her shower, using the spare toothbrush Leah had given him, and took out his contacts. He padded into her room in the dark. After stripping off his clothes, he draped them over a chair and slid beneath the covers.

Leah rolled over and curled against his side.

"You aren't asleep yet?"

She shook her head, soft hair brushing across his bare chest. "No, I was waiting for you." Her voice slurred. "Now, I feel . . . safe." Slow breathing followed.

Ryan held her close and pressed a kiss to the top of her head, but it was a long time before he was able to relax into sleep.

Chapter Seventeen

Leah sat across from her grandma and Magnus Lindgren, sipping the last of her coffee and feeling like a third wheel. She was pretty sure the two were holding hands beneath the table, and Gram had made several suggestive comments indicating they held a whole lot more than that in private. Leah wasn't sure if she should be shocked, offended, or give them both an A for effort. Admiration for her grandma's spunky determination to live life to the fullest filled her. She should take lessons.

"You've been quiet, dear. Are you missing that nice young man, Ryan? Maybe you should have brought him along with you to brunch."

Leah pushed aside her empty plate and planted one elbow on the table. "He took a quick trip up to Portland on Thursday. Some problem at his company headquarters, but he called earlier to tell me the complication had been ironed out, and he's on his way back now."

Magnus set down his cup. "Evie mentioned the man you're dating is the founder of Crossroads. That site is far superior to its social media predecessors. Much smoother to navigate and more functional. Your friend must be a genius at coding."

Leah smiled at the man who, it seemed, knew his way around a computer. "Ryan is a genius, period." She paused as the waitress approached the table with their check. "The pancakes were delicious."

The woman shot her a quick grin as she cleared their plates. "I'll be sure to tell our chef her efforts were appreciated."

"We all like to hear that." Gram wiggled her brows, sending color rushing to Magnus's cheeks.

He slicked back his silver hair and coughed. When Leah reached toward the bill, he swooped in to grab it from the tray. "No, no, brunch is my treat."

She withdrew her hand. "Well, thank you. The meal was lovely, and I certainly enjoyed meeting you."

"The same. Evie talks about you all the time." He pulled out his wallet. "Shall we go? We don't have much time before our scuba session."

Leah slung her bag over her shoulder as she rose to her feet, then turned to stare at her grandma. "You're taking scuba lessons?"

"This is our third one. At my age, squeezing into a wetsuit is no easy feat, but the view underwater is worth the effort."

"I'm impressed." Leah followed the pair to the

cashier at the front of the coffee shop. "Sounds like fun. By the way, I like the purple. Very chic."

Her grandma patted her curls. "Flo did a terrific job." She hooked her arm through Magnus's after he returned his wallet to his jacket pocket, then led the way outside. "Oh, that nice policeman came by with sketches the other day to see if I recognized the other two men who robbed foolish seniors like me."

"Not foolish, Gram, just a little too trusting." Leah pulled her bike out of the rack near the door. "Did you?"

"No, just Thomas Woodward. I told Officer Long one of the other names sounded familiar, but I can't put my finger on why."

"Which name?"

"Anthony Benedetto. I looked in the phone book after the officer left, but no one named Benedetto lives in Siren Cove. Maybe he used to and is dead now." Her grandma shrugged. "When you get to be in your eighties, old acquaintances start dropping like flies."

Leah winced at her matter-of-fact tone. "I suppose so, but the man who swindled you was around my age."

"Could be a relative of the one I'm remembering." She patted Leah's arm. "Well, I won't worry about it since I know everyone is doing their best to find that asshat Woodward and recover my money. I have great faith in the system."

Which is a whole lot more than I have. Leah smiled despite her doubts. "I'm keeping my fingers crossed. At this point, we'll take all the luck we can get."

Magnus gave her a sympathetic look. "I know you're worried, but everything will work out for the best." He slipped an arm around her grandma's waist. "Come along, Evie, or we'll be late for our class."

"I'll see you soon, Gram. Bye, Magnus, and thanks again for brunch."

"You're very welcome." He opened the door of his smoke-gray Bentley for her grandmother and gave a toot on the horn a minute later as they pulled away.

Leah couldn't help grinning, even though she wasn't nearly as optimistic about the future as her grandma and her new beau seemed to be. Straddling the bike, she pushed off and headed for home, enjoying the breeze blowing off the ocean as she rode.

Life wasn't all bad. No one had tried to brain her or rob her in the last few days. Definitely a plus. And Ryan would be back soon. She couldn't believe how much she'd missed him in the forty-eight hours since he'd left. Imagining what it would be like after he went home for good made her chest ache. She forced the thought away and pedaled harder. By the time she reached her house, she was breathless.

Barney greeted her with shrill barks of joy as she wheeled her bike into the carport. Pushing the dog away when he continued to dance around like a lunatic, she dug her keys out of her bag to unlock the back door. Her lips tightened at the reminder that leaving her home unsecured was no longer an option.

Once inside, she dropped her bag on the counter and rubbed her dog's ears. "I love you, too. We'll go for a walk later, but first I need to work in the garden."

With a moan, he followed her up the stairs and waited while she changed into old jeans and a sweatshirt. Amusement curled her lips at his woebegone expression while she braided her hair into one long plait. Returning to the kitchen, she glanced around and frowned. Dishes filled the sink, and somehow a pile of junk mail, jackets, and shoes had accumulated in the corner. She really should clean up . . .

"Later." With a smile at the dog, she sorted through a basket of odds and ends to locate her gardening gloves. "Got them. Let's go, Barney."

The sun shone warmly on her shoulders as she knelt in the dirt to dig up potatoes, but there was a bite to the wind. The weatherman was forecasting a hard freeze. She needed to get the tubers out of the ground, not to mention hauling in the squash and pumpkins. Beside her, Barney dug furiously and stuck his nose in the hole.

"If only I could harness all that energy into productive gardening." She unearthed the first hill of potatoes, then glanced over at her dog. "Hey, what do you have there?"

Barney clamped his jaws around something small and black and scurried backward. Making a lunging grab, Leah caught hold of his collar and pried his mouth open.

"Ha, got it!" She held up a plastic container

dripping slobber. "Oh, good grief. So, that's what happened to the film from the time capsule. You buried it!"

When an engine rumbled louder before cutting off, Leah stood and stuck the container into her pocket. A car door slammed, and footsteps crunched gravel.

"I'm back here," she called out.

A few moments later, Ryan rounded the side of the carport. His smile grew when she jerked off her gloves and ran toward him.

"You're back!"

He caught her in his arms and swung her around, then bent to kiss her. She responded with enthusiasm, turning a simple greeting into a whole lot more.

"I missed you." He cupped her face and kissed her again. "You taste good. Sweet."

"Probably maple syrup. I had brunch with my grandma and her . . . gentleman friend." She grimaced. "What the heck am I supposed to call the man my eighty-two-year-old grandmother is sleeping with?"

Ryan grinned. "Go, Evie. Does this dude have a name?"

"Magnus Lindgren." She leaned against the hands he linked behind her back. "He seems nice. I'm just thankful you're here because it would be downright embarrassing if Gram was getting more action than me."

"You crack me up. What else have you been doing?"

She shrugged. "The usual. Work and . . . I guess

just work. Right now, I'm bringing in the last of my fall vegetables. If you like, you can help me dig potatoes and gather squash."

"Sure." He glanced down at his button-up shirt and khakis. "Am I going to get filthy?"

"You do look a little dressier than your usual jeans and a T-shirt."

"I had a breakfast meeting with my management team before I left. I guess it wouldn't kill me to get dirty, but—"

"Are my less than tidy habits rubbing off on you?"

He grimaced. "I wouldn't go that far. Dirty knees are one thing. Clutter, on the other hand—"

"Stop right there." She pressed a finger to his lips. "You may want to avoid my kitchen."

"Good to know, but what I was going to say is I can change. I have clothes from my trip in the Jeep, since I haven't been back to my mom's yet."

Knowing he'd come straight to see her the minute he arrived in town filled Leah with warmth despite the cold wind. She kissed him again and stepped back. "Go change." She paused to pull the film canister from her pocket. "On your way through, can you please put this on the table? Barney buried it in the garden."

"What have you got there?"

"The film roll we found in the time capsule. I couldn't imagine what had happened to it. Now I can get the pictures developed."

He took it from her and popped the lid. "There's some corrosion on the casing. Dampness might have damaged the negatives. I'm not sure a technician would want to touch this."

"No? That sucks. I was looking forward to seeing those photos. Do you think they're all ruined?"

"I really don't know. Some of the roll might have survived." He frowned. "I could try to develop the film. I've done a little photography, including the technical side, but I don't have access to a darkroom here."

"There's one at the high school, and I know the woman who teaches the photography and art classes. I could ask her if she'll let you use their darkroom."

"Sure. I'm curious to see if any of the negatives can be salvaged, too."

"Then I'll call her. In the meantime, go change. I need to finish in the garden, and I promised Barney a walk later."

"Sounds good. I'll be back in a few minutes."

Leah did a happy dance down the row between the pumpkins and the squash before dropping to her knees beside the potato hills. Slowly her smile faded. She couldn't deny her feelings for Ryan had escalated far beyond friendship and attraction. His presence made her day complete. And his absence, well . . .

She picked up the trowel and stared blankly at the loosened earth around the plants. He cared about her. A lot. But she couldn't help wondering if all those dirty dishes in the sink would be a deal breaker. Nor did she have any desire to start making her bed every morning. She couldn't change who she was any more than he could.

Did something as petty as cleaning habits even matter? She had a job in Siren Cove, one she enjoyed most days, one she had no intention of quitting. Not that she could afford to, anyway. And Ryan had made no mention of staying in town after his mom got her cast removed.

She glanced over at Barney, tail waving as he stuck his nose down a gopher hole, not a care in the world. Right now, all she wanted was to be like her dog and bury her head in the sand—or more accurately, the dirt—and pretend the problem didn't exist. So when Ryan returned, wearing faded jeans and a smile, she pushed her worries to the back of her mind as her heartbeat quickened. She'd ignore her fears, at least for today . . .

Ryan stared at the row of prints laid out on the counter in the high school darkroom. Only five had been salvageable, and the quality of those was pretty horrible after twenty years buried in the ground. Blurry and distorted, he tried to make out the images in the dim light. Maybe photos from a Halloween party? Figures dressed in costumes stood around a bonfire. Not kids, though. He was pretty certain they were adult-sized. He picked up one picture by the edge and held it closer to the light. Strange, all the figures seemed to be dressed in long robes. Not white like ghost costumes. Gray, with a single man—or possibly a woman—garbed in black in the center of the group.

When a rap echoed through the room, he laid

the photo down with the others and stepped around the center island to open the door. "Hey, Britt, come on in."

Britt Forsythe didn't look old enough to be a high school teacher. Hell, she barely looked old enough to be one of her own students. The photography teacher pushed heavy, horn-rimmed glasses up her nose and snapped her gum. "How'd it go?"

"Only five negatives from the center of the roll came out. The rest weren't salvageable."

"That's too bad. Anything good on the ones you printed?"

"They're sort of odd." He waved a hand toward the counter. "Come have a look."

"I would, but I'm running a little late. If you're finished . . ."

"Sure. Sorry to keep you waiting." Ryan gathered up the prints and slid them into a folder along with the negatives. "I really appreciate you letting me use your lab."

Britt gave him a shy smile. "Happy to help out our most successful alumnus to date." She flipped off the light in the darkroom and walked beside him between groupings of tables. "Old Mr. Anderson, the computer science teacher, uses you as an example of what can happen if students apply themselves to their studies."

Ryan grinned back at her. "That's hilarious since I seem to remember spending more time in his class daydreaming than listening to his lectures."

"Apparently all that dreaming paid off." She shut the classroom door behind them and locked it.

"I like to think so." He reached into his pocket and pulled out a folded check. "Here's a donation for photography and art supplies for your classes. Thanks again for helping me out."

"You don't need to—"

"I want to. I appreciate your time."

She took a quick peek at the check, and her eyes widened. "Oh, my. You can use my darkroom anytime you want."

"I'll keep that in mind." He followed her outside and headed straight to his Jeep. After starting the engine, he pulled out his cell to call Leah. "Are you home from work yet?"

"Just got here. Did any of the photos turn out?"

"A few of them. Can I come over?"

"Of course. I'll just straighten up . . ." Her voice faded.

He frowned then shifted into gear. "Okay. I'll be there in a few minutes."

"Great."

Ryan dropped the phone on the seat as he cruised slowly over the speed bumps in the parking lot and headed out to the main road. Leah had been acting a little odd since he'd returned from Portland. Jittery. He'd love to chalk it up to nerves after having been clocked on the head, but he had a sinking feeling the problem was more personal. Almost like she was afraid of . . . something. He didn't have a clue what. Or maybe his imagination was working overtime. She'd certainly seemed happy enough to have him around.

A few minutes later, he turned down her driveway and stopped in front of the carport. After grabbing the folder off the dash, he got out, slammed the door, and greeted Barney. "Hey, bud."

The dog licked his hand before running off toward the back of the house.

"Over here, Ryan."

He changed directions to approach the front porch, where Leah leaned against the railing. "How was your day?" He took the steps two at a time and pulled her close to drop a kiss on her upturned lips.

"Good." She pointed toward the rattan couch. "It's such a nice afternoon, I thought we'd sit outside. I can't wait to see those photos."

He followed her over to the seat and dropped down beside her. "The pictures aren't of our classmates. They're actually pretty weird."

Leah pushed a long strand of hair behind one ear and frowned. "What do you mean?"

"See for yourself." He opened the folder across his knees. "The images are a little difficult to make out, but it looks like some sort of costume party in the woods. There are trees in the background."

She picked up the top photo then glanced through the others. "These *are* strange. They look like adults or teens, not kids. What's that dark shape in the center? A table of some sort?"

Ryan pulled out one of the other photos. "This one has a slightly better view. It's definitely something large and flat. Is there someone lying on top of it?" He touched a whitish blur. "Those look like legs."

"I'm getting a little creeped out here." Leah shuddered. "You can't see any faces. Those hoods cast shadows that distort their features in the dark." She touched each figure and counted. "Eight in gray plus the one in black. Then whoever was taking the pictures."

"Unless the camera was set up on a tripod. The angle is exactly the same in each photo. Only the people have moved." He touched one hooded figure. "This guy is a little taller than the others, and that one is beefier. Their positions shift from shot to shot, so maybe they were taken over time."

"I wonder why one person is dressed in black."

"Haven't a clue." Ryan held up a picture. "In this one, it looks like there's something shiny in his hand, but the photo's so blurred it's hard to tell what it is."

Leah rose to her feet. "I'll get a magnifying glass. Maybe that'll help, although I'm not too sure I want to see exactly what they're doing." Her eyes widened. "Some kind of frat house initiation ceremony?"

"Could be, but how would film belonging to students at the university wind up in our time capsule? That's over an hour's drive from here"

"Good point." She turned away. A moment later, the screen door slapped shut behind her as she entered the house.

Standing, he laid out each photo on the porch railing where the setting sun cast direct rays on the pictures. When Leah returned, she handed him an old-fashioned magnifying glass with a long black handle.

"Let's see what we have." He focused on the photo with the clearest view of the black-robed figure. Enlarged, the object in his hand appeared to be—

"Is that a knife?" Leah's voice rose. "The firelight reflects off it the way it would on shiny metal."

"Yeah, I think you're right." He studied each hooded figure in turn. "I'm not sure why, but I'd say they're all men."

"It's the way they stand. Anyway, I'd swear this one has a beard."

"Yeah, there's a dark shadow on his chin. No way to identify any of them, though."

"What about the person lying down? Maybe with the magnifying glass . . ."

He held it over the center of each photo in turn. "Yeah, those are legs and feet. You can see them clearly between the two figures on the right in this shot."

Leah gripped his hand. "Here." She positioned the magnifying glass above the third photo. "Check the gap between the guy in black and the tall one. Is that what I think it is?"

"Looks like a bare breast."

"Yeah, it does, and I'd swear that's long, pale hair hanging down over the edge of the table or whatever it is."

"There's some kind of cloth draped over it. Too bad you can't see the woman's face in any of the photos."

Leah jerked back and rubbed her hands up and down her arms. "Ryan." Her voice broke. "What are they doing to that poor woman?"

He dropped the magnifying glass and pulled her against his chest. His heart pounded as he held her close. "Nothing good."

She pressed her face to his shoulder. Her words came out in a whisper. "Something . . . evil."

Chapter Eighteen

"Shouldn't we call the police?" Leah scrubbed a pan crusted with oatmeal and wondered why no one had patented the adhesive quality to use as glue. Maybe if she'd washed the dishes this morning instead of leaving the pan to sit on the stove . . . She gripped the handle with shaking fingers. She needed to pull herself together.

Ryan jotted something down on the pad of paper resting next to the pictures he'd spread across the table before glancing up. "I'd like to consider what we know first. These photos were taken twenty years ago. There's no rush to turn them over to the authorities this second."

He had a point. Whoever the woman stretched out naked in the pictures was, they certainly couldn't help her after all this time. A shudder rippled through her, and she turned back to the sink full of dishes. Just looking at those images made her feel sick.

"What, precisely, do we know?"

"Well, the exact date the roll of film was put in the time capsule is established. Identifying the people in these pictures may not be possible, but we can figure out who had access to the box our class buried twenty years ago."

She sloshed water as she rinsed the oatmeal pan and set it on the drain rack. "Why would anyone put undeveloped film of sicko photos like that in our time capsule? It makes no sense."

"I can only think of one reason." Ryan's voice hardened. "To hide it. Dropping it in the box must have been a spur-of-the-moment decision and implies the person was desperate or frightened."

Tamping down her emotions, she tried to look at the facts like a puzzle. How did each piece fit? "Okay, I agree with your hypothesis. Whoever was carrying around that film put it in the time capsule to get rid of it in a hurry, knowing it wouldn't be found for years . . . if ever."

"Exactly. So the challenge is to determine who had access to the box before it was buried. I'm making a list."

"Of course you are."

"What was that?"

"Nothing." Leah waved a hand. "You're organized, and I'm not. The state of my kitchen is ample proof of that. Sorry, but I'm a little on edge." She rinsed the last of the dishes and dried her hands on a towel. "So, who's on your suspect list? Us?"

He regarded her steadily as she walked over to pull out the chair next to him. "Are you okay?"

"I guess. Those photographs bother me . . . a lot, but I'm not going to lose it on you."

"You aren't the only one feeling disgusted and angry. That's why I want to figure this out."

She squeezed his arm. "I know. Tell me what you're thinking."

"I believe we can eliminate the twenty-odd kids who were in Sloan Manning's class. We were ten at the time, and we've agreed the people in these pictures aren't children. So, let's focus on the adults who had access to the time capsule."

"Okay. Obviously Sloan did."

"He's at the top of my list."

Her stomach knotted. "I don't like this."

"Neither do I, but it has to be done."

She pressed fingers to her eyes and forced herself to think before glancing up. "Edgar Vargas was in and out of the room. I remember he went to get a hammer to nail down the lid."

Ryan made a note on his list. "We had a party. There were parent helpers in the classroom, including my mom."

"Paige's mom brought frosted sugar cookies."

He nodded. "I remember those cookies. Delicious, and she always decorated them for the holidays. I seem to recall the room was all decked out for Halloween."

"It was actually early November when we buried the time capsule, and we hadn't taken down the witch and skeleton art projects yet. We planned our reunion over the Fall Festival weekend, hoping to get a better turnout, so we were a few weeks shy of twenty years when we unveiled the time capsule." Leah planted an elbow on the table. "We didn't wait for the exact anniversary."

"Obviously you have a better memory than I do. Which other moms were present?"

"Don't be sexist. A couple of dads dug the hole." Her brow wrinkled as she tried to picture that day so long ago. "I think Pete's father was one of them."

"Interesting." Ryan added Waylon Brewster to the list then pulled his phone out of his pocket. "I'll ask my mom. Maybe she'll remember the other parents since she helped that day."

Leah couldn't control the bitter edge to her voice. "Are you going to put her name and Ava Shephard's on that list?"

"I guess I should." He was silent for a moment. "You really hate this, don't you?"

"I look for the best in people instead of the worst." She stood. "I'm not very hungry, but I suppose I should start dinner while you talk to her."

Ryan rose slowly and placed a firm hand on her shoulder. "Sit. You can pick my mom's brain while I cook. Tell her I haven't forgotten she has her book club meeting tonight, and I'll be home in an hour to drive her there."

"Fine." She returned to her chair. "How much of this situation do you want me to explain?"

"Whatever you feel comfortable with." He pulled a bowl off the cupboard shelf then opened the refrigerator door.

Leah took out her phone and scrolled through her contacts to dial. Marion answered on the second ring.

"Hi, Mrs. A. It's Leah."

"Well, hello there. How are you, dear?"

Her cheerful tone eased some of Leah's tension, and she loosened her grip on the cell. "Fine."

"Are you looking for Ryan? I'm afraid he isn't here right now, but—"

"Actually, he's with me. He asked me to tell you he'll be home shortly to take you to your book club meeting."

"No need. Flo is picking me up. I've told that boy time and again I'm perfectly capable of getting along on my own, but he won't listen. Not that I want him to go home. Still . . ."

Leah pressed a hand to the ache in her chest as Ryan's mother chatted away. Apparently his time in Siren Cove might be even shorter than she'd thought. When Marion paused to take a breath, Leah broke in, "Uh, we were wondering if you could help clear up a few facts about the day we buried the time capsule all those years ago."

"Well, sure, if I can. I remember taking an extra-long lunch break from work at the travel agency to help with the class party. That was back before everyone booked their own vacations online. What did you want to know?"

"Which other adults were around that day? I know Paige's mom helped, and I think Waylon Brewster was there."

"That's right. Let me think." She paused for a moment. "Three dads were out digging the hole where they buried the time capsule. I remember thinking they were acting like little boys, bickering over who should do what, while Tina Radcliff, Ava Shephard, and I worked together inside like a well-oiled machine."

Leah smiled. "I'd forgotten Quentin's mom helped out. Who were the fathers, do you remember?"

"Waylon Brewster, Arnold Dorsey, and... Kimmy Long's father. What was his name?" Seconds ticked by. "Rodney Long. I think he and his wife still live in town, but I haven't seen him in years. Why all the interest in that day, Leah?"

She juggled the phone to write down the names on Ryan's list. "Uh, we found a roll of film in the time capsule, and the pictures made us curious. There are people we didn't recognize in them." Maybe not the whole truth, but she couldn't bring herself to explain further.

"Probably the detectives who were at the school that day."

Her jaw sagged open. "What?"

"Oh, it was quite exciting, not that we all weren't worried to death about the poor girl they were looking for."

"Mrs. A, I've no idea what you're talking about."

"Of course no one said anything to the students... Such a shame. A young woman from just south of here was hitchhiking in the area and went missing a couple of weeks before your class buried the time capsule. I still remember her name, Merry—spelled like the adjective rather than the traditional way—Bright. So cheerful, in stark contrast to the awfulness of her disappearance. The police never did find that girl."

Leah noted the name on the pad and drew a line under it. "That's horrible, but why were detectives at the school?"

"I guess Mrs. Winston, the principal, had watched a follow-up story on the morning news and called to report she'd seen the girl on the highway. Apparently, she'd driven by Merry Bright just as a car coming from the opposite direction pulled over, presumably to pick her up. For some reason, Nola Winston hadn't seen a picture of this pretty blond woman when the story originally broke."

The breath stalled in Leah's throat. "So the detectives on the case came to question Mrs. Winston?"

"That's right. The detectives were there along with our current police chief. Not that Irving Stackhouse was chief at the time, of course, but he was on the force. Ava and I pulled him aside to ask what was going on, but he wouldn't give us any information. The whole story leaked out eventually, but I'm afraid the information Mrs. Winston provided never led to the girl's recovery or an arrest in the case."

"Wow. I guess all the kids were completely clueless, totally focused on the excitement of burying the time capsule. At least I was."

"As it should be. The authorities had no reason to upset the students."

Leah let out a shaky breath. "You certainly satisfied my curiosity. Thanks, Mrs. A. I'll tell Ryan you already have a ride to your meeting."

"Thank you, dear. Have a nice evening."

"We will. You, too." Leah disconnected and set down her phone. "Oh. My. God. Unbelievable."

Ryan slid a cast iron skillet into the oven. "What was that all about?"

She gave him a brief recap and then added, "Oh, and your mom has a ride tonight, so you don't need to hurry away. Unless you want to."

He gave her a long look. "I don't want to. You're as nervous as a cat in a room full of attack dogs. Seems like you could use some company, despite your earlier snarkiness."

"I'm sorry. I didn't mean . . ." She rubbed the back of her neck in a futile attempt to ease her tension. "Those pictures are a little terrifying. I keep imagining what that poor woman was thinking, lying there naked and vulnerable . . ."

"Don't." He pulled her to her feet and into his arms. "There's no reason to torment yourself."

"I guess not." She leaned against his chest. "I shouldn't have taken my anger out on you." She forced a smile. "What's for dinner?"

"A frittata with tomatoes, mushrooms, chives, zucchini, and peppers."

"Yum. I guess calling the police can wait until after we eat. I bet everyone in the department is sick of seeing my name pop up on their reports, anyway."

"I've been thinking about that." His voice took on a grim edge. "Maybe we shouldn't contact them."

She pulled back to meet his troubled gaze. "Why not? We have new information related to a crime."

"Yes, we do. We also have nine faceless individuals who were more than likely involved in the disappearance of Merry Bright, *if* that's who the naked blonde in the pictures was."

"Seems like a pretty safe assumption. Detectives

were at the school questioning Mrs. Winston about this young woman and the car that stopped to pick her up. Someone who had the film in his possession freaked out, maybe believing the principal would point the police in his direction, so he buried the evidence in our time capsule."

"Makes a whole lot of sense to me. You said he. You think it was a man, not a woman?"

Leah resisted the urge to shout. "I *will not* consider either your mom or Paige's or Quentin's is one of the hooded figures in those pictures."

"Easy." He cupped her chin and stroked her cheek with one finger before dropping his hands to her shoulders. "I don't believe it either."

"Then why did you say—"

"Just making a point. If we eliminate the women, there are five names left on our list."

"Sloan Manning, Edgar Vargas, Waylon Brewster, Arnold Dorsey, and Rodney Long." Leah shook her head. "I can't imagine any of those men would kidnap and hold some poor girl captive in the woods. That's just sick."

"The woman is naked and seems to be the centerpiece of some twisted ceremony. Sick doesn't begin to describe it."

"Agreed. So, we report what we know and let the police question them. I hate to throw any innocent person under the bus by bringing up his name, but this is too horrible to keep to ourselves."

"One problem. Siren Cove has a small department, and one of their own could very well be involved."

"Are you talking about Chief Stackhouse? Your

mom said he was with the detectives who came to question Mrs. Winston."

Ryan shook his head. "No, I mean your buddy, Chris Long, the cop who's always on hand to investigate all your problems. His dad's name is on our list. If Rodney Long is the one responsible . . ."

"Chris could find a way to bury this a lot deeper than the time capsule." A chill slithered down her spine. "Maybe he already tried."

In the silence that followed her words, the timer dinged.

Ryan's grip on her shoulders tightened. "What do you mean?"

"Someone searched my house, my car, and my bag, and he wasn't afraid to hurt me when I got in the way. Also, your Jeep was broken into. What if that person was looking for the film? What if he never wanted those pictures to see the light of day? It could have been Chris Long, covering up for his dad."

"Yes, or it could have been one of the others, since we're short on concrete evidence. Edgar Vargas might have knocked you senseless then pretended to find you when his son arrived. Or, Sloan Manning didn't really leave the school and circled back on foot to hit you over the head."

"I don't believe that." Her voice broke. "I can't and won't."

"Well, you'd damn well better start because one of these men is responsible." Ryan gave her a shake. "Merry Bright was never found. Someone on this list isn't the person you believe he is. One of those five men may very well be a cold-blooded killer."

*   *   *

He slowed to a stop beside the compact car pulled to the side of the road and lowered his window. "Need some help?"

The woman crouched beside the front tire dropped the jack and rose to her feet. The glare of his headlights illuminated long, dark hair and a face streaked with tears. Young. Pretty.

Perfect.

"Oh, thank God. I don't have a clue how to change a flat. I can't even get the stupid jack in place. Wouldn't you know I had the bad luck to puncture my tire in a dead zone, so my cell doesn't work to call roadside assistance." She moved closer and bent to look through the open window. "I was just about ready to lose it when you stopped. Thank you so much."

"Happy to help a lady in distress. I'll just pull over and park."

When she stepped back, he cruised to the edge of the road in front of her car and turned off the engine. Taking a moment, he controlled the jitters of excitement quivering through him. Talk about fate—or Satan himself—throwing him a bone. He was getting a hard-on just thinking about his unbelievable luck.

Drawing in a deep breath, he let it out slowly, opened the door, and got out. The girl was there, waiting for him with a smile. She shivered and ran her hands up and down her arms.

"It sure is chilly out tonight. Do you think you can fix the tire for me?"

"Oh, I can fix it, all right. What's your name, miss?"

"Yvonne." Her smile faded as she backed up a few feet and glanced down the empty road. "I really appreciate this."

He bent to retrieve the jack and held it by the handle. "No problem at all. I was having a crappy day, but do you know what? You just made my night."

Her dark eyes widened. As she turned to run, a cry ripped from her throat.

Her scream echoed in the night before he swung the jack with a delicate touch. Metal connected to flesh and bone with a satisfying *thunk* before she crumpled into his arms. Not hard enough to kill her. Not so easy she'd offer up any resistance on the drive to their holding room. He'd had practice perfecting his technique.

Perfect.

Chapter Nineteen

Hints of dawn filtered into the room, highlighting the sleeping face of the woman on the pillow next to his. Leah mumbled something indecipherable, and Ryan held her a little closer. She tensed then relaxed against him. When he shifted slightly, her lashes fluttered before her eyes slowly opened.

He bent to kiss the tempting lips so close to his. "Did I wake you?"

"I was dreaming. Men in robes chased me through the woods. Then you appeared and scooped me up, and we galloped away on . . . Barney. Except he was bigger."

A smile formed. "Freud would have a field day with that one."

"I expect so. What time is it?"

Ryan glanced at the illuminated digital numbers on the bedside clock. "Nearly six."

"Not enough time to go back to sleep before I have to get up for work."

"But plenty of time for this." He kissed her again,

this time with purpose, as he aligned her curves to his angles.

She kissed him back with almost a hint of desperation, wrapping her arms around his neck to cling tight. He slid his hands over warm, smooth skin, down her back to cup the firm muscles of her ass until they blended into one. Holding still, he fought the urge to go deeper, harder. Instead, he savored the connection as his lips found hers in a long, drugging kiss. He nipped the lobe of her ear and licked the delicate skin of her neck.

Shivers coursed through her before she pushed hard to roll them over and lie flat upon his chest. Her deep brown gaze dug into his soul, searching for . . . something. Relief mixed with desire in her eyes when she apparently found whatever reassurance she needed.

"I love you, Ryan."

"I love you, too."

She slid over him, rising and falling in a measured rhythm he felt certain would destroy him. He held on, nearly crying with the need for relief, until she quaked with the force of her release and collapsed on top of him. Only then did he let go, wrapped up in the sanctuary of Leah's body.

They lay together for long minutes as coherent thoughts dissolved before they could take hold, and his breathing slowed. He never wanted to move again.

"Ryan?"

"Hmm." He inched his face downward to nuzzle the bare breast pressing against him.

"Not to kill the mood, but I have to get ready for work soon, and we need to make a few decisions."

His tongue swirled around one pink tip before he drew back. "About?"

Her breath hissed out as she slid off him. "Those photos. Merry Bright."

His burgeoning desire wilted as he propped himself up on one elbow. The fear in Leah's eyes ate at him.

"I'll do a little research, maybe go have a chat with our former principal to see what she told those detectives the day we buried the time capsule. If there was any evidence that might lead back to one of the men on our list, we'll at least have a place to start."

Her brows drew together over worried eyes. "All right. Maybe you can find out who the detectives were on the case and confide in them. Since they weren't from our local station . . ."

"That might be an option, but I know cops share information. If we could eliminate Chris Long's father as a potential suspect, I'd feel better about taking this to the authorities. I'd like to feel out the situation and gather more information before we show those photos to anyone."

She nodded. "I'll let you take the lead on this and do it your way."

"Good. You just go to work, and don't stress about anything." He dropped a kiss on her lips before flinging back the covers to lever out of bed. "I have time at my disposal, and I'm good at digging for the truth. We'll figure this out."

"I hope so because not worrying isn't an option. Those pictures are disturbing and offensive. What if the men in them are still doing . . . whatever it is they were doing?"

Ryan paused on the way to the bathroom and turned back. "That ceremony, or whatever the hell it was, took place twenty years ago. I can't imagine . . ." He broke off as a chill slid through him. "At least I hope not. Keeping anything that twisted a secret for so long in Siren Cove seems impossible."

Leah sat up against the pillows and crossed her arms over her chest. "I pray you're right."

Two hours later, he was still thinking about her words as he parked his Jeep at the senior apartments, got out, and slammed the door. Apparently Mrs. Winston had been retired for quite a few years, and she was currently a neighbor of Evie's. He kicked the fall leaves scattered across the sidewalk beneath a row of maple trees as he looked for unit thirty-two. Finding the correct residence, he approached and rapped sharply.

The woman who opened the door looked vaguely familiar. The dark hair he remembered was gray now, and she seemed shorter than the formidable figure who'd stood near her office door as the kids filed inside after recess. Or maybe he'd simply gotten a whole lot taller.

"My goodness, Ryan Alexander all grown up." She stepped back and waved him inside. "Please come in. I'll admit your phone call stirred my curiosity."

"It's good to see you, Mrs. Winston. Thanks for having me over on such short notice."

"One of the benefits to retirement is I don't have to race off anywhere at the crack of dawn." She led the way to the bar counter separating the kitchen from the living area. "Have a seat. I made a fresh pot of coffee if you're interested."

"Thanks, I'd love a cup."

She poured two steaming mugs and nudged the sugar bowl and cream pitcher his way as she settled on the second stool. "Help yourself, then tell me what you'd like to know about the time capsule your fifth-grade class buried."

He stirred in a splash of cream before sipping the strong brew. "Not so much the time capsule as the day we buried it. I'm doing a little research into the events that fall, and my mom mentioned two detectives questioned you about a woman who went missing a couple weeks prior to that day."

"Merry Bright." The former principal's eyes darkened. "Goodness, I haven't thought about that tragic young woman in years. Wondering what happened to her gave me quite a few sleepless nights, since I was probably one of the last people to see her before she disappeared."

He eyed her soberly. "Sorry to bring up bad memories, but if you could describe the car you saw . . ."

"There was nothing remarkable about the vehicle, and I wasn't paying much attention when I passed it. I'd just glimpsed the girl at the side of the road and remember thinking she looked like a Barbie Doll with all that long, pale hair shining in my headlights. I glanced in my rearview mirror as a car pulled over next to her and had the fleeting thought that hitchhiking wasn't safe for pretty young women."

"I guess not."

"A real tragedy that could have been avoided, or at least that was the conclusion I drew since, to my knowledge, no one ever found her. As for the car that stopped, it was a sedan. Maybe a Chevy or a Ford, though I wouldn't swear to it, dark in color. Navy, green, or brown. Possibly black." She shrugged. "I didn't see the driver, and my description of the vehicle didn't exactly thrill the detectives who questioned me, but it was a moonless night."

"So, you weren't able to help them in their investigation?"

"I'm afraid not. One of them gave me his card and told me to call if I remembered anything else. I didn't."

"I don't suppose you still have the card?"

Mrs. Winston snorted. "Are you kidding? I got rid of thirty years' worth of crap when I moved in here. But I have a mind for details, and my memory hasn't started to go yet. They were Detectives Stannard and Hutch from down in Coos Bay. Of course I joked that Stannard should have been Starsky, and he said if only he had a nickel for every time he'd heard that line." She patted Ryan's arm. "Those old TV show references are before your time, I'm afraid. Why did you want to know about Merry Bright?"

He hesitated and sipped his coffee before going with the version of the story Leah had told his mother. "We found a roll of film in the time capsule and didn't recognize the people in it. My mother mentioned the detectives who'd been at the school that day, and I was curious to hear exactly what had happened."

"From the horse's mouth, so to speak." She grinned. "Well, I hope I satisfied your quest for knowledge."

"Definitely." He finished his coffee and stood. "Thanks for chatting with me, Mrs. Winston."

"Oh, I enjoyed our talk. It's always fun to catch up with my former students." She rose and followed him to the entry. "By the way, I love Crossroads. You're a clever young man, Ryan, but then you always were."

He smiled back at her. "Good to hear. You have a great day."

"I intend to."

He shut the door behind him and hurried down the path, only to stop when Leah's grandmother left her apartment and turned in his direction.

Keen eyes widened beneath purple curls. "Hello there, Ryan. Should I tell my granddaughter you've been stepping out on her with an older woman?"

His mouth dropped open. "I was just—"

"Kidding!" She slapped her thigh. "You should see your face. Did you come for a visit? I was headed over to meet Magnus, but I don't mind making him wait."

"Actually, I was talking to Mrs. Winston about something, but it's great to see you, Evie."

"Walk with me then." She took his arm and turned him in the opposite direction from the parking lot. "I had a real enjoyable evening with my book club last night. I told them all about that brash young man who robbed me blind. Of course they were horrified. But your mom, who may be even sharper than you are, came up with the solution to a mystery that had been puzzling me."

Ryan stopped walking. "She did? What mystery was that?"

"One of the aliases the con man used has been driving me crazy because it sounded familiar." She grinned broadly. "Leah would tell you that's a short trip."

"What . . . oh, I get it." He smiled back. "Crazy like a fox, maybe. What insights did my mom share?"

"Anthony Benedetto was one of the names that fool used to bilk susceptible old ladies like me who are too darn trusting for our own good." Evie pulled him along, shuffling through the scattered leaves. "Tony Bennett."

"Excuse me?"

"Tony Bennett was born Anthony Benedetto. *That's* why the name sounded familiar to me, not because I'd met him before."

"Huh, odd. Maybe not very helpful in catching the con man, but still interesting."

"Not useful at all since I don't imagine Mr. Bennett's younger incarnation is out scamming senior citizens." She stopped in front of a short walkway leading to a corner apartment. "This is Magnus's place. I'll let you go on your way now."

Ryan smiled and bent to drop a kiss on her cheek. "Bye, Evie. I'll be sure to give Leah an update on the name."

"You do that. And tell her I said not to be a stranger. Oh, I also need to talk to her about expenses. Maybe I shouldn't have bought that new wetsuit."

He opened his mouth then shut it. He wouldn't even ask. "I'll give her the message. Take care, Evie."

She waved, then continued up the walk to the door and entered the apartment without knock-

ing. The door shut with a thump. Swiveling on the
heel of his running shoe, Ryan hurried back toward his Jeep. Before he reached it, his steps
slowed. No point in rushing when he wasn't sure
where to go next. Without knowing the type of car
each of the suspects drove twenty years before, he
had no way of eliminating anyone from their pool
of potential homicidal maniacs . . . if that's what
the man was. Of course, there was always the possibility the person who picked up Merry Bright had
borrowed a car from a friend or relative. Basically,
he didn't have shit to go on.

He thumped a fist down on the hood before unlocking his vehicle to climb inside. What he really
wanted to know was if any other women had disappeared from the area in the last twenty years. He
could try searching through old newspaper ac-
counts, but access to police files would be far more
efficient. Staring through the windshield at the
falling leaves as a strong gust of wind shook his
Jeep, he spent about thirty seconds considering the
feasibility of hacking into law enforcement comput-
ers. He might be able to manage it, but if he got
busted, the idea of time spent in prison with a
roommate named Big Bubba didn't appeal.

Ryan started the engine and backed out of the
parking spot. He'd have to risk talking to the authorities. But not the local ones. He'd take a drive
down to Coos Bay to look up Stannard and Hutch.
Hopefully they'd have a few insights into the cold
case. Because he damn sure didn't.

*   *   *

Leah shut her classroom door and nearly jumped out of her skin when Sloan did the same only a few yards away. She clutched her bag in a tight grip and pressed her free hand to her chest as she forced herself to breathe. Her nerves were shot, and all she wanted to do was scurry home to hide.

"Sorry, did I startle you?" He waited for her to join him. "I'll walk out with you. What a day."

She gave him a sidelong glance. "Oh?"

"The kids were all wound up over Halloween costumes and trick-or-treating, and we still have a week to go before the big day. I'll be happy when the holiday is over and we can focus on Pilgrims instead of skeletons and ghosts."

A shiver slid through her. *Does Sloan have any skeletons in his closet?* The thought angered and depressed her, but as much as she wanted to, she couldn't dismiss her suspicions.

"Are you okay, Leah? You've acted a little off all day." Gray eyes regarded her from behind his glasses. "Is something bothering you?"

"No, why would anything be bothering me?" *Cool it, Leah. He isn't accusing you of thinking he might be a psycho murderer.* She let out a shaky breath. "I'm fine. As you said, it's been a long day."

"Hey, I heard Ryan Alexander was up at the high school to use their dark room. Was he developing the film we found in the time capsule?"

She froze as they reached the front doors. When Edgar appeared from around the front counter, carrying a bulging trash bag, she stammered out a response. "No, I'm afraid I lost that roll for good. I don't know what happened to it. Ryan was developing sunset pictures he took down on the beach with an old film camera he found in a closet at his mom's place."

For God's sake, don't overexplain.

"Well, that's too bad. About the lost film, I mean. I guess we'll never know who took pictures for our time capsule." Sloan held the door wide as a gust of wind swept through. "Hey, Edgar, how's it going?"

"Not so good." He slung the black plastic bag over his shoulder. "Jesse worries me. He lost his latest job after only a couple of weeks, right after he bought a new motorcycle. If that boy doesn't settle down . . ." He shrugged. "You don't want to hear my problems."

Leah led the way down the steps. "I'm sorry Jesse's having troubles. Hopefully he'll find work soon."

"He'd better." The janitor turned to head toward the dumpsters. "Have a good evening, Leah. You, too, Sloan."

Sloan clapped him on the shoulder. "Don't worry too much about your boy. That kid always has a way of coming out on top."

"Let's hope so."

Leah was quiet until she reached her car, then glanced over at her colleague. "I'll see you tomorrow."

He waved a hand toward her Audi. "You haven't ridden your bike to work lately."

"No time. Seems like I'm always running behind in the morning."

"I know the feeling. Good night, Leah."

"Good night." She let out a relieved breath,

tossed her bag filled with vocabulary tests on the passenger seat, and slid inside. Surely Edgar wasn't one of the men in the pictures. Or Sloan, even though he'd asked about the film . . ." The key dug into her palm as she started the engine and drove out of the lot. She'd go home and call Ryan . . . right after she stopped at the grocery store, since the damn refrigerator was practically empty. Nothing about this day was going right.

A half hour later she pushed her cart loaded with bags out of the store and nearly nailed a man in a suit standing just beyond the door, talking on his cell.

"Oops, excuse me."

Waylon Brewster turned and frowned. "Good to know. Yeah, I'll definitely be there." After tucking his phone in his jacket pocket, he stepped out of her path. "Leah, how are you?"

"Fine, and you?"

He ignored her polite question as his blue gaze narrowed. "Pete mentioned you treated poor Brock like a dog turd when he was in town last week. Not very nice, parading your lover in front of him the way you did."

Leah gripped the bar on the cart so hard her knuckles turned white. "I guess that's better than what he did with other women *while we were still married.*"

Brewster shrugged. "Once in a while a man has a lapse in judgment. No reason to be unforgiving about it."

Leah tried to think of a suitable response that didn't involve swearing or slapping his smug face, and failed. She pushed past him and nearly rammed a van in her rush to get to her car. After loading the groceries into the back with shaking hands, she took a few deep breaths and glanced skyward.

"Please let it be him," she muttered. "I so want that loser to be the guilty party." She climbed into the car and slammed the door. "So we can nail his ass."

Chapter Twenty

"I'm down in Coos Bay, waiting to talk to Detective Stannard. Doesn't look like I'll be back anytime soon."

Leah closed her eyes and propped an elbow on the counter as she clutched the cell phone in her other hand. "That's too bad. I take it your conversation with Mrs. Winston wasn't very productive?"

"Not at all. After twenty years, she didn't have any stunning new revelations." Ryan chuckled. "I did speak to your grandma while I was at the apartment complex. She was in rare form. By the way, you're to call her. She mentioned something about money problems and a wetsuit. I didn't even try to figure out what she was talking about."

Leah cringed. "I know what she means. Damn." She wondered how much the wetsuit for the scuba lessons had cost and if more of her grandma's checks would soon be bouncing higher than a freaking kangaroo on meth. Drawing and quarter-

ing was too good for that low-life son of a bitch
who'd—

"Leah, are you still there?"

"Yeah." She forced her grandma's financial issues to the back of her mind and focused on Ryan.
"I miss you. I've gotten used to having you around
when I get home from work. It's been . . . nice."

"More than nice. Pretty damn special." He
paused for a moment. "Oh, I was also supposed to
tell you that one of the con man's aliases, Anthony
Benedetto, is Tony Bennett's birth name. You
know, the singer. That's why your grandma recognized it."

Leah couldn't help smiling even though she
felt like smashing something. "So, a world-famous
crooner is bilking old ladies out of their nest
eggs? Isn't that special?"

"It would be funny if the situation wasn't so serious. I'll probably be back pretty late tonight. One
of the detectives on the Merry Bright case died of
a heart attack not long after we buried that time
capsule. The other is out interviewing witnesses in
relation to a current crime and isn't expected back
to the precinct for a couple more hours."

"Let's hope your wait pays off with a little information, then. If nothing else, you can give him
those sick photos. I don't want to ever see them
again."

"I only brought two with me. The others are in
the folder on your kitchen counter. I wasn't sure
how I'd want to handle this."

Leah glanced toward the coffeepot and wondered how the plain manila folder beside it could look so menacing. "Oh."

"I'm worried about your safety. If the person who dropped the film in the time capsule is the same man who knocked you out and searched your house and car, there's no guarantee he's given up. And if he finds out we printed those pictures—"

"I told Sloan I lost the film for good, and Edgar heard me say it. Maybe I should take out an announcement in the local paper so the rest of the suspects get the message."

"I don't like this. Can you find someone to keep you company this evening? Until we know exactly what we're up against, I don't want you hanging out by yourself at home."

"I'm not alone." She eyed Barney, sprawled on the kitchen floor near his food bowl. "I have my fearless canine protector."

"That would be great if I thought he'd bite an intruder instead of licking him to death."

She smiled. "Fine, I'll call Nina or Paige. Will that ease your mind?"

"Yeah." His voice softened. "I'll talk to you before I head back. Be careful, okay?"

"I will. Bye, Ryan."

"Bye."

She set the cell down on the counter and wondered why she hadn't said what she was really thinking. That she loved him. Maybe their feelings were a little too new and fragile for casual declarations of love over the phone. As disheartening and at times downright frightening as her life had been lately, she was almost afraid to hope something wonderful with Ryan could result from it.

Leah straightened. "On the topic of overwhelming problems . . ." She headed into the living room to retrieve her laptop and powered it up. Dread settled in the pit of her stomach as she waited to pull up her grandmother's checking account. She wasn't sure if asking for the password after their fruitless trip to the bank had been a smart move or not. She'd almost rather not know the truth . . .

The balance left her gasping for breath. A check written to the local surf shop—for the wetsuit, she assumed—sent a chill through her. Had her grandma even looked at the price tag before she bought the damn thing? She only had half her latest retirement check left, and rent would be due in another week. Leah slammed the laptop shut. Gram would have to give up her apartment and move in here. There really was no other solution. Since the management company probably had a hefty security deposit, she might be able to stay there long enough to get all her stuff packed . . .

"I am *so* not going to think about this tonight."

Springing to her feet, she went back to the kitchen, detoured over to feed Barney, then picked up her cell to call Paige. When her friend answered on the first ring, she let out a sigh of relief and didn't bother with a greeting.

"What are you doing this evening?"

"Celebrating. I sold that giant buffet that was taking up half a wall in my shop. I don't know what possessed me to buy it in the first place, but I turned a terrific profit."

"Congratulations. Are you at home popping open the champagne?"

"I'm not that pathetic." Her voice turned ironic. "Okay, maybe I am, but I'm not drinking alone tonight. Nina is meeting me at Poseidon's for dinner at six thirty. Want to join us, or are you hanging out with Ryan?"

"He's busy, and I'd love to join you." She scratched her elbow and frowned. "I feel like I've been neglecting my BFFs lately."

"You really have, but we might be willing to forgive you. Great sex trumps girls' night out every time. I'd ditch you, too, if I had a hot guy waiting for me at home."

Leah sputtered with laughter. "I can't believe you just said that."

"We tell each other everything, right? This evening you can dish the dirt on what you and Ryan have been up to, and Nina and I will live vicariously while we drink that champagne."

"Maybe not everything, but I'll see you in an hour." She disconnected and turned to stare at Barney, who'd finished wolfing down his dinner. "I guess I'd better grade those vocab tests, pronto."

Leah was only fifteen minutes late when she pulled into the parking lot next to the Poseidon Grill. Maybe Ryan's promptness was beginning to rub off on her. Slamming the car door, she hurried through the swirling fog toward the glow of the lighted entrance, wishing Paige had chosen any restaurant other than this one for her celebration dinner, since the owner was one of the men on their list. Still, she obviously couldn't avoid any of the potential suspects, not in a town the size of Siren Cove,

not when she worked with two of them ...
Wrenching open the door, she stepped inside and
approached the hostess stand.

Rebecca, a young woman who'd been a student
in Leah's class her first year teaching, flashed her a
broad smile. "Hi, Miss Grayson. Your friends told
me to keep an eye out for you. You look fantastic,
very sixties retro."

She glanced down at the clingy knit dress over
colored tights, and smiled. "I was going for warmth
over style, but I'm glad you approve. What grade
are you in now?"

"Senior." Rebecca tapped the open calculus
book on the podium. "This job is going to help pay
college tuition next year, and Mr. Dorsey is nice
enough to let me study between customers."

"Good for you, but you make me feel really old."
Leah held up a hand. "Stay where you are. I can
find my dinner companions on my own."

Her former student nodded and handed her a
menu. "They're at a table by the windows. Have a
nice evening."

"Thanks." Leah headed into the dining room
and nearly dropped the menu when her gaze col-
lided with Waylon Brewster's. "Are you freaking kidding me," she mumbled beneath her breath. "Twice
in the same day?" Ignoring him, she nodded to Dr.
Carlton, who was seated with the attorney and
their local judge, as she passed their table. With a
sigh of relief, she pulled out the empty chair between Paige and Nina and dropped onto the seat.
"What are we drinking?"

Nina eyed her up and down. "Cute dress. Very
trendy. What's with the scowl?"

Paige poured champagne from the open bottle on the table and handed her the flute. "Are you going to ruin my good mood? I thought we established earlier you're the only one getting any, so you should be all smiles."

Leah's lips curved as she took a sip. "Sorry. Waylon Brewster pissed me off earlier when I ran into him at the store. Made a snarky comment about Brock." She angled her head toward the trio of men not far away. "Not the first face I wanted to see when I walked in here tonight."

"Then don't look at him." Paige topped off her glass and Nina's. "I agree the man is a jerk, just like his son." She glanced over her shoulder. "I wonder what a nice guy like Dr. Carlton is doing with him."

"Doesn't matter. We're celebrating." Nina raised her glass. "Here's to you selling that giant buffet. Now you'll have all sorts of room to display new stock."

"You've got that right." Paige tapped her glass against the other two before taking a sip. "Here comes our server. Check the menu, Leah. We waited for you to order."

"I already know what I want. The spinach soufflé is unbelievable."

After they'd placed their orders, Nina sat back in her chair and studied Leah. "Is something wrong? You look . . . tense. Are you still having headaches from the concussion?"

"Concussion? Oh, no." She let out a breath. "Was it only last week I got knocked on the skull? Seems longer."

Paige squeezed her arm. "Then what's bothering you? Are you and Ryan having problems? I hoped this time you two would stick."

"We're okay . . . better than okay, but we haven't talked about the future." She swallowed hard as tears burned the back of her throat. "Right now the present is such a mess . . ."

"Hey, tell us what's wrong." Nina's green eyes darkened. "We'll help you fix it. Isn't that what we always do for each other?"

Leah's smile shook a little. "If only this were as simple as copying homework." She opened her mouth to spill her guts about the pictures, then caught a glimpse of Arnold Dorsey crossing the restaurant toward the table where Waylon Brewster sat. *Too risky.* If they overheard her . . . She changed mental gears.

"It's my grandma."

"Oh, no. What crazy thing has Evie done now?" Paige asked.

"For once, the problem isn't totally Gram's fault."

The story of the con man took the conversation through the salad course. By the time Leah had explained about Tony Bennett, their waiter had served their dinners and departed.

Nina poked a scallop in cream sauce then twirled the accompanying fettuccini around her fork. "What a sleazeball. Is Evie going to be okay financially? I sold a couple of paintings during the Fall Festival. I could donate—"

"Thanks, Nina, but no. I appreciate your generosity, but that would only be a temporary fix. Without her investment income, Gram can't afford the senior apartments. She's going to have to move in with me."

"How will that work out?"

Leah blew on a bite of her soufflé before glancing back at her friend. "Fine. We get along well. She has a more active social life than I do. Once Ryan heads home, chances are I'll cramp Grandma's style more than she will mine."

"Ouch. Is Ryan leaving soon?" Nina asked.

"I'm not sure—"

"What was the other alias?"

"Huh?" Leah turned to stare at Paige.

"You mentioned Thomas Woodward and Anthony Benedetto. What was the third name that creep used?"

"I can't remember." Leah frowned. "Wait, it was Williams."

Paige's blue eyes brightened. "Andrew Williams?"

"That doesn't sound right." Leah snapped her fingers. "Howard. Howard Williams."

Paige pulled out her cell and tapped the screen.

"What are you doing?" Nina bit into a scallop and chewed. "Your pork tenderloin is getting cold, and you're being very mysterious."

"I have a theory . . . hold on . . ." Paige set down her phone and let out a whoop, then cringed when diners at nearby tables glanced their way. "Oops, sorry, I got a little carried away."

"About what?" When Arnold Dorsey turned to frown in their direction, Leah lowered her voice even more. "Geez, you're going to get us blacklisted from this place."

"Doubtful. Not while we're spending money. Anyway, I figured out the connection between the names. You know how I have a head for useless facts . . ."

Nina laughed. "That's because you look up the history of all your antiques. What does that have to do with the cretin who robbed Evie?"

"This isn't about antiques. Do you remember when my mom and a couple of her old college friends went to Vegas together? Well, they saw Tom Jones in concert."

Leah frowned. "Who?"

"An early version of a pop star back in the late sixties and early seventies. I remember seeing his real name somewhere. Thomas Woodward."

"You're kidding!" Leah dropped her fork. "First Tony Bennett and now another singer?"

Paige tapped a few times then held up her phone. "This is Tom Jones back in the day when he was considered a sex symbol."

"Oh, my God! That sort of looks like the police artist's sketch of the con man."

"Does it?"

Leah nodded. "I don't understand what's going on."

Nina balled up her napkin and set it on the table. "Where does the Williams guy come into the picture?"

"That's what I was checking. Andy Williams, who was another famous crooner from the same general era, was born Howard Williams."

Leah stared at Paige. "Grandma listens to Andy Williams on her old stereo. She has a whole collection of records that are practically antiques."

"So, this guy who has been robbing seniors impersonates singers from our grandparents' heyday?" Nina's gaze darted over Paige's shoulder, and she lowered her voice. "But he uses their birth names, not their stage names. Why?"

"Maybe the crook likes taking risks but is a chicken at heart." Paige picked up her fork. "He knows most of the seniors he scams would recognize these stage names but counts on them not knowing the names each man was born with. He's playing a game and getting some sort of satisfaction from fooling people."

"Interesting theory. I guess you're using your psych degree after all." Leah stopped speaking as Arnold Dorsey paused beside their table.

"Evening, ladies." He spoke in a well-modulated tone. "How are your dinners?"

"Wonderful, Mr. Dorsey." Nina smiled at him. "Your chef always turns out a top-rate meal."

"Excellent." He took a step back. "Enjoy your evening."

"Thank you," Paige said. After he had walked away, she added, "Hey, he didn't even kick me out for shouting and disturbing the ambiance."

"Not a chance." Leah ate a bite of her soufflé. "While I'm extremely impressed with your powers of deduction, how are these new insights going to help catch the con man?"

Nina shrugged. "Tell the police and let them figure it out. That's their job."

"That would be my advice." Paige smiled. "Although it was fun solving the mystery."

"Fine, I will." Leah dug into her soufflé. "Let's eat and talk about something else. We spent too much on this dinner not to enjoy it."

"True that," Paige agreed. "You promised an update on your relationship with Ryan. Spill it."

"All we've done is talk about me and my problems. Surely you two have something to contribute to the conversation."

"Selling the buffet was the highlight of my week. That and advising Quentin about his latest woman problems. He seems to really like this one." She sighed. "Obviously I need to get a life. How about you, Nina?"

"Let's see. A For Sale sign went up on the house next door to mine, which totally sucks. I've enjoyed not having close neighbors since the wannabe rock star moved out."

"That place needs a lot of work, so maybe it'll take a while to sell." Paige sipped her champagne. "Didn't you mention something about a date with Clayton Smith a while back? How'd that go?"

"Horrible."

Leah frowned at her friend. "Why? He's good-looking, has his own business, and is plenty sharp. What was the problem?"

Her face tightened. "He's not Keith."

Paige scooted her chair closer and gave Nina a quick, hard hug. "It's been nearly five years. Keith would want you to be happy."

"I know, and I gave it a shot. Clay was sweet and tried really hard, but . . . ." She shrugged. "I'm just not ready to let myself feel again."

Leah couldn't think of anything to say in the face of her friend's determined martyrdom, at least nothing Nina would want to hear. She clamped down on the urge to shout and changed the subject. "Fine, we'll talk about Ryan. Maybe that will motivate you two to put yourselves out there instead of wallowing in work or . . . whatever. Have I mentioned he's really great—"

Paige slapped her hands over her ears. "TMI! I was kidding about you dishing the dirt."

Leah laughed. "You're actually blushing. What did you think I was going to say?"

"That Ryan's an animal in bed?" Nina suggested.

"Kissing and telling isn't my style. You'll have to keep wondering about that." She eyed Paige's still pink cheeks. "Or not. I was going to say Ryan is great for my ego. It's awfully nice to have a man around who tells me I'm wonderful instead of constantly criticizing."

Nina pushed back her plate. "You *are* wonderful, and Brock is an asshole. Old news. Is your relationship with Ryan serious?"

"I think so." A pain tweaked somewhere near her heart. "I sure hope so, but we have other . . . complications to work out before we can talk about the future." Her attention strayed to the table several yards away when Waylon Brewster and his companions rose to their feet. As their gazes locked, the man's lips twisted in a smile, and he gave a brief, acknowledging nod.

"Don't wait."

"Huh?" Leah glanced over at Nina.

"Life is short. Keith and I thought we had plenty of time to get married, have a family . . . If you love Ryan, seize the day. There might not be a tomorrow."

Chapter Twenty-one

"That's quite an interesting story."

Ryan sat across from Detective Stannard with the two photos displayed on the battered desk between them. The man was as beat up by time and the stress of his job as his desk. Deep grooves etched stubbled cheeks and bracketed his lips, but the pale blue eyes beneath thinning silver hair were sharp with intelligence. When he shifted in his swivel chair to reach for one of the pictures, his back cracked.

"I'm sorry to spring these photos and my suspicions on you so late in the day. I'm sure you'd like to go home."

Stannard didn't even glance up. "No one except a cat to go home to since my wife walked out ten years ago. And I honestly don't think Bruiser cares if I show up or not as long as his food dish doesn't run empty."

"Most cats have the art of subtle revenge mastered when they're unhappy."

The detective leaned back in his chair and eyed Ryan steadily. "Sneaky bastards, but even Bruiser beats coming home to an empty house."

"I'd have to agree." He tapped the pale hair just visible in the photo remaining on the desk. "What do you think? Could this woman be Merry Bright?"

"Based on what you've told me, it's a definite possibility. The fact that we never solved that case has bothered me for years."

"No other unsolved missing persons cases involving young women since then?"

"Well, of course there've been a few. That's a twenty-year time span." Stannard closed his eyes for a moment. "I recall one case from ten or so years back. A local girl, early twenties, had a fight with her boyfriend and demanded he let her out of his car south of town near the beach . . . or so the jilted lover said. The woman disappeared that night. He was our prime suspect, but we never could pin it on him. No substantial proof, so the DA refused to file charges." The detective's frown deepened. "This victim and Merry Bright were each last seen a good forty miles apart, but it might be worth checking with other law enforcement agencies in the region to see if there's any pattern to similar unsolved crimes."

"God, I hope not."

"I'd much rather believe these pictures were taken over near the university at some perverted frat party that had nothing to do with Merry Bright. You said the time capsule was buried in early November, so the likelihood is high this was a Halloween bash turned orgy."

"True, but no one with access to the time capsule was a college student at the time." Ryan planted his elbows on the desk. "They were all men . . . and women . . . mostly in their late thirties and early forties with young children. Except Sloan Manning, who was probably still in his twenties. If those pictures were from some kind of sex party, it was thrown by middle-aged adults, not college kids."

Stannard straightened in his chair. "Do you mind if I keep these photos?"

"Of course not. I have a few others that are similar. My main concern is for the safety of Leah Grayson. If the break-ins and assault she suffered are related to a twenty-year-old crime, and the person responsible believes she has evidence—"

"I'll look into the individuals who had access to that box you buried." He slid the photos along with the list of names he'd written down into a folder.

Ryan didn't like the fact that his own mother's name was on the list. But Stannard had insisted he include everyone, even the kids in his class. He'd tried to remember them all . . .

"One of the students could have swiped his older brother's film and dropped it into the time capsule."

Apparently the detective was also a mind reader.

"If I forgot any of my former classmates, you can probably contact the school for old enrollment records."

"I'm sure I can." He held out a hand. "Thanks for bringing this to my attention."

Ryan shook the extended palm. "You'll tread

carefully with the police in Siren Cove? If Officer Long's father was involved—"

"I'll be cautious sharing information outside this office."

"I appreciate that."

"Still, both you and Ms. Grayson could be potential targets." Stannard's gaze held steady on Ryan. "Please be conscious of your surroundings at all times."

A chill crept down his back. "I've already warned Leah about spending time alone. We'll be wary."

"Great." The detective stood and glanced toward the doorway when a heavyset cop knocked on the partially opened door. "What's up, Fenton?"

"You have a call. I told him you were occupied, but—"

"We're just finishing up here, so I'll take it. If you could walk Mr. Alexander out . . ."

The man nodded as Ryan rose to his feet. "Happy to. Right this way."

A few minutes later, Ryan drove away from the police station. The marine layer hung clear to the ground, so thick his headlights barely penetrated the fog. Shivering in the clammy interior of the Jeep, he hoped his heater would warm the frigid air soon.

The trip home promised to be a slow one. Pulling out his cell, he placed it on speaker and called Leah.

"Ryan?" She sounded breathless. "How'd it go with the detective?"

"He listened and didn't act like I'd lost my mind. I don't know if that's good or bad. I almost wish he'd told me I was crazy to believe the woman in the pictures could be Merry Bright."

"I know what you mean. I'd like to think we're delusional, too."

"However, he did theorize it might just have been some sort of Halloween bash." Ryan squinted, staying well to the left of the white line at the edge of the road so he wouldn't land in a ditch. "I'm on my way home now. Are you still with one of your friends?"

"I went out to dinner with Paige and Nina. In fact, we just left the restaurant. I was hurrying to get to my car when you called. The fog is horrendous."

"Down this way, too. Don't go home alone. In these conditions, I probably won't get back for at least another couple of hours."

"They both left the parking lot while I was talking to you. Anyway, I'm tired and just want to crash on my couch."

"Follow one of them—"

"I have Barney for protection. Besides, no one knows we developed those pictures, and it's been a week since that freak hit me and searched my purse, with no further incidents."

Ryan's grip on the wheel tightened. "I don't know . . ."

"I'll be fine. Please drive carefully. In fact, maybe you should get a room—"

"No, I'm coming back. Stay alert. Please."

"I will." Her voice softened. "I love you, Ryan."

Heat that had nothing to do with the tepid air blowing through the vents suffused him. "I love you, too."

He stepped out of the shower just as the cell sitting next to the sink rang. Grabbing the towel off the rack, he wrapped it around himself before answering. "Yeah, hello."

"We have a problem."

"What, now?"

"Ryan Alexander took a trip down to Coos Bay tonight and did a lot of talking."

"Shit."

"He brought a couple of photos with him." The voice on the other end of the connection grew louder. "So your theory that the damn film wound up in the trash is just that . . . garbage."

"Only two pictures?"

"Exactly. Where do you suppose the rest of them are?"

He closed his eyes and leaned both elbows on the counter. "The interfering bitch has them."

"That would be my guess."

"What's the current status on the photos he turned over?"

"They've mysteriously disappeared." The hint of humor in his tone faded. "However, we need to recover the rest of those prints."

"I'll take a trip over to Leah's place. If she's home . . ."

"Do whatever it takes to get those damn pictures back."

When the dial tone buzzed in his ear, he set the cell back on the counter. Goose bumps pebbled his chilled skin, and a hard, hot knot formed in his stomach. Offering up a sacrifice once every decade was part of the deal their forefathers had made, but this—

Spinning, he opened the toilet lid and puked up his dinner. After a moment, he wiped the back of a shaking hand across his mouth. No time to indulge a weak stomach. He'd get the job done.

One way or the other.

Leah brushed her teeth and spit, then slowly raised her head. A thump had sounded from somewhere downstairs. Or possibly outside. Had Barney jumped off the couch? Maybe the wind had picked up and was finally blowing out the fog. She'd meant to screw down that loose shutter . . .

She rinsed her mouth and left the bathroom. When a shiver worked through her, she tightened the belt on her robe and stopped in her bedroom doorway. Not Barney. Her dog was stretched out on the bed. He rolled over and opened one eye to stare at her. Obviously, he didn't have a care in the world.

From the TV in the corner of the room, a reporter droned on about Yvonne Ames, a young woman who had gone missing nearly forty-eight hours earlier after leaving the motel in Eugene where she worked as a desk clerk. A picture of a pretty brunette flashed on the screen. Lifting the remote from the top of the dresser, Leah turned off the TV and debated going down to see what had caused the thump.

Damn Ryan for planting crazy suspicions in my head.

She wouldn't be able to sleep until she made doubly sure the house was secure. Squaring her shoulders, she turned to head downstairs. With a moan, the dog jumped down and followed her. The stairs creaked as she descended.

Oh, my God, get a grip, Leah. It's an old house.

Thoroughly annoyed with her case of nerves, she crossed the dark entry to the front door and flipped on the porch light to peer through the small window. Outside, fog shrouded the rattan furniture and hung like a curtain, obscuring the yard.

Not the wind, then. Maybe she'd imagined the thump, or the noise had come from the TV. Probably her own damn heart beating overtime as she pictured bogeymen in every closet. If someone was sneaking around the house, wouldn't Barney be barking—or at least running to greet them—not sitting on his butt, scratching furiously behind one ear?

Even so, it wouldn't hurt to check the lock on the kitchen door. Surely she'd flipped the dead bolt once her dog came inside after his nightly stroll. Latching the doggy door didn't mean she was a coward, did it? Just smart.

Smart would have been going home with Nina or Paige.

She bit down on her lip as she turned toward the kitchen, where she'd at least had the sense to leave on a light. When a soft rattle sounded, she nearly peed herself. Pressing a hand to her chest, she stopped beside the table and stared across the room at the doorknob. Had it jiggled slightly?

Barney brushed past her and ran toward the door, barking to wake the dead. When the knob turned, Leah let out a whimper and debated flight or fight for the two seconds it took to grab the cast-iron skillet she'd left on the stove. Raising it over her head, she took aim as the door opened—and just missed braining Ryan when Barney jumped against him. The pan hit his arm instead and knocked him off balance.

"Oh, my God." The skillet slid from her fingers to hit the tile with a thud.

"Down, boy." Ryan pushed the dog away then reached for her. "Are you okay?"

Leah nodded and pressed her face against his shoulder. She didn't even try to stop the tears. "You scared me to death. Did I hurt you?"

He flexed his arm. "I expect I'll have a bruise. You swung that thing like you were aiming for the fence."

"Sorry." She sniffed hard. "Really, really sorry."

"Don't be. It's my fault. When the only light I saw was in the kitchen, I thought maybe you'd gone up to bed. I hunted for the spare key you leave under the mat so I wouldn't wake you." He stroked her hair. "By the way, didn't I suggest you find a better hiding spot?"

"I meant to . . ." She let out a shaking breath. "I'm just happy you don't have brain damage."

Keeping one arm around her, he pushed the door shut and locked it, then reached down to rub Barney's ears. "I can thank your dog for saving me from head trauma." Turning, he cupped her chin and wiped the tears off her cheeks. "Hey, don't cry. The bruise I'll have tomorrow is nothing compared to some of the ones I've gotten rock climbing."

"That doesn't make me feel any better. Honestly, I don't know how much longer I can stand this. Afraid in my own home. Jumping at shadows."

"Better to be wary than a victim. If the person coming through that door had been a threat, you would have clobbered him." Ryan hugged her tight. "You're a strong, resourceful woman. I admire the hell out of you."

"Great, but being Wonder Woman is exhausting."

He smiled. "Then we'll go to bed."

"I want to hear what that detective had to say first. Since I have to work tomorrow, we won't have time to discuss it in the morning."

"Stannard intends to check out the people who had access to the time capsule. He'll also research missing persons cases in the surrounding area that occurred over the past couple of decades to see if there's a pattern." Wrapping an arm around her, Ryan guided her across the room. "That was the gist of our conversation. He promised to let me know what he uncovers."

Leah turned off the kitchen light and leaned against him as they headed toward the stairs with

Barney following. "Two decades . . . I can't even think about the possibility without feeling sick to my stomach."

"I know. I hope he doesn't find anything to connect other missing women to Merry Bright. I hope whatever ugliness happened on that night twenty years ago was an isolated incident."

When they reached her room, Leah climbed into bed while Ryan used the bathroom. He joined her a few minutes later and clicked off the lamp. Darkness settled around them as she cuddled close and rested her cheek on his chest.

"Ryan?"

"Hmm."

"I don't want to lose what we have together."

He tightened his arms around her. "I don't, either."

"But you live in Sisters, which is a good three-hour drive. That's quite a commute."

"I don't know what you want me to say."

She pressed her eyelids tightly closed and fought tears. "I don't know, either. I'm not sure why I brought up the subject now." Her throat ached. "I'm scared . . . of the psycho who wants the pictures, of what those awful images represent." The truth tumbled out. "I'm afraid our relationship will fizzle when you go home."

"It won't. I can stay with you as often as we want. I get plenty of work done while you're teaching."

"Probably because there isn't any rock climbing in the area. Tell me you don't miss it."

"I won't because I do miss climbing." He

touched her cheek with his thumb and wiped away the dampness. "I'd miss you more."

The tears came faster. "One problem—"

"Not tonight." His voice was firm. "You're tired and stressed and frightened. So am I. We'll finish this discussion later and talk about our options when we're both thinking more rationally."

She nodded, and her hair caught on the rough stubble covering his chin. "Can I say one more thing?"

He pressed a kiss to her hair. "I'm not trying to muzzle you."

"Good, since I'd probably bite you if you did." She smiled and let herself relax. "I love you."

He held her tight. "I love you, too."

Maybe nothing had been resolved between them. Maybe a dangerous psychopath was still out there somewhere in the night. But for the moment, Leah pushed her troubles away. She would lie in Ryan's arms and simply be thankful . . .

Light streamed through the window when Leah woke the next morning. Squinting against the brightness, she stretched and smiled when her foot brushed against a hairy leg. Nestling closer, she pressed her nose against one hard pec and breathed in the intoxicating scent of male in the morning.

Ryan ran a big hand down her back to cup her butt beneath the oversized T-shirt. "Time to get up?" His lips grazed her ear.

She smiled and wiggled against him. "Feels like you already are."

"Oh, yeah." Rolling her over, he slid between her legs and kissed her.

Lost in a haze of need, Leah blinked then focused on the numbers displayed on the digital clock. Her eyes widened, and she shoved hard. "Oh, my God!"

"What?" He drew in a breath as she scrambled out from under him. "What's wrong?"

"The time! Holy hell. I'm going to be late for work." She yanked off the shirt she'd slept in and ran toward the closet. "I forgot to turn on the alarm last night."

"Oh." He propped up the pillows and leaned back against them.

When she turned, holding a long paisley skirt, his eyes glazed as he stared at her bare breasts.

"Leah?"

"What?" She snatched a lacy bra from the open dresser drawer and slid her arms through the straps.

"Naked and frantic is a good look on you. I can't begin to tell you how hot you are right now."

His sultry blue eyes gave her pause . . . but only for a moment. "We can't. The kids will be lining up at the classroom door in exactly fifteen minutes." She shimmied into purple panties before yanking a black shirt over her head.

"Fine, but I'm going to walk around all day with a hard-on, just thinking about how you look when you roll out of bed in the morning."

Leah fastened the waistband of her skirt and shoved her feet into ankle boots without bothering with socks. "I sympathize." Her gaze dropped to the sheet tented over his lap. "But I'm still leaving." She hustled into the bathroom, swirled mouthwash and spit, then attacked her hair with a brush. "Okay, I'm out of here."

He strolled out into the hall wearing nothing but his jeans. He hadn't bothered to button them, and the fact that he didn't have anything on underneath was evident. She gripped the doorframe and swallowed hard.

His eyes sparkled. "No time for coffee?"

"Afraid not." She dragged her gaze upward and ran down the stairs. Sprinting into the living room, she picked up the folder full of vocabulary tests and stuck them in the top of the bag she'd left on the end of the couch.

Ryan grabbed her as she dashed past on the way to the front door and dropped a kiss on her lips. "Have a good day. I'll see you this afternoon." He held up her car keys.

"Thanks. You, too."

Flinging open the front door, she took two steps and stopped. The big planter that held petunias during the summer was tipped on its side. Dirt was scattered across the porch.

"That was the thump I heard last night." She glanced over her shoulder. "Did you trip over the planter before going around to the back door?"

Ryan stopped beside her and frowned. "No, I went straight through the carport to the kitchen entrance."

"If you didn't knock it over . . ." She gripped his arm. "I wasn't imagining a bogeyman last night. Someone was out here in the fog, sneaking around my house."

He slammed a hand down on the porch railing. "That means whoever wants those pictures hasn't given up."

Chapter Twenty-two

Ryan wiped off the counter, hung up the rag, then glanced at his watch. School would be letting out shortly. Picking up his phone, he texted Leah. **Are you going straight home?**

"What's in the pot? It smells good in here."

He looked up when his mom strolled into the kitchen. "I made vegetarian chili."

"Hmm, Leah must be converting you."

When his phone dinged, Ryan glanced at the display. An unfamiliar number, so he let it go to voice mail. "Or, I just like making her happy." When his cell chimed a second time, he smiled.

Homework to correct. Home in thirty.

He unlocked his phone and tapped a response. **Come to my mom's. Veggie chili.**

Yum. Barney first. Be there soon.

He set the phone back on the table then glanced over at his mom. "Leah's coming here for dinner."

"Excellent. I'm going outside to finish cutting

back my roses." She tapped her cast. "A slow job with one good arm."

"I can help you."

"No need. It's a beautiful day, and I'll enjoy the fresh air."

"In that case, maybe I'll walk Leah's dog for her. Can you give the chili a stir every now and then?"

"Of course. Have a good time."

After she left the room, he checked the unknown number on his cell and listened to the message.

"This is Bill Stannard with the Coos Bay Police Department. Please give me a call at your earliest convenience."

Had the man uncovered new information already? Crossing his fingers, Ryan tapped his screen to respond. "Detective Stannard, this is Ryan Alexander returning your call."

"Thanks for getting back to me. You said you have other copies of those photos?"

"We have three more similar to the ones I gave you, along with the negatives. Why?"

There was a pause before the detective cleared his throat. "Someone broke into my desk drawer last night and took the pictures you left."

"You're kidding?"

"I wish. Under the circumstances, I have to assume it was a fellow cop. Either that or someone on the janitorial staff who has access to my office. We're investigating, but I wanted to make sure the other photos were someplace safe."

"They are." Ryan stared out the window over the kitchen sink as his mom appeared in the yard carrying gloves, a pair of clippers, and a flat basket. The folder with the photos was locked up in his Jeep. "An intruder may have been sneaking around Leah Grayson's yard last night shortly before I got back. Possibly he was looking for a way into the house."

"Was her property damaged?"

"Just a tipped-over planter. I must have scared him away when I pulled into the driveway. The timing was right."

"Damn." Stannard let out a harsh breath. "Do you want to bring those pictures down here so you won't be a target?"

"Not really. I'm busy right now, and—"

"You don't intend to turn them over to your local police force?"

Ryan scowled. "Not when you suspect a cop took the other two. I don't know who I can trust anymore."

"Point taken. I have commitments the rest of the day, but I'll try to drive up to Siren Cove first thing tomorrow morning. I'm concerned about your safety while you have those photos in your possession."

"I know you weren't prowling around Leah's house last night. Since I can't say that about anyone else, I'm fine with handing them over to you."

"I'll be in touch."

Ryan disconnected and shoved his phone in his pocket. At the rate he was going, he'd barely get to Leah's place before she did. And the last thing he wanted was for her to walk into an empty house. Or worse, one that wasn't empty at all.

* * *

Leah drove straight through town and left behind what little traffic there was as she headed down the empty stretch of road toward home. Despite the worry that had eaten at her all day, a smile formed. Maybe she and Ryan had plenty to work out between them, but he'd certainly been a rock when she needed one. That was reason enough to love the man.

A road construction vehicle parked along the edge of the highway pulled out behind her and accelerated with a roar of exhaust. Her brows shot up in surprise. Rock slides usually only happened during bad weather, and it hadn't rained recently.

Her thoughts returned to Ryan. He cooked. Reason number two to be crazy about him. He also looked extremely hot lying against rumpled sheets first thing in the morning . . .

A blur of movement in her rearview mirror caught her attention just before a jolting impact sent her car careening across the road toward the cliff. Flung forward against the steering wheel, a scream wrenched from her throat as she struggled to correct the skid. A second hard slam pushed her into the guardrail with a shriek of metal on metal. Before she could react—or even think—the barrier gave way, and her car nosedived over the edge of the cliff. It pitched downward at a steep angle and smashed into a boulder at the base with a tremendous crunch.

At some point, her airbag had deployed. Leah coughed and choked as white dust settled over her. Her ears rang, and her head ached. Something damp ran down the side of her face. She lifted a shaking hand to touch her hair, winced, and stared at the blood on her fingers.

Her teeth chattered as she shoved against the door, but it only budged a few inches. When the passenger side opened a minute later, she nearly cried in relief. A fluorescent yellow vest filled her field of vision.

"Thank heavens. I'm stuck." Her voice sounded wobbly, even to her own ears.

"Shit. You're like the freaking Energizer Bunny. Nothing stops you. Where the fuck are those pictures?"

Leah cringed back against the seat. She couldn't breathe. Couldn't force words past the knot of fear lodged in her throat.

A hand in a leather work glove grabbed her purse off the floor on the passenger side and up-ended it onto the seat. Half the contents slid out of the car and clattered onto the rocks below. "They aren't in here. Where the hell are they?"

"Leah!" The faint shout, along with deep barks, carried on the breeze from far down the beach.

The yellow vest disappeared, and boots smacked against the rocks. A running figure was just visible through the windshield, fractured like a giant spiderweb in front of her face.

Fighting off panic, she tried to shout out a response, but her voice broke. "Help. Help!"

Footsteps slapped the sand, growing closer. Whining sounded as nails scratched against rocks before a furry face thrust through the door opening.

"Barney." Tears ran down her cheeks. "I'm okay, baby." She stroked his head as he licked her chin.

"Leah." Breathing hard, Ryan pushed the dog away and crouched down to look in at her. "How badly are you hurt?"

"I don't know. I cut my head, but it isn't bleeding too horribly. My legs are jammed against the dash, but nothing hurts." She shifted and winced. "Not much, anyway. My door won't open."

He reached over to release her seat belt. "Let's see if I can pull you out." His worried gaze met hers. "Can you feel everything? Both your legs will move?"

"Yeah. I'm just kind of wedged in."

"Okay, then I'll try a little gentle force." He grasped her under the arms and tugged until she sprawled halfway across the passenger seat.

"I think my skirt's caught."

He took hold of the material and ripped. "There. I got it loose." Holding tight around her middle, he pulled steadily.

Her legs slid out from under the steering wheel, and she landed on top of him. When they fell backward against a boulder, Barney danced and barked in a circle around them.

Ryan kissed her forehead and let out a shaky breath. "When your car smashed against the rocks like a squashed tin can, I nearly had a heart attack. Jesus, Leah."

"You saw me go over the cliff?"

He nodded. "I'd just gotten to your house, and Barney was running around the yard, acting all hyper. I planned to take him for a quick walk and had just started down the trail to the beach when I heard a loud impact. I glanced up as your car broke through the guardrail."

"It all happened so fast." She pressed her face against his shoulder. "I didn't have time to be frightened until it was over."

In the distance, a siren wailed, growing louder.

She huddled closer to Ryan's chest as his arms tightened around her. "Someone must have called nine-one-one."

"I reported the accident while I was sprinting up the beach."

"Did you see the man running away from my car?"

Ryan jerked back. "No! What the hell?"

She nodded. "A plow truck rammed me. Then the freak driving it climbed down to search for those pictures. He was shocked to find me still alive."

"Who was he?" Ryan bit off each word. "Give me a name, and I'll kill the bastard."

"I don't know." Her words ended on a tearful sob. "I only saw the fluorescent vest he was wearing. Then you shouted, and he ran off. But I couldn't make out any details through the shattered windshield."

"I was focused on the trail when I yelled. I didn't want to fall on my face. He must have stayed close to the base of the cliff to avoid being visible."

The sirens suddenly cut off, and loud voices drifted on the breeze.

Ryan kissed her again, a gentle caress. "I'm just so damn thankful you survived that crash." He shifted out from behind her. "Stay put while I go talk to the emergency responders, then we'll get you out of here."

The next two hours passed in a blur. The paramedics assessed her injuries and concluded she had a badly bruised knee and diaphragm, a gash at her hairline, and possible internal injuries. Once they hauled her up the cliff face in a sling, Leah agreed to go to the ER. After being subjected to a series of tests, the doctor in charge determined her spleen was bruised but not ruptured. The nurse cleaned and bandaged the cut at her temple and iced her knee. Pronounced fit to go home, she leaned back in the wheelchair as Ryan pushed her toward the exit.

"Leah, are you feeling up to giving me a statement now?" Chris Long stood near the sliding glass doors leading to the parking lot. "I wanted to question you earlier, but the staff refused to let me go back there while you were being examined. I know you're probably exhausted and in pain, but I need your account of the incident."

"Can we do this back at Leah's house?" Ryan asked abruptly.

Chris gave her another quick once-over and must have decided she looked like crap. He gave a quick nod. "Fine. I'll follow you there."

"Thank you. I appreciate that." Leah reached up to pat Ryan's hand. "Let's go, but you'll have to keep it under eighty since we'll have a cop on our tail."

The officer cracked a smile. "At least you can still joke. I'll see you shortly."

After Ryan helped her into his Jeep and returned the wheelchair, she settled carefully against the seat and forced her mind to go blank. For the length of time it took to drive home from the hospital, she didn't want to think about . . . anything. Ryan seemed to understand. He kept quiet as he started the engine and pulled out of the parking lot onto the road. They'd gone a good five miles before she opened her eyes to stare out into the dark. The headlights slashed through the night, illuminating the winding road ahead.

"Thank you for being there for me through this. Odd, but that's what I was thinking when that homicidal maniac slammed into my car. You've been a rock when I needed you." She waved a hand toward the three stone monoliths in the cove, outlined in the moonlight. "As steadfast as one of the Sirens."

"Hopefully I haven't been the one drawing you closer to disaster. I don't know why that asshole went after you instead of me. Why did he think you were the one who had the pictures?"

"Kind of makes sense." Leah sighed. "I had the film originally, and you turned over two of the prints to the cops in Coos Bay."

"So, he reasoned you were holding on to any remaining photos." He slammed his hand down on the steering wheel. "Damn, I hate this."

"Me, too." Her head ached, and thinking was an effort. "What should we tell Chris Long?"

Ryan glanced over before returning his attention to the road. "A version of the truth, I guess."

"And if his dad is involved? What if Chris is willing to do anything to conceal his father's crime?"

"Then we'll cover our asses and call the police

chief ourselves. We'll tell Long we want Chief Stack-house to hear what happened straight from us."

"Smart. Very smart." Leah pulled her phone out of her purse, thankful she'd had the presence of mind to ask Ryan to collect all her belongings before she abandoned her car to the wrecker. "I have his personal number. I'll call him right now."

By the time they parked in her driveway, Chief Stackhouse had assured her he was on his way. She dropped her phone back in her bag and glanced over her shoulder as Chris Long pulled up behind them.

"Don't move. I'll help you inside." Ryan opened his door. "I don't want you putting any pressure on that knee."

She nodded and waited as he hurried around to her side of the car. "Good thing I have a pair of crutches in one of the closets from when my grandpa had hip surgery a dozen years ago."

"I'll find them for you after the cops leave." Ryan slid his arm around her waist and fended off Barney, who barked and jumped in excitement. "Do you have your keys?"

Leah sorted through her bag and handed them over before sliding off the seat. Leaning on him, she limped into the carport. Behind them, a door slammed and gravel crunched. She turned and forced a smile as the officer approached.

"I'll be happy to have this over with. I gave Chief Stackhouse a call." Her mouth strained to keep the smile in place. "I didn't want to have to repeat the whole story again."

The officer nodded and eyed the dog when Barney growled and stared out into the dark. "Good idea."

Ryan unlocked the kitchen door, pushed it open, then reached inside to flip on the light. He took one step and stopped so fast, Leah smacked up against him.

"Holy hell."

"What?" She peered around him and gasped.

"Someone trashed the place. Again."

Chapter Twenty-three

"Where, exactly, are the rest of the photos now?"

Ryan gripped Leah's hand as he faced the police chief across the coffee table and lied through his teeth. "That's the thing. There aren't any more pictures. The film was damp, and most of the roll was unsalvageable. I gave the only two prints I was able to recover to Detective Stannard."

Officer Long glanced up from his notepad. "And the negatives?"

"I had them in a folder open on the counter, and I'm afraid I splashed coffee on them. I chucked the ruined negatives in the trash before I took the prints to Stannard. Otherwise, I would have given those to him, too."

Stackhouse glanced from Ryan to Leah and back. "Now, why is it you drove all the way down to Coos Bay to turn over those photographs when you could just as easily have given them to Chris here, or to me?" The chief hunched forward and planted his elbows on his knees. "Am I missing a piece of the puzzle?"

"Curiosity." Leah gave a nervous laugh. "And you know what they say about curiosity killing the cat. I think I used up one of my nine lives today."

Stackhouse frowned. "I'm afraid I don't understand."

Ryan jumped in before Leah could speak. "My mom told me about the detectives who questioned Mrs. Winston, our school principal, back when we buried the time capsule. I got to wondering about that, since those photos were so strange."

"You said the pictures showed men in hooded cloaks around a bonfire." Chris Long frowned. "Sounds like a Halloween party to me."

Ryan squeezed Leah's fingers so hard she winced. "Except there was a naked woman stretched out in the center of the ring."

The clock over the mantel ticked loudly in the ensuing silence.

"Jesus," the younger cop said softly.

"As I said, strange and . . . disturbing." Ryan let out a breath and relaxed his grip on Leah's hand. "Our curiosity was roused, so I talked to Mrs. Winston. She mentioned the hitchhiker who'd vanished that October, the girl she'd passed, out on the highway. I couldn't help wondering if there was any connection between her disappearance and the photos on the film buried in the time capsule. I figured taking the pictures to the original detective in charge of the case was the right move."

"Except the pictures were stolen out of his possession." Stackhouse grunted. "I would have been more careful with evidence."

"Honestly, at this point, I couldn't care less. They're gone for good." Tears thickened Leah's voice. "I just wish whoever wants the damned things knew we don't have them anymore so he'd stop trying to kill me."

Officer Long glanced at his superior. "Chief, maybe we can try to spread the word. I don't like the idea that someone might come after either Leah or Ryan again."

"That might work. This is a small community. If all my men drop a casual comment here and there around town, the news will spread faster than fleas on a hound." His lips curled as he gazed at Barney, scratching furiously behind one ear. "My guess is you'll be safe enough in short order." His attention returned to Leah. "You're certain you aren't able to identify the man who ran you off the road?"

"He was probably of average height and weight. He wore jeans with a fluorescent yellow vest over a dark shirt, and gloves. That's all I saw."

"What about his voice?" Long held his pen poised over the notebook. "He spoke to you, so possibly you noticed something distinctive."

"He was yelling. Swearing. I was so scared I didn't pay much attention to his diction." She closed her eyes. "No odd accent, I'm certain of that. People sound different when they shout—high and whiny—and he only said a few words. I don't know if I'd be able to identify him if he spoke in a normal tone, but I'd certainly be willing to try."

The officer closed his notebook and slipped it into his pocket. "If you remember anything else, call us."

Stackhouse rose to his feet and smiled at Leah. "We'll need to process your home for evidence. At least the perp didn't make as big of a mess this time. I assume you have someplace you can go for the night?"

"My mom's house." Ryan released her hand and stood. "I'll go get Leah a change of clothes and a pair of crutches, if that's okay, and then we'll get out of your way."

"I'll come with you." Chris Long followed him from the room and up the stairs.

Ryan found the crutches in a closet in one of the spare bedrooms, then efficiently loaded an overnight bag with the bare essentials. At least he hoped he'd gotten everything Leah would need. Officer Long leaned against the doorframe while he packed. *To make sure I don't sneak the missing photos into the bag along with her clean underwear?* He had no idea if the two cops had believed his lies, but he sure as hell hoped so.

"That should do it." He shut the dresser drawer and lifted the crutches off the bed.

Long straightened. "Great. We'll do our best to keep the mess to a minimum when we dust for prints, but it has to be done. Hopefully the perp screwed up this time and left evidence."

"The guy seems pretty damned cautious. I'm surprised he spoke in Leah's presence."

"Could be he wasn't planning to leave her there alive, but you screwed up his plans."

A chill blasted through Ryan as he snapped off the bedroom light and headed downstairs with the cop following him. "You mentioned earlier this freak just walked onto the lot where the road crews leave their vehicles and drove off in one of them?"

"Yes. A few of the men we questioned admitted to leaving the keys in the ignition of the trucks since the gates are locked after hours."

Ryan stopped at the foot of the stairs. "But this SOB swiped the plow truck before they closed the gates and probably wore the vest so a casual observer wouldn't see anything unusual."

"Pretty damned smart," Long agreed. "They're easier to catch when they're stupid."

"I imagine. You'll contact us if there's any news?"

"Of course."

As the cop turned toward the kitchen, Ryan hurried into the living room. Approaching the couch, he held out the crutches to Leah. "Here you go."

"Thanks." She rose with a slight wince to take them from him, then glanced over at the chief. "Unless you need anything else?"

"Not right now." He patted her arm. "I'm sorry you were hurt, but after a crash like that, I'd say you were pretty fortunate it wasn't a whole lot worse."

"I guess so, but I certainly don't feel lucky. Thanks for coming out to personally supervise my case. I appreciate it."

"You bet. Take care, Leah."

Ryan nodded as he passed. With a moan, Barney surged to his feet and followed them out of the house into the chilly night air.

"All I want is to wake up in the morning to discover this whole day was nothing but a nightmare." She leaned against the Jeep, head hanging, as he unlocked the door.

"We'll deal with all the complications." He raised her chin with a gentle hand and dropped a kiss on her lips. "Together." After Barney jumped into the back, Ryan stowed the crutches before helping Leah onto the passenger seat. "I know it sucks. The last time I felt like my life was this out of control was when Jay stole Intersect out from under me."

She glanced over and smiled. "I guess that didn't turn out so badly."

"No, and we'll get through this ordeal, too."

"One can only hope."

"You know I can't simply run away from all my problems, right?" Leah rolled down the window and breathed in the scent of pine as they bumped down the narrow road. "Not that I wouldn't like to."

"We're simply putting them on hold for the weekend. No harm in that."

Ryan drove into a small clearing and parked in front of an adorable cabin that reminded Leah of a fairy-tale cottage. In the distance, the Three Sisters towered over the forest of evergreens that backed up to Ryan's property.

"I love your home." She opened the door, then grunted when Barney jumped across the center console onto her lap before leaping to freedom. "Do you have seven dwarves stashed somewhere?"

"Funny." Ryan climbed out and lifted the cat carrier from the back seat. "My house is small but functional. Charlie and I don't need a lot of room."

"I don't know about that. Charlie's presence is immeasurable, despite his physical size. Barney is terrified of him."

"Your dog's a big chicken." Ryan released the latch on the gated front of the container and lifted his cat to the ground. Charlie strolled toward the cabin, tail twitching as Barney backed cautiously away.

"Apparently, Barney knows who's boss."

Ryan circled the Jeep and slipped an arm around her waist. "Let's head inside. I'll get the bags later."

"I wish I could go for a hike in the woods with you. It really is beautiful here." Leah clamped her teeth together as a twinge of pain zinged through her knee.

"Next time." Pulling the keys from his pocket, he unlocked the front door and waited for the cat to precede them inside. "You should still be using those crutches."

"My knee feels a whole lot better, the swelling has gone down, and after a full day of walking with crutches, I'm over the damned things. I know it'll be a while before I can do anything strenuous, but I can get around the house unaided."

He squeezed her to his side. "I like aiding you,

but I'd rather take you rock climbing. That'll have to wait."

"For me, yes, but I know you're dying to go." Leah glanced around the main room of his perfectly tidy cabin. "Wow, I really am an unorganized mess. I'm surprised you can stand hanging out in my house."

"I'm learning I can put up with a lot when I have the right motivation." He led her to a stool at the kitchen counter. "Sit."

She followed orders. "Should I be flattered or appalled that I'm corrupting you?"

"Flattered. Shall we have lunch?"

"After that huge breakfast? I'm not hungry."

His gaze slid toward the ropes and harnesses and other paraphernalia hanging on hooks in the mudroom. "We can play cards or work on a puzzle or—"

She dropped a hand onto his arm. "Go. Do your own thing. Please. I agreed to come with you because I needed a break from stressing over who might try to kill me next." Her grip tightened. "But if you hover over me all weekend, I may scream."

He grinned. "Can't have you turning into a raving lunatic. Fine, I'll go. I expect you can entertain yourself."

"Thank you." She rolled her eyes. "I'm a big girl now."

"Funny."

"I try." She waved a hand. "We can go out to dinner after you get home, since I doubt you have much food in the house. Then maybe stop by the store for milk and eggs and a few other necessities."

"I have nonperishables in the pantry. You can heat up a can of soup if you get hungry later." He cupped her face in his hands and kissed her. "You rock. You know that, right?"

"What, because I don't cling? That's not my style. Have a good time, but try not to hurt yourself. Can't have both of us gimping around."

He grinned. "I do love your sense of humor." He kissed her again. "I'll change, grab a couple of protein bars and my equipment, then I'm out of here."

"Great, but bring those bags in first."

Twenty minutes later, Leah was alone with the cat—who seemed to delight in tormenting her dog by stalking his every move—and a quivering canine. She eyed Charlie. "You're just plain mean. You know that, right?"

The cat narrowed his eyes at her.

"Fine." She limped to the door. "Out, Barney. Go chase a squirrel or something."

Her cell phone rang as she headed back toward the kitchen. Hobbling as fast as she could go, she scooped it up just before it went to voice mail.

"Hello."

"You'll never guess who just called me."

Leah rounded the end of the counter and opened the freezer door. "Hi, Grandma. Who?"

"Do you remember Milly Harrington? Your grandpa and I used to play bridge with Milly and Fred." Her voice lowered. "You didn't hear this from me, but the Harringtons were swingers back in the day."

"I remember her." After searching through two pullout bins, Leah extracted a bag of frozen mangos. Her damn knee had started to ache again.

"Milly's a widow now, too. A few years back, she moved to a senior community similar to mine up in Astoria to be closer to her daughter." Gram's tone filled with a hint of superiority. "I guess everyone isn't as self-sufficient as I am."

Leah's smile faded as she hitched herself up onto a stool, extended her leg across a second seat, and slapped the frozen fruit onto her knee. Her grandma wouldn't be able to live alone much longer, either, now that she was broke. "Astoria? That's where Brock lives."

"He does? I'd forgotten. That man . . . well, never mind. You know my feelings on the subject of your ex-husband."

"Only too well."

"Anyway, Milly heard I got taken by that con man back in September. Flo, who does my hair, is the worst sort of gossip, and they're friends."

Her knee was going numb, which, Leah supposed, was the point. She wasn't certain Gram's rambling narrative had one. "Uh, is there a reason you called to chat about Milly?"

"Well, of course. One of Milly's neighbors stopped by to tell her all about this handsome young man who'd offered her an investment opportunity she simply couldn't pass up. Sometime during the conversation, Milly remembered Flo's story about me."

Leah straightened and clenched the cell a little tighter. "Investing in real estate?"

"That's right."

"What was this man's name?"

"Eric Hilliard. But Milly's neighbor mentioned something funny. She said the man reminded her of Ricky Nelson, who was a big heartthrob back in the fifties and sixties."

The mangos slipped out of Leah's hand and smacked against the floor. "You're kidding?"

"I'm not. Do you think there might be a connection to my con man?"

"I certainly do. Did Milly contact her neighbor and urge her to report this guy?"

"Since I gave her an earful, she definitely plans to." Her grandma chuckled. "She was all atwitter, talking about busting this case wide open. I think Milly's been watching too many cop shows. Anyway, I called you as soon as I hung up."

"This could be the break we've been waiting for. If Hilliard, or whatever he's calling himself, makes a second trip to see this woman . . ."

"The police could nab him . . . and I might get all my money back."

Leah frowned. "It's a little strange this jerk is hitting another retirement community so soon after robbing you. It was months between his previous cons."

"Maybe he needs more cash for some reason. I hope it doesn't mean he spent all of mine."

"Grandma, can you call our local police station? They should be brought up-to-date since they're investigating this man . . . if he's the same person. Just tell them everything you told me."

"I still have that nice Officer Long's business card. I'll call him directly."

"You do that. I'll touch base with you tomorrow night after Ryan and I get home."

"Okay. Bye, Leah."

She set down her cell then swooped to grab the bag of mangos off the floor. Closing her eyes, she said a little prayer the cops would soon catch the bastard stealing from seniors. When her phone rang again, she answered without checking the display. "Did you forget something, Gram?"

"It's Brock."

Her eyes popped open. "I mention your name, and suddenly you call me? Weird. What do you want?"

"I guess the reports of your near demise were exaggerated. You're your usual snarky self."

She scowled. "Someone told you I was in a car wreck?"

"Pete mentioned it. I know we aren't on the best terms, but I didn't like hearing you'd been hauled off to the hospital in an ambulance."

A long breath hissed out. "I appreciate that. Apparently someone else isn't nearly as concerned for my health."

"Huh?"

"The crash was no accident. Someone shoved my car off that cliff on purpose."

"Why the hell would anyone do that?"

She pressed a hand to her forehead as her head began to throb. "Long story. This person thought I had incriminating evidence from an old crime. Some photos."

"Do you?"

Leah hesitated for a moment as her mind flashed to Ryan handing over the remaining pictures and negatives to Detective Stannard the previous morning. "No, I don't, thank God."

"Then why—"

"As I said before, long story. But hopefully word has spread by now, and this freak will leave me alone in the future."

"I really don't wish you ill, Leah."

He probably believed every word of his declaration. In Brock's small mind, emotional wounds didn't count for much.

"Great. Thanks for calling."

His voice rose. "Wait. Why'd you mention my name?"

"What?"

"When you answered the phone, you said you'd just mentioned my name."

"Oh, yeah." Leah massaged her temples. "My grandma called. I don't know if you heard, but some bastard scammed her and robbed her blind."

"If you think I—"

"That's not what I was implying. Gram would have recognized you, so don't get your shorts in a knot. Anyway, this loser is now preying on elderly women in Astoria. I mentioned you live there."

"Oh. Evie isn't exactly a fan of mine, so I thought . . . Never mind. Someone stole all her money?"

"Damn near every cent. She's going to have to move in with me."

"Unfortunate." Brock's tone dripped sarcasm. "I guess that'll kill your sex life with good old Ryan."

"You're a jerk." Leah hung up the phone. "Ass."

Charlie strolled into the room and jumped up onto the stool next to her injured knee. When she reached out to pet him, he batted her hand with his paw, claws extended. A faint line of blood appeared.

Leah rolled her eyes. "Perfect."

Chapter Twenty-four

Leah sat across the table from Ryan, picking at a plate full of chiles rellenos and black beans, while he worked his way through a giant burrito. She glanced up when a blonde, a redhead, and a brunette walked into the restaurant and sat at a table a short distance away. The redhead's gaze zeroed in on the back of Ryan's head before she said something to her companions. All three women looked their way.

"Leah."

"Huh?" She jerked her attention back to Ryan.

"What happened when this bastard's latest victim called the cops in Astoria?"

"Hilliard had promised to meet the woman at her home with the contract to sign and asked her to have a check ready. The cops were waiting for him, but he never showed."

Ryan set down his fork and frowned. "That's odd. You'd think he'd be punctual when it came to cashing in on his scam. Did he contact her about a different meeting time?"

"He hadn't when I spoke to Chris Long. Chris filled me in on the details while you were in the shower. The police think maybe the guy was tipped off."

"Who would have told him? No one knew Hilliard was under investigation except your grandma and her friend, the cops in Siren Cove, and the police in Astoria."

"It doesn't make any sense. I'm sure Milly didn't blab the news around town." Leah poked at her relleno as her appetite faded. "I'd so hoped they would nail the jerk. By the way, I looked up this new alias online. What do you know, Ricky Nelson's real name was Eric Hilliard Nelson, so the crook in Astoria is definitely the same guy who conned my grandma."

"Idiot. He must think he's clever using these old singers' names. Hopefully it'll trip him up eventually."

"Now would be good. Later isn't going to help us a whole hell of a lot since we can't pay my grandma's November rent."

"I could—" Ryan let out a breath and glanced away. "This conversation is obviously upsetting you." Reaching across the table, he squeezed her arm. "Let's talk about something else. You need to relax."

"Not much chance of that happening." Leah dropped her napkin beside her plate and stood. "I'm going to use the ladies' room. I'll be right back."

His eyes darkened as he met her gaze. "Are you okay?"

"Yeah, I'm fine. Grandma will be, too. Everything will work out somehow." She limped a little as she made her way past the table where the three women sat drinking cocktails. Once she reached the restroom, she used the toilet, then washed her hands at the sink. Worried brown eyes stared back at her as she glanced in the mirror. When the door opened, her gaze shifted, and she gave a little nod to the redhead who walked into the room.

The woman joined her at the sinks and studied her reflection in the mirror for a long moment, opened her mouth, then pressed her lips tightly together.

Leah pulled a paper towel out of the dispenser and dried her hands before wadding it into a ball. Turning, she met the woman's gaze head-on. "Did you want to say something to me?"

"I don't know why I followed you in here. It was a mistake."

"Okay." She tossed the towel in the trash and took two steps toward the door.

"Curiosity, I guess. Or maybe the need to poke a wound that isn't completely healed."

Leah pivoted slowly and eyed the woman, from her red hair twisted into an elegant knot, past hazel eyes that held a hint of defiance, over a tidy suit jacket and pencil skirt, to a pair of heels that made the most of her long legs. "Since I'm pretty certain I've never seen you before, I have to assume you know Ryan."

"We broke up last month."

The breath left her in a rush as she reached out to hold on to the edge of the counter. "He's never talked much about a recent relationship."

"Why am I not surprised? I don't want to cause trouble. I'll go back to my table now." She drew in a couple of quick breaths but made no move to leave. Finally her gaze rose again to meet Leah's. "It's just that you're the exact opposite of me, so I couldn't help wondering if the problem all along wasn't Ryan's issues with commitment and intimacy but the fact that I simply wasn't his type."

This lady had a point. She exuded elegant sophistication. Leah had dressed for comfort in a bright pink sweater over black leggings tucked into heelless suede boots. Subtle makeup made the most of the woman's quiet attraction, while Leah hadn't bothered to do much more than dab a little foundation over the worst of the scabs on the side of her forehead. She still looked like she'd come out the loser in a street brawl.

"Ryan's not into battered waifs, if that's what you're thinking. I was in a car accident a couple of days ago."

The hazel eyes widened. "I just meant you don't look like the uptight sort. I hope you weren't badly injured."

"Scrapes and bruises. I'll live. I'm Leah, by the way."

"Ursula." She held out a hand.

Leah shook it. "Nice to meet you. Commitment and intimacy issues, huh?"

"Look, Ryan's a great guy, but I got the feeling some woman did a real number on him in his past. Trust doesn't come easy for that man." Ursula shrugged. "Maybe you'll be the one to heal those old wounds. I certainly wasn't."

Leah swallowed hard. Any possible response stuck in her throat.

"Unless you only want no-strings fun. Then Ryan fills the bill." Ursula's smile looked forced. "Anyway, have a nice evening."

Leah nodded. "Yeah, you, too."

After the other woman left the room, Leah took a few moments to compose herself. If Ryan had trust issues, she was more than likely the cause. Closing her eyes, she pressed her fingers to her lids to hold back tears. Maybe she'd done more damage to him than she realized all those years ago. The knowledge cut deep.

But there wasn't much she could do about it now . . . except try to make it up to him.

Ryan finished his burrito and pushed back his plate, wondering what was taking Leah so long in the bathroom. She'd been visibly upset talking about the con man evading arrest. Tight lines had bracketed her lips, and the hand she used to push her hair behind her ear had been a little unsteady. He'd almost offered to give her a chunk of cash to pay her grandma's rent but had stopped himself at the last second. If he'd learned one thing in his experience with his old college roommate, it was that mixing money into a personal friendship could end in disaster. As much as he wanted to ease Leah's financial concerns, he wouldn't risk screwing up their developing feelings. He cared about her too much.

Glancing over his shoulder, he wondered if he should go check on her. A movement caught his attention, but his relief faded as the woman leaving the restroom turned his way. Not Leah. Ursula. Their gazes locked as she approached. She paused for a moment at a table where two other women sat before continuing toward him.

Slowly he stood. "It's good to see you, Ursula. How are you?"

"Busy as usual. I haven't bumped into you since . . . well, in a while."

"My mom broke her arm. I've been staying in Siren Cove to help her out."

"I'm sorry to hear that. Is that where the woman you're with is from?"

"Leah? Yes." He gripped the back of his chair. "Did you—"

"We spoke in the restroom. She seems nice."

"She is. Ursula, I—"

"I won't intrude on your evening. See you around, Ryan."

She walked away before he could respond, and when he tore his gaze from her stiff shoulders, Leah was halfway across the room. He offered a hesitant smile when she reached their table. "I guess you met Ursula."

Leah nodded, her eyes sober. When she glanced down at the food remaining on her plate, her lips twisted. "If you're finished eating, maybe we can go?"

A knot of dread tightened in his stomach. *What the hell did Ursula say to her?* "Sure."

He stopped at the cashier's stand on their way out to pay the bill, then took Leah's arm as they walked outside and crossed the parking lot. A cold wind sent dead leaves scattering across the pavement ahead of them. After he unlocked his Jeep and helped her inside, he ran around the front. By the time he was seated, his nerves were completely shot. He started the engine but made no move to leave.

"Are we going to sit here or drive?"

At Leah's words, he shifted into gear and pulled out of the lot. The minutes ticked by with only the sound of the tires on the asphalt to break the silence. When he couldn't stand the suspense another moment, he spoke. "What did she say to you?"

Leah glanced over. "Ursula? Just that you used to date her. Nice woman."

"Oh."

"And that you have intimacy problems."

He nearly drove off the side of the road. "Are you kidding!" He jerked the wheel and breathed hard through his nose. "Okay, maybe we didn't spend all our time in bed, but—"

"Eww, stop right there!" Leah's voice rose in a screech. "I don't want to hear about that. How would you feel if I told you about my sex life with other men?"

His stomach protested, and he wished he hadn't eaten all of his giant burrito. "A little ill. It's not something I want to think about, but you said—"

"Ursula meant you weren't open about your feelings, not that you couldn't . . . Eww, just eww."

"Okay, I get it. Sorry."

"Are your trust issues my fault?" She turned to stare out the window into the dark forest. "Did I destroy your confidence in women?"

He wanted to deny her words, to take away the misery coloring her voice. But he couldn't lie. "Maybe I'm more cautious than I would have been if you hadn't dumped me our senior year. I don't think that's such a bad thing."

"Closing your heart to love isn't bad?"

"The door isn't completely shut. Maybe just not wide-open." He slowed to turn onto the dirt track leading to his house. "If you hadn't taught me a lesson in relationship reality early on, someone else would have. I learned not to have unrealistic expectations."

Turning in her seat, she dropped a hand on his thigh. "If you won't allow yourself to be vulnerable, you aren't able to experience the joy of totally surrendering your emotional well-being to another person. How can you be happy holding part of yourself back? How can you make the person you love happy?"

"Does it seem like I'm holding back with you? I'd have to say I've been pretty damn open." He pulled up in front of his home and cut the engine. In the silence that followed, the motor ticked as it cooled. "You didn't ruin me for other women, if that's what you're thinking."

"I'm not that egotistical." Her lashes fluttered across her cheeks before she opened her eyes and seemed to stare straight into his soul. "Anyway, if I did, I sort of screwed myself in the process. Ironic, don't you think."

He covered the hand still resting on his leg and squeezed. "This is me, putting myself out there. I love you, Leah. If I held back with Ursula, it was because my feelings weren't . . . engaged. She didn't twist me up inside like a pretzel the way you do. Are you happy?"

A slow smile spread. "Yeah, I'm happy. That's about the sweetest thing anyone has ever said to me."

"Great. Can we go in now?"

"Yep." She opened her door and stepped out, then regarded him across the hood of the Jeep when he joined her. "I'm going to make your night worth every one of those knots."

"You are?"

"I am." She held out her hand. "Let's go make it happen."

His heart beat faster as he walked beside her to the door. When he opened it, Barney pushed through, knocking Leah against him. The dog ran in circles, barking and wagging in a frenzy of joy, like a convict released early for good behavior. Ryan spared a moment to wonder what the cat had done to him in their absence, before ushering Leah inside with a hand on the warm curve of her waist.

"I guess bed will have to wait."

He snapped on the light in the entry as disappointment filled him. "Okay."

Reaching up, she ran a finger across his lower lip. "Only until Barney stops going crazy. He's not used to being stuck in the house, but I was worried he'd run off and get lost if I left him outside."

"Oh, I thought maybe you changed your mind."

"Why would I do that?"

"You haven't exactly had a peaceful evening. I know you're stressed."

"Yeah, I am." Her eyes glimmered with a teasing light. "There's nothing like a little crazy sex to relax a person."

Ryan pulled her close. "You never fail to make me smile." He kissed her, deepening the contact when she let out a little moan. After the dog strolled back inside, he kicked the door shut and scooped her into his arms.

"Don't hurt yourself!" She clung to his shoulders as he started up the stairs.

"Don't worry. I'm not going to drop you." He reached the top, only slightly out of breath, and turned into his loft bedroom.

"I'm not worried." She stroked the back of his neck with her thumb. "I trust you completely. Ryan?"

"Hmm?" He lowered her onto his bed, sat down next to her, then clicked on the bedside lamp before stretching out at her side.

"I was young and stupid back in high school. Believing we wouldn't be able to make our relationship work simply because we're different was the biggest mistake I've ever made. I'm sorry I hurt you. I'm sorry we lost all those years together."

He tucked her close to his chest. "Maybe it was for the best."

She stared up at him, her eyes wide. "Why?"

"You're right. We were both young. Maybe we needed to experience life before we could see that what we have together is strong and beautiful and damn near perfect."

"I had to marry a toad before I could have my prince?"

"I guess so."

"Since it appears you dated lovely women like Ursula rather than slimeballs, I can only be thankful none of them broke through your walls. Maybe that's horrible, but you're the missing ingredient in my recipe for happiness. Maybe my life wouldn't have been ruined if we hadn't found each other again, but it would always have lacked . . . heart."

He kissed her, more grateful for Leah than he could express in words. "If you'd still been married to Brock—"

She pressed a finger to his lips. "Not a chance."

"I guess we both have a lot to be thankful for."

"So, maybe we can show each other how we feel after we shed a few layers of clothes."

He smiled. "I need to take out my contacts first."

"And I want to brush my teeth." She laughed. "The movies always gloss over the mundane details."

He levered up off the bed and held out a hand to pull her up beside him. "But this is reality, and in my book, that's a whole lot better than any fantasy."

"Agreed."

There was something incredibly sexy about watching Leah brush her teeth while wearing nothing but a skimpy black bra and panties. After Ryan removed his contacts, her image blurred around the edges, but the soft haze only added to the mystery.

She rinsed her mouth, then moved behind him to wrap her arms around his waist and lean against his bare back. His fist clenched, shooting out a stream of toothpaste into the sink.

"Oops."

"A little premature, don't you think?"

He grinned at her reflection as she peeked over his shoulder, brown eyes alight with humor. "Your fault entirely."

She kissed the back of his neck. "Hurry."

Ryan brushed his teeth in record time then reached down to unfasten his jeans. He slid them over his hips and kicked them toward the clothes basket in the corner. When they missed, he didn't even care. Turning to pull Leah into his arms, his entire focus was on the beautiful woman he held. "I'm ready."

She pressed closer. "I'll say."

He fumbled with the clasp of her bra. A moment later, it fell to the floor at their feet. Sliding his hands down her smooth skin, he hooked his fingers beneath the elastic of her panties and tugged. The lace ripped, and he tossed the scrap of cloth on the tile before spinning around to lift her up onto the counter next to the sink. Heat suffused him as she tossed her head back to let her silky hair puddle around her hips.

"Oh, God." The tips of her breasts pearled into hard peaks.

Eyes wide open, he pushed into her and nearly came apart as her face went slack with desire. Gripping her firm flesh, he pumped hard, never taking his eyes off her until she cried out and slumped against him. Then, and only then, did he let himself explode . . .

"Your son is a freaking idiot. I told you using those names was a huge risk, but he thought he was so clever. And what the hell was he thinking, striking again so soon after the last con? That's just asking for trouble."

"I'll speak to him." The pulse throbbed at his temples as he slumped against the counter with his head in his hands, his cell phone clamped to one ear. "He says he wants to relocate and start his own business, and he's stockpiling the funds to do it."

"Screw him and his plans. Samhain is nearly here. It's been ten long years, and we have our sacrifice waiting. The last thing we need is to have anyone come snooping around, following leads. I'd turn him in myself before I let that happen."

His voice came out in a hiss. "Don't threaten me or mine. My boy's been generous about funding the Brotherhood with his proceeds."

"Only because I saved his hide last year by convincing a buddy of mine to hide evidence."

"I suppose that sounds better than blackmail."

The seconds ticked by in silence before the cool voice filled his ear. "Are you complaining?"

"No, of course not." He let out a slow breath. "I'm grateful."

"Then keep your kid under control. In fact, tell him his little game is over. I won't risk him bringing unwanted attention our way." The voice on the other end of the line lashed out. "I won't see a centuries-old tradition destroyed because of your greedy whelp. Got it?"

"Yeah, I got it. He had a close call up in Astoria, and it shook him. He won't do anything stupid."

"He better not."

When the line went dead, he dropped the phone on the counter. He'd had enough of this shit storm that never seemed to let up. At least he could relax, knowing those damn photographs were no longer a threat. He'd given himself an ulcer for nothing.

Maybe he was blowing this latest problem out of proportion, too. He'd make sure his son didn't take any more risks, and their Samhain celebration would go off without a hitch.

Anything less was unthinkable.

Chapter Twenty-five

Leah covered the knickknacks with a final layer of newspaper, closed the flaps on the box, and sealed it with a piece of packing tape. Straightening from her bent position, she stretched to work the kinks out of her back and glanced around the apartment. "I think we're making progress."

Her grandma turned away from the half-empty bookshelf and nodded. "It looks barren in here with only furniture. No pizzazz."

Leah smiled. "You do have a style all your own."

"Magnus calls my *style* Early American Clutter, but what does he know. His apartment looks like a monk's chamber. It'll benefit from a few trinkets to dress it up." Hands on her hips, her grandma surveyed the living room. "I don't think there's enough room to move over most of my furniture, though."

"We can fit your rocker by the window and re-place my coffee table, since yours is nicer. What furniture we don't sell at the yard sale, we can donate to charity if it comes to that. Have you decided if you want to keep your bedroom set?"

"Definitely. There isn't much of anything other than a desk in the spare room, so my stuff will outfit it in style."

Leah frowned. "What spare room? All the bedrooms have furniture."

"Magnus's second bedroom. His apartment is bigger than mine."

"So you're giving him your furniture? I guess that's one way to get rid of it. Less to move to my house."

"Why would I move my furniture to your house?"

Leah wondered if Gram was beginning to lose it. "Am I missing something? What the heck are you talking about?"

"Geez, Leah, I *told* you I'm staying put." She returned to packing books. "I *told* you not to worry, that I had the situation under control and wouldn't need to move in with you."

"Yes, but that was when we thought the police were going to bust the con artist. They didn't, so your money wasn't recovered."

"I'm not happy about that, but my basic plan didn't change. Over the weekend, Magnus asked me to move in with him. It only took a little nudging on my part." She glanced over her shoulder. "Do you think this box will be too heavy to lift?"

"When, exactly, were you planning to tell me this?"

"I did tell you, but I don't think you were paying attention."

Probably because I was thinking about Ryan.

"Gram, you can't move in with Magnus." Her voice rose. "You've only known him a few months."

"So? At our age, why waste time. We aren't going crazy and planning a wedding or anything." Her eyes gleamed. "We intend to live in sin."

Leah slumped into the nearest chair. "I don't know what to say."

"Why say anything? You pack faster when you aren't talking. Since you had a minimum day today at school, we'll be able to finish up in the living room before my scuba lesson this afternoon."

Nonplussed, Leah shook her head. "I may need a few minutes to process all this. Have you told Mom and Dad?"

"Not yet. I plan to wait until it's a done deal so they can't try to talk me out of it. Of course, they'll be worried about a *strange* man taking advantage of me." Her grandma gave an unladylike snort. "Magnus certainly isn't after my money, since that horse already left the barn. As for anything else, he takes advantage very nicely."

Leah held up a hand. "Stop right there. TMI!" When her cell vibrated in her pocket, she pulled it out. "Uh, that means—"

"Too much information. I'm hip to all this texting lingo."

Leah couldn't help but smile, though she refrained from pointing out that "hip" wasn't hip. Instead, she glanced at her phone display. "It's Ryan. I need to talk to him."

"I'm not stopping you."

Gram was certainly in a feisty mood. Leah shook her head and answered, "Hey, Ryan."

"Hey, yourself. Are you riding your bike home, or would you like me to come pick you up?"

"Neither. We had a minimum day, so I'm over at my grandma's helping her pack. We plan to put in another couple of hours before I head home." Standing, she skirted boxes on her way to the door. Once she'd shut it behind her, she let out a breath. "Do you mind if I whine a little? That woman has more vintage crap than Paige's antique store. And don't get me started on all the furniture we need to sell. The only bright note is we don't have very far to haul everything."

"Your grandma's moving out of her apartment?"

She frowned. "I told you we don't have the money to cover her rent for next month. I could maybe squeeze out another payment or two, but then I'd be up against it in an emergency. And let's not forget I have to buy a new car."

"Surely the insurance—"

"The Audi was so old I didn't carry anything but liability, so, no, I won't be getting a check from the insurance company." She pressed the heel of her palm to her forehead. "No one cares that the accident wasn't my fault, that I was the victim of a crime."

"Hey, calm down."

"I am calm. I'm not screaming, am I?" She leaned against the wall and let the cool wind that fluttered her skirt around her knees defuse her temper. "Sorry. I didn't mean to snap at you. You've been terrific through all this."

"I guess I could—"

"Help?" She straightened. "If you wouldn't mind—"

"I don't mind."

Leah frowned. He certainly didn't sound very enthusiastic. "If it's a problem—"

"No problem. I'll be over shortly."

"Great. Thanks." She disconnected, stuffed her phone back in her pocket, then went inside. "Ryan's coming over to help. We can use his muscle to move boxes, since I'm still a little sore from the crash." She fisted her hands on her hips. "Are you going somewhere?"

Gram nodded and pushed her arm through the sleeve of her coat. "Magnus just called to remind me our scuba lesson was rescheduled for earlier today. I'd completely forgotten." She held out a key. "If Ryan wants to haul boxes over to Magnus's place, you can keep packing. Tell him to put everything in the small bedroom with the desk."

"Sure." Leah bent to drop a kiss on her grandma's cheek as she took the key from her. "Don't you need your wetsuit?"

"All our gear is in Magnus's car. Bye, dear. Thanks for your help this afternoon."

"Of course. Have fun."

"We always do." The door shut behind her with a thud.

"Good God, I can't keep up with that woman." Shaking her head, Leah went to work on the second bookshelf and smiled as she loaded the box full of paperbacks with half-naked men on the covers. The fact that her grandma was moving in with Magnus probably shouldn't have surprised her. The woman was a born romantic.

When a knock sounded, she glanced up and called out, "Come on in."

Ryan entered the apartment and stared around the main room before giving her a quick smile. "Unpacking everything is going to take a while. I guess I should have called sooner."

"Huh?" Leah scooted around to face him and rose to her feet. "Thanks for coming over. We aren't unloading the boxes today, just moving them. You'll never guess what new twist my grandma threw at me. My head is spinning."

He pulled a checkbook and a pen out of his jacket pocket and dropped onto the couch. "More financial woes? How much does she need to keep her in her apartment and weather the latest crisis?" He glanced up, pen poised.

Leah frowned. "What are you talking about?"

"Should I make the check out to you or Evie?"

"Why would you write a check to either of us?" Leah pressed fingers to her temples when they started to throb. "I feel like I'm in some alternate universe. First with Gram, and now you're talking in circles. Am I just being dense?"

His gaze held steady on hers. "Look, your grandma is in trouble, and you asked me to help. So, I'm here to give you the money. How much do you need?"

She stiffened, fists clenched at her sides. "Fifty grand ought to do it."

He didn't even blink, just bent his head and started writing.

"Are you kidding me?" Her voice came out in a screech.

"What's wrong?" He stopped writing to look up as confusion darkened his eyes.

"What's wrong?" She kicked a box then winced

when her toe smarted on impact. "This whole situation, that's what's wrong. You're sitting there writing a check with a look on your face like you just bit into something rotten. I was kidding about the fifty grand. I just said that to get a reaction. Jesus!"

He leaned back against the cushions. "I'm afraid I don't understand. You asked for my help, and I agreed. Granted, I have a few concerns about bringing money into our relationship. That didn't work out so well with Jay, but I hate seeing you worried sick about finances."

"So you figured all my problems would go away with a big, fat check?" She swallowed hard as her throat burned with tears. "I can't believe your opinion of me is so low you thought I'd expect you to give me money. What am I looking for, a sugar daddy?"

"Hardly, and I don't think badly of you." He surged to his feet and dropped the checkbook onto the coffee table. "You're the one who asked for my help, so why are you all bent out of shape that I agreed?"

"Help moving boxes! They're freaking heavy, and I'm still sore from the damn car crash. I never said anything about money."

"You said you couldn't afford your grandma's rent." His voice rose. "What did you expect me to think?"

"Excuse me for wanting to complain a little. God!" She rubbed a hand across her eyes. "I think you should leave."

He shoved his hands in his pockets. "I'm sorry if I misunderstood. Can we talk about this?"

She wiped away more tears. "Probably not a great idea right now. I need to cool off."

"Leah . . ." He stepped around the coffee table and held out a hand.

"No." She backed against the bookcase. "Just take your checkbook and go. My heart hurts right now, and I don't want to talk."

He didn't say anything else, just regarded her with a look she couldn't interpret.

"Let me know when you're ready to discuss it." He grabbed his checkbook off the table, strode to the door, and opened it. After one final glance over his shoulder, he shut it behind him with a quiet click.

Leah stepped over to the couch on shaking legs and curled up in the corner. She pressed a hand to the ache in her chest beneath her soft wool sweater, then wiped away tears as they slid down her cheeks. When her cell chimed, she whooshed out a shuddering breath.

What part of no doesn't he understand?

She snatched the phone from her skirt pocket and answered. "I told you not now."

"Leah? Uh, is this a bad time?" The voice on the other end of the line was hesitant.

"Oh, God, I'm sorry, Nina. I thought you were Ryan."

"Trouble in paradise?" Her friend's tone held a deep layer of sympathy. "What did he do to you?"

A small smile tilted Leah's lips. "Thanks for being so certain this is all Ryan's fault."

"Hey, I'll always have your back. I called because I heard about a good deal on a used car, but we can talk about that later. Do you need to vent?"

"In a big way." She glanced around the mess in the living room. "I also need a stiff dose of fresh air. Do you want to go for a hike? My knee's feeling almost back to normal."

"Sure. I've been slaving over my latest project, and I could use a break."

"I'm at my grandma's apartment, but I'll meet you at my house so we can take Barney with us."

"Sounds good. See you in a few."

Leah went hunting for a pad of paper and jotted a quick note. She hated leaving the apartment in shambles, but she'd go crazy if she didn't get outside. Fifteen minutes later, she pedaled down her driveway and leaned her bike against the wall in the now empty carport. She was still petting her ecstatic dog when Nina drove up and parked her Mini Cooper nearby.

She got out, slammed the door, and approached with a hand stretched out to ward off Barney's dirty paws. "Down, boy. Yes, I'll rub your ears, but no jumping." Once she'd greeted the dog, she faced Leah. Clear green eyes regarded her for a long moment. "You've been crying. I may have to kick Ryan's ass."

"I'm probably making mountains out of molehills. Anyway, riding my bike into the wind caused my eyes to water."

Nina's gaze held a wealth of skepticism. "I'll decide if you overreacted. You can tell me what he did while we walk. Are you planning to wear that?"

Leah glanced down at her skirt and sweater. "No, I haven't had time to change since I got off work. Give me a minute. You can fill a couple of water bottles and grab some energy bars out of the pantry while you wait. I may need sustenance." She headed toward the back door, unlocked it, then pulled a daypack off the row of hooks. "Here you go."

Nina took the pack and glanced around. "Is it my imagination, or is this place a whole lot tidier than usual? No piles of miscellaneous crap heaped on the table. No mound of shoes and boots on the floor. Is Ryan the neat-freak rubbing off on you?"

"No, he just cleans up when I don't. Be right back."

A short time later, they set a quick pace through the forest with Barney leading the way. Leah's knee ached a little, but the exercise was worth any pain. She breathed in the scent of damp earth and evergreens.

"You're not limping."

She glanced over at Nina. "My knee twinges now and then, and my ribs are still sore from the impact of the airbag, but I guess I should be thankful my injuries weren't worse."

"They were bad enough. So, are you going to tell me what Ryan did to upset you?"

"He tried to give me fifty grand."

"What!"

"To help out with my grandma's financial situation." She kicked a fir cone, then gave her friend a nudge to keep her moving. "And he wasn't all that gracious about it."

Nina glanced back. "No silver platter beneath the check?"

Leah snorted and choked on a laugh. "Hardly, but I'm hurt and angry he believed I *expected* money from him. It was all a big misunderstanding, but the way he assumed I'd simply take his cash bothered me. Am I really that shallow? Does he think I'm dating him for his bank account?"

"Did you ask him how he feels?"

"No. He wanted to talk, but I sort of kicked him out. I wasn't feeling terribly reasonable at the time. Honestly, I was a total bitch."

Nina laid a hand on her arm and squeezed. "You'll have a conversation and work it out. Bitchiness aside, Ryan is a good guy, so maybe you should listen to what he has to say before you judge."

"I know. Maybe getting me to quit whining and complaining all the time was worth fifty thousand bucks to him. I haven't exactly been Miss Congeniality lately."

"You have every reason to bitch and moan. Christ, Leah, your grandma was robbed of her life's savings, and then someone tried to kill you. Give yourself a break."

"Still, no one likes a whiner."

Nina rolled her eyes. "You stuck by me when I lost Keith, and I did nothing but cry and rail against fate and mope for a good six months. You and Paige both deserve sainthood for that."

"We probably do."

Her friend's laughter rang through the trees. "I expect Ryan was just trying to help in his own inept male way. Point out his error and move on." She gave her a sideways glance. "Maybe keep the check, since he can certainly afford it."

"You're hilarious. You know I'd never do that."

"I'm kidding." Nina was quiet for several minutes as they trod silently along the path covered with fir needles. "He really is a good guy. You're lucky to have found each other again."

"I know, but I may let him stew for a while before I apologize for yelling at him." Leah kicked a stick to send it ricocheting off a tree trunk. "I'm still angry he misjudged me, and I want to make it clear he'd damn well better not do it again."

"Good for you. Oh, and for the record, you didn't overreact. Not much, anyway." Nina gave her shoulder a nudge. "I still think he should have served up that check on a silver platter. Just saying."

"And hold the side of grudging toleration. He wasn't any happier about writing the check than I was to take it." Leah scowled. "He said something about his old business partner, and how money ruined their friendship. If Ryan thinks I could *ever* care more about cold, hard cash than our feelings for each other, then he—"

"Wow, the man really did blow it. Sounds like he may have a few unresolved issues to work out that have nothing to do with you."

"You think?" Leah let out a long breath. "His exgirlfriend mentioned commitment and intimacy problems. I'm beginning to think he's holding on to a whole lot of insecurities."

"You talked to his ex-girlfriend?"

Her knee tweaked a little as they climbed steadily uphill, and she winced. "I ran into her in the ladies' room of a restaurant in Sisters on Saturday. She seemed nice."

"Interesting. You weren't even a tad jealous?"

"No, why would I be?"

"You wouldn't be because you trust what you and Ryan have together. That's pretty amazing, so hold on to that knowledge when you talk to him. Okay?"

"I will. Thanks, Nina. Discussing this whole sorry mess with you helped."

"Good." Her friend reached out to give her a quick hug then glanced around. "The sun is beginning to set, and it'll be dark in under an hour. How far are we going?"

"There's a viewpoint not far from here, and I have a flashlight in my pack." Leah stumbled over a tree root and stopped. "Hey, where's Barney?"

"Somewhere up ahead. Apparently we weren't hiking fast enough to suit him."

"Well, crap. I hope he comes when I call him. I should have been paying more attention." She raised her voice to shout, "Barney!"

The wind rustled tree branches in the silence.

Nina touched her arm. "Let's keep going. Maybe he's out of earshot."

"Damn, I hope he didn't go too far."

They hiked until they reached the viewpoint where Leah and Ryan had stopped before, but encroaching darkness hid the ocean vista. When she yelled again for Barney, a snuffling bark answered her.

"Oh, thank God. I know where he is." Leah pushed through the manzanita bushes. "He's obsessed with this spot. There must be a nest of squirrels or something." Breaking through into the clearing with the large stone, she let out a breath. "You're a total pain. You know that?"

Barney whined and dug furiously near a large fir tree on the far side of the open area, butt upended and tail wagging. Dirt flew in all directions.

"Whatever rodent you're after, leave it alone."

Barney turned with a stick in his mouth, long and nearly black in the fading light. When Leah walked around the stone and reached for it, the dog sidestepped her and dashed toward the bushes.

"Fine, but I can't throw your stick if you won't drop it."

Nina laughed. "Your dog is an idiot."

"I know, but I still love him." Leah shrugged off her pack and unzipped the compartment to pull out a flashlight. "We'll definitely need this on the way down."

"I'd prefer not to fall on my head, so lead the way."

"Happily. This place has an eerie feel to it, secluded with the trees towering over us."

Nina nodded as she held back the bushes. "You'd never know there was a clearing here if the dog hadn't found it. If this is an actual trail, it's super overgrown."

"Ouch." Leah rubbed her arm when a branch scratched her. She flashed the light down the main path and caught Barney in the gleam, chewing on his stick. He jumped up and trotted off when she called out, "Stay close, boy. I don't want to look for you again."

"God forbid, especially with the fog rolling in." Nina shivered. "It's going to be a cold night."

Such an innocent comment, yet Leah's heart ached. Ryan wouldn't be around to keep her warm. Not that she was willing to simply forgive and forget. Not yet, anyway. "That wind cuts like a knife. Let's go home."

Chapter Twenty-six

Ryan sat in Castaways with his elbows planted on the bar as he nursed a beer along with a piss-poor mood. All he'd done was try to help Leah, despite his misgivings, and *he* was the bad guy? Just went to prove money and friendship didn't mix. Apparently love only made the problem worse.

When someone plunked a glass down on the bar and claimed the stool next to his, he glanced up and met Pete Brewster's slightly glazed stare. Obviously the cocktail wasn't his first of the evening.

"Drinking alone, Ryan?"

"Apparently not anymore."

The irony in his tone was lost on Pete. "I don't mind keeping you company while I wait for George and Brock. They're late."

Ryan stiffened. "Brock's in town again? He was just here a couple of weeks ago."

"Last time I checked, hanging out in Siren Cove wasn't a federal offense. Astoria is only a few hours away, and he has friends here."

"Astoria?" Ryan frowned at his old classmate. "Brock lives in Astoria?"

"That's where he moved after that bi . . ." Pete's voice faded beneath Ryan's hard stare. "Uh, I mean after Leah divorced him and took him to the cleaners, despite my best efforts in the courtroom. Brock went into business with his uncle who lives there."

"Un-freaking-believable." Ryan pulled out his wallet and dropped a ten-dollar bill on the bar.

"You leaving without finishing your beer? What has your shorts in a wad? Afraid Leah's going to cheat on you with her ex?" Pete's smirk held little humor. "Hey, maybe that's why my buddy's late. He had a better offer."

"Go to hell, Brewster." Ryan strode out of the bar, letting the door slam shut behind him. The fog closed in around him as he headed toward his Jeep, climbed in, and started the engine.

Could Brock be the asshole conning seniors?

It didn't seem likely he would have risked approaching Evie, even in disguise, but the man had always been brash. His headlights cut through the fog as Ryan pulled out onto the road and turned toward Leah's house. One thing was certain, he intended to have a discussion with her . . . whether she liked it or not.

Tension thrummed across his nerves as he parked in her empty driveway a few minutes later. Obviously she was home alone, not that he'd believed Pete's insinuations for a minute. After climbing out and pocketing his keys, he headed up onto the porch and knocked. A few hours before, he would have simply walked inside. Tonight, he didn't plan to push his luck.

The door opened slowly, and Leah regarded him with wary eyes. She wore fleece pajama pants and an oversized sweatshirt with her SOU college emblem on the front. Obviously she hadn't dressed for company.

"Can I come in?"

With a nod, she held the door wide then shut it behind him. Without speaking, she led the way into the living room and curled up on one corner of the couch. He sat on the opposite end and tried to ignore the ache in his chest.

He met her gaze head-on. "I'm sorry, honestly and truly sorry if you think I questioned your character. I didn't mean my gesture that way. I only wanted to help."

"You consider fifty thousand dollars a gesture?"

When her voice rose, he cringed. "One meant to ease your anxiety. I only want you to be happy, and I know you hoped your grandma could stay in the senior apartments where her social life is centered."

Leah's feet hit the floor with a thump as she stood to pace the room. "She is staying there. I started to tell you she plans to move in with Magnus, her boyfriend . . . or whatever the heck you want to call him. You interrupted me with the check before I could explain." Her hands shook a little as she fisted them on her hips. "Along with a helping of attitude. Don't pretend you were thrilled with your noble gesture."

"Evie's moving in with Magnus? You're okay with that?"

"It's not my place to judge. She's a fully competent adult who's capable of making her own decisions. They seem to get along well, and I have the feeling they spend most of their nights together, anyway. If this man makes her happy and takes away the loneliness losing my grandpa caused her, then I'm going to support her choice."

"Good for you. I wish my mom had remarried after my dad died. I know she struggled with depression over the years but battled her way out of it." He shrugged. "Now she says she likes living alone. To each his . . . or her . . . own, I guess."

"Exactly. We all make our own choices, and sometimes they're mistakes. We learn from them, grow stronger, and move on. Having friends and family around to support us helps."

He eyed her as she stopped by the window to stare out into the darkness. "I've admitted I made a mistake. Can we move past it? Please?"

"I'd like to think we can, and I apologize for snapping at you." She turned to face him. "But I'm a little concerned. Do you believe everyone you meet is after your millions—or is it billions? Don't you know me better than that?"

The hurt coloring her tone tied his stomach in knots. "I trusted Jay implicitly, and he screwed me over. Obviously the end result is I'm slower to place faith in people, but that doesn't mean I don't believe in your integrity." He patted the cushion next to him. "Can you please sit down and stop pacing like a caged animal? Even Barney is disturbed."

They both glanced over at the dog lying on the

rug with his nose on his paws. Sad brown eyes followed Leah's every step.

"He senses the tension between us." She crossed the room and dropped down beside Ryan. "Okay, I'm listening."

"Thank you." Reaching out, he took her hand and held tight. "I realize we have a few things to settle between us. I love you, and I know you love me, but love doesn't solve every problem. We loved each other back in high school, too."

"Yes, we did, but don't you think we're smarter now and more willing to compromise?"

"I would certainly hope so. However, I didn't want to confuse the situation between us by bringing any sense of obligation into play. My intention was to give you the money with no strings attached. The last thing I'd ever want is for you to feel beholden. However our relationship works out, I need to be one hundred percent certain you're in it because I'm what your heart wants."

"If you believe—"

He raised his voice. "Come on, Leah, don't flip out on me again. If you did a big favor for me, don't you think I'd want to respond in kind? It's human nature to be grateful."

She slumped against the cushions. "I suppose."

"That's why I was reluctant to broach the subject of helping your grandma out of her financial bind. This time around, I want nothing between us but honest feelings." His grip on her fingers tightened as he tugged her closer and slipped an arm around her. "I guess I should have said all this before I pulled out my checkbook."

Leah rested her head against his shoulder. "That

would have been nice." She waved a hand. "Look at my home, Ryan. Most of my possessions are hand-me-downs older than I am. My car was a relic. I dress like I shop at the thrift store, which I've been known to do on occasion. I'm in a profession where I take joy from inspiring kids, not in the size of my paycheck. Money is not my top priority in life."

"I know that."

"Yes, I've been worried, but only because I want my grandma to be happy. I'm not dismissive of financial security, but I also don't let it rule my world."

He laid his palm under her chin and tilted her face to look into her eyes. "You make me feel like a total schmuck."

Leaning forward, she kissed him then stroked his cheek with her thumb. "You don't need to feel bad about anything. What I want is for you to let go of Jay's betrayal and learn to trust again. Hauling around baggage like that isn't healthy."

"Probably not, and I do trust you." He kissed her back, a lingering caress that almost made him forget what he'd been about to say. "You're everything I want. Everything I need, and I do believe we're smarter now."

"Obviously I haven't gotten over my tendency to go ballistic before I think things through. *And* I'm still messy."

"Yes, you are. And I'm still a neat freak." His smile had a self-deprecating edge. "I hold grudges longer than I should. Still, I'm willing to make an effort to let go of the small stuff."

"If we can both do that, the larger problems

have a way of working themselves out with a little effort." She slid her hand around to the back of his neck. "Thanks for being big enough to make the first move after I told you to take a hike. I *literally* took a hike with Nina and cooled off. I was planning to call you."

"I'm glad, but I did have another reason for coming over. I stopped by Castaways for a beer and had a brief conversation with Pete while I was there."

"I can't imagine any good coming from that."

"Apparently Brock's in town again."

"Ugh." She screwed up her lips. "He didn't mention anything about it when I talked to him over the weekend."

Ryan frowned. "Why'd you talk to Brock?"

"He called after he heard about my wreck to express concern for my welfare. That was decent of him, actually."

"Pete mentioned your ex lives in Astoria. Don't you think it's a bit of a coincidence the con man struck there so soon after he fleeced elderly residents, including your grandma, here in Siren Cove?"

"I did mention it to Brock. Of course he thought I was insinuating—"

"You told him?" Ryan reared back. "Before or after that dirtbag bailed on the meeting with his intended victim?"

"I think it was before. Why?"

"I don't know." He tried to ease off the sarcasm and failed. "Maybe because I'm wondering if Brock is the one robbing seniors."

"Are you kidding?" She pushed his arm aside

and jumped up from the couch. "Don't you think Gram would have recognized my ex-husband, for crying out loud?"

"If his disguise was good enough—"

"Brock may be a cheating weasel, but he doesn't have the IQ of a stump. If he was the man running the con, he would never have approached my grandmother. Maybe he would have risked targeting her neighbor, but not someone guaranteed to nail his ass! Geez."

"If you're sure . . ."

"Positive."

"I still don't like the coincidence of this guy hitting elderly targets both here and in Brock's new hometown. Something about the whole situation doesn't feel right. If the guilty party isn't Brock, maybe he's someone your ex knows. I'd bet my damn business he's the one who tipped off the con artist before the police could arrest him. Nothing else makes any sense."

"I don't know . . ." She collapsed onto the couch. "You think this person is someone he met up in Astoria?"

"Or he could be a buddy from around here. Or an old college friend. Who the hell knows, but you told Brock, and the suspect bolted. Unless someone on the police force tipped off the dude, it must have been Brock."

Leah held her head in her hands and let out a low moan. "God, I feel like an idiot. I never thought—"

Ryan scooted over beside her. "This isn't your fault."

She let out a breath and glanced up. Eyes dark

with worry regarded him. "Then why do I feel like I totally blew it? Should we tell the police what we suspect?"

"Let's not rush into anything without facts. Maybe we can figure this out ourselves, going off the assumption Brock helped this whack job evade arrest." Ryan squeezed her shoulder. "Quit beating yourself up and think. You probably know most of your ex-husband's friends. Let's start with that and this game he plays with aliases. Why would any of Brock's good buddies assume the birth names of vintage pop stars as a disguise?"

"I don't know. Brock is a country music fan. No one our age listens to Tom Jones or Tony Bennett or any of the others. That music wasn't even popular with our parents' generation. More likely it was our grandparents who listened to them."

"True. His victims are from the age group most familiar with those singers. Do you think this guy gets off on tempting fate? Some people live for an element of danger."

"I suppose that could be it. But why use their birth names? Why singers and not movie stars? It all seems so random."

"Okay, let's go at this from a different angle. Who are Brock's friends and relatives he's tight with, men he would be willing to protect even if they committed a crime?"

Leah leaned back against the cushions and unclenched her fists. When Ryan picked up one hand to hold, she squeezed back. "His uncle Craig and cousin Del. Craig took him into their business after our divorce. I always liked both men, and I can't imagine either one of them would commit a crime against the elderly."

"We're looking for a man around our age, so let's consider Del." Ryan pulled his phone out of his pocket and released her hand to type. "Is his full name Delbert Hooker?"

Leah nodded.

"Hmm, nothing pops. Of course, I can't check to see if this guy has a record, but the police will do that." He glanced up. "Let's try a few other options. Who are Brock's closest friends?"

"I don't know who he's hooked up with in the years since our divorce. As for old college buddies, he never kept in touch with anyone in particular after graduation. He spent his free time here in Siren Cove hanging out with Pete, and he'd get together with George whenever he was in town to visit his dad."

"Okay, let's start there." He typed Peter Brewster into his phone and hit enter. "Hmm, that's too bad. No flashing neon indicators to tell me Pete's the guilty party. That idiot seriously rubs me the wrong way."

"He was always a bad influence on Brock, encouraging him to party with the boys to the detriment of our relationship. Then he tried to shaft me during our divorce. That didn't work out so well for either of them, since I had a better attorney."

Ryan grinned. "Good for you."

Her smile held a hint of old pain. "Water under the bridge now."

"If we can't nail Pete for this, let's check out

George." He typed George Dorsey into his phone then scanned the results. When the name Arnold George Dorsey caught his eye, he paused. "Isn't George's dad named Arnold?"

"Yeah, why?" Leah leaned in to peer at his screen as he clicked on the entry.

"Well, holy shit, look at that."

Leah read out loud, "Engelbert Humperdinck was born Arnold George Dorsey." She turned to stare at him. "Oh, my God!"

"So, George knew he had the same name as a famous singer and thought he'd be clever by using the birth names of other similar performers as aliases." Ryan dropped his phone on the coffee table. "What an idiot. If he'd used a bunch of random names and disguises, we'd never have figured it out."

"You have to love an arrogant criminal who thinks he's smarter than everyone else. Even back in school, George was kind of an irritating know-it-all." Leah turned to face him with a thoughtful frown. "George moved back to town not that long ago. I wonder if he lived near any of the places where the other scams took place."

"Pretty easy to find out. Even with this much information, we need to go to the police. Hopefully they can get a warrant to search his place and find enough evidence to make an arrest."

"*And* recover my grandma's money." Leah pushed down on his thigh to lever to her feet. "Should we call now or go report this in person?"

"Let's drive into town. I'll feel more comfortable talking to someone face-to-face. Do you know how late the police station stays open?"

"Damn, I'm sure the office is closed by now, but I have Chris Long's cell number. I'll call to see if he can meet us, but first I need to go get dressed." She glanced over at Barney, who lay on the floor whining, with one paw stuck under the end of the couch. "You okay, boy?"

"What's his problem?"

She walked around the coffee table to crouch beside the dog. "Can't you reach your stick?" Rising to her feet, she regarded the dog with a frown. "He brought home a stick from our walk earlier and hid it under the couch before I could take it away. He's going to scratch up the floor if we don't get it out for him."

"I'll move the couch. That thing is heavy." Ryan stood and nudged her aside to grip the padded arm and swing the bulky sofa forward. "Can you reach it now?"

Barney lunged between them and came out with the prize clamped between his teeth.

"What the hell?" Dropping the couch with a thud, Ryan grabbed the dog's collar. "That's not a stick."

"It's not?"

"No, it looks like a charred bone. Drop it, Barney."

The dog whined and tried to jerk away.

When Leah knelt to pry open his jaws, the object fell to the floor. Ryan scooped up the bone before the dog could retrieve it. Turning the grimy, blackened thing in his hands, he frowned.

"Looks like a femur that's been through a fire and is splintered on one end. Barney might have caused some of the damage, chewing on it."

When the dog jumped up and whined, Leah fended off her pet. "Is it a deer leg?"

Ryan set the bone on the back of the couch, out of Barney's reach, then wiped his hands down the legs of his jeans and shuddered. "I'm no anatomy expert, but I'd swear that bone is human."

Chapter Twenty-seven

Leah rubbed her hands up and down her arms and shivered. "That's just so freaky. Ugh. Why would there be a human bone in the woods? Do you suppose Barney dug up an old Native American burial site?"

Ryan eyed the femur the way he probably would a glitch in his computer system. One part suspicion combined with determination to solve the puzzle.

"It doesn't look that old to me, but what do I know? Where, exactly, did he find it?"

"That spot with the big rock we discovered on our hike a few weeks ago. You remember Barney was sniffing around the base of the stone, and we had to drag him away. This time he was digging over by the trees on the edge of the clearing. I swear he's part bloodhound with that nose of his."

"I remember. That place gave me the—" His eyes widened, and he took a step away from the couch. "Oh, hell."

"What?" Goose bumps broke out on her arms. "You're freaking me out, Ryan."

"The pictures from the time capsule. They were taken in a small clearing, and we thought the woman was lying on a table or platform of some sort covered with a cloth. What if it was that rock? It would be about the right height."

Leah pressed a hand to her mouth as she stared in horror at the bone. Her voice was muffled when she spoke. "Oh, God, I'm going to be sick." Turning, she ran from the room and barely made it to the bathroom before she heaved up her guts. When her stomach stopped contracting, she reached out a shaky hand to flush the toilet.

"Here." Ryan handed her a wet hand towel.

She took the dripping cloth and wiped her face, then closed her eyes. "Sorry."

"Don't be. I'm barely holding it together, myself."

"I couldn't stop thinking about that poor girl who disappeared all those years ago, Merry Bright, wondering if that bone was part of her leg." Leah let out a shuddering breath and stared at Ryan. "What are we going to do?"

"Maybe I'm wrong and the femur isn't human. We can hope we're way off base."

"Either way, we still need to take it to the police."

He stepped aside when she stood and tossed the towel in the sink. "I guess so, but our concerns about who might have been involved back then haven't changed."

"So we stay away from Chris Long, since we don't know if his dad was the one who put the film in the time capsule. We can take the bone and our suspicions directly to Chief Stackhouse."

Ryan nodded, but his eyes were troubled. "I think I'd rather report this to Detective Stannard and leave the local police out of it."

She left the bathroom on shaky legs. "You want to drive all the way down to Coos Bay tonight? I don't imagine he's on duty this late."

"Probably not." Ryan paused beside her at the foot of the stairs. "Maybe we should hike up to that clearing tomorrow to see if there's anything else buried in the spot where Barney was digging. Neither of us are forensic experts. We might be freaking out over nothing. Then, depending on what we find, we can call Stannard or go in to see Chief Stackhouse."

"Except I have to work. Tomorrow is Halloween, and the kids are excited for their costume parade and party. I can't disappoint them by asking for a substitute."

"I can hike up alone—"

A chill shook her. "Call that detective and take him with you."

"I doubt he'll want to drive all the way to Siren Cove simply because your dog found a bone that looks like it's been on the grill too long."

"Ugh. Don't say things like that."

"Sorry." He wrapped an arm around her and squeezed. "I'll call Stannard in the morning, and we can take it from there. Obviously that bone has been buried for a while, so it isn't like we have to make a quick decision tonight or panic and do something stupid. Right?"

"I suppose not, although I'm not thrilled to

have that thing in my house. Also, there's still the matter of reporting George Dorsey."

"Crap, I'd already forgotten about him. Yeah, we need to tell the police about George's connection to those aliases." Ryan slid his hand down to her pajama-clad hip. "Are you going up to get dressed?"

Leah nodded. "Can you call Chris Long while I change? His number is in my phone, and he knows all about my grandma's case."

"I'll take care of it. What's your password?"

"My birthday." She glanced toward the living room where the bone still lay on the back of the couch. "Uh, do you mind putting that thing somewhere out of sight? Maybe in the carport. Honestly, I can't bear to look at it, and I certainly don't want Barney trying to get hold of it again."

"Sure."

After dressing in jeans and a sweater, she brushed her teeth and stared at her reflection in the mirror. Dark shadows beneath her eyes looked like bruises against her still pale complexion. She took a moment to comb her hair, then gave her head a shake. Time to suck it up, forget about the charred femur, and go get justice for her grandma and the other seniors fleeced by George. Not that she didn't feel sick knowing Brock had aided and abetted a criminal. The whole situation turned her stomach.

She flipped off the light and headed downstairs. Ryan stood near the front door holding her jacket. She gave him a grateful smile as she slid her arms through the sleeves. "Thanks."

"You bet." He handed over her phone. "Chris was working late and said he'd meet us at the station."

"Great. Let's get this over with."

They drove into town, the twin beams barely penetrating the dense fog. Ryan braked before turning into the lot next to the police station as a cruiser pulled out with lights flashing.

"Someone's in a rush."

"Probably a car accident caused by this fog." He parked and turned off the engine. "Ready?"

"Yeah." When her phone pinged, she pulled it out of her pocket. "Damn it. Chris just texted. He was called out on an emergency. Now what?"

"That must have been him leaving just now. I guess we can hang around until he returns. The station looks like it's locked up tight. No lights on inside."

"Well, hell. I just want to be done with this."

"It's damn frustrating." He leaned forward when a marked vehicle turned into the lot and parked. "Hey, is Long back already?" Ryan unbuckled his seat belt and got out of the Jeep. "Must have been a false alarm."

The driver slammed his door and turned to face them. The outdoor spotlights illuminated Chief Stackhouse as he approached. His steps slowed, and his brows shot up. "This is a surprise. What brings you two out at this hour? Not another problem, I hope."

"Oh, thank heavens." Leah hurried toward him. "We have new information regarding the man who conned my grandma, and we had planned to meet Officer Long, but—"

"Chris just headed out on a domestic disturbance call. I heard it over the scanner when I was on my way over. I think I left my damn phone on my desk. I've been at home hunting for it for an hour." The chief waved an arm toward the station. "Come along with me, and I'll take your information."

Leah hesitated. "If you're not on duty—"

"I'm always on duty." After they followed him across the parking lot, he unlocked the door and held it open. "We'll head back to my office." He led the way toward the rear of the building, flipping on the lights as he went. "Right where I left it. Wouldn't you know." Stackhouse scooped the cell off a pile of folders and gestured toward a pair of club chairs. "Have a seat and tell me what the problem is now."

They sat, and Ryan laid a hand on her thigh and squeezed. "Not a problem. We believe we know who was responsible for conning seniors, including Leah's grandma. You know those aliases he used were the birth names of singers popular in the sixties, right?"

"You bet. I read Long's report."

"Well, we just figured out Engelbert Humperdinck was born Arnold George Dorsey. Quite a coincidence, don't you think?"

The chief's eyes narrowed. "You're certain about this?"

"About the name, definitely. It only took a few seconds to verify over the internet."

"Then, I'd say that's enough to at least question George. I'll need to get a warrant to look into his finances. That boy must have shit for brains, using disguises that could be traced back to him. Does he think cops are stupid?"

"Apparently." Leah clenched her fists at her

sides. "I'm only sorry we didn't figure it out sooner. What are the chances we'll be able to recover my grandma's money?"

"I guess it'll depend on what's left in his account." Chief Stackhouse paused to lean back in his chair. "Of course, we'll have to find evidence he's guilty first. I'll get on that warrant right away." With a creak of leather, he rose to his feet. "Thanks for bringing this to my attention. You can be sure I'll take it from here and nail the little bas . . . uh, the suspect."

Ryan stood, and pulled Leah up beside him. "Thank you, Chief. We appreciate your personal attention to the matter."

"Have you confided in anyone else about this yet?" He rounded his desk and put a hand on Leah's back to guide her toward the door.

"No, we just figured it out a short time ago and called Officer Long."

"I'll fill Chris in on the details, but you might not want to talk out of turn until we can get that warrant. This is a small community, and I don't want anyone to tip off Dorsey."

"We'll keep quiet about it. I learned my lesson on that front already."

The chief's grip on her shoulder tightened. "How's that?"

"I think my ex-husband knows what George has been doing. I had a conversation with Brock before the police tried to make an arrest up in Astoria." Her voice broke. "I would never have said anything if—"

"You think Brock warned his buddy?"

Ryan nodded. "Yes."

"I'll look into that aspect of the situation, as well. You've both been very helpful."

"I just want George brought to justice," Leah said. "This whole nightmare can't be over soon enough to suit me."

"Agreed." The chief walked them to the door and held it open. "I'll be in touch."

"Thank you." Taking Leah's hand, Ryan led the way through the dense fog to his Jeep and clicked the remote to unlock it. "Let's go home."

She leaned against the window as they drove through the night. Her stomach still ached with none of the relief she'd expected to feel after unburdening herself and hearing the chief's promise of action. "Maybe we should have told him about the bone, too."

"Huh?" Ryan glanced over as he slowed to turn into her driveway.

"My insides are all tied up in knots."

"Yeah, mine, too." He shifted to look over his shoulder when headlights shone in the rearview mirror. "I wonder who that is."

"I don't want to talk to anyone." Leah's voice cracked. "Not until I've had a chance to wrap my head around all this. Honestly, I feel like I might lose it completely."

"Go inside, and I'll deal with whoever's back there."

She bolted out of the car and practically ran through the carport to the kitchen door. Once inside, she switched on the light, then dropped onto a chair at the table and buried her face in her hands. When Barney poked his nose against her side and whined, she stroked his soft head with trembling fingers.

A few minutes later, the door opened, and Ryan sat down next to her. "You okay?"

"Yes. I'm being a baby to let everything bother me so much. First we solve the con man mystery, but then discover that horrible bone." She shuddered. "It's just one thing after another with no break."

"It'll be over tomorrow. I promise. I'll give the femur to Stannard and be done with it, even if it means driving down to Coos Bay. None of this is our problem. Let the cops handle it."

"If that's how you feel, why didn't you tell Chief Stackhouse?"

"Honestly, I was tempted. But when I opened my mouth, something made me stop. Probably an excess of caution, along with fear the news might spread to the wrong ears if that bone is in any way tied to the men in the pictures from the time capsule."

"I guess better safe than sorry." She turned to face him. "Who was outside?"

"It was Chris Long, following up after my call earlier. I gave him a brief rundown on George Dorsey and told him we'd talked to the chief."

"Good." She glanced at her watch. "It's not even eight o'clock, and all I want to do is go to bed."

Ryan tilted her chin to look into her eyes. "You're not hungry? We didn't eat dinner."

She shook her head. "I couldn't possibly, but go ahead and make yourself something."

He stood and pulled her into his arms to gather

her close. "Go upstairs and take a hot bath to relax. I'll be with you shortly."

She wound her arms around his neck and held tight. "Thank you."

"For what?"

"Being here. Being *you.* For not letting me push you away. I love you so much, Ryan."

He kissed her, then wiped away the tears that slid down her cheeks. "I won't let anything come between us this time. Not your stubbornness or my stupidity. I'm sorry I was a jerk about the money."

"I'm sorry, too. At least all this drama has shown me what's important in life. You and me together. Nothing else matters more than that."

"You're right. Now go unwind while I make a sandwich. You look completely worn out."

"I'm emotionally drained, that's for sure." She pressed a quick kiss to his lips then pulled away. "Don't be too long."

"I won't."

Barney followed Leah up the stairs and into her bedroom. He flopped down on the rug with a sigh while she stripped off her clothes and shrugged into a warm fleece robe. The idea of a bath had merit, but she settled for a hot shower to take away the deep-seated chill in her bones.

Minutes later, she stood beneath the stinging spray with her head hanging and let the water wash away her exhaustion. She'd had a few moments of weakness, but no more. Straightening, she squared her shoulders, shut off the water, and stepped out onto the mat. She was still drying her hair in the steamy bathroom when Ryan cracked open the door and poked his head through.

"Are you okay?"

She clicked off the blow dryer and laid it on the counter. "Yes. I'm over letting everything bother me. If George is a criminal, he deserves to be locked up. I already knew Brock has zero morals, so I'm not sure why I let another example of his tendency to make horrible decisions bother me. His problem, not mine."

Ryan stepped farther into the room and slid his arms around her waist, taking care not to squeeze her still sore ribs. "You have an enviable strength. Don't beat yourself up because you allowed yourself to be vulnerable for a change."

"I'm sick of feeling like a victim. The scumbag who tried to steal back those pictures has hurt me for the last time. If that bone has any connection to whatever perverted ceremony was going on in those woods twenty years ago, then they all deserve to rot in hell." She met his gaze in the mirror. "You were right to be cautious about turning over possible evidence. I want justice for the woman in those pictures. Maybe we're no longer in any danger, but it's our duty as responsible citizens to see that the crime committed that night is punished."

"Agreed. I'll call Detective Stannard first thing in the morning."

She turned to face him and wrapped her arms around his neck. A fierce love filled her, along with a sense of righting old wrongs. "We'll make those bastards pay."

Ryan cupped her face in his hands and kissed her. "Time to let go of the past and focus on the future. We've got this, Leah."

She smiled into his eyes. "Damn right."

*   *   *

"Tell your idiot son to get the hell out of town. Now."

Arnold Dorsey dropped his beer bottle on the card table, and foam spewed out of the top. He scooped up his cell before it could get soaked. "What the hell are you talking about?"

"Leah and Ryan Alexander just figured out the connection between your name and the game George was playing with those aliases, and reported it. I told you your kid was beyond stupid to think no one would catch on."

"Shit. Can't you do something to squash an investigation?" His hand shook as he righted the bottle and sopped up the mess with a wad of napkins. "You owe me that much."

"Unfortunately, a report has already been filed. The last thing I want is outsiders snooping around before tomorrow night, but your son left victims all over the state. Everyone and his brother will be looking into this."

"Can't you—"

"I'll do everything possible to head off an official investigation until the Samhain is over, but I can't promise more than that. Tell your kid to get on a plane to . . . wherever. I don't want to know anything more about it."

"Should we cancel tomorrow night's ceremony? Seems a little risky at this juncture." He met the terrified gaze of the other occupant of the room. "I can eliminate—"

"I'm not willing to do that. We'll celebrate as planned. I trust our sacrifice is still secure?"

"Yes." He rubbed his temple as the throbbing

behind his eyes strengthened. "I'll need more than a day to—"

"You aren't going to get it. Tell George to cut his losses, take what cash he can, and get out now. Access to that report is widespread. The best I can do is use my resources to throw up a few roadblocks."

Arnold slammed his fist down on the table with enough force to rattle the beer bottle. "Let me guess who's responsible for the report. Chris Long, always the Boy Scout."

His answer was a grunt.

"We have leverage to use against him."

"I won't threaten a brother. Your son dug his own grave. Now deal with it."

The phone went dead.

Arnold stared at the young woman, bound and gagged on a mattress in the corner. She stared back at him in stark horror.

"I'll deal, all right." His lips curled. "Count on it."

Chapter Twenty-eight

"Why the heck can't Stannard meet with you?" Leah tightened her grip on her cell and lowered her voice as Sloan approached from across the playground. Between them, costume-clad kids ran screaming, all hyped up on sugar and holiday excitement. "He has something more important than buried human remains to keep him busy?"

"He promised to drive up here, but not until early evening," Ryan answered. "They're dealing with a reported hate crime, and he can't get away any sooner."

"Well, that sucks." She shivered in her hippy costume as a cold wind fluttered the fringe on her suede vest. "What now?"

"I still want to hike up to the clearing to see what else is buried near that rock."

Leah forced a smile when Sloan joined her. "If you can wait a couple hours, I'll go with you. I should be finished here by three."

"I guess there's no rush. I'll pick you up after school lets out."

"Okay. Bye, Ryan." She clicked off her phone and stuffed it in the pocket of her flowered bell-bottom pants.

"Do you and Ryan have plans for this evening? I've heard there are quite a few parties, despite the fact it's a work night." Sloan rolled his eyes. "My invitations must have gotten lost in the mail."

"No, this is . . . something else." She shot him a quick smile. "Maybe if your go-to costume wasn't a nerd you'd be more popular."

"Hey, dressing up is easy when I can simply pull my regular clothes out of the closet, add a little tape to my glasses, and voilà, instant geek."

She smoothed the fringe. "Maybe that's why I usually dress as a flower child . . . it's not much of a stretch." When the bell rang, she clapped her hands. "Line up, kids. Lunch is over."

"We should just send them home now. It's not like they're going to learn anything this afternoon."

"Don't be such a pessimist. You never know when someone will surprise you."

Two hours later, Leah's enthusiasm for trying to teach had disappeared completely. When the final bell rang, she cheered nearly as loudly as her students. "Make sure you have all the pieces to your costumes." She raised her voice to be heard over the clamor of excited voices. "Have fun trick-or-treating tonight, and remember the safety rules we talked about." When the last fairy princess and devil disappeared through the classroom doorway, she slumped in her chair. "Oh, thank God."

"Rough day?"

She glanced up as Ryan entered the room, and her fatigue evaporated. "They were understandably unruly."

"I'll say. I was nearly trampled by a stampede of skeletons and witches on my way down the hall."

"You're here ahead of schedule." She stood and walked around her desk to meet him halfway. "I need to clean up the party mess before I can leave."

"I came early to help." Pulling her into his arms, he dropped a kiss on her upturned lips . . . then a second and a third lingering caress involving tongue. His voice was slightly hoarse when he finally turned her loose. "Put me to work."

She blinked and took a deep breath. "Sure, work."

They straightened the room in record time and had just finished cramming used paper plates and black and orange crepe paper into a garbage bag when Edgar pushed a wheeled trash container through the doorway.

Leah held up the bulging plastic bag. "Tada! It's all yours." She lobbed it into the bin.

He glanced around the room and nodded at Ryan. "You win the prize for quickest clean-up today."

"That's because I had help."

Edgar dipped his mop up and down in a bucket of cleaning solution strong enough to burn the inside of her nose. "My shoes are sticking to the floor. How many cups of punch did the kids spill?" he asked.

"I lost count. You deserve hazard pay for a day like this."

"Tell that to the schoolboard. Go on home, Leah." His gaze shifted to Ryan. "I imagine you two have somewhere better than this to be."

She pointed at the bucket. "We're off on a hike. A little fresh air and exercise to clear the fumes out of my head will be welcome. You should try it."

His lips curved in a quick smile. "I might just do that."

Ryan handed over her denim jacket. "On that note, let's get out of here. Have a nice evening, Edgar."

Leah pulled her tote bag out of her bottom desk drawer, slung the strap over her shoulder, then glanced up when Sloan entered the room. "Ryan and I were just leaving. Do you need something?"

"Just a minute of Edgar's time. I'll talk to you tomorrow, Leah." He nodded as they passed. "Good to see you, Ryan."

"Likewise." Slipping an arm around Leah's shoulders, he guided her from the room. "I want to get moving. It'll be dark in a couple of hours, and we won't be able to see squat."

"We can take a couple of heavy-duty flashlights with us, just in case." She waved to the office staff as they headed toward the front doors. "Any word from Detective Stannard?"

"I told him we intend to hike up to that clearing. Since he wants to take a look around, he offered to meet us there. Apparently he lived in Siren Cove when he was a kid and is familiar with the trail."

"Good." Leah shivered as a cold breeze hit her the minute Ryan held open the door. "Brrr. It's going to be a chilly hike."

An hour later she had warmed considerably as they set a fast pace up the trail, carrying packs loaded with flashlights, snacks, water bottles, and a shovel with a folding handle. Barney ran ahead but returned when she called him.

Leah glanced over at Ryan. "Maybe we should have left him at home. I don't want my dog chewing any more suspicious-looking bones."

"There may not be any bones to find, but if that femur is part of a larger stash, Barney will sniff it out. Why not take what help we can get?"

"I suppose." She let out a sigh. "God, I hope we don't discover anything too horribly gruesome."

"Me, too." Ryan nodded toward the shifting shadows crisscrossing the trail as tree branches waved in the wind. "At least there's no fog this afternoon, but we probably don't have much more than another hour of daylight left."

"I hurried as fast as I could." She stubbed her toe on a protruding root and winced. "Oh, I forgot to tell you Chief Stackhouse left a message on my cell earlier that there was a glitch in getting the warrant to search George Dorsey's financial records, something about Judge Reardon being indisposed. He expects to have his signature by tomorrow. If the evidence is there, the chief will make an arrest."

"I sure hope so. Did you talk to your grandma?"

Leah shook her head, huffing a little as they hiked up the last steep incline. "I didn't tell her because I don't want to get her hopes up too soon. Since her packing isn't finished yet, we did ask the management company for a week extension on the apartment. They don't have her unit rented until December, so they were happy to oblige."

"Maybe she'll be able to stay, after all."

"I'm not sure she'll want to, even if the police do recover her money. Gram seems pretty happy about moving in with Magnus."

"Whatever makes Evie happy, right?"

"Absolutely." Leah waved a hand as they reached the top of the climb. "We've arrived. Barney, get over here right now."

The dog cast a guilty look back at her before bolting through the bushes.

"Damn it, Barney."

"I'll get him." Ryan pushed through the manzanita in pursuit of the dog, with Leah following. "What the hell?"

She jerked free of a prickly branch snagged on her jacket, stepped into the clearing, and drew in a sharp breath. Dead wood was heaped in a tall pile near the mammoth stone, apparently waiting only for a match to turn the pyre into a flaming beacon. A white cloth covered the rock's flat surface. A black star inside a circle stood out in stark relief.

"What is that thing?"

"A pentagram."

Leah stared at the satanic symbol as fear crawled up her spine. "Let's get out of here."

"Too late for that, I'm afraid. I was told you'd be hiking up here." A man in a hooded gray cloak stepped out of the trees. His face was hidden in the gathering twilight, but the muzzle of an ugly black revolver protruded from the sleeve of his garment.

Barney stopped sniffing the heap of branches and growled as the fur stood up along his back.

"I like dogs, but I won't hesitate to put a bullet through his head."

The conversational tone struck a note of recognition . . . and disbelief. Surely the hooded figure couldn't be—

Barney barked low in his throat and bared gleaming teeth.

"Don't hurt him!" Leah stepped closer on shaking legs. "Come here, Barney." Her voice rose when her dog hesitated. "Now!"

Ryan pushed her behind him and lunged forward to grab Barney's collar. Turning, he unzipped her backpack and yanked out a leash, then tied the still growling dog to the nearest tree. "This doesn't have to end badly. If you let us go—"

"You know far too much to let you walk away. Any threat to the Brotherhood must be eliminated, but I'd prefer to wait for the others to get here to decide how to handle this." He waved the gun. "However, if you don't cooperate, I'll shoot first and figure it out later. Understood?"

Ryan grabbed Leah around the waist and pulled her close to him. "We'll cooperate. Maybe the others will listen to reason."

"I wouldn't count on it." He pointed with the revolver. "Both of you, over to that big fir." He bent for something behind the stone and straightened holding a coil of rope. "Leah, I want you to tie Ryan up nice and tight. I'll be checking to make sure you do a good job, so don't waste time trying something stupid that will only make me angry."

She caught the rope he tossed her way. They left Barney whining and tugging against his leash to approach the tree he indicated. Her hands shook so badly, she fumbled to unwind the rope.

"Easy, babe. Just do what the doctor says." Ryan's voice was barely above a whisper. "We have to stay alive long enough for Stannard to get here."

"You recognized Dr. Carlton's voice?" Her lips practically touched his ear as she looped the rope around him and the tree.

"He used that same calm tone when I was a kid getting a shot. Obviously something seriously twisted has been going on in Siren Cove for years."

"How did he know we were coming up here?"

"Sloan Manning and Edgar Vargas both heard us talking about taking a hike. One of them could have figured it out," he whispered.

"I can't believe—"

"Quit talking and get the job finished." The doctor's voice slashed through the falling darkness.

"I'm trying." Leah pulled the rope tight and knotted it. "There, Ryan's secure."

Carlton set his weapon on top of the pentagram. "I'm going to tie you up now. If you make any attempt to escape, I'll shoot your boyfriend. Are we clear?"

"Crystal." She stood perfectly still while this man she'd always liked and admired tied her next to Ryan. "Can I ask why you're doing this?"

He checked to make sure the rope was tight without cutting into her arms, then stepped back.

"I don't mind satisfying your curiosity since the information won't leave this spot." He picked up the gun and dropped it into a bag he pulled out from behind the rock, then laid a knife with a long, serrated blade on the pentagram in its place. "By the way, that pistol shoots pellets. At close range, it might have injured you. Nothing more. I don't believe in firearms, but I figured it would be a handy way to contain you."

"Shit." Ryan's frustration gave the single word an ugly undertone.

The doctor lifted a container of lighter fluid out of the bag and squirted streams onto the pyre. Stepping back, he tossed a lit match, and the piled branches exploded in flames.

"The others should be here shortly, but back to your question. The Brotherhood was organized by the group of men who founded Siren Cove a hundred and fifty years ago. They were the sole survivors of a massacre on the trail west, and witnessed their fellow travelers die in agony as the savages scalped them." Carlton's voice hardened. "Our ancestors renounced God that fateful day and promised their souls to Satan in exchange for the lives of their families going forward. We've all prospered ever since."

Leah stared at him in horror. "Surely you don't believe devil worship is the reason for your success."

"Oh, I believe. Once every decade we offer up a sacrifice to Satan, and our families continue to thrive. In order to keep our numbers strong, we've brought a few carefully vetted newcomers into our ranks over the years, but the core group is still the male descendants of those original men."

"That's sick." Ryan's words rang out, echoing through the forest. "Twisted and ugly."

A burning lump filled Leah's throat. She wiggled her hand until she could just touch his fingers and held tight.

"Twenty years ago we were nearly found out, but thankfully our current leader was able to neutralize a suspicious cop. He picked up the knife and turned it over as the firelight gleamed along the blade's length. "With a little help from me. The right drugs will mimic a heart attack every time. After that, we stopped photographing the ceremony. Too risky. I'm happy to say our sacrifice last decade went off without a hitch. Too bad this year you insisted on digging up that damn time capsule where the film was buried."

"Sorry to inconvenience you." Leah's voice rose. "You and your brotherhood are nothing but a bunch of sick—"

The doctor held up his hand and turned as lights flashed and voices carried on a gust of wind. "Your insults don't faze me in the least. Here come my brothers now."

The bushes parted, and a robed figure entered the clearing carrying a naked woman. Long, dark hair streamed over the sleeve of his robe, and her mouth hung slack, eyes open mere slits.

Carlton spoke up to be heard over Barney's barking. "And so the tradition continues with a sacrifice to appease our lord and master."

"Oh, my God." Leah breathed hard through her

nose as the world swayed around her. "I saw that woman on the news. Is she dead?"

Ryan shook his head and spoke in a low tone. "Maybe just drugged for the trip through the woods. I have a feeling they'll want her alive for whatever perverted ritual is planned."

Six more hooded figures followed the man carrying the unconscious woman. The final member of the group wore a black robe instead of gray.

Ryan squeezed Leah's hand. "He must be the head of this freak show. I'd sure like to know who he is."

"I'd like to know who they all are. It's too dark to see anything that isn't directly in the firelight." She shivered and pressed closer against Ryan's side. "I wonder why Barney stopped barking. One of those men is standing next to him. If he hurts my dog—"

"Barney looks okay. The guy isn't doing anything, but if Stannard doesn't get here soon . . ."

"They'll kill that poor woman *and* us. I can't believe this is happening. I can't believe our town has been harboring this kind of evil. To think Dr. Carlton and—"

"Pete." Ryan let out a harsh breath. "The one to the left of the leader. See how he stands with his arms akimbo. I'd swear that's Pete Brewster."

"Then I'd bet money his father is in the group, too."

She stiffened when Dr. Carlton raised the knife in both hands in some kind of salute before sheathing it in the folds of his robe. With a grunt, the man holding the unconscious woman lifted her onto the rock. One of her arms dangled limply over the edge as she let out a low moan.

"She's definitely all drugged up. Damn, the head freak is looking this way." Ryan tugged harder against their restraints. "I've got a tiny bit of slack going on the rope binding you. Can you slide your hands free?"

Leah pressed back against the tree and wiggled one wrist. "No, but almost. Keep working on it."

Ryan's breath brushed her cheek. "Look, the man who was near Barney is arguing with the one in black. I don't know if that's a good thing or not."

". . . can't just kill her." The words fell into a sudden silence.

"Shit. Definitely not good." Ryan twisted harder against the ropes. "Try now."

The hemp dug into her wrist, but Leah barely felt the burning pain as she wrenched her hand free. She couldn't breathe through the tightness in her chest. "That's Brock."

Ryan stopped moving. "You're sure?"

"Yes." Her voice broke. "Oh, God."

"Leah."

She stared across the towering fire at the man she'd once loved, and her stomach convulsed. She swallowed hard against the hot bile.

"Leah!" Ryan's voice was low but sharp. "Work your other wrist loose then untie the knots holding me. Keep your hands behind you so they can't see what you're doing. The firelight doesn't reach this far, but I don't want to take any chances."

She nodded and forced back the surge of nausea. Gritting her teeth, she went to work on the knots. With numb fingers, she picked at the rope, loosening it a little at a time. When the hooded figures formed an organized circle around the woman on the makeshift altar, and the leader held up his arms, a whimper slipped from her throat.

"Where the hell is Stannard? He should be here by now." Ryan pressed his lips to her ear. "Forget about me, scramble out of these ropes and run like hell."

"No, I won't leave you." She sniffed back tears as the first knot came loose.

"You damn well will."

"Reveal yourselves to our lord and master as we let the blood of our sacrifice." The leader's voice rang out before he slowly lowered his hood.

Ryan's breath left in a rush. "Shit."

"What?" Leah's whisper was fierce. "Who is he?"

"No one will be coming to save us. The head freak is Detective Stannard."

The lump in her stomach grew heavier as each man lowered his hood and revealed himself: Arnold Dorsey and Judge Reardon, Waylon and Pete Brewster, the manager from the bank, Brock . . . Her heart pounded so hard, she could barely breathe. "Dr. Carlton has his knife out again . . ."

"Now, Leah. You have to get the hell out of here while they're focused on their . . . sacrifice." Ryan's tone was unyielding. "We can't wait any longer. Try to get out of the ropes without drawing attention this way."

The blade of the knife glinted in the firelight as the group chanted softly, their voices rising in unison.

Her tears fell faster. "I won't leave you here."

Carlton held the knife high before bringing it slashing down to pierce the woman's thigh. A shrill scream echoed through the trees, ending on a sob as the doctor passed the bloody knife to the man beside him.

"Oh, God, I have to help her." Leah worked the ropes down her arms.

"There's nothing you can do for her, and I won't watch them carve you up, too. I love you more than my life. Please, go." Ryan's whisper was harsh against her ear. "Please."

She jerked her arms free and shimmied out of the rope. When another shrill scream rang through the night, she glanced toward the sick ceremony, met Brock's feverish gaze, and froze. When he didn't so much as blink, she dived behind the tree.

"Damn it, Leah. Run!"

"No!" Ignoring Ryan's quiet cursing, she worked at the knots binding him to the tree.

"Stop her! That bitch is free." Waylon Brewster's voice rose in a shout.

"Leah, go!"

With a cry, she spun around and slammed into a solid chest as men ran out of the woods. Shots echoed, and a hard shove pushed her to the ground as all hell broke loose. Crawling to her feet, she threw herself against Ryan, wrapped her arms around him, and prayed.

Chapter Twenty-nine

"Mr. Alexander! Mr. Alexander!" The reporter shoved a mic toward his face as he reached the top of the stairs leading up from the beach. "What was it like being tied to a tree, believing you were about to die?"

"What do you think it was like?" Ryan held tight to the leash as Barney growled at the man. "This is private property, and you're trespassing. Back off."

"Are you aware Crossroads' stock has plummeted since word broke you were involved in the situation with the satanic cult operating out of your hometown?"

"I don't have any comment." As the dog strained forward, Ryan practically sprinted the final few yards to Leah's porch and ran up the steps. When the front door opened, he shot through behind Barney and turned to slam it shut.

"Wow, you're a whole lot braver than I would be."

He leaned against the door as Nina unhooked the leash from the dog's collar. "More like stupid. I thought I'd be safe going for a walk on the beach. Turns out I underestimated the persistence of the press."

"When I was at the grocery store, I ran into a TV crew out of Portland who somehow learned I was friends with you and Leah. Talk about piranhas scenting blood . . ."

Ryan followed her into the living room where Paige stood beside the window, peaking out through the blinds. Leah sat on the couch with her phone clamped to her ear. She gave him a quick smile before returning to her conversation.

"Yeah, one of them is on my property now. If you could . . . okay. Thanks, Chris." She laid her cell on the coffee table and leaned back against the couch cushions. "How'd the walk go?"

"Barney seemed to enjoy himself. I think he likes barking at reporters." Ryan took a seat beside her and picked up her hand.

Leah looked worn to the bone. Dark circles marred the skin beneath her eyes, and her hand shook as she hooked a strand of hair behind her ear. He knew she hadn't slept well the last few nights, probably because he'd been awake, too. In the dark, they'd clung to each other in an effort to hold back the nightmares.

"Besides promising to chase off the reporter out there, Chris also gave me an update."

"Do tell." Nina sat opposite them.

Paige left her post at the window to drop down onto the rug beside Barney. "I'm almost hoping for some kind of natural disaster to distract the media's interest away from Siren Cove."

Leah's grip on his hand tightened. "I know what

you mean. Every time I turn on the news, they're replaying footage of some of our most esteemed citizens being loaded into patrol cars in handcuffs. While I have no trouble believing Waylon and Pete Brewster were part of that sick cult, it still kills me to think Doctor Carlton was a member, that for years he condoned—"

"Try not to think about it." Ryan bent to press a kiss to the top of her head.

"The whole town is in shock. I heard Dr. Carlton's wife packed her bags and left to go live with their daughter in California," Nina said.

Paige stroked Barney's ears when he laid his head in her lap. "Is it any wonder the rest of the men involved are currently divorced? Even if their wives didn't know the specifics, they must have felt something was seriously wrong."

"Except for Rodney Long. The guilt of what they'd done probably contributed to his stroke. If he hadn't turned on his 'brothers' and confessed to his son when he did . . ." Leah broke off, and her whole body quivered as Ryan let go of her hand to wrap his arm around her.

"Seems like Chris was the only male offspring the group didn't try to indoctrinate."

Leah met Nina's thoughtful gaze and nodded. "Probably because the man's morals were evident from an early age. I've never been more thankful than I was when he and Chief Stackhouse and the rest of the department ran out of the woods to save us along with that poor woman."

Ryan held Leah a little tighter as another tremor shook her. "You mentioned you had new information?"

"I do. Chris said Yvonne Ames is scheduled to be released from the hospital tomorrow and is expected to make a full recovery from her injuries."

"That's good news, at least."

"She was the lucky one, unlike the others they killed over the years." Paige's tone was somber.

"Knowing they buried their *sacrifices* up there makes me ill just thinking about it, but at least those families will have closure once the remains are identified." Leah let out a long sigh. "Merry Bright was one of them. I guess Leonard Wilkinson, the manager from the bank, went a little crazy and started shooting his mouth off before his lawyer shut him up. He ratted out Arnold Dorsey, who was behind the attacks on me."

"I wonder what's going to happen to them." Nina spoke quietly. "The manager closed the Poseidon Grill after the police arrested George Dorsey at the airport, so who knows when the restaurant will reopen. Is there any news yet on recovering your grandma's money from that scumbag?"

"Earlier, I talked to the attorney Magnus hired for Gram. Once the warrant finally came through, the bank froze George's account. What with all the elderly victims he's fleeced over the last couple of years, her lawyer expects her share will be about half of what he originally stole."

Ryan frowned. "That sucks."

"Yeah, it does, but we discussed the situation, and she and Magnus are both happy to be cohabiting. They moved the last of Gram's stuff into his apartment yesterday."

"Go, Evie!" Paige pushed up off the floor. "Seems like she made the best of a bad situation. I hate to take off, but I need to get back to my shop. If that idiot reporter is still out there, I intend to give him a piece of my mind. Haven't you both been through enough without all the added media harassment?"

"You'd think." Pressing down on Ryan's thigh, Leah rose to her feet. "Thanks for coming over to keep me company."

"You bet."

Nina followed them into the entry. "I should go, too."

Ryan stayed where he was, figuring Leah could use a few minutes alone with her friends. Both Nina and Paige had been solid bulwarks of support since the minute he and Leah had emerged from the woods, shaken and more than a little traumatized.

Has it only been three days? It seemed like a lifetime.

The women's voices carried from the entry, breaking through his thoughts. Or maybe it was a single name that had caught his attention. He mouthed an obscenity.

"Have you heard from Brock?" Paige's voice was hesitant.

"He actually called me and broke down crying. He said he didn't know what Pete and George were getting him into. They were drunk and all hopped up on something when he agreed to join their sick cult. Then he was afraid to back out once he sobered up."

"Didn't the police arrest him?" Nina asked.

"Of course, but he hasn't been charged with murder or kidnapping like the others since he had no part in abducting Yvonne Ames, and this was his first time up in the woods with those freaks." Leah's voice broke. "I'm sure he'll still do jail time, but at least he tried to talk the group out of killing me and Ryan. Not that I'll ever forgive him for his part in the whole nightmare."

"I hope they lock them all up and throw away the keys. None of them deserve to live."

Ryan clenched and unclenched his fists at his sides. He agreed with Nina. Their perverted cult had contaminated the whole town, and it would take a long time for the residents to recover.

"Are you going to be okay?" Paige's soft question penetrated his anger.

"Honestly, if it wasn't for Ryan, I don't know if I would be. I feel like such an idiot. I *hate* that I once loved a man who's so messed up. What does that say about me?"

"That you look only for the best in people. Don't beat yourself up over someone else's failings. Anyway, you dumped him years ago, so you saw the light," Paige answered.

Leah's voice was tearful. "I appreciate the vote of confidence, but I still feel like a fool."

"What does Ryan have to say about it?" Nina asked.

"Nothing. He just supports me, lets me cry, and holds me when I wake up in a cold sweat."

"That's all you need right now. Look, I can stay if—"

"No, I'll be fine. Go back to your shop. You, too, Nina. Ryan will be here if I start to lose it again."

"If you're sure . . ."

"I'm sure. I have Ryan."

The door opened, and their voices faded as they

walked out onto the porch. Ryan hoped the reporter had left. If not, he'd be tempted to punch
the jerk. He closed his eyes and willed himself to
calm the hell down. Leah needed his patience
right now, not his anger.

When the door shut, he opened his eyes again
and met her gaze head-on when she stopped in
the doorway.

"Did you hear all that?" At his nod, she continued, "I should have told you I talked to Brock."

"You don't owe me an explanation if you choose
to speak to someone. Even an asshole like your ex."

Leah returned to the couch and sat down beside him. "Since Brock used his one call from jail
to contact me, I felt like I should take it. I guess it's
something that he was horrified they intended to
kill the two of us."

"Not much, but something."

"Knowing he was a part of that group makes me
sick." She pressed a hand to her stomach. "Actually physically ill."

She wasn't exaggerating. She'd run to the bathroom more than once when he'd tried to per-
suade her to eat something. But the fact that she
cared about Brock's actions at all killed him.

"If you still have feelings for your ex-husband . . ."

"What!" Leah jerked upright and stared at him.
"What are you talking about?"

"This whole situation is turning you inside out.
If you didn't care—"

"Care!" She rose to her feet and faced him with
fists clenched. "I *care* that I married that man. I
care that I was capable of being fooled into thinking he was a decent human being. My stomach is

in knots wondering what other horrible decisions I've made in my life. How can I ever trust my own judgment again?"

"Am I a mistake? Do you question loving me?"

"No, of course not." Tears slid down her face. "You—your love—is the only thing holding me together. You're the one bright spot of hope I have."

Ryan stood and walked around the coffee table to take her into his arms. Pressing her face against his chest, he simply held her. "Stop torturing yourself. Don't think about the past. Look toward the future. Our future."

"I'll try. I really will."

"That's all I ask." He held her far enough away to look into her troubled eyes. "Right now, I think we both could use a little time to recover."

"At least the school board was nice about giving me the rest of the week off. I have to pull my act together by Monday, though. The kids in my class will be worried about me. After everything that's happened, they need normalcy in their lives."

"We all do."

Leah held Ryan's hand as they strolled down the beach. Ahead of them, Barney chased a flock of seagulls that squawked in indignation and flew away long before her dog reached them. With a cold wind blowing off the ocean, they had the entire strip of sand to themselves. She stopped and turned to face the three Sirens out in the cove, then leaned against Ryan's chest when he wrapped his arms around her.

As it did all too often, her mind turned to the

horrific night when they'd both nearly died. Dreams of hooded figures still plagued her sleep, but the times she woke up shaking and gasping for breath came fewer and farther between. She was finally beginning to heal.

"I'll never take *this* for granted again." Ryan turned her in his arms and brushed strands of blowing hair off her cheek with a gentle finger, obviously picking up on her thoughts, as he so often did. "If there's one positive to take away from what happened last month, it's an appreciation of each moment we have together."

"Many, many moments." She smiled up at him. "Hopefully, years and years." Looping her arms around his neck, she stood on her toes to kiss him. "I'll never leave you, Ryan. In those petrifying minutes when I thought we both might die, I knew with complete certainty living without you wasn't an option. That's the positive I gained from the whole nightmare."

"Nothing and no one will come between us again. Of that, I'm certain."

"I love you so much. Thank you for standing by me this last month. I know it wasn't easy because I was a complete basket case for quite a while, *and* you had work problems to deal with, just to make matters worse."

"You'll always be my top priority. Never doubt that. Anyway, now that my shareholders have been reassured I wasn't part of the cult as was first reported, stock in Crossroads has bounced back." His grip on her tightened. "I'd like to know which moron reported that version of events."

"I guess it sold more papers than the retraction they printed on page ten."

"You think?"

"I think." She stroked the back of his neck with her thumb. "I also think you have amazing fortitude to have faced all the crap thrown at you, plus my insecurities, and not put your fist through a wall. You deserve a medal."

"How about if I give you something instead." Releasing her, he slid his hand into his pocket. After pulling it out, he turned his palm upward. On it rested a twisted gold band with an inset ruby. "It's a promise ring with your birthstone. I bought it our senior year before . . ."

"Before we broke up?" Tears burned her eyes

"I kept it all these years and have been carrying it around since I came back home to you. I want you to have it as a token of what we've always meant to each other."

She touched the shiny band with a shaking finger. "I don't know what to say."

"Before you say anything, there's something else I need to tell you." His eyes were full of promises as he smiled at her. "I love you, Leah. I want to be the person you turn to for support when you need it most. The one you run to when you're happy. I want to be your everything, now and always."

He reached into his other pocket, pulled out a small black box, and flipped open the lid. "Maybe you'd like to wear this one, too. Will you marry me and make me happier than I ever believed possible?"

She stared down at the diamond solitaire glinting in a ray of sunlight. Her heart swelled with pure joy as she met his gaze. Speechless, she nodded.

He slid both rings onto her finger with shaking hands. "My heart is yours to keep."

"And mine belongs to you." She reached up and kissed him. "This is where I belong, where I've always belonged. In your arms and by your side. It's the only place I ever want to be. Loving you, Ryan. Forever."

Don't miss the next book in Jannine Gallant's
Siren Cove series

LOST INNOCENCE

A Lyrical Press mass-market and e-book
on sale July 2018!

Connect with U(s)

Visit us online at
KensingtonBooks.com
to read more from your favorite authors, see books
by series, view reading group guides, and more.

Join us on social media

for sneak peeks, chances to win books and prize packs,
and to share your thoughts with other readers.

facebook.com/kensingtonpublishing
twitter.com/kensingtonbooks

Tell us what you think!

To share your thoughts, submit a review,
or sign up for our eNewsletters, please visit:
KensingtonBooks.com/TellUs.